ITALIAN SURGEON TO THE STARS

BY
MELANIE MILBURNE

HER GREEK DOCTOR'S PROPOSAL

BY
ROBIN GIANNA

MILLS
&
D0233754

From as soon as **Melanie Milburne** could pick up a pen she knew she wanted to write. It was when she picked up her first Mills & Boon® at seventeen that she realised she wanted to write romance. After being distracted for a few years by meeting and marrying her own handsome hero, surgeon husband Steve, and having two boys, plus completing a Masters of Education and becoming a nationally ranked athlete (Masters' swimming), she decided to write. Five submissions later she sold her first book and is now a multi-published, bestselling, award-winning *USA TODAY* author. In 2008 she won the Australian Readers' Association most popular category/series romance, and in 2011 she won the prestigious Romance Writers of Australia R*BY award.

Melanie loves to hear from her readers via her website, melaniemilburne.com.au, or on Facebook: facebook.com/melanie.milburne

After completing a degree in journalism, working in the advertising industry, then becoming a stay-at-home mum, **Robin Gianna** had what she calls her 'midlife awakening'. She decided she wanted to write the romance novels she'd loved since her teens, and embarked on that quest by joining RWA, Central Ohio Fiction Writers, and working hard at learning the craft.

She loves sharing the journey with her characters, helping them through obstacles and problems to find their own happily-ever-afters. When not writing, Robin likes to create in her kitchen, dig in the dirt, and enjoy life with her tolerant husband, three great kids, drooling bulldog and grouchy Siamese cat.

To learn more about her work visit her website: RobinGianna.com

ITALIAN SURGEON TO THE STARS

BY
MELANIE MILBURNE

MILLS & BOON

Published in Great Britain 2015
by Mills & Boon, an imprint of Harlequin (UK) Limited,
Eton House, 18-24 Paradise Road, Richmond, Surrey, TW9 1SR

© 2015 Melanie Milburne

ISBN: 978-0-263-24712-1

Dear Reader,

One of the things I love about being a writer is that I never have to look very far for the characters for my stories. They nearly always come looking for me. Jem Clark is one such character.

I wrote Jem's younger sister Bertie's story, *A Date with Her Valentine Doc*, with the intention of it being a one-off first person Mills & Boon® Medical Romance™ especially for St Valentine's Day. (By the way, I had so much fun writing that story!) But right from the start Jem was there, with her story just waiting to be told. In fact she was so real to me I sent an email to my editor using her voice!

Jem is a strong and sharp-tongued young woman, with a take-no-prisoners attitude. You have been warned!

Thankfully, I didn't have to look very far for my hero, Alessandro Lucioni. My Mills & Boon® Modern™ Romance readers will already know how much I love an Italian alpha hero—and a deeply tortured one even more so.

I hope you enjoy *Italian Surgeon to the Stars* as much as I enjoyed writing it.

Warmest wishes

Melanie Milburne

**Praise for
Melanie Milburne**

'Fast-paced, passionate and simply irresistible, *Sydney Harbour Hospital: Lexi's Secret* is a powerful tale of redemption, hope and second chances that sparkles with richly drawn characters, warm-hearted pathos, tender emotion, sizzling sensuality and uplifting romance.'
—*CataRomance*

'A tale of new beginnings, redemption and hope that will make readers chuckle as well as wipe away a tear. A compelling medical drama about letting go of the past and seizing the day, it is fast-paced and sparkles with mesmerising emotion and intense passion.'
—*GoodReads* on
Their Most Forbidden Fling

To Amy Thompson—a fellow poodle-lover,
a fantastic friend and a fabulous beauty therapist. You
are one of the sweetest and kindest people I know. xxx

CHAPTER ONE

EVEN THOUGH I'M a fully qualified teacher I still hate getting called into the headmistress's office. I get this nervous prickle in my stomach, like a bunch of ants are tiptoeing around in there on stilettos. My knees feel woolly and unstable. My heart starts to hammer.

It's a programmed response from my childhood. I was rubbish at school. I mean *really* rubbish. Which is kind of ironic since I ended up a teacher at the prestigious Emily Sudgrove School for Girls in Bath, but that's another story.

Being called in to the office nearly always means there's a problem with one of the parents—a complaint or a criticism over how I'm handling one of their little darlings. Everyone knows helicopter parents are bad news. But, believe me, fighter pilot ones are even worse.

I stood outside the closed door and took a calming breath before I knocked on the door and entered.

'Ah, here she is now,' said Miss Fletcher, the headmistress, with a polished professional smile. 'Jem, this is Dr Alessandro Lucioni—a new parent.'

The words were like a closed-fist punch to my heart. *Bang*. I'm sure it missed a beat. Maybe two. Possibly three. I stood there with a blank expression on my face...

or at least I hoped it was blank. God forbid I should show any sign of the shock that was currently rocketing through me.

Alessandro was a parent? A father? He was married? He was in love?

The words were like a ticker tape running through my head. But then it flipped off its spool and flickered in a tangled knot inside my head. One of the stray tapes wrapped itself around my heart and squeezed until it hurt.

Alessandro gave a formal nod and held out a hand. 'Miss Clark.'

I stared at his hand. That hand had known every inch of my body. That hand had coached me to my first orgasm. Those long, clever fingers had made me feel things I hadn't felt before or since. The sight of that hand made memories I'd locked away twist and writhe and wriggle out of their shackles and run amok with my emotions. I could feel the spread of heat flowing through me. Furnace-hot heat. Heat that made me acutely aware of my sexuality and the needs and urges I usually staunchly, stubbornly, *furiously* ignored.

I brought my gaze up to his unreadable one. So he wasn't going to let on that he knew me. Biblically or literally. Fine. I would play the same game.

'Welcome to Emily Sudgrove,' I said, and put my hand in his. His fingers were cool and strong, and closed around mine with just enough pressure to remind me of the sensual power he'd once had over me.

Okay. Forget about once. I admit it. He *still* had it over me. I felt the tingle of the contact. The nerves of my fingers and hand were lighting up like fairy lights on a tree. Sparking. Fizzing. Wanting.

'Thank you,' he said, with a brief flicker of his lips

that passed for a smile—but I noticed it didn't make the distance to his eyes.

Oh, dear Lordy me, his eyes! They were a dark lustrous brown. Darker than chocolate. Strong eyes. Eyes that could melt frozen butter like a blowtorch. Eyes that could be sexily hooded and smouldering when he was in the mood for sex. Eyes that could make my blood sing through my veins with just a look.

I felt his gaze move over my face in an assessing manner. I hoped he wasn't noticing my eyebrows needed shaping. Why hadn't I made the time for a bit of lady landscaping? Why, oh, why hadn't I used the hair straightener that morning? My hair is my biggest bugbear. I *hate* my corkscrew curls. For most of my life I've had to endure dumb blonde jokes. At least when I tame my hair it gives me a little more credibility, or so I like to think.

Think. Now, there's an idea. But my brain wasn't capable of rational thought. I was in fight-or-flight mode. I wanted to get away from Alessandro—as I'd been doing for the last five years.

I'd seen glimpses of him from time to time. He'd saved the life of a London theatre actor a couple of years ago, which had made him into a celebrity doctor. He's a heart surgeon. A pretty darn good one too—I have to give him that. He ripped *my* heart right out of my chest without anaesthetic. Oh, and the reason he's called 'Dr', and not Mr like other surgeons, is because he's done a PhD on top of his arduous training.

Talk about an overachiever. And people think *I'm* a workaholic. I reckon his business card would have to be one of those fold-out concertina ones, like those old-fashioned postcards, to accommodate all the letters after his name.

I saw him just a couple of weeks ago in Knightsbridge, when I was having lunch with my younger sister Bertie. He didn't see me, thank God. He was with a blonde. A gorgeous supermodel type, with legs up to her armpits and perfect skin, perfectly shaped eyebrows and perfectly smooth straight hair. The type of woman he's been seen out and about with ever since our relationship. Luckily my sister didn't recognise him—or if she did she knew better than to say anything.

Urgh. I hate thinking about my relationship with Alessandro. I hate even using that term. It wasn't a relationship—not for him, anyway. I was a rebound. That's another word I loathe. I was a consolation prize. Not Miss Right, but Miss Will Do.

'Dr Lucioni has enrolled his niece into your class, Jem,' Miss Fletcher said into the canyon of silence.

Niece?

An inexplicable sense of relief collided with shock. He had a sister? A niece? Relatives? He'd told me he was an orphan.

I'd been amazed at how well he had done for himself when he had no one to back him. Not many people get to where he has without a leg-up somewhere along the way. But on the rare occasions when he spoke of his past he'd told me his parents died when he was a teenager and he had put himself through school and then medical school by working three jobs. There was no family money. No extended family support.

What other lies had he fed me?

I looked at him with a quizzical frown. 'You have a sister?'

Something moved at the back of his eyes, like a stagehand darting back into the shadows behind the curtains between acts.

'Yes,' he said. 'She's currently unwell, and I'm taking care of Claudia until she recovers.'

His voice... *Holy guacamole*. His voice was like a caress to my sex-starved body. It stroked over me like a sensual hand, making the base of my spine melt like a marshmallow in front of a campfire. The deepness of it, the mellifluous tone of it, the Sicilian accent even years living outside his homeland hadn't been able to remove.

That voice had told me things I had no business believing. I had fallen for every word. Every shallow promise I had taken to heart. I was ashamed of how stupid I'd been. Deeply and cringingly ashamed.

I'd spent years scoffing at my hippie parents for falling for the latest fad and then I'd gone and done the same. I'd latched on to Alessandro like a directionless follower does a guru. I'd worshipped him. I'd been prepared to give up all I had to be with him. I would have walked— no, crawled on my knees—over glass or razorblades or burning coals or a pit of hissing vipers to be with him.

But what I'd thought we had was a sham. It was all smoke and mirrors. He hadn't loved me at all. I was payback to the woman who'd dumped him for a richer man.

'Claudia will be boarding with us,' Miss Fletcher said.

I swung my gaze back to Alessandro's. 'Boarding?'

His expression gave nothing away. 'I work long, sometimes unpredictable, hours at the hospital.'

I teach six and seven-year-olds. Key Stage One as we call it in the UK. Grade One in the US and other parts of the world. I know children in the UK go to boarding school a lot younger than anywhere else, but sometimes it's a good thing. *Sometimes*. If a family is dysfunctional or not coping with the demands of kids then a well-run boarding school is a good option. Maybe even the best option in some cases. But I worry about kids who are shunted off before they're emotionally ready.

Boarding school can be a brutal place for a child who is overly sensitive. I have a history of oversensitivity, so I kind of know about these things.

Mind you, I never went to boarding school. Maybe if I had my childhood would have been a little less chaotic. My sister and I were hauled out of school when we were six and seven respectively and taken off to live in a commune in the Yorkshire moors, where we were supposed to learn through play. We were there two whole years before the authorities tracked us down and stepped in.

My sister Bertie's playing and learning was clearly of a much higher standard than mine, because she was a year ahead of her peers when she was placed back in the system. Unfortunately I was behind. Way, *way* behind. It took me years to catch up, and even now whenever I don't know the answer to something I get that same sinking sensation in the pit of my stomach—a feeling of inadequacy, of not being smart enough, of not quite making the grade.

It doesn't take a psychotherapist to understand why I chose to teach at a posh girls' school. I needed to prove to myself that I was good enough to teach in one of the best schools in the country. But the thing I've come to realise is that it doesn't matter how rich or poor your parents are—children are the same the world over. Some are strong academically; others, like me, can wangle the social side to their advantage. I made the art of fitting in into a science. I totally nailed it. Even though at times I compromised myself.

Alessandro was watching me with that same unfathomable expression on his face. Why had he chosen my school? There were dozens of boarding schools across the country. Why The Emily Sudgrove School for Girls in Bath? He worked in one of London's top hospitals. He lived in Belgravia. Yes, Belgravia. I told you he'd done well for himself. Why didn't he enrol his niece in a school closer to where he lived?

'Dr Lucioni would like a tour of the school,' Miss Fletcher said.

Her name was Clementine, but no one was allowed to call her that. She was proudly single and preferred Miss to Ms. She believed in formal address from her staff to establish respect, although she always called us by our Christian names when the children weren't around.

'Will you see to that, Jem?' she added.

'Sure,' I said brightly.

See how good I am at playing the game? Show no fear. That was my credo. It comes in pretty useful as a teacher too. You'd be surprised at how knee-knockingly scary some six or seven-year-olds can be. Although nothing compares to a six-foot-three hot Sicilian guy you once had monkey sex with, but still...

'Come this way,' I said.

I felt him just behind me as I walked out of the office. If I stopped he would cannon into me. I was tempted to stop. It had been a long time since a man had touched me, even by accident. I'm no nun, but neither have I been getting out there much. Not lately. Not since...

I had to really think before I could remember. Ah, yes, I remember now. I had a blind date with a friend of a friend's older brother a couple of years ago. God, what a disaster *that* was. No wonder I don't like remembering it. He was on something illegal and kept leaving the table where we were having dinner to have another snort. It took me a while to realise what was going on. The third time he said he needed the bathroom I ordered the most expensive wine on the wine list, drank half a glass and then left him to sort out the bill. I don't let men walk all over me any more. I get in first.

Speaking of illegal… There should be a law against men as good-looking at Alessandro Lucioni. I know the tall, dark and handsome tag is a bit of a cliché, but he's exactly that. Tall and olive-skinned, and with the sort of looks that would make any woman between the ages of fourteen and fifty throw herself on the nearest bed and beg to be ravished by him.

He has sharply chiselled cheekbones and a prominent brow that gives him a slightly intimidating air whenever he frowns. His hair is thick and plentiful and not quite short, not quite long, but somewhere fashionably in between. He looks like one of those dishy European aftershave models. That day his hair was brushed back off his forehead, and it looked like the last time he'd done it he had used his fingers.

I wished I could stop thinking about his fingers. I was breaking out into a hot flush. I could feel it deep in my core. That subtle tensing of my girly bits as I recalled the way he had stroked me there. I pressed my knees together, but that only made it worse.

'This is the…erm…library,' I said as I pushed open the door.

He stood waiting for me to go in before him. He had excellent manners. That's another thing I have to give him. Ladies first—that's his credo. *Yikes*, why couldn't I stop thinking about sex?

I turned on my heel and walked in with my head high, waving my hand to encompass the shelves and shelves of books. 'We at Emily Sudgrove Academy pride ourselves on giving our girls a broad choice in reading material which is both age-appropriate while giving them the opportunity in which to extend their reading range.'

I sounded like I was reading it from the school information booklet—which is not surprising since I was the one who rewrote the latest edition.

'Jem.'

I get called by my name, or at least the shortened version of it, all the time. There was no reason why my legs should suddenly feel as if the bones had been taken out. Or for my heart to beat extra quickly and my chest to feel tight, as if something rapidly expanding had taken up all the space in there. But something about the way Alessandro said my name made the base of my spine tingle.

I took a slow deep breath and turned to face him with my Key Stage One teacher face on. My sister Bertie calls it my Miss Prim and Proper face. Apparently I've been doing it since I was a little kid, which is kind of ironic since nothing about our childhood was anywhere close to being prim and proper.

'Miss Clark,' I said, with a tight smile that didn't reveal my teeth. 'We at Emily Sudgrove believe in teaching our girls proper forms of address, so as to equip them with the necessary tools to—'

'Why did you run away the other week in London?'

I tried to keep my expression composed. I hadn't realised he'd seen me that day. It made me cringe to think he'd witnessed my panicked bolt via the kitchen of the restaurant Bertie and I had been lunching in. But I hated seeing him with his lovers, either in the press or in the flesh. He was in and out of relationships like a cab driver in and out of his cab. I swear to God he should have a revolving door in his bedroom. Or a ticketing machine—like the ones in the deli to keep people from jumping the queue.

'I'm afraid I have no idea what you're talking about,' I said. 'You must have mistaken someone else for me.'

The corner of his mouth tipped up in a knowing smile. It was only a slight hitch of his lips but it was enough to set my pulse racing.

'I could never mistake you for anyone else, *cara mio.*'

This time I didn't bother with the composed expression. I frowned. I glared. I bristled. 'Do *not* call me that. It's Miss Clark.'

The hitch of his lips went higher, as if he found my stand-off amusing. 'How long have you been teaching here?' he asked.

I made an effort to relax my shoulders. *Keep it cool and professional.* I could do this as long as I forgot about our history. 'Five years.'

His brows moved together over his dark eyes. 'Since Paris, then?'

Paris. The city of love.

Yeah, right. The city of bitter disappointment, if you ask me. I hate Paris now. I can't even bring myself to look at a baguette without wanting to throw up or hit someone over the head with it. Or both.

I brought up my chin. 'I was ready for a change.'

His frown had melted away as if it had never been, but I got the feeling he was thinking about our time together. Shuffling through the memories like someone searching for something in a long neglected drawer. I could see the distant look in his gaze. I got the same look in mine if I allowed myself to think of that whirlwind month in Paris.

But then he blinked and rearranged his features into a cool mask. 'I chose this school because it's close to where I live.'

My heart gave a lurch. 'You live nearby?'

'I've bought a property in the countryside, just outside of Bath,' he said.

'Then why are you boarding your niece?'

'It's being renovated at present,' he said. 'I don't think it's a safe place for a young child.'

'So what will you do once it is?' I asked. 'Take her to live with you? Or will you be too busy travelling back and forth to London?' *And sleeping with anyone with a pulse*, I wanted to add but didn't.

He'd selected a book from the bookshelves and was turning it over in his hands. It was a Beatrix Potter book. My mother had a thing about Beatrix Potter. Hence Bertie's name—Beatrix, but don't call her that unless you want her to hate you—and my name. Had he chosen the book deliberately? Reminding me of the connection we'd once had?

I hadn't told him *everything* about my childhood but I'd told him a lot. Well, maybe not a lot—more like a bit. There was stuff I hadn't even told Bertie, close as we were. There were some things it was best not to talk about. Best not to even think about. I'm good at avoidance. Avoidance is my middle name… Well, it's not—but it could be.

Bertie and I don't have middle names. Our parents didn't believe in them. I suspect it's because they have about four or five apiece and can never remember them. My parents both come from aristocratic backgrounds. I figure it's a whole lot easier being a hippie when some-one else is paying the bills. But don't get me started…

I watched as Alessandro slid the book back into place on the shelf. As his index fingertip slowly slid down the slim spine I felt a traitorous quake of lust roll through me. I squeezed my thighs together to stop the thrumming sensation. Like *that* was ever going to work. Just being in the same room as him was enough to make me come. That voice. Those eyes. Those hands. That delicious body…

I drank in the sight of him. The broad shoulders, the strong back and lean hips, the long legs and taut buttocks. I had run my hands and lips and tongue over every inch of that body. I had learned how to give and receive pleasure instead of being frozen with fear. A fear I hadn't told him about. Well, not the truth, anyway.

I told him my first time had been 'a bit unpleasant'. I didn't go into the details of exactly *how* unpleasant. I refuse to see myself as a victim. I don't even see myself as a survivor. I'm a fighter. I'm strong and tough and I take no crap from anyone.

Alessandro turned and his gaze locked with mine. 'You look good, Jem.'

That's another thing I hate. Compliments. I never believe them.

I've never considered myself beautiful. Even though I'm blonde and blue-eyed and slim, with a decent set of boobs—who I am to talk about clichés?—I have hang-ups about my looks. I've got my father's nose and my mother's cheekbones. I've got my maternal grandmother's hair and my paternal grandfather's chin. I don't know whose eyes I've got, but I sure hope they can see without them! Seriously, it's like all the bad bits of everyone in my family were cobbled together to make me. Thanks a bunch, God, or whoever it is in charge of genetics.

Bertie's the beautiful one in our family—not that she thinks so or anything. She would say I'm the good-looking one, but that's because she's a sweetheart. She has gorgeous brown hair and brown eyes, and the cutest smile with tiny dimples. When I smile it looks more like a grimace.

I have to remind myself that's it okay to show my teeth because for most of my childhood my teeth were like a picket fence. They were so wide apart I could have flossed with hessian rope. My parents went through a 'no medical intervention' phase, which unfortunately included dentistry. They believed my teeth would eventually find their rightful position all by themselves. Well, let me tell you they didn't. I had to endure braces and a night-time plate for three and a half years during my late teens and early adulthood. Yes. *Three and a half years!*

God, talk about excruciating torture—socially *and* physically. No wonder my sex life was a little on the barren side when I met Alessandro. Not that I cared about it all that much then—or now. If I remove my memory of Alessandro's lovemaking—which is darn near impossible to do—I think sex is horribly overrated.

I shrugged off his compliment like I did everyone else's. 'I'll show you the boarding house. Please come this way.'

I led the way out of the library, but before I could get through the door he put a hand on my arm. I was wearing a silk shirt and a cotton cardigan, but even so I could feel the heat of his long fingers as they wrapped around my wrist like a set of handcuffs. I looked at his hand on my wrist like someone would look at a cockroach on a piece of cake. I brought my gaze up to his. How had I forgotten how tall he was? I was going to have get myself a decent set of heels or a neck brace.

'Do you mind?' I said, with a crisp note to my voice. Bertie calls it my schoolmarm tone.

His fingers didn't budge. If anything I thought they tightened a fraction. I lost myself for a moment in the bottomless depths of his coal-black gaze. I could feel his eyes drawing me in, like a magnet does a piece of metal. I could even feel my body leaning towards him, as if an unseen force was pushing me from behind.

Hell's bells. I'm starting to sound like my mother, with her paranormal take on things. She would have a field day with his aura. He was sending off vibes even I could read. Although his eyes were dark and inscrutable it felt like he was watching me from behind a closed door that had once been open.

But hadn't I always felt that way about him? He had shadows in his eyes I had chosen to ignore five years ago. I hadn't liked to press him because I knew how awful it was to talk about stuff you didn't want to talk about. I figured that, him being an orphan and all—how had I fallen for *that* lie?—meant he wasn't comfortable talking about his childhood.

Why had he lied to me? What sort of family did he come from? Surely it couldn't be half as weird and wacky as mine.

Alessandro's thumb found my leaping pulse. *Damn.* No way of hiding that involuntary reaction from him. It didn't matter how determined I was in my brain to armour up, because he could always find a way to ambush my senses. That was why I'd so assiduously avoided him over the years. I didn't go to places I knew he frequented.

I didn't want to run into him like we were old friends. Making polite conversation, talking about the weather or current affairs, as if he *hadn't* torn my heart out of my chest and ground it under the heel of one of his handmade Italian leather shoes.

I had way more self-respect than that. *No second chances* was another credo of mine. One strike and you're out. You don't get to screw over Jem Clark more than once.

I suppressed a shiver as his thumb began a slow stroke, back and forth, making every nerve beneath my skin shiver and shriek out for more. He had a mesmerising touch, gentle and yet strong. Confident. Assured. As if he knew my body like a maestro knows his favourite instrument.

Actually, it was a pretty accurate analogy, because I was as strung up as an over-tuned violin. I could feel every nerve and muscle in my body pulling taut. My insides practically shuddered with longing.

How could he possibly have that effect on me after all this time? I hated him for how he'd used me. I detested his smooth-talking artifice. Saying he wanted to spend the rest of his life with me when all he'd wanted to do was send a message to his stunningly beautiful ex that he'd moved on.

Why had I been so dumb as to fall for that? I wasn't proud of my history for falling for charming lies. The event during my early teens which I refuse to mention came about because of my naivety when it came to men and their lies.

But I'm older and wiser now. Tough as old goat's knees, that's me. No one can charm me nowadays— which is kind of why I haven't been out on a date in years.

I don't care if men are put off by me. I'm fine with it. I don't want the fairy tale, like my sister. I'm not hankering after some guy to lock me away in the suburbs with two-point-five kids and a mortgage.

Besides, I have more than enough kids to take care of at school. Mothering at a distance. I can handle that. I'm darn good at it too.

I unpeeled Alessandro's fingers as I gave him a look of utter contempt. 'I don't think you heard me, Dr Lucioni.'

Dr Lucioni? Snort. Who was I kidding? No amount of formality was going to wipe away the memory of our affair. It was a presence in the room.

Sheesh. There I went with the paranormal thing again. But really—it was. I felt the erotic tension in the air like a singing wire. The memories of how we were together were swirling around inside my head. From behind the wall of my resolve I caught glimpses of our bodies locked together in passion. Rocking together, straining, writhing, climbing the summit of human pleasure until we both came apart. His long, tanned hairy legs entwined intimately with mine. His arms wrapped around me, holding me to him as if he never wanted to let me go. His mouth…

I should *not* have thought about his mouth. His mouth had wreaked such havoc on my senses. He had used his mouth in ways I had not experienced before. No one had ever pleasured me that way. I hadn't allowed them to. But with him it had felt natural. Damn it, it had felt like he was worshipping my body. It had added a level of sanctity to our lovemaking that was sadly lacking in my past experiences…especially the one I refuse to mention.

Alessandro gave me one of his half smiles—a twitch of his lips that was borderline mocking. 'You think you can erase what we had?'

I rubbed at my wrist as if it had been stung, glaring at him so hard my eyes hurt. 'I would appreciate it if you would refrain from referring to our...association whilst within the parameters of this school.'

I sounded so priggish I almost laughed out loud. Bertie would have been doubled over at me.

His eyes took on a glint that did serious damage to my equilibrium—if indeed I had any in the first place, which I suspect I didn't.

'I've told my niece we're old friends,' he said. 'I thought it would help her to feel less threatened by coming here.'

I widened my eyes. I'm not talking cup-and-saucer wide. I'm talking satellite-dish wide, like those ones on the International Space Station.

'What?'

'You have a problem with making a small child feel a little more secure?'

I whooshed out a stormy breath. 'I have a problem with you fabricating a relationship between us that doesn't exist.'

'It did once.'

I sent him another death-adder stare. 'I beg to differ. How can you stand there and say we had something together when you failed to mention the fact that you'd recently broken up with your gold-digging fiancée? Not to mention your lies about not having a family. You lied to me from day one, Alessandro.'

I mentally kicked myself for using his Christian name. It was too personal. Too informal. Too intimate.

'You have a sister and a niece and God knows who else. That's not what people in a relationship do. They share stuff. Important stuff.'

I felt a teeny-weeny twinge of guilt at my statement. I hadn't told him *my* important stuff, but I refused to see it as important. It was not worth thinking about. I *hated* thinking about it. It gave me nightmares to think about it. It was so long ago. I had packed away the sickening memories behind layers of I'm-a-tough-girl-don't-mess-with-me bravado.

'I would've told you in time.'

I rolled my eyes in disdain. 'Like when?' I said. 'On our fiftieth wedding anniversary?'

Ack! There's another word I loathe. Wedding.

'But there wasn't going to *be* a wedding, was there? Or even an engagement. Our quick-fire affair was all for show. After you'd achieved your aim of royally annoying your ex you would've neatly extricated yourself from our—' I put my fingers up in air quotation marks '—"relationship" and moved on to your next conquest. You're just annoyed I saw through you and got out first.'

His eyes held mine in a dark, unreadable lock. 'I'm not here to talk about the past. I'm here to talk about my niece's future.'

I gave him a narrow look. 'Why this school?'

His eyes didn't waver as they held mine. 'I told you. It's convenient for where I'll living.'

'So you're thinking of settling down at some point?'

Why are you asking that? I thought. *You. Do. Not. Care.*

'At some point.'

I was like a dog with a bone. A terrier, that's me. Now I had him here I wanted to know everything—even the stuff I didn't want to know. Maybe it wasn't a bone I was hanging on to. It was a smelly old carcass I was rolling in.

'Are you in a relationship with someone at present?' I said.

'No.'

'What about the blonde the other week?'

His eyes glinted as if in triumph. 'Was that your sister with you?'

I glowered at him. Why had I allowed myself to fall into his trap so easily? But then, I thought, what was the point in denying I'd seen him? It was making me look foolish, and the last thing I wanted was to appear foolish and gauche in front of him.

'Yes. Who was your date?'

'The practice manager from my consulting rooms.'

I only just managed to stop myself from rolling my eyes. I could just imagine the 'practice' they'd get up to.

'I'd love to see her job description.'

His jaw tensed as if he found my comment irritating. 'It was her birthday. Now, let's get on with the tour, shall we?'

It annoyed me that he'd made me look petty and unprofessional. 'This way,' I said, and turned smartly on my heels.

But I was all too acutely aware of his tall, commanding frame following close behind.

CHAPTER TWO

I COULD SMELL the lemon and spice of his aftershave as I led the way to the dormitories on the second floor. It was a subtle scent, redolent of warm summer afternoons in a lemon grove. I thought of that brief time in Paris— the way we'd met by accident when I'd run into him as I was coming out of a shop late on a Saturday afternoon. He steadied me with his hands and I looked up into his face and my heart all but stopped.

I'm the last person who would ever believe in love at first sight, but something happened at that moment I still can't explain. I felt something shift inside me as his dark brown eyes met mine. He spoke to me in fluent French, so that might have explained it. It made me fall all the faster. And then he was so gallant, bending down to help me pick up the tote bag that had slipped off my shoulder, spilling its contents all over the cobblestones.

When he handed me my wand of lip gloss our fingers touched. I felt a fizzing sensation that travelled all the way up my arm and somehow ended in a molten pool between my legs.

He led me to a quiet table in the shade of a leafy tree outside a café on the Rue de Seine and ordered sparkling mineral water for me and an espresso for himself. We talked for two hours but it felt like two minutes.

He told me how he had grown up in Sicily but had studied and trained in London, and was spending that year working at Paris's top cardiac centre to complete his PhD before heading back to London. Most surgeons found the specialty hard enough, but he'd taken on even more study.

He fascinated me. I was spellbound by his warm, intelligent brown eyes and his long-fingered hands that had so briefly touched mine. I thought of those hands, how they performed intricate surgery and saved countless lives. I sat there aching for him to touch me again. I must have communicated it silently, for he suddenly reached across the table and took my hand in his, stroking his thumb over the back of it as his eyes meshed with mine.

He didn't have to say a word. I could see it in his gaze. I knew it was the same in mine. There was a connection between us that transcended the primal attraction of two healthy consenting adults. I had never felt a surge of lust so overpowering, and yet I could feel something else as well, which was less easily defined.

Looking back, I suspect I recognised some quality in him that spoke to the lonely outsider in me, which I prided myself on keeping well hidden. My mother would say it was fate, or kismet, or the planets aligning or something. My father would say it had something to do with our chakras being balanced. Whatever it was, the world seemed to carry on without us as we sat there gazing into each other's eyes.

I gave myself a mental slap and pushed open the first dormitory door. 'We sleep the Key Stage One and Two girls two to a room to encourage close friendship,' I said.

'The older girls can request single rooms, but we encourage sharing to maintain a sense of family.'

Alessandro gave the dormitory a cursory look before meeting my gaze. I wondered if he could see any trace of the nostalgia that had momentarily sideswiped me. His eyes moved back and forth between each of mine as if searching for something.

'Are you happy, *ma petite*?'

I felt my knees weaken at the French endearment. I covered it quickly by pasting a poised and professional look on my face. I could *not* allow myself to be lured back into his sensual orbit. His voice, no matter what language he spoke—French, Italian, English or a combination of all three—made a frisson of delight shimmy down my spine.

I wondered if my voice had the same effect on him. Not flipping likely. I might have smoothed over my Yorkshire vowels after years of living in London, but even so there was no way anyone would want to listen to me reading the phone directory.

'What's wrong with Claudia's mother?' I asked, to steer the conversation away from my emotional health.

An impenetrable sheen came over his eyes and he turned away to look at the dormitory, with its two neatly made beds and the waist-high bookshelf that doubled as a bedside table between. There were two teddy bears in pink and purple tutus sitting side by side on the top. It might have been any bedroom in the suburbs except for the sound of schoolchildren playing in the playground outside.

'She's receiving treatment for a protracted illness,' he said after a long moment.

Something in my stomach slipped. 'Terminal?'

'I hope not.'

I bit my lip as I thought of six-year-old Claudia losing her mother. My mother—both my parents, actually—drove me nuts, but I couldn't imagine not having her around any more.

What would it do to a little girl so young to have no one but her uncle to watch out for her? Who would help her with the issues of growing up? Who would tell her about the birds and the bees, not to mention the blowflies who could destroy her innocence in…? Well, I'm not going to go there. Who would she turn to when the world seemed to be against her? Or when she got her heart broken for the first time? Who would hold her and tell her they loved her more than life itself?

'What about Claudia's father?' I asked.

Alessandro's top lip developed an unmistakable curl of disdain. 'He's not in the picture. Never has been. Claudia has never met him.'

'What about grandparents?'

The line of his mouth tightened until it was almost flat. 'There are none on either side.'

None? Or none he wanted to acknowledge? I wondered. 'Why didn't you tell me you had a sister five years ago?' I said.

He drew in a deep breath and slowly released it. I watched as his broad shoulders went down on the long exhale and what looked like a tiny flicker of pain passed over his features.

'We weren't in contact at that point.'

'Why?'

'It's complicated.'

'It sounds it.'

He gave me a level look. 'It's important to me that Claudia settles in as quickly and seamlessly as possible.'

'What have you told her about her mother's illness?'

He held my gaze for a moment before he looked away again. He let out another long breath. 'Not much. I didn't want her overburdened with worry about things she can't change. She's a sensitive child.'

'Then she'll join the dots for herself but probably come up with the wrong picture,' I said. 'You should be honest with her. Kids are much more resilient than you realise.'

His eyes collided again with mine, one of his brows going up in an arc. '*Are* they?'

It was a pointed question that hung suspended in the air.

I found myself going back in time to my own childhood, thinking of all the times when a bit of resilience would have come in handy. My parents' hippie lifestyle was fine for them, but it hadn't been fine for me or for my younger sister Bertie. So many times I'd had to take on a parenting role for Bertie's sake because our parents were missing in action, so to speak.

It's not that they weren't loving parents—if anything they were too indulgent. We didn't have any proper boundaries—not just to keep us in line, but also to give others a clear message that someone was watching out for us. Mum and Dad were dreamers—drifters who never stayed in one place long enough to put down roots— which meant Bertie and I had little stability during our childhood. We would no sooner make friends at one place before we'd be shuffled on to another location where some visionary guru was setting up a new lifestyle commune our parents were keen to join.

I was always watching out for Bertie, who got bullied a lot. I did too, until I learned to stand up for myself. I had to pretend to be tougher than I really was in order to survive. It's a good skill to have, but it has its downside. After all those years of playing tough it's hard to find my soft centre. It's been bricked in, like a vault cemented into a wall. I don't know if you can call that resilience or not.

I stopped thinking about my childhood and started speculating on Alessandro's. Was that why he had posed the question? Was there something about *his* childhood that made him sceptical of a child's ability to cope with what life dished up? I had always seen him as a strong, invincible sort of person. He had brushed off his 'orphan' status with a casual it-happened-a-long-time-ago-and-I'm-over-it shrug. But what had made him pretend to be alone in the world?

I didn't think it had been to garner sympathy. He was too self-reliant to want or need anyone else's comfort. That was what I'd found so attractive about him. He didn't care what people thought of him other than in a professional sense. He'd told me he wasn't out to win a popularity contest but to save lives. He got on with his life as if other people's opinions were irrelevant.

I secretly envied him as I'd spent so much of my life trying to fit in. I'd learned to morph into whatever I needed to be in order to belong. My chameleon-like behaviour had turned me into someone I didn't always like, but I wasn't sure how to go back to being the warm and friendly and open girl I had once been. To be perfectly honest, I wasn't sure if I even wanted to be that girl any more. That girl had got herself into trouble, and the last thing I wanted to attract was trouble.

Alessandro might have been in any sort of career and I would still have been attracted to him. I had been totally swept away by him—charmed and captivated by his take-charge, can-do attitude, which was so at odds

with the way I had been raised. He was goal-orientated
and disciplined. He didn't dream or drift aimlessly, or
wait for someone else to tell him what he should do. He
made plans and set about fulfilling them. He hadn't let
his background or lack of family money stop him from
becoming one of London's top heart specialists. He had
laid down a career path as a young boy and got on with
making it happen.

His intelligence was the biggest turn-on for me. I don't
mean his doctor status, because that sort of thing doesn't
impress me. I loved it that he was well read and well informed on topics I had barely even thought of before.
But it was the physical intensity between us that took me
completely by surprise. I had never considered myself a
sensual person. The event I refuse to talk about put paid
to that when I was thirteen. I wasn't the touchy-feely sort.
I didn't hug or kiss. I didn't seek affection and I didn't
give it—unless there was no avoiding it, like at Christ-
mas and on birthdays.

But with Alessandro I embraced my sexuality. I cel-
ebrated my womanhood with every cell of my body. I
bloomed and burned and blazed under his touch. I discovered things about my body I had no idea it was capable of—wickedly delightful things that left my skin
tingling for hours afterwards. I loved exploring the hard
contours of Alessandro's body. I just about crawled into
his skin once I lost my first flutter of fear.

I had never seen a man more beautifully made. Although I'm not a doctor like my sister Bertie, who sees
naked men all the time, I've seen a few. My parents went
through a naturalist stage when I was in my early teens,
so the male form is no stranger to me. Talk about embarrassing... Most of those men had the sort of bodies

one would think they would be desperate to cover up with clothes—layers and layers of them. But, no, it was all out on show. However, none of the men I had seen in their birthday suits had looked anywhere as perfect as Alessandro. He wasn't gym-obsessed perfect, but rather healthy and virile and in-his-prime perfect.

I had to give myself another mental slap to keep my mind on the conversation. Images of his naked body were flooding my brain to such a degree I could feel warmth blooming in my cheeks. I rarely blush. I lost my innocence a long time ago. But something about Alessandro's penetrating gaze made me feel as if he could see exactly where my mind was taking me.

I realised then with a little jolt that the intimacy we'd shared would always be between us. We had 'A History'. It wasn't as if I could wipe it away, like I do the day's lesson from the whiteboard in the classroom. There was a permanent record of it in my flesh.

I was tattooed with his touch, indelibly marked, so that when any other man touched me I automatically compared it to Alessandro's and found it sadly lacking. It's basically why I haven't bothered dating. I don't see the point. Quite frankly, I could do without being reminded I'm basically dead from the waist down with anyone else.

'I'll…erm…show you the bathrooms,' I said, and made to turn away.

But his hand stalled me again. I had folded my arms across my body, which meant his hand was tantalisingly close to my breasts. I felt the stirring tingle of my flesh, as if my breasts had picked up his proximity like some sort of finely tuned radar.

My breath stalled somewhere in the middle of my throat. I brought my gaze up to his. His eyes were so dark it was impossible to make out his pupils. A girl could get lost in those eyes. Disappear and never be found again.

My gaze went to his mouth as if of its own volition. My stomach did a rollercoaster loop and drop as I recalled how his lips had felt against mine. The taste of him, the feel of him, the sensual power of him had made everything so tight and bound up inside me unwind. His lips were evenly shaped—neither too thick or too thin. He had shaved that morning, but even so I could see the urgent pinpricks of stubble surrounding his mouth and on his lean jaw.

My fingers twitched to slide over it, to remind myself of the erotic feel of his prickly male skin against the softness my female flesh.

I dragged in a ragged breath and brought my gaze back to his, but he was now looking at *my* mouth, a small frown tugging at his brow. I ran the tip of my tongue over my lips and my stomach did another crazy somersault as I saw his sexily hooded eyes follow its pathway.

I swear to God someone had sucked all the oxygen out of the air. I was finding it hard to breathe. I was standing there as if I'd been snap freeze-dried. I couldn't have move if I'd tried.

His hand reached out and ever so gently cupped my cheek. A shiver of reaction coursed through me, but for some reason I still didn't move away. It was like I was under his spell. Totally under his control, with no will to snap out of it. The pad of his thumb moved over the circle of my chin, not quite touching my lower lip but close enough for it to go into raptures of tingling, fizzing anticipation. His eyes remained focused on my mouth, as if he too were recalling how it had felt against his.

Was he going to kiss me? Would I allow him to? I was

in a conundrum. I wanted to feel his mouth on mine if for no other reason than to prove to myself that I'd been imagining it had felt far more amazing than it actually had. I guess I also wanted to prove to myself that I could resist him. That I could withstand the commanding pressure of his mouth and not melt into a pool of mush.

But another shockingly traitorous part of me wanted to close the distance between our mouths and give myself up to the storm of passion I could feel building inside my body. It was surging through my blood, firing up all my senses, making me giddy with longing. A longing I could feel pounding deep in my core. The relentless ache of it was part pleasure, part pain. It had been so long since I'd felt desire I was shocked at how powerful it was.

I realised then how base I was. How utterly primal my urges were that, for all my prim and proper fastidiousness, I was as earthy and lust driven as anyone else.

Alessandro's thumb pressed against my lower lip and I all but whimpered. I smothered it as best I could but I saw the gleam of satisfaction in his eyes as they meshed with mine.

'Have dinner with me tonight,' he said.

The fact he'd issued it as a command rather than asked me was enough to break the spell. I stepped out of his light hold and sent him an icy glare.

'The staff at Emily Sudgrove are prohibited from fraternising with the parents or guardians of the girls,' I said.

That wasn't strictly true, but it sounded like it could be. I hoped he wouldn't find out about Kate McManus, a young widow who had recently started dating our Physical Education teacher, Rob Canning. We were delighted with the budding romance, because Rob had gone through a really painful divorce a few years ago and Kate was the only woman he'd dated since.

'Are you involved with someone?' Alessandro said.

I put on my best haughty look. Bertie reckons no one can do haughty better than me. I can arch my brows and look down my nose and send sparks of scorn from my gaze like a blue-blooded aristocrat staring down an impudent underling.

'I have no idea what makes you think you have the right to ask me such an impertinently personal question, Dr Lucioni,' I said.

His mouth tipped up at one corner, as if he found me amusing rather than threatening. 'So that's a no,' he said.

I wished I could deny it, but he would only have to ask around to find out my dating track record was abysmal. My life was a cycle of work, eat and sleep. I occasionally threw in a bit of exercise to break it up a bit. But the fact is I love my job. I don't want to be distracted from it. As far as I can see, having a relationship is one big time suck.

I didn't have the time or the inclination to be someone's date for a few weeks or months, until they found someone more attractive or more interesting. I had much more important things to do with my time. I was proud of the work I did with the girls—especially the ones who struggled to fulfil their high-flying, high-achieving parents' dreams for them. I spent a lot of time planning lessons and writing up programmes and exercises.

I'm not a chalk-and-talk teacher. I'm interactive and creative and I thrive on seeing the girls in my charge blossom and play to their strengths. I would much rather give my girls an A for effort and attitude than an A for academic prowess.

My mother laments the fact that my life has no balance but who is she to talk? She hasn't held down a job since before Bertie and I were born. Nor has my father. They've lived on their parents' trust funds while meditating their mostly peaceful way around the country. I say 'mostly' because there was one occasion a couple of years back when I had to bail both of them out of a county court after a forestry expansion protest got a little ugly. It was quite a while before I could turn on the television without expecting to see an image of my parents chained to a tree, dressed in hemp clothing and waving placards.

Lately even Bertie has been banging on about me finding someone now she's got herself engaged to a fellow doctor. I must admit when I met her fiancé I did feel a teeny-weeny twinge of envy. The way Matt Bishop looked at my sister made me feel all squishy and gooey inside. But I quickly squashed the feeling. Bertie has always been a romantic, with her head in the clouds. I'm much more down to earth and practical. Believe me, I've had to be. Someone in our family had to have their head screwed on.

I pursed my lips at Alessandro. One thing I did have in common with my little sister was that I did not appreciate being laughed at.

'You find it funny that I choose to be single?' I said. '*You're* currently single, are you not?'

His brows lifted slightly. 'I didn't realise you took such an interest and followed my love-life in the press.'

I could have kicked myself. I had as good as admitted to poring over every inch of the tabloids for news of him. Mind you, he kept a much lower profile than some others of his ilk. Being a celebrity doctor and a bachelor made men like him a juicy target for the press.

Every time I saw a photo of him with some gorgeous model-type I would seethe and quake with rage. It would reopen all the wounds I'd tried so hard to heal. It was like rock salt being pummelled into them.

But why he had never settled for long with anyone since me puzzled me. The ex he had been so keen to prove a point to had married the man she'd left Alessandro for—a high-profile businessman who was superduper wealthy. But I'd heard whispers in the press that the marriage was in trouble. Was he waiting for her to divorce her husband so they could be together?

I glowered at Alessandro as I stalked past to lead the way on the rest of the tour. I pointed out the bathrooms, and then the games room, and the juniors' and the seniors' common rooms. I spoke in a flat monotone, stripping my expression of anything other than excruciating boredom.

If he was annoyed by my little show of defiance he didn't show it on his face. His expression was mostly blank, apart from that faraway look I caught a glimpse of now and again. Finally we made our way outside into the sunshine, where the children were playing just before the lunch break ended.

One of my pupils, a little girl called Harriet, came gambolling up with a cheeky grin on her freckled face. 'Is that man your boyfriend, Miss Clark?'

I'm not one to blush easily, but right then I could feel heat spreading like a grass fire across my cheeks.

When I was a little kid I didn't think teachers were anything but teachers. I didn't think they had a personal life. To me they were like police or firemen or other authority figures. They didn't seem like real people. Not so today's kids. They know too damn much and way too early.

'No, Harriet,' I said. 'Dr Lucioni is enrolling his niece into our school. I'm giving him a guided tour.'

Harriet scrunched up her face as she peered at Alessandro. 'Are you a movie star?'

Alessandro's smile at Harriet made something at the backs of my knees go fizzy.

'No, I'm afraid not.'

Harriet wasn't convinced. 'You *look* famous.'

'Run along, Harriet,' I said. 'The bell is about to ring.'

As if I'd summoned it, the bell sounded, and Harriet scampered off to join the rest of the girls as they prepared to enter the building for the afternoon's lessons.

I turned to face Alessandro. 'That's my cue as well. When shall I expect Claudia to come to class?'

'I'll bring her tomorrow.'

'Where is she now?'

'With a temporary nanny.'

'Why didn't you bring her with you today?' I said. 'It would've helped her to get her bearings. Meeting the other girls and so on.'

His eyes tethered mine in a lock that made my insides flutter as if a handful of flustered moths were trapped in the cavity of my stomach.

'I thought it best for us to meet alone first,' he said.

I didn't think it was wise for me to *ever* be alone with him. I didn't trust myself. He had a frightening way of dismantling my self-control with a look or a casual touch. My chin was still tingling from where his thumb had stroked. My wrist was still burning as if he had left a brand on my flesh. My inner core was still pulsating with the memory of how his body had moved within mine.

Again I wondered if he was remembering all we had shared in that brief mad fling I'd stupidly thought would last for ever.

His gaze was dark and bottomless…inscrutable, enigmatic. Mesmerising.

The sound of the second end-of-lunch bell startled me out of my stasis. 'Excuse me,' I said with a formal quirk of my lips that passed for a smile. 'I have to get to class.'

He put out his hand, and because we were in full view of the school admin office, as well as Miss Fletcher's office, I had no choice but to slide mine into it.

His fingers closed around mine in the same way they had before. There was nothing formal or polite about it. It was purely erotic. Wickedly, shamelessly erotic.

I drew my hand away from the temptation of his touch and turned and walked into the school building. But it was not until school finished that day that my hand finally stopped tingling.

CHAPTER THREE

I WAS AT SCHOOL early the next morning…earlier than usual. So shoot me. I'm a lark, not an owl. I like to get on with the day from the get-go. I bounce out of bed and hit the ground like a lightning bolt. It's because I'm a list-maker. I thrive on being organised. It's like an addiction. I even write down things I've already done, just so I can get that little buzz of satisfaction at seeing it ticked off.

My parents think I'm crazy not to start my day with some peaceful mindfulness practice or yoga poses or chanting. They sleep in until midday when they come to stay, which drives me completely nuts. And I use the term 'sleep in' loosely. They do a lot of things in bed when they come to stay, and not much of it involves sleeping.

Everyone thinks their parents don't 'do it', but my parents make sure everyone knows they do. At least these days they're only doing it with each other. Up until a couple of years ago they had an 'open relationship', which meant they could have sex with anyone they fancied and the other wouldn't mind. Bertie and I found it completely and utterly weird.

My mother is embarrassingly open about sex. My dad too, although he doesn't drop it into every conversation like my mother does. It's the first thing she asks me when she calls. 'How's your sex life?' Or, yesterday's cracker: 'Did you know having an orgasm every day is good for your pelvic floor?'

Seriously, I think she's obsessed or something.

I like being at school early because I like being prepared. I like getting my lessons organised, with all the little extra touches I've designed that are tailor-made to each child's learning style and personality. I like watching the girls come in through the school gate or walk over from the boarding house. I guess it's my version of people-watching.

I learn a lot about the dynamic between parents and their children by watching what happens in the hand over. You can see the parents who have a tendency to do too much for their kids. They're the one carrying the kid's backpack or tennis racket or lacrosse stick or musical instrument. I have nothing against parents helping little kids with their things, but senior girls…? Honestly…

I also learn a lot about the dynamic between the girls and what sort of mood they are in as they file into the building. I can tell which girl has had a bad night, or which one is homesick, or which one is lauding it over another. I can almost read their little minds.

Maybe I'm more like my mother than I realise. Scary thought.

After a few of the regulars had arrived I noticed a shiny black sports car pull up in front of the school. A lot of expensive cars pull up in front of the Emily Sudgrove School for Girls, but this one stood out. It was a top-model Maserati, with tinted windows so you couldn't see who was behind the wheel or inside the car. It had a throaty roar I swear you'd be able to hear from the next suburb. Possibly from across the English Channel.

I watched as Alessandro got out from behind the wheel with the sort of athletic grace I privately envied. It's not that I'm clumsy or anything, but I've never mastered the art of alighting from a vehicle without showing too much leg or, on one spectacularly embarrassing occasion, my underwear—which was unfortunately not the sensible sort.

Alessandro opened the back passenger door and leaned down to speak to the little girl inside. I saw him take her by the hand and gently help her from the car. When I saw him smile at his niece a hand reached deep inside my chest and squeezed my heart. He gave Claudia's ponytail a little tug and then led her by the hand towards the entrance of school, carrying a suitcase, presumably full of her belongings, in the other.

When we'd been together Alessandro had spoken openly about his desire for a family. I'd been ecstatic. So many men were either not ready or didn't want kids at all. I was so thrilled that I'd found a man who wanted the things I wanted. Back then I wanted to have kids and do all the things with them my parents hadn't done with Bertie and I.

I wanted to live with them in a proper house—not a commune or a tree house or a bark hut. I wanted to toilet train them instead of letting them go wherever or whenever nature called. Don't ask, but rest assured I'd sorted it out by the time I was four and taught Bertie in the process. I wanted to be interested in their education, supervising it so they got the help and encouragement they needed. I wanted to go on holidays—not communal ones, with a guru dictating the programme, but relaxing ones where I could play with my kids and enjoy the magic of their childhood.

And I wanted to share the whole experience with a man I loved and trusted to stand by me no matter what.

Yeah, I know. What a deluded fool I was.

I was waiting in my classroom, pretending to be sorting out flashcards, when Alessandro arrived at the door. I put the flashcards down and smiled at the little girl standing meekly by his side.

'Hello, Claudia,' I said, and squatted down so we were eye to eye. 'My name is Miss Clark. It's lovely to have you in my class.'

Claudia had the biggest brown eyes I'd ever seen, fringed with thick lashes that were like miniature black fans. Her skin was olive toned but quite pale, as if she spent a lot of time indoors. She was small for her age, delicate and finely made, with thin wrists and ankles, and she had a pretty little cupid's bow mouth that was currently finding it difficult to smile.

'Go on, Claudia,' Alessandro prompted gently. 'Say hello to Miss Clark.'

Claudia's little cheeks turned bright red and she bent her chin to her chest as she mumbled so softly I could barely hear her. 'Hello, Mith C-C-C-C-Clark.'

My heart gave another painful squeeze when I heard that shy little voice with its lisp and stutter. It reminded me of myself at that age, when I had a terrible speech impediment. I was mercilessly teased about it.

There are times when I can still hear the mean kids imitating my inability to say certain words. Anything starting with a hard-sounding consonant was torture for me. I finally got control of it by the time I was ten—and not because my parents sent me to a speech therapist. They flatly refused to. They believed my stutter was a voice from one of my past lives trying to be heard and that I had to be patient and allow them to channel through me. *Yeah, right.* Why is it that everyone's been a prince or princess in a past life and never a penniless pauper?

Anyway, back to my stutter. It was because of a teacher I had—once we were placed back in school— who was really fabulous at teaching drama. She used to give me the best roles to play and like magic my stutter would disappear. It was as if by playing someone else I could forget about my speech impediment. I've since done a special education diploma in language and learning difficulties, which I've found enormously helpful as a classroom teacher.

I straightened so I could speak to Alessandro. I had to keep my friendly and open smile in place, but it nearly killed me.

'There's just enough time for me to take Claudia over to the boarding house to meet the house mistress,' I said. 'It would be good to get her settled in before class starts. Her roommate, Phoebe Milton, is looking forward to meeting her.'

A pleated frown appeared between his eyes. 'You're right. I should've thought of that yesterday. But there's been so much to do over the last few days.'

I realised then that looking after a small child of six was a probably a relatively new experience for him. He was out of his depth and doing everything he could not to show it. It made me feel a flicker of compassion for him I wasn't expecting to feel. I didn't want to feel a flicker of *anything* for him, but seeing him with his little niece took the sharp edges off my bitterness—like a file does a ragged fingernail.

He was so kind and tender and protective of her. He hadn't once let go of her tiny hand. Just seeing his large tanned hand gently holding that tiny pale one made my heart contract again. There was so much I wanted to ask him, but with his little charge there to hear every word I had to hold my tongue. I also didn't want to let little Claudia pick up on anything untoward between Alessandro and I.

He had already said she was a sensitive child and I could well believe it. Her obvious shame at her lisp and her stutter was making my chest ache with sympathy so badly it hurt every time I took a breath. It would be irresponsible of me, not to mention unprofessional, to give Claudia the impression I was at odds with her uncle— even though it was true. From what I'd gathered so far, he was the only anchor she had right now.

Once we got to the boarding house I introduced Alessandro and Claudia to Jennifer Lancaster, the boarding-house mistress. Once pleasantries were exchanged, Jennifer took Claudia by the hand and showed her where she would be sleeping.

'How long has Claudia been with you?' I asked Alessandro, once we were out of his niece's hearing.

'Two weeks.'

Yikes, I thought. That would certainly have put the brakes on his playboy lifestyle.

'You mentioned you'd lost contact with Claudia's mother,' I said. 'How long have you been back in contact?'

'About a month,' he said. 'She called me out of the blue and said she needed my help.'

I sent him a sideways glance but he was looking at his niece, who was standing quietly as Jennifer unpacked her belongings. Claudia was biting down on her bottom lip, and even though we were a few feet away I could see the distinct wobble of her little chin.

'Should I go to her?' he asked, turning to look at me.

I was tempted to bite my own lip in sympathy for the poor little kid. But I knew from experience that drawing too much attention to the imminent separation of parent/ guardian and child sometimes made it worse.

'The first couple of days will be hard, but she'll soon settle in,' I said. 'Jennifer's put her with a lovely little kid. They'll be best friends before you know it.'

Fortunately Phoebe came in at that point, so the two girls had a chance to meet before class. Phoebe was as ebullient as a friendly puppy, thankfully doing enough of the talking for Claudia simply to stand there and smile shyly.

'At least it's not for long,' Alessandro said as he and I watched the two girls interact. 'I hope to have the house ready in a month, tops.'

Was it the dream house we had talked about while lying in bed in Paris on those wonderful mornings when I'd basked in the glow of his lovemaking? Who would he share it with now? A knife stabbed me under the ribs. Why couldn't I move on? So what if he found someone to have babies with? I. Did. Not. Care.

'How long do you think you'll have Claudia?' I asked.

'It depends on how my sister responds to treatment.' He turned and looked at me again. 'I would appreciate it if you'd call me immediately if you have any concerns about my niece.' He handed me a business card with his contact details on it. 'You can call me any time. Day or night.'

I pocketed the card as Jennifer came over with Claudia and Phoebe, who were holding hands.

'Ready to meet the rest of your classmates?' I said with a bright, enthusiastic smile.

Claudia gave a tiny nod without speaking, her big soulful eyes making that knife under my ribs jab a little harder.

'How's your new pupil settling in?' asked Lucy Gatton, the Reception/Kindergarten class teacher, when I came into the staffroom at lunchtime.

I gave Lucy a brief rundown on what I'd observed about Claudia and her speech impediment, and the way she compensated for it by allowing others to speak for her.

'She's a little on the shy side, but she seems to be fitting in without too much trouble,' I said. 'Phoebe Milton's taken her under her wing.'

I could have kissed Phoebe for how brilliantly she was looking after Alessandro's niece. Phoebe's parents were missionaries in Sierra Leone. She had been sent to England with her brother to be educated after an Ebola virus outbreak a few months ago. I was amazed at how easily she had adapted to boarding school. It was as if she was on her own little mission—taking care of the natives, so to speak. She was a born nurturer who was always on the watch for anyone who needed a bit of love and care.

She reminded me of Bertie at that age—always eager to please and friendly to a fault—and I was hopeful that Claudia and Phoebe would become best buddies once Claudia developed some confidence. It was only the first day and the poor little munchkin had been through a lot just recently.

It's hard as a teacher not to become emotionally involved. *Too* emotionally involved, I mean. The kids feel like *my* kids. I want to protect them like a mother hen.

I hate seeing them struggle. I feel actual physical pain when I see them cry or hurt themselves or get hurt by others. I could tell Claudia was going to be one of those kids I would be lying awake at night worrying about. She had a haunted look in those big brown eyes—as if she'd seen things no child of her age should ever have seen.

'Was that her father who brought her to school?' Lucy asked.

'No, her uncle.'

I could feel the probe of Lucy's gaze as I set about making myself a cup of tea. I had tried to keep my expression suitably composed when dealing with Alessandro earlier, but anyone who knew anything about body language would have known I wasn't entirely at ease with him. Half the time my body had been giving off signals I had absolutely no control over.

How was I going to maintain a professional standing when he was around? How much would he *be* around? Although Claudia was boarding at Emily Sudgrove it was solely for practical reasons. Would he come and visit her regularly? How was I going to avoid him? At the very least there would be the parent-teacher interviews, which we do twice a term—more frequently if there's a problem.

And the more I saw of little Claudia the more I realised there *was* a problem…

'He looks kind of familiar…' Lucy tapped her chin for a moment. 'Of *course*! He's that celebrity doctor, isn't he? I didn't recognise him, dressed in civvies. I saw a couple of press interviews but he was wearing scrubs. He's gorgeous looking, isn't he?'

'Is he?' I reached for a tea bag from the box on the shelf. 'I hadn't noticed.'

Lucy gave a snorting laugh. 'Pull the other one, Jem.

Tell you what—I wish one of *my* uncles looked like him. Is he single?'

'Apparently.' I spent an inordinate amount of time jiggling the tea bag in my cup.

'So how come he's looking after his niece?' Lucy asked.

'Her mother's ill.'

'Cancer?'

'He didn't say, and I didn't like to pry,' I said. 'I got the feeling it was painful for him to discuss.'

'Poor little kid.' Lucy sighed. 'But is boarding school the right place for her?'

'Al—Dr Lucioni is renovating his house,' I said, just catching myself from saying his Christian name in time. 'Claudia will live with him once it's completed, or until her mother is out of hospital—whichever happens first.'

'But if the kid's mother's in hospital and she's boarding he won't be able to take her to see her.'

I'd been thinking the very same thing. Years ago no one took children to visit their loved ones in hospital in the belief that it would terrify them or make them too upset. It was the same with funerals. Children were kept away in an effort to shield them. But children needed to process the same emotions that adults felt, with plenty of support at hand.

'I know,' I said to Lucy. 'I guess he thinks it's for the best. Perhaps the mother's on a ventilator or something. That would be pretty distressing to see as a little kid.'

'Maybe she's in a psych ward?' Lucy said.

A ghostly hand touched the back of my neck with icy fingers. Was that why Alessandro was keeping his little niece away? Was Claudia's mother mentally unstable?

Mental illness is possibly the most difficult of all

conditions for a child to understand. The impact of medication can often make things worse before it makes things better. It's harrowing for everyone involved, let alone a small child who looks to their parent for safety and security.

I frowned into my cup and saw the tea-leaves had spilled out of the tea bag from all the jiggling. They'd made a weird swirly pattern on the bottom of my cup.

I couldn't help wondering what my mother would make of it.

I stayed late at school—there was nothing unusual in that—to check that Claudia was settling in to the boarding house. I found her and Phoebe sitting on the floor of their bedroom with a bunch of Barbies in various states of dress and undress.

I didn't interrupt them for long. As usual Phoebe was doing all the talking, but Claudia was handing her articles of clothing and tiny high-heeled shoes, and seemed to be enjoying herself. I suspected Phoebe's friendly chatter relaxed Claudia as it took the pressure off her to speak. After all, there are speakers and there are listeners. Some people are much more comfortable doing all the talking. Others like to take time to listen and reflect. I suspected that even without her speech impediment Claudia would still be a reserved and reflective child.

On the way out I had a chat with Jennifer to make sure everything was going fine, and was reassured to hear Claudia had eaten a healthy after-school snack and had even smiled a couple of times at something Phoebe had said. I wondered if the boarding house was providing the sort of security and routine Claudia might have been missing in her life with her mother. I couldn't let it go. I *had* to find out what was wrong with her mother.

But the only way I could do that was to meet with Alessandro. In private.

I found his address on the school's computer system. I had his number on the business card he'd given me, but I didn't want to give him a heads-up about me coming to visit. I wanted simply to show up. I know it was cynical of me, but I wanted to cold-call him to see if he really *was* renovating—not trying to keep some sexy little model-type a secret while his little niece languished at boarding school.

I know. I'm a hard case. But it's his fault.

I drove about twenty minutes out of Bath into the countryside that makes England so famous. Verdant rolling fields, birds twittering in the hedgerows and late-afternoon sunlight casting everything in a golden hue that looked as picturesque as a postcard.

I turned up a tree-lined driveway that had a creamy-coloured Georgian mansion at the end of it. The trees' overarching limbs with their fresh spring growth created a lime-green canopy overhead. It was like driving through a long, leafy tunnel.

The mansion, on closer inspection, was indeed in the throes of being renovated. Tradesmen's tools such as ladders and sawhorses and scaffolding surrounded the building, and stonemasons had clearly been doing their thing. However, they weren't currently doing their thing as it was way past knock-off time. The place looked deserted.

I parked the car and got out, waiting for a sign of anyone responding to my arrival. Not that my car gave anything like the roar Alessandro's had done outside school that morning. My car is more of the coughing and spluttering type, although today was a good day. So far.

I stood there for five minutes… Well, it was probably closer to thirty seconds, but it felt like five years. In case you haven't already guessed by now, I'm not the most patient person on the planet.

I walked across the gravel courtyard to the front door, my footsteps sounding like I was walking over bubble wrap in spiky heels. There was a brass doorbell on the left-hand side of the door, which I noted needed a good polish. It made no sound at all that I could tell from where I was standing. I gave the door a rap with my knuckles but—unlike in all those period dramas my sister loves watching—no uniformed butler answered my summons.

I looked at the door for a moment before reaching out and turning the doorknob. The door opened with a ghostly creak that made the hairs on the back of my neck stand up. The sensible, law-abiding side of my brain was asking, *What the hell are you doing trespassing on private property?* But the other side was saying, *Go on. Have a good old snoop. You know you want to.*

I stepped over the threshold and peered around in the failing light. Thousands of dust motes were floating in the air, as if my entry had disturbed them from a century-long slumber. I stepped further inside, and the floorboards announced my presence with a screech of protest. It gave me such a fright that I let go of the doorknob and a tiny gust of wind—it might even have been a ghost, but don't tell my mother I said that—closed the door behind me with a snap that sounded as loud as a rifle shot.

My heart was suddenly not where it was supposed to be. It had leapt from my chest to my throat and was fluttering there like a pigeon stuck in a pipe. I gave myself a good old talking-to and reached for the doorknob. It wouldn't budge. I rattled it a couple of times. I turned it this way and that. I tugged on it. Then I put both hands on it and rattled it some more.

The rattles echoed throughout the foyer like chains in a dungeon. I could feel perspiration breaking out between my shoulder blades even though the temperature inside the house was cool. Ghost cool, if you were the type to believe in all that nonsense—which, of course, I wasn't. I knew for sure that my parents' seances were staged. I'd seen my father's finger pushing the glass across the board. I'd pushed the thing myself, to spell out 'this sucks' when my mother had pressured me to join in the last time I visited.

I pulled on the doorknob with one almighty tug and stumbled backwards as it came off in my hands. I regained my balance and stood staring down at the brass ball of the doorknob as if it were a hand grenade.

I tried to put it back where it belonged, but part of the mechanism had come away with the knob. My heart began its frantic flapping up in my throat again. I was trapped inside Alessandro Lucioni's house and night was falling. How on earth was I going to get out? What if he found me skulking around in there? I would look like a complete nutcase. A stalker. A prowler. A first-class idiot.

The windows. *Of course!* I put the doorknob down on the dust-ridden surface of a hall table and went to the nearest windows, which were in a reception/drawing room off the hall. I tried the catches but they looked like they had all been painted over. None of them would budge at all.

I went to the next room along but, while I was able to get one catch undone, the sash of the window must have been broken because it wouldn't lift up. I let out a very rude word—and turned around to see a tall, silent figure framed in the doorway. This time my heart almost leapt out of my throat and bounced along the floor. Then I realised it was Alessandro, and not some ghostly spectre from the past.

But then, he *was* a spectre from the past.

'You scared the freaking hell out of me!' I said.

He cocked an eyebrow in a wry manner. 'Same.'

Quite frankly, I was annoyed he wasn't showing any of the fear or shock he'd alleged I'd caused him. My heart was still hammering so fast I could feel it in my fingertips, and my stomach was like a butter churn set on too fast a speed.

When I'm cornered I always go on the offensive. 'What sort of place *is* this?' I said. 'It's not safe for an adult, let alone a child. You should have hazard signs up, with skulls and crossbones on them. How on earth are you going to have this house ready in a *month*? Have you got rocks in your head?'

He moved further into the room. It was a large room. A very large room. But when he entered it felt like we were in a dolls' house. Or maybe even a matchbox. He came to stand in front of me. I resisted the urge to back away. There wasn't anywhere to go other than through the window that had stubbornly refused to provide me with an escape route.

The closer he got the more my heart raced. *Boom. Boom. Boom.* It was not just pounding in my fingertips but between my legs as well. I could feel the memory of him pulsing through me, heating me inside out. My flesh was hungry, starved, just about gagging for his touch. I could feel its restiveness against the covering of my clothes, as if my body couldn't wait to get naked and feel his wickedly clever hands gliding over every inch of it.

His eyes were dark and inscrutable as they held mine. 'Why are you sneaking around my house?'

I gave him an affronted look. 'I wasn't sneaking. I called on you but no one answered the door.'

'So you let yourself in?'

The way he said it made it sound like I'd committed a crime. But then, breaking and entering was—and I was guilty on both counts. I'd entered his house and I'd broken his door.

'I was just taking a look around,' I said, quickly thinking on my feet. 'I was checking to see if the place was suitable. We at Emily Sudgrove often do home visits.'

One of his dark brows went up again. 'Unannounced?'

'Well, yes, of course,' I said. 'We like to make sure our girls come from good homes. *Safe* homes.' I emphasised the word 'safe'.

Something in his gaze hardened to onyx. 'I can assure you my niece's safety is my primary concern, Miss Clark.'

It was kind of weird, having him call me Miss Clark—even though I'd been the one to insist on it. It was like we were each playing a role in a play. And right now it was feeling more and more like a melodrama. He was looking all stern and irritated, as if he wanted to remove me bodily from the premises, and I felt like a petty thief caught red-handed.

But I could also feel something else pulsing between us. Not just hostility, because that was coming mostly from me. I'm no mind-reader, but I got a sense that he was brooding over something that had nothing to do with our history. There was a wall around him—an invisible fortress that made him appear untouchable. It was like he was weighed down with something. It was in the way he held himself: the braced posture, the rigid set of his jaw, the guardedness about his expression and the shadows that came and went at the back of his eyes.

Was it concern about his sister and his niece? It was an enormous responsibility to be appointed *in loco parentis*. He was used to being a playboy, free to live his life without having to answer to anyone.

He walked back to the door of the drawing room and held it open in a pointed manner. 'I have things to do. I trust you'll make your own way out?'

I gave him a sheepish look. 'Actually, I had a bit of a problem with your front door.'

A muscle ticked near the corner of his mouth. I wasn't sure if it was anger or amusement. It was hard to tell from his expression.

'Oh?'

'Yes, it sort of broke. That's how I got locked in. That's why I was in here, trying to get out of the window.'

It was definitely amusement, I decided. I could see the corners of his mouth twitching and a gleam had come into his darker-than-night eyes.

'There *is* a back entrance.'

Now, why didn't I think of that? I wondered. 'Oh, right…well. Maybe I'll go out that way.'

I made to go past him in the doorway but he put out his arm like a railway-crossing barrier.

'When Beauty trespasses on the Beast's property there's a forfeit to pay,' he said.

I wasn't sure what version of *Beauty and the Beast* he was working from, but it certainly wasn't the same as mine. I looked at the strongly corded muscles of his arm, blocking my escape. He was wearing a light grey cotton T-shirt that clung to his chest and shoulders like cling film. Every sculpted muscle was showcased to perfection—especially his pectorals and biceps. *Oh, dear God, his biceps.*

He had patches of perspiration on his chest and beneath his armpits, and his arms were dusty—as if he had been working on the house. How could someone look so good when they were so hot and sweaty? My insides did a little shuffling thing at the thought of those arms pinning me to a bed while he had his wicked, wonderfully heart-stopping way with me.

I made the mistake of lifting my gaze to his mouth. He hadn't shaved since that morning and his stubble was rich and plentiful, reminding me of the way it had felt scraping along my skin in the past.

I had to curl my fingers into tight balls to stop myself from touching him. I surreptitiously breathed in the scent of him—that beguiling mix of citrus and hard-working male that was as intoxicating as a drug. Not that I've ever *done* drugs. I leave that sort of stuff to my parents.

I curled my fists even harder. So hard I could feel my nails digging into my palms—which is really saying something, as I don't have any nails to speak of. I've been a nail-biter since… Well, since way back.

The urge to touch him was overwhelming. It was like my body was set on automatic. It wanted to do all the things it used to do. Touch him. Stroke him. Kiss him until we were tearing at each other's clothes. My inner core was throbbing with need and he hadn't even touched me.

Alessandro's gaze went to my mouth. I knew that look so well. I hadn't been able to erase that look from my memory even though I had so desperately tried. The smouldering heat of it, the electrifying erotic promise of it, was enough to make my girly bits shiver in rapture.

He lifted his hand and ever so slowly grazed my face with his knuckles. It was such a light touch, barely touching my face at all, but it was as if he had set alive every nerve beneath my skin with an electrode. I felt the pulse of it shoot like a hot wire straight to my core.

'You should've left while you had the chance,' he said, in a voice that sounded like it had been dragged over his gravel driveway before being swirled around in a pot of honey.

I could have pointed out that he hadn't given me the chance to leave, but right then winning an argument wasn't high on my list of priorities. I found myself transfixed by his mouth as it came inexorably closer to mine. My breath hitched and stuttered and then stalled. My heart leapt and then galloped as our breaths mingled in that infinitesimal moment before final touchdown.

My lips all but exploded with fiery sensation as his covered mine. The pressure of his mouth was not too hard nor too soft, but—to borrow from another popular fairy tale—just right. His tongue stroked along the seam of my mouth but he needn't have bothered asking for entry. I was already opening to him with a sound of encouragement that was part whimper, part gasp of delighted surprise.

How could I have forgotten how wonderful his mouth tasted? It was like rediscovering a favourite flavour. My tastebuds tingled and danced and exploded with delight. My tongue met his, darting against it in a come-play-with-me action that made him growl deep at the back of his throat.

He took control of the kiss by spinning me around so my back was against the nearest wall, pinning my hands either side of my head as his mouth supped and sucked on mine. The seductive pressure on my mouth incited me to arch my back and press my pelvis against his in a totally instinctive, utterly primal manner. I wanted to feel his response to me. The swell of his flesh, the arousal that signalled his need for me, which I desperately hoped was as fervent and out of control as mine.

It was.

He was hard and getting harder. I could feel the hardened swell of his erection growing against my body, making me ache with a bone-deep longing. I moved against him wantonly, urging him to take things to the next level. It had been so long since I'd felt desire like this. It was pulsing through me like a force I had no power to control.

There was an element of desperation about his kiss— as if he'd been waiting a long time to feast on my mouth and was making up for lost time. His tongue stabbed and stroked at mine, ramping up my desire until my whole body was trembling with it.

He reached for the tie at the back of my head and my hair fell in a mass of curls around my shoulders. He fisted one of his hands in my hair as he worked his magic on my mouth. The slight tug on the roots of my hair triggered a wave of intense longing deep in my womb.

His mouth moved from mine to blaze a hot, moist pathway down the sensitive skin of my neck. His stubble grazed, his teeth scraped, his tongue salved. I whimpered and melted against him. My legs were like two strands of overcooked fettuccine. I would have slithered to the floor if it hadn't been for him holding me upright.

He moved further down to my décolletage; ruthlessly

pulling aside the sensible cotton blouse I was wearing to access the upper curve of my breasts. His tongue licked the valley between before moving up in a fiery blast of heat over each of my curves in turn. He didn't expose my nipples. He didn't have to. They were doing their own little happy dance behind the lace cups of my bra.

His mouth came back to mine as he tugged my blouse out of the waistband of my cotton trousers so he could access my naked skin. I shuddered with delight as his hands glided over my waist and rib cage. His hands were slightly callused, and that added roughness gave his touch a primal, almost dangerous element to it that made my knees feel as weak and wobbly as a newborn foal on ice skates.

His tongue tangled with mine in a heated duel that reminded me of two opponents battling it out for supremacy. I'm not so sure if I was fighting him or myself. My brain had gone into its left-side, right-side dialogue again. The logical side of my brain was saying, *Stop it. Stop it right now.* The other was saying, *Seize the day.*

Alessandro's hands were on my hips now, holding me against his arousal while his lips played with mine in little nips and nibbles and playful nudges.

'Tell the truth, *cara mio*,' he said, in a husky burr that did even more serious damage to the stability of my legs. Possibly permanently. '*This* is what you came here for.'

It was shamefully close enough to the truth for me to push him away with a mocking laugh that unfortunately didn't sound too convincing. 'Nice try, Lucioni, but no. I came here to talk to you.'

He leaned indolently against the door jamb with his arms folded across his broad chest. It was annoying that he showed no sign of our recent lust-fest. I was still trying to tuck my blouse into my trousers and put some order to my hair, but I couldn't find the tie he'd taken out of it. I would have to leave it bouncing around my face like a clown's wig. *Argh!* Why hadn't I made the time to book in for my three-monthly chemical straightening session?

He held something up in his hand. 'Is this what you're looking for?'

I was wary about getting too close to him again. My senses were still screaming in protest because I'd cut short their titillation. Besides, I didn't trust myself. It was galling to think he had such sensual power over me. I didn't let *anyone* have *any* sort of power over me. How could he undo me with one kiss?

My body was still thrumming like a tuning fork struck too hard. The wanting was an ache deep inside, like a hunger only he could satiate. Why had I allowed him to reawaken those wretched needs? It was like being planted in front of an all-you-can-eat smorgasbord after a five-year diet. For years I'd been able to ignore my needs, deaden them, deep-freeze them. But one look, one touch, one potently passionate kiss, and they were active again.

'Throw it to me,' I said.

The corner of his mouth tilted. 'Come and get it.'

I wasn't sure if we were still talking about my hair tie or not. There was a sardonic glint in his eyes that made my stomach free-fall. The air was crackling with the sexual energy of the primal need we had stirred in each other. It was a palpable force that made me hyperaware of every cell of my body, as if my skin had been turned inside out.

I felt it on my lips, where his had pressed and played and plundered. I felt it on my face, where his hand had cupped my cheek. I felt it at the roots of my hair, where his fingers had splayed along my scalp. I could still taste him on my tongue—the hint of mint and good-quality coffee and maleness that was like a potent elixir to me. My breasts were tingling inside my bra, my lady land was contracting, my thighs were quivering, my spine was threatening to unlock vertebra by vertebra.

How could I have walked into this situation so blindly? But maybe I hadn't. Maybe my subconscious had known all along that something like this would happen once Alessandro and I were alone.

'Put it on the table over there,' I said, nodding towards a leather-topped drum table.

He held his hand out with my hair tie right in the middle of his palm. 'You want it? You come and get it.'

That was another thing I could feel pulsing in the air—the collision of two strong wills. We were both driven and competitive people who hated losing. I had already lost considerable ground by responding to him so wantonly. No wonder he was looking so darn smug. He'd crooked his metaphorical little finger and I had come running. But I wasn't going to let him win this. Not on his terms.

Although how I was going to get past him in order to leave was presenting me with a rather perplexing problem.

'Why are you doing this?' I said, clenching my teeth and my fists.

'Doing what?'

I narrowed my eyes to hairpin slits. 'You know what.'

He gave me a guileless smile. 'It's just a hair tie, *tesoro*.'

My lips were pinched so tight I could barely get the words out. 'It's not just about the hair tie, damn it. It's you. You're playing games.'

He tossed the tie in the air and deftly caught it. Once,

twice, three times. His eyes were still holding mine. 'You said you came here to talk. So talk.'

I compressed my lips for a moment. The light was fading outside, which made the shadows inside the house all the more menacing. Goose bumps rose and raced along the flesh of my arms.

I crossed my arms over my body and glared at him. 'Why don't you turn on the light?'

'You came all this way to ask me that?'

I gave him a cutting look. 'Don't be a smartass.'

'Right back at you, sweetheart.'

I poked my tongue out at him. Childish, I know, but he had that effect on me.

I knew he was only using those tender endearments to annoy me. I had believed them once. I had really *felt* like his sweetheart. His treasure. His darling. I had loved hearing him say the words. His trace of a Sicilian accent had given them a spine-tingling quality. But they were false—just like his promises of for ever.

My anger blistered inside me, peeling off a layer of my stomach like acid. How could I have been so gullible as to believe he loved me? He hadn't even *told* me. Not in so many words. He had acted like he did. That had been enough for me. I've always been a great believer in actions speaking louder than words. Words are so cheap. Anyone can say *I love you*. It's demonstrating it that's important.

All he had demonstrated was that he was a master at manipulation. He'd charmed me into believing I was the best thing that had ever happened to him. When I'd ended things he hadn't even *acted* being devastated. He'd shrugged it off in an easy-come, easy-go manner that still rankled with me. If he'd felt anything for me—

anything at all—wouldn't he have fought for me? Defended himself?

But, no. He'd listened to my spitting tirade and gone all stony-faced and tight-lipped. And why wouldn't he? The woman he'd really wanted had got away. I was just the backup plan. The face-saving fling. What did it matter if I stormed off in a huff? Our four-week fling had achieved what he'd wanted it to achieve. It had showed his ex he'd well and truly moved on.

The trouble was I *hadn't* moved on. I was stuck. My life was on pause. I couldn't go forward because I was too frightened to open myself up to caring about someone enough for them to hurt me. I was watching life from the sidelines. Watching as friends fell in love and got married. Set up homes together. Had babies.

Even my sister was talking about babies. She and Matt were getting married in September, and I was going to be the maid of honour. I was dreading it. It wasn't that I wasn't happy for her. I was. I was thrilled she'd found Matt after that two-timing twat Andy she'd been with before. But it was the thought of everyone asking me if I was seeing anyone. Of everyone looking at me and pitying me for still being single at twenty-nine.

I struck a don't-mess-with-me pose: one hip pushed forward, my arms still crossed over my chest. 'You can't keep me here all night.'

That wickedly sexy gleam was back in his espresso-dark eyes. 'Can't I?'

A frisson of traitorous excitement shot down the length of my spine. 'Holding someone against their will is a crime.'

He moved away from the door and came over to where I was standing. 'Open your hand.'

I didn't care for his commanding tone, but I opened my hand regardless. The sooner I got out of there the better. He placed my hair tie in the middle of my palm and then gently closed my fingers over it, giving my hand a tiny squeeze before releasing it.

'I like your hair loose,' he said.

'I'm thinking of getting it cut off for the wedding.'

His eyebrows snapped together. 'Whose wedding?'

'My sister's.'

'Oh...' Something about the way he said it gave me the impression he was distracted. But then he seemed to gather himself. 'No. Don't do that. Your hair is beautiful.'

I raised my brows at him. 'It's *my* hair. I can do what I damn well like.'

He picked up one of my curls and slowly wound it around his finger. I should have moved away. But apart from the risk of having my hair pulled out by the roots I was having trouble getting my body to respond to the commands from my brain. My body was acting of its own accord, standing close enough to touch him, my hips almost brushing his.

I looked at his mouth and a shudder of longing went through me like the tremor of an earthquake. I knew if he kissed me a second time I might not be able to control myself. I put my hands against his chest, but instead of pushing him back, my fingers curled into the fabric of his T-shirt.

'Don't...' I said in a breathless little whisper that kind of belied my plea.

His mouth hovered just above mine, his eyes hooded in a way that made every feminine cell in my body sit up and beg. His warm breath danced over the surface of my lips, teasing my senses into a mad frenzy.

'Don't what?'

My fingers tightened their grip on his shirt. 'We shouldn't be doing this.' *I shouldn't be doing this. Not again. Never again.*

His lips nudged mine—a playful, teasing little movement that made my lips buzz with sensation. 'You want me so bad you're shaking with it.'

The fact that it was true was just the impetus I needed to get the hell out of there while I still could. Pride came to my rescue.

I gave his chest a hard shove and stepped back from him, flashing him one of my trademark haughty looks. 'I wouldn't sleep with you again if you paid me a million pounds.'

His smile was deliberately—irritatingly—mocking. 'How about two?'

I put my hands on my hips in a combative manner. There's nothing I like more than a fight-to-the-death contest. I was *so* going to win this.

'Make it five and you've got yourself a deal,' I said, privately congratulating myself on calling his bluff. I even did a couple of mental fist pumps in victory.

But then he held out one of his hands, and my stomach fell through the floor as he said, 'Done.'

CHAPTER FOUR

To say I was gobsmacked would be an understatement. I stood gaping at him as if he'd just offered me five million pounds. Hang on a minute. He *had* just offered me five million pounds.

Five million pounds!

My head was spinning. My mouth opened and closed but I couldn't locate my voice. My heart was thumping as if I'd just sprinted up the Empire State Building during an asthma attack. Not that I get asthma or anything, but you get the idea.

'Are you *serious*?' I finally managed to ask—although to be perfectly honest it was more of a squeak.

His gaze was unwavering as it held mine, his expression as enigmatic as ever. 'Don't you think you're worth it?'

I licked my lips. Not in anticipation of all that money, or even the sex—although the thought of having smoking hot jungle sex with him *did* make my pulse skyrocket like crazy—but in panic. I couldn't possibly agree to such an outrageous proposal. *Could I?* The sex I could handle. No-strings sex. No-promises sex. No-plans-for-the-future sex. The fact that money would be exchanged for it made me feel a little uncomfortable…but, heck, it was a *lot* of money. A truckload of money. Besides, it had been ages since I'd had sex. Years, actually. Why *shouldn't* I indulge in a hot fling with him?

Because he broke your heart the last time, you idiot!

Yes, well, there was that to consider. But five million pounds was nothing to be sneezed at.

I could buy my own Georgian mansion with loads of acreage, instead of living in a tiny flat where I could hear every petty little argument my neighbours had. I could wear ridiculously flashy jewellery and be driven around by a chauffeur in a Bentley or a Rolls-Royce with personalised number plates. I could wear bespoke designer clothes and have a flock of servants to see to my every whim. I could have my very own beautician and nail technician. I could have my hair washed and styled and straightened every day.

My capitalist-hating parents would probably never speak to me again, but still…

I stared at Alessandro's outstretched hand while this inner dialogue ran through my head. With that sort of money I could have anything I wanted…except the thing I *most* wanted.

I brought my gaze back up to his and gave him a tight smile. 'Wow. You nearly had me there.'

'You think I don't mean it?'

I gave a tinny-sounding laugh. 'You must have a very expensive sex-life if you have to dish out that amount of money every time you want to get laid.'

His dark eyes smouldered as they went from my mouth to my gaze and back again. 'I've never had to pay until now.'

I turned away to scrape my hair back into a knot on top of my head, using the hair tie. It gave me something to do with my hands, because I was worried one of them might be tempted to reach out and shake on his deal.

He surely wasn't serious? He was playing with me. Teasing me. Of course he was. I was an idiot to think he would pay five pounds, let alone five million. He was just stringing me along, making me out to be some sort of greedy little gold-digger. The fact that I'd started it by using that old cliché was beside the point.

'You've got the wrong person, Alessandro,' I said, swinging back round with another forced smile. 'Thanks, but no thanks.'

If he was disappointed or annoyed, nothing in his expression showed it. In fact I thought I saw a gleam of respect shining there. 'Would you like a look around the house before you leave?' he asked.

'Sure—why not?' I said, thinking it best to keep casually cool and easygoing in spite of the fact that I might have just rejected—*gulp*—five million pounds.

Alessandro led me out of the reception room into the hall. 'As you can see, there's still a lot of work to be done,' he said. 'There's a lot of structural stuff that has to be sorted before I can get the painters and decorators in.'

'My sister does a bit of home renovating,' I said as I looked around at the paint-stripped hall and bare floors that were in need of a polish and stain. 'She finds it relaxing. But I can't think of anything worse. I guess I'm not so good with my hands.'

His eyes met mine across the distance that separated us. 'I disagree. I seem to remember your hands had very special skills. Skills I haven't come across before or since.'

I turned my face away so he wouldn't see the blush I could feel creeping all over my cheeks. The same heat was pooling between my thighs. Pulsating need was like a raging fire, racing out of control. I could feel it licking along my flesh with hot, fiery tongues. Why was he so determined to remind me of our past? Surely he realised by now that I was not interested in resuming it.

Although I had to admit I'd been giving him mixed messages. Kissing him the way I had had hardly helped my cause. I'd come across as a wanton desperado. I mentally cringed. How could I have let my guard down like that?

I pushed the toe of my shoe against a bit of broken plaster on the floor. 'Do you really think you'll have this place ready in a month? It looks like it could take six months—maybe even more. It must be costing you a veritable fortune.'

'Money's not an object for me when I have my heart set on something I want.'

His statement had an element of ruthless determination about it that sent another frisson dancing down my spine. I didn't have the courage to look at him. If I looked at him I would cave in and reveal how pathetically weak I was.

I stared fixedly at the peeling paint on the skirting boards instead. 'Clearly not.'

He moved towards another door that led into an east-facing room. 'This is the morning room,' he said. 'It has a nice view over the garden—well, it will once the gardeners get control of the weeding and pruning.'

I looked out of the windows at the garden, where the weeds were almost waist-high. There was a yew hedge surrounding a fountain, but it looked like it hadn't been pruned in years. There were roses in another section, their skeletons spindly and long-armed from lack of winter pruning. There were clusters of bulbs here and there—

narcissus and jonquils, and an early daffodil or two offering the only bit of colour and cheer in the neglected landscape.

I turned to look at Alessandro. 'Who owned the house before you?'

'An elderly man who had neither family nor funds nor the health to keep things in shape.'

I thought of all the gorgeous properties in and surrounding Bath. With the sort of money he apparently had at his disposal he could have bought any of his choosing. Why choose a house that needed such a lot of work?

'So why this house?' I asked, voicing my thoughts out loud.

He turned from looking out of the window, his eyes meeting mine. 'It was where my mother grew up as a child.'

I blinked at him in stunned surprise. My mother would be doing cartwheels at this. She would say there was some supernatural force at work that had led me to work and live in Bath because it was where Alessandro's mother had lived as a child. I must admit it was a little freaky, even for a hardened sceptic like me.

'This was her home?'

'My grandparents', actually,' he said. 'She was supposed to inherit it on their death.'

Something about his tone alerted me to an undercurrent of bitterness. His jaw had a locked look about it, as if he were grinding his molars together.

'So what happened?' I said.

A diamond-hard look came into his eyes. 'She got swindled out of it by my father.'

I frowned. 'How did that happen?'

His mouth had an embittered set to it. 'When my

grandparents died soon after each other, from cancer and a heart attack, my father tricked her into signing the house over to him. As soon as she signed he divorced her.'

I gasped in disgust. 'That's *despicable*.'

'Yes…he's a class act, is my father.'

'So he's still alive?'

'Not to me.'

The implacable way in which he said the words and the black look on his face made a shiver pass over the back of my neck. 'You really hate him,' I said, rather un-necessarily.

His coal-black eyes pulsated with it. 'Six months after the divorce my mother had a fatal car accident. After the funeral Bianca and I went to live with our father and his new wife.'

'How old were you?'

'Ten. Bianca was seven.'

I pictured him as a ten-year-old boy. Devastated by the divorce of his parents, shattered by the loss of his mother, traumatised by being forced to live with a parent he no longer respected and a new stepmother who might well have resented having to care for two children who weren't her own.

I could see why he hadn't wanted to tell me about his background. It was probably too painful even to think about, much less talk about. And now he had the worry of his sister's health and the responsibility of caring for his little niece.

'I'm really sorry,' I said. 'It must've been a terrible time for you and your sister.'

He moved to the door. 'Come on. I'll show you the kitchen.'

I tried a couple more times to draw him out about his

past as we went through each of the rooms, but it seemed the subject was now well and truly closed. He showed me the rest of the house in much the same way as I'd shown him around the school. In a bored tour-guide manner that made me feel I was being a nuisance to him.

Under any other circumstances I would have been angry with him, but after finding out about his bleak childhood it made my emotions towards him somewhat confusing, to say the least. For so long I'd blistered and bubbled with bitterness towards him. My anger had become such an entrenched part of my personality I wasn't sure how to live without it. It was my armour. Stepping out of it would be like being naked in public.

But wasn't his reluctance to dredge over the past more than a little like mine? I was the high priestess of avoidance. How could I blame him for not telling me about *his* childhood when I hadn't told him what had happened in mine?

Once the tour was over Alessandro accompanied me out to my car. He held the door open for me.

'Thanks for showing me around,' I said. 'It's a really nice house. It has loads of potential. I can see why you want to get it back in the family.'

'It's what my mother would've wanted. To see her grandchild enjoy the place as much as she did.'

I put my hand on the top of the car door and then half turned to look at him. In the heat of the moment I'd forgotten my whole purpose for being there. 'How long has Claudia had her stutter?'

'I'm not sure.'

I raised my brows. 'You haven't asked her mother?'

His expression tightened. 'My sister isn't well enough to handle much conversation right now.'

'She must be very ill.'

'She is.'

I rolled my lips together for a moment. 'Look, I think I can help with Claudia's speech. I've done a special course on language and learning problems.'

I wondered if I should tell him about my own experience. But just as swiftly decided against it. I wasn't going to be fooled into being too open with him. I would treat him like any other parent or guardian at my school. Which meant I would have to erase that kiss out of my memory as soon as possible.

I was about to slip in behind the wheel when his hand came down on mine, where it was resting on the top of the car door.

'Thank you for what you're doing for my niece,' he said.

I glanced at his tanned hand, covering my paler one. A traitorous pulse of longing passed like a current through my body. It was as if he had direct access to my core by that simple touch. It had always been that way between us. I'd felt it the first time he'd touched me outside that café in Paris. I had no immunity from him. For all these years I'd kidded myself I was over him. But every time he touched me I felt that same jolt of awareness. No one else had the same effect on me. I was beginning to suspect no one else ever would.

I brought my gaze up to his. 'I'm not doing anything I wouldn't do for any other child under my care.'

'I called the boarding house before you came,' he said. 'The house mistress told me you'd dropped in after school to see how Claudia was getting on.'

I dismissed his comment with a shrug. 'I often call in on the boarders—especially the young ones.'

His lips lifted in a little sideways smile. 'I would have done it, you know.'

I frowned in puzzlement. 'Done what?'

'Paid you five million.'

I swallowed thickly. 'I'm sure you're not lacking in available and willing partners.'

He lifted a hand to brush back one of my escaping curls and carefully tucked it back behind my ear. 'No. But none quite like you.'

I couldn't drag my eyes away from his lustrous brown gaze. I moistened my lips with a quick dart of my tongue, my pulse doing one of its mad sprints that made me feel light-headed and a little off-balance.

'This is all types of crazy. You. Me. It's not going to happen.'

He traced a spine-tingling pathway along my jawbone from below my ear to my chin. There was no reason why I couldn't have pulled back from his touch but somehow I didn't. I couldn't. There was something in his caress that was almost wistful. Nostalgic.

'Have you been back to Paris since?' he asked.

'No.'

His mouth took on a rueful twist. 'Have I ruined it for you?'

I made a scoffing noise. 'Of course not.'

His eyes searched mine. 'Sure?'

'Absolutely,' I said. 'I was over you as soon as I boarded the plane back home.'

It's a pretty handy skill to be good at lying. My sister and I are masters at it. We've had to be. Years of trying to pretend we had normal parents gave us an edge in the lying stakes. All those schools we had to fit in to made us experts.

We learned early on how to lie through our teeth and how to control our giveaway body language. No nose-rubbing or face-touching. Always maintaining eye contact. No fidgeting. No looking to the right. I've told some porkies in my time, and no one's caught me out.

But for all that I didn't think Alessandro was buying it. His fingertip skated over the vermilion border of my lower lip, triggering sensations I felt all the way to my core.

'So why no steady relationship since me?' he asked.

'I'm a career girl—that's why.'

'Can't women have it all these days?'

I decided against maintaining eye contact. I'm good at lying, but not *that* good. I looked at his tanned neck instead.

'Why do you keep touching me?'

'I like touching you.'

'It's not appropriate, given our…circumstances.' I was going to say *relationship* but thought better of it.

He put his finger underneath my chin until our gazes met. 'You like it too. I can feel it. It's always been like that between us, hasn't it?'

I wanted to deny it. It was just a matter of saying the words. But my voice refused to work. I could feel myself being drawn into that coal-black gaze until I was all but mesmerised. His thumb brushed over my lower lip, sending a riot of sensations through me.

'How much do I have to pay you to have dinner with me?' he said.

'You don't have to pay me,' I said, suddenly embarrassed at the way I'd handled things.

What did money have to do with what I felt about him? If I wanted to spend the evening with him I would. It didn't have to mean we were resuming our fling. Besides, I wanted to dig a little deeper into his background, find out a little more about his sister. A dinner on neutral ground would be just the ticket.

'That's crazy. Dinner's just dinner. We can split the bill.'

His half smile made something in my stomach slip sideways. 'I'll pick you up at eight tomorrow night.'

Why not tonight? I thought with a little pang of disappointment.

As if he could read my mind, he added, 'I have to go to London to check on a transplant patient.'

'How are you managing your work with all this?' I nodded towards the house.

He gave me a weary-looking smile. 'It's a balancing act—probably no different from what your average working woman does every day.'

'True, but surely you've got help? A nanny organised for the holidays and a housekeeper and so on?'

'Can you recommend anyone?'

'As a nanny?'

He nodded. 'I've interviewed four or five, but I can't seem to find what I'm looking for.'

I gave him a cynical look. 'Yes, well, I expect all the blonde busty bombshells are signed on at modelling agencies instead.'

His dark eyes glinted. 'Or teaching.'

I pursed my lips. 'Flattery doesn't work with me, Alessandro. You should know that by now.'

His knuckles lightly grazed my cheek again, his eyes still holding mine in a lock that tethered much more than my gaze. It was like he was pulling on my most intimate muscles every time he looked at me. The memory of him inside me—stretching me, pleasuring me, filling me and completing me—consumed my senses. I couldn't escape the feelings he stirred in me. I couldn't run away from them and pretend they didn't exist. They did, and they clamoured for attention like baying hungry hounds.

'You don't see yourself as others see you,' he said. 'You find fault where others find perfection.'

I gave a little snort and pulled out of his hold. 'I have to go. I've got lessons to prepare.'

I slipped behind the wheel and reached for my seat belt and snapped it into place. Alessandro closed the door and stepped back from the car. I put my keys in the ignition and prayed. Yes, you read that correctly. I might not believe in the supernatural, but when it comes to my car my feeling is a little prayer never goes astray.

The engine kicked over without a cough or a splutter. Maybe I'd have to rethink my atheist stance, I thought. But as I drove away my car gave a cacophonous backfire that was as loud as a thunderclap.

I glanced in my rear-view mirror to see Alessandro smiling crookedly. *Damn.*

CHAPTER FIVE

I WAS ON my way to my classroom the next morning when my mother phoned. I've told her hundreds of times never to call me during school hours, but she has no concept of the nine-to-five working day. I normally switch my phone off or to silent the moment I get to school, but my mother has this uncanny ability to call me just as I reach for the 'off' button. It's as if she knows I'm about to go incommunicado so she gets in first.

'Poppet, you won't *believe* the vision I had last night.' That was her opening gambit.

Why my mother continues to call me poppet when I've got a perfectly fine name—if you use Jem, not Jemima, that is—is a mystery to me.

'Mum, I'm at school. I can't talk right now.'

'But it's only seven-thirty in the morning!'

'Yes, well…I have to get the classroom ready and—'

'You have no *balance*,' she said. 'I was only saying to your father the other day, you're going to work yourself into an early grave. People can have heart attacks and strokes in their twenties, you know and you're nearly thirty.'

Thanks for reminding me, I thought. 'I'm fine, Mum, really. Now, I really must go as I—'

'But I have to tell you about my vision,' my mother said. 'You were having wild kinky sex with a man.'

I always try to be logical and rational when my mother shares one of her visions with me—especially any that involve sex. She has a very overactive imagination, and the stuff she imagines wouldn't even be allowed in the *Kama Sutra*.

'That's not a vision,' I said. 'It's a dream. It's just your subconscious making a narrative out of what you've been thinking about during the day. That's basically what dreams are.'

'I wasn't dreaming,' my mother insisted. 'I was having a vision. There's a big difference. I know when I'm receiving a sign from the cosmos. It always happens like that. I get this fizzy feeling that won't go away. Last night I closed my eyes and focused on the images coming to me. I could see him clear as day. He was tall and dark and handsome, with really dark brown eyes.'

I felt a little shiver go over my skin in spite of my sandbags of logic. 'That certainly narrows it down a bit,' I said.

'Not only that,' my mother said, 'he looked like that famous doctor. You know—the one who saved Richard Ravensdale the stage actor? It could have been his twin.'

My sandbags were in a sorry shape, but for all that I persisted. 'There's a perfectly logical explanation for your dream…erm…vision. You've probably read something in a gossip magazine about him at the hairdresser's and the image has stuck in your mind. Plus Bertie's Matt is a doctor, so you've—'

'I haven't been to a hairdresser in years,' my mother said. Which is true.

She has dreadlocks—long ones, with beads woven in.

At least she washes them now. There was a time when my parents were anti-shampoo, because they believed toxic chemicals would give us all cancer. Thankfully Bertie and I got head lice, so we were allowed a few toxic chemicals to sort them out.

I glanced at my watch. 'Mum, I really have to dash. Say hi to Dad and I'll call you soon. 'Bye.'

I ended the call and then spent the next hour or two feeling guilty. I always feel like that over my parents. They frustrate me. I know I should accept people for who they are, but there's a part of me that can't accept my parents' lifestyle. They drive me nuts because they have zero ambition. They just want to sit around and navel-gaze, or meditate, or have sex in weird positions while chanting ridiculous chants. Bertie is much more accepting of them, but then I did a lot to protect her from the worst of it.

The rest of the day passed without drama, but I noticed Claudia was still not speaking. I didn't pressure her, for I knew the stress would make her stutter worse.

I spoke to Jennifer at the boarding house and she told me Claudia had slept well and was not showing any signs of homesickness other than seeming reluctant to speak. We talked about my plan to help Claudia with some drama therapy and I told her I would suggest that Alessandro engage a speech therapist as well. Of course I didn't tell Jennifer I was having dinner with him that night.

The prospect of our 'date' had had me in a state of restlessness all day. Whenever there was a moment when I wasn't fully engaged in teaching the girls—when they were working on their own or something—my mind would drift... I would start thinking of how he would look. Would he wear a suit or dress casually? How would he smell? Of lemons or lime or sandalwood or soap? How would his hand feel in the small of my back as he led me to his car?

I was like a lovesick teenager. Talk about nauseating. I kept telling myself we were just having dinner to discuss Claudia's management. It was perfectly legitimate and aboveboard. It didn't mean I had to take it any further. It wasn't as if I was going to jump into an affair with him after what had happened last time.

But no amount of self-talk could take away my attraction to him. It was as feverish as ever—maybe even worse than five years ago. I only had to think of him and my flesh would tingle all over.

I got home late after a staff meeting ran overtime. Normally I enjoy staff meetings. It's a good chance to chat through any issues that have come up with the pupils or concerns about the curriculum. But this time I was fidgeting like I had a bad case of intestinal worms. Miss Fletcher had glanced at me once or twice from over the top of her bifocals and asked if I was all right. I assured her everything was just fine and concentrated harder on taking down the minutes of the meeting.

Once inside the door of my flat I had just enough time to have a shower and do something with my hair. I rummaged through my wardrobe for something to wear, pointedly ignoring the wedding dress bagged in a silk bag, hanging at the back behind my hiking jacket. I selected the classic little black dress I'd bought in a sale when shopping with Bertie.

I'm not a slave to fashion. Unlike Bertie, who adores bright colours and quirky clothes, I have very little colour in my wardrobe. I stick to the basics: black, white, navy and grey. Boring as hell, but I'm not out to impress anyone.

I had only just finished with the hair straightener when the doorbell rang. My heart lurched as I glanced at my watch. It was only seven-thirty. Alessandro had said eight o'clock. I hadn't even done my make-up. Not that I use a lot at the best of times, but I'd figured a bit of facial armour wouldn't go astray—especially since I'd blushed more in the last twenty-four hours than I had in the last five years.

I put down the straighteners and smoothed my hands down my dress, slipped my feet into a pair of heels. He'd seen me without make-up so what did it matter? He'd seen me without *anything*.

I opened the door and found my parents standing there, with big cheesy grins on their faces.

'Surprise!' they said in unison.

I mentally rolled my eyes. I think I did it in reality as well. My parents love surprises. I hate them. Not my parents. Just surprises. I don't like anything spontaneous. I'm a planner. Surprises do not fit into neat plans.

'What are you doing here?' I said. 'I thought you were on a yoga retreat in Salisbury?'

'We cancelled,' my father said. 'Your mother was worried about you. We thought we'd come and stay for a few days.'

Stay? My brain was like a neon sign, flashing PANIC in big red letters. I was about to say it was totally inconvenient and inappropriate of them to turn up announced when I suddenly realised how tired Dad looked. He would have been driving for hours, because my mother had lost her licence a few months ago for speeding. I know... Talk about irresponsible. She maintains she was driving well under the limit, but because she got into a 'discussion', as she called it, with the traffic cop things got a little testy.

'Aren't you going to ask us in?' Mum said with a beaming smile.

'Oh, right—sure,' I said, and stood stiffly as they both crushed me in bear hugs and smacked noisy kisses on my cheeks.

Mum did a full circle of my sitting room once I'd closed the front door. 'Poppet, the feng shui in here is dreadful.' She gave a little shudder. 'That mirror is facing the wrong way.'

'How can it be facing the wrong way?' I said. 'It won't reflect anything if I turn it around the other way.'

My mother gave me a despairing look. 'It should be on *that* wall. It's bad luck to have it facing that way. All the energy will drain out through the front door.'

This time I did roll my eyes. Twice. 'Look, I'm about to go out, so why don't you guys make yourselves comfortable and—?'

'Out?' My mother's eyes were suddenly as bright as searchlights.

'Yes. I have a parent-teacher meeting.'

'Dressed like that?' my father said.

I frowned. 'What's wrong with the way I'm dressed?'

'Nothing,' he said. 'You look lovely. Like you're going on a date or something.'

'See?' My mother said to my father. 'I told you she's seeing someone. A mother just *knows* these things.'

'I am not seeing anyone,' I said. 'I'm just having dinner with…a friend.'

'Don't worry about us,' my mother said. 'We'll make ourselves at home. I'll make some kale and quinoa muffins for you. We can chat when you get back.'

I glanced at the clock on the wall. 'Erm…you don't

want to go and stretch your legs after being in the car all that time?'

'It's dark outside,' my father said.

'And it's starting to rain,' my mother chipped in.

'Right… Well, then, you guys settle in while I put on some make-up,' I said, and headed back to my room.

My mother followed and stood watching me as I applied a bit of powder and bronzer. I mentally prepared myself for one of her lectures on how using make-up was totally unnecessary and just a ploy for cosmetic companies to make loads of money out of women who felt insecure about their looks. But instead of lecturing me she handed me the bronzer brush like a scrub nurse hands a surgeon a scalpel.

'What's wrong, poppet?' she said after a moment or two. 'You seem so tense. I mean, more tense than normal.'

'I'm fine.' I put down the brush and picked up my mascara. It was almost empty, but I managed to get enough out to coat my lashes from practically invisible blonde to brown.

My mother tilted her head on one side as she took in my outfit. 'You know, black really isn't your colour. It washes you out too much. Have you got anything a little more colourful?'

She made a move towards my wardrobe but I cut her off at the pass. I moved so fast I was like greased lightning.

'Don't,' I said, flattening my back against the wardrobe with my arms outstretched like I was guarding the Crown Jewels.

My mother looked at me oddly for a moment, and then with sparkling intrigue. 'What on earth are you hiding in there?'

I worked hard to keep my expression clear of any of the dread I was feeling. The wedding dress was my skeleton in the closet. A taffeta and tulle skeleton of my hopes and dreams.

'I've…erm…got your birthday present in there. I don't want you to see it.'

My mother screwed up her forehead. 'But it's not my birthday until November.'

'I know, but you know how I like to be super-organised.'

The doorbell sounded and my heart slammed against my breastbone. The choice between my mother rifling through my wardrobe or having my father answer the door to Alessandro was an easy one.

I snatched up my purse and dashed out of my bedroom—but my father was already doing the honours.

'Well, howdy-do,' he said to Alessandro, not just shaking his hand but clasping it between both of his as if Alessandro was the Prodigal Son. Or a big-time prophet. '*So* delighted to meet you. Well, well, well—look at you. A fine specimen of manhood. Mighty fine indeed. Jem hasn't been on a date in *years*—or none that we've known about. I'm Charlie and that's Annabel.'

Thankfully my mother had followed me out of my bedroom and now stood with her hands clasped to each side of her face. 'Oh, my God! It's *him*! It's the man in my vision!'

I wanted the floor to open up and swallow me and spit me out in some other country. Outer Mongolia, preferably. Outer space would have been even better.

'Pleased to meet you, Mr Clark…Mrs Clark,' Alessandro said, somehow getting his hand out of the grip of my father's and offering it to my mother. 'I'm Alessandro Lucioni.'

'Oh, please call me Annabel,' my mother said. 'We're not married. We don't believe in—'

'Right, let's go,' I said, grabbing Alessandro by the arm and all but marching him out of the house before my mother read his mind, his palm, his aura, or whipped out a set of tarot cards and predicted his future.

'Don't do anything we wouldn't do!' my mother called out in a singsong voice.

'They seem like nice people,' Alessandro said once we were in his car. 'Do they live with you?'

'God, no,' I said barely able to suppress a shudder. 'They've just dropped in to stay for a few days.'

I felt his glance come my way.

'You don't like it when they visit?'

I looked at my hands, gripping my evening purse. My knuckles were bone white. I forced myself to relax my grip but the tension was still in the rest of my body. It was like concrete setting along the column of my neck and spine. I get that way every time my parents land unannounced on my doorstep.

I'm a private person. I like my own space. My own routine and timetable. My parents have no concept of personal boundaries. It's not that I don't love my parents. But I like them in small doses—and preferably on neutral territory.

'I would've liked a heads up first,' I said. 'They don't seem to understand that I have a job that means the world to me. Their life is one big holiday. They flit from place to place like a couple of stoned butterflies. They drive me completely nuts. I'll come home and find my furniture all rearranged because the feng shui isn't right. Or my fridge and pantry will be cleaned out so there's no processed food.'

I suddenly gasped.

'Oh, my God!'

The car slowed as he applied the brakes. 'What's wrong?'

'I forgot to hide the steak.'

He glanced at me quizzically. 'The steak?'

'My parents are vegans,' I said. 'They were vegetarian before that. My sister and I used to sneak in a steak when they weren't looking. I just bought the most delicious eye fillet. It cost me a fortune and now my mother will throw it in the rubbish.' I groaned and banged my head against the headrest. '*Why* couldn't I have normal parents?'

'You don't get to choose your family—only your friends.' It was a well-used axiom, but the way he said it gave it a level of gravitas.

'Tell me about it.' I swivelled in my seat to look at him. 'Tell me about *your* family.'

His expression got that boxed-up look on it. 'I don't want to ruin your appetite for dinner,' he said. 'How did Claudia go today?'

'She was quiet in class, but she seems to be settling in,' I said.

I explained about the speech therapist we had as a consultant to the school and how we would need his approval to engage her services.

'Fine—do whatever needs to be done,' he said. 'I don't care about the cost.'

'For a kid you hadn't met until a couple of weeks ago, you seem to really care,' I said.

He lifted the shoulder nearest me in an indifferent shrug but it didn't fool me for a second.

'She's an innocent child,' he said. 'She deserves a

chance to be the best she can be, no matter what her circumstances. As does any other child.'

I let silence slip past while I studied him covertly. He had a grimly determined look on his face. It etched his features into harsh lines that gave him an intimidating air. I liked the fact he was prepared to do anything to protect and provide for his niece. I didn't want to like anything about him, but how could I not admire him for that? Didn't I have the very same values?

'Claudia is a little behind academically, but that's probably because of her language difficulties,' I said. 'I'm working on a special programme for her. She'll get extra tuition from me, and from Jennifer at the boarding house.'

There was a long silence as the car's tyres swished over the rain-lashed roads.

'My sister has a drug problem,' Alessandro said heavily. 'She's had it since she was sixteen.'

'I'm so sorry.'

He flicked me a bleak look. 'I blame myself for not doing more to protect her.'

I frowned. 'But how can it be your fault? You're not her parent. You're her brother. Besides, sometimes teenagers do stuff regardless of the parenting they've received.'

He let out a jagged-sounding sigh. 'I spent most of my life resenting her. My father spoilt her. She could have anything and do anything she wanted. There were no boundaries.'

'Wasn't he like that with you?'

He gave a scornful laugh that had a sharp edge of bitterness to it. 'No.'

There was a lot of information in that one word, I thought. Not just the way he said it, as if spitting out something vile-tasting, but also the way his body was set. His hands were gripping the steering wheel so tightly I could see each of the tendons bulging on the backs of his hands. And there was a storm of suppressed anger in his gaze as it fixed on the road ahead.

I had an unbearable urge to reach out and touch him. To soothe the pain he was obviously feeling. It was unlike me to be so sympathetic—especially to someone who had hurt me so badly. I would have to watch myself. I wasn't as armoured up as I wanted to be.

I shifted in my seat and held my purse a little tighter. 'What was he like with you?' I asked.

'Tough.' The tendons on his hands now looked like they were going to burst out of his skin. 'Demanding. Strict.' He paused for a beat. 'Occasionally violent.'

I swallowed thickly. 'That's awful… It must've been so hard, having to live with him after your mother died.'

There was another swishing silence. I watched the windscreen wipers go back and forth like twin metronome arms. I couldn't stop thinking about his childhood. How had he coped with his mother's death? How had his sister coped? What responsibilities had Alessandro taken on that made him feel so guilty for his sister's problems? How difficult must it have been to live with the man who had exploited his mother? Was that why he hadn't told me anything of his childhood? Because it had been too bleak and lonely and Dickensian to verbalise?

'He hated me for defending my mother,' he said finally. 'He believed a son should stick with his father, no matter what. He was of the opinion that women were inferior. That they only existed to service the needs of men.'

'Yes, well, I've met a few of that type in my time.' I couldn't stop myself from saying it.

His eyes cut to mine. 'I didn't use you, Jem. I know it

probably felt like it at the time, but I really wanted things to work out for us.'

I wanted to believe him. Even after all this time, and with all the simmering hurt that weighed me down so much, I still wanted to believe him. The foolish hope that refused to die annoyed the hell out of me. I thought I'd packed that part of myself away and thrown away the key.

'So why didn't you tell me about your ex-fiancée?'

He looked back at the road. 'I wanted to put it behind me. To move on. I hated thinking about how I'd failed to make someone I cared about happy.' He let out a whoosh of a breath. 'But you're right. I should have told you. It's yet another regret I have to live with.'

'How long had you been with her?'

'All through my specialist training—which, looking back, was part of the problem,' he said. 'I was doing a PhD as well as my fellowship. Work and study took up most of my time. I invested in my career, not in our relationship. She got bored.'

I waited a beat before asking, 'Did you love her?'

There was a pause that seemed to go on for ever, but it was probably only a second or two.

'I think what I loved was being in a relationship,' he said. 'Coming from the background I had, I wanted the security of it. Knowing there was someone who wanted the same things in life. Who had the same values. Although on reflection her values were not the same as mine. It was only when I met you that I realised that.'

Did you love me?

The words were balanced on the end of my tongue like a terrified novice diver on the ten-metre springboard. But of course I didn't say them. I sat there staring at my hands and wondering how different my life would have been if I hadn't met him that day in Paris.

I would probably be married to some guy—a fellow teacher, perhaps—and living in the suburbs. I might even have a baby by now. I would have an ordinary life. A predictable, ordinary life that would have been exactly what I'd wanted right up until I met Alessandro. But meeting him had changed everything. It had changed me.

He had changed me.

He suddenly reached across the console and picked up my right hand. He brought it to his chest, holding it against the deep, steady throb of his heart.

'There were so many times I wanted to call you. To apologise for how I handled things.'

I should have pulled my hand away, but something about the solid warmth of his chest and the husky honey depth of his voice stopped me. It occurred to me then that we had communicated more about our backgrounds in the last few minutes than we had in the whole month we'd been together. It was like we'd been pretending to be other people back then—happy, carefree people who didn't have difficult relatives or issues from the past.

'Why didn't you?' I said, but strangely not in the accusatory tone I'd intended to use.

His hand squeezed mine and I swear I felt the contraction as if his long, strong fingers had surrounded my heart.

'The usual reasons,' he said. 'Pride. Stubbornness. Regret that I'd screwed up yet another relationship so why bother trying to salvage it. Stupid reasons.'

What was he saying? That he had loved me after all?

I could feel my resolve slipping like a silk wrap sliding off a bare shoulder. But then I pulled myself up short.

So what if we were communicating now? As far as I was concerned it was too little, too late. I wasn't handing out second chances. No way.

'Careful, Alessandro,' I said, with a return to my mother tongue: sarcasm. 'You might fool me into thinking you were really in love with me back then.'

There was another beat or two of telling silence. A pulsing, simmering silence that made the air tighten.

'Why haven't you had a date in years?' he asked.

I decided I was going to kill my father when I got home. I had it all planned. I would force-feed him my steak. I'd pump him full of chocolate and ice cream and frozen yoghurt. I would stuff a loaf of white bread down his throat. I would tie my mother up and make her watch. It would be death by a thousand processed calories.

'I told you the other day. I'm a career girl. I don't have time for a full-time relationship.'

'What about a fling? Had any of those?'

'Not recently—but, hey, if a guy comes along and offers me five million quid to open my legs I'll do it. No problem.'

He threw me a hardened glance. 'Don't play the cheap hooker with me, Jem.'

I raised my brows in an exaggerated fashion. 'Cheap? At five million? You could get a blow job around here for two hundred pounds.'

'And you know that *how*?' he asked, with a distinct curl of his lip.

I wasn't sure what demon was riding on my back, but I wanted to push Alessandro into expressing some of the anger I could feel brooding in him. Or maybe it was my own anger I wanted to unleash. God knew I had enough of it.

How *dared* he tell me he had regrets over the way he'd handled things? I'd spent the last five years trying to forget him. How dared he waltz back into my life and apologise? To *communicate*, for pity's sake? It was too late.

'I've slept with men for money,' I said. 'Isn't that what a girl does when a guy pays for dinner?'

His jaw locked so tightly I heard his molars grind together. 'I know what you're doing.'

I glided a fingertip from the top of his shoulder down to his thigh. 'What *am* I doing, big guy?' I said in a smoky whisper.

He sucked in air through his nostrils. 'Stop it. I'm driving.'

'What if I don't want to stop?' I sent my fingertip closer to the swollen heat of him, tracing over the tented fabric of his trousers.

To tell you the truth I was a little shocked at myself, but I couldn't seem to stop my wanton come-and-get-me behaviour. I was relishing in the rush of power it gave me. So far he had been the one with all the power. Now it was my turn to show him he had more than met his match.

He let out a muttered curse and turned the car into a side street so quickly I was thrown back against the seat.

But I wasn't there for long.

The engine hadn't even died when Alessandro's strong arms pulled me towards him and his mouth came crashing down on mine.

CHAPTER SIX

HIS MOUTH TASTED of mint and anger and lust and longing. The same intense longing I could feel throbbing through my own veins. His lips moved over mine with devastating expertise, demanding I open to him with a bold stab of his tongue.

I had recklessly taunted the tiger and now I was experiencing the full force of his reaction. And, quite frankly, I was loving every pulse-racing second of it.

I received him with a sound of approval that came from somewhere deep inside me. I wound my arms around his neck, fisting my hands into the thickness of his hair, and kissed him back with all the pent-up passion that had been lying in hibernation for what seemed like most of my life.

His freshly shaved jaw scraped the skin of my face as he changed position to deepen the kiss. His arms relaxed their iron grip on me and moved to cup one of my breasts in a caressing and yet possessive movement that made my insides twist and contort with lust. His other hand went to the nape of my neck, underneath my hair. He knew instinctively that it was one of my most sensitive erogenous zones. As his fingers moved in amongst those finer hairs, I tingled all over and my toes curled in my shoes.

His mouth softened against mine, his kiss less punishing now, but no less passionate. Our tongues danced around each other in a cat-and-mouse caper, stopping to play every now and again before doing another round. I heard myself whimper as his lips nipped at mine in playful little nudges and bites that made every cell in my body shudder with delight. His warm breath mingled with mine, his taste lingering in my mouth like the bouquet of a top-shelf wine.

I wanted more. I wanted to get drunk on his kiss. To be completely and utterly intoxicated with him.

He slowly pulled back from me, but my lips clung to his as if they didn't want to let him go. He cradled my face in his hands—a gesture that was sure to win any girl's heart, in my opinion. I looked into molasses-dark eyes that were glittering with hot-blooded desire and felt another fissure open like a fault line in the cold, hard armour around my heart.

His thumbs stroked over my cheeks in slow motion, back and forth in a mesmerising caress that made it impossible for me to think of anything witty or pithy to say. I was in a sensual stupor. Stoned on the power and potency of his masterful mouth and the combustion of passion it had triggered in me.

There was a pleated frown between his brows. 'That was...' he paused for a moment, as if searching for the right word '...unforgivable.'

Unforgettable, more like, I thought.

I moistened my lips with a quick dart of my tongue. 'It's fine,' I said. 'It was just a kiss. No big deal.'

One of his hands cupped my cheek as if it were a

priceless piece of porcelain. His touch was so gentle it made the tight knot of my bitterness towards him unfurl like satin ribbon spilling away from its spool. The pad of his thumb pressed ever so lightly against my lower lip. The desire to suck his thumb into my mouth was almost unbearable. His eyes met mine and I felt a jolt of something hot and electric run through me from head to foot and back again.

'I'm sorry,' he said.

'For…?' I could barely get my voice to work, let alone sound normal. It came out husky and breathy. So *not* like matter-of-fact me.

He drew in a deep breath and let it out on a sigh, his hand still cradling my cheek. 'I don't want it to be like this between us,' he said. 'Fighting. Scoring points. Being bitter.'

I moistened my lips again. 'So…what are you saying?'

His eyes went to my mouth, as if he found it the most fascinating thing in the world. And I must admit I found his pretty fascinating—especially when I could see a trace of my lip gloss on his lower lip.

I lifted my hand and blotted it away. 'Buy your own lip gloss,' I said, with an attempt to lighten things.

I was feeling threatened by his disarming gentleness. It was reminding me of how easily I had fallen in love with him in the past. It was his gentle sensuality that had bewitched me. He wasn't a man to lose control of his emotions or his passions. He had always been in control. He had shown me that in so many ways. It had built my confidence, made me feel secure and safe and able to express my own sensuality without fear of exploitation. He hadn't steamrollered me or pressured me.

And yet he was a deeply passionate man. I could feel the heat of that simmering passion in his body, sitting so close to mine. I could see it in his gaze when it meshed with mine. I was left in no doubt of his desire for me. I suspected he was in no doubt of mine for him, in spite of all of my paltry attempts to disguise it.

His smile was canted to one side. 'Is it so impossible for us to be friends?'

I cocked my head in a guarded manner. 'What sort of friends?'

His eyes measured mine for a long moment. The back and forth movement of his gaze to each of my eyes in turn made me feel as if he was seeing beyond the starchy, don't-mess-with-me facade I'd erected over the last few years. I got the feeling he was looking for the girl he'd met in Paris.

But I was no longer that girl…or was I?

Was there a faint trace of the old-fashioned romantic in me? Like an old sweater I should have thrown out long ago but had kept just because…just because it was warm and comforting and stirred a lot of memories.

Why else was I finding it so impossible to resist Alessandro's touch? He had come back into my life and turned it upside down. I couldn't control my response to him. It was programmed in my DNA to respond to him on a primal level. I wanted him—no matter how much he had hurt me. I wanted him regardless. I wanted to feel the passion only he evoked in me. I wanted to experience the rapture of being desired by a man who could have anyone he wanted but for some reason had chosen me.

Wasn't that the thing I found most thrilling? Alessandro Lucioni wanted *me*. I was an ordinary girl and he was an extraordinary man—a gifted man who had saved so many lives, changed numerous lives for the better. He was a leader in his field—a giant on whose shoulders others would one day stand. How could I not be flattered that he wanted me? How could I possibly resist the longing he triggered in me?

I wanted to feel alive again. To feel passion and excitement and the hot rush of lust and release race through my body until I was boneless and mindless and breathless.

'The sort of friends who can put the mistakes of the past aside and move forward,' he said.

'Forward into what?'

My voice was back to normal now. Shoot-from-the-hip normal. Don't-mess-with-me normal. Even though I wanted him, I wasn't going to spring into anything serious. Why would I set myself up for heartbreak and disappointment again? I know how to take care of myself these days. I can separate my emotions from my physical needs. Sure I can. No problem. Men do it all the time. Sex is just sex. It's like eating or drinking. You do it when you're hungry or thirsty.

Sex was just another appetite and I could satisfy it—*temporarily*—with him.

A one-off binge—that was what it would be. A gourmet feast of the senses that would hopefully overload my system so the craving stopped. That's how I cured my chocolate addiction. I ate two family-size blocks and was so sick afterwards I was frothing chocolate at the mouth like one of those chocolate fountains you see at a party.

The reason I ate those two blocks was that I'd seen Alessandro walk into the restaurant where Bertie and I were having lunch that day. I'm not normally a comfort eater, but seeing him with that blonde had been like a rusty dagger to my heart. They had looked so good together. Like they'd stepped straight out of the pages of a glossy magazine. I could scrub up pretty well if I worked at it, but there was no way on earth I could compete with the sort of glamorous arm candy he squired around. Or employed. Or whatever the case might be.

Reading Alessandro's expression was like trying to read a closed book. I knew there was a lot going on between the covers of his mind, but he was showing none of it on his face.

'Would you be interested in taking it a day at a time to see how things go?' he said.

I screwed my mouth up and shifted my lips from side to side in a musing manner. I didn't want to look too keen. I wanted to appear cool and in control, even though my body was already leaping with excitement.

'What about the school's "no fraternising with the parents" clause?' I said, even though none existed and I was pretty sure he knew it.

He would have done his research. He was that sort of person. He would make it his business to find out everything he could in order to get what he wanted.

His smile was sexily lopsided again. 'Rules can be bent a little to accommodate specific needs, *n'est-ce pas*?'

I wish he wouldn't do that. Speak in French, I mean. How was I supposed to act cool and composed when he made my spine go all squishy and tingly? His voice was not the only thing that undid me. It was that look in his eyes that made my body vibrate with longing. The look that said, *I want you. Now.*

I forced myself to sit primly. My mouth was set in a pursed fashion. My hands were clasped in my lap to stop them from wandering over to where I could see the tenting of his trousers. *Be still, my pulse.*

'You seem pretty confident I'll say yes,' I said.

He picked up a stray wisp of my hair and gently

tucked it behind my ear. That and the face-cupping and the speaking French were enough to make any hard-case cynic melt, let me tell you. Every muscle in my body felt like it had turned into a blob of hair mousse.

His eyes went to my mouth in that hooded manner that communicated much more than words could ever do. It was the body language of sex and he was totally fluent.

'It would be a shame to ignore what's still there between us,' he said.

The only thing between us right then was the car's middle console and the gearshift, but I didn't point that out. I knew exactly what he was referring to. I could feel it. I'd felt it the first time we met and every time I'd come in contact with him since. The air changed. The atmosphere became charged. *I* became charged.

My blood pounded through my veins as if I had been injected with a potent drug. I could feel my heart beating against my rib cage like a sparrow trapped in someone's hand. My skin tightened all over my body, as if the bones of my skeleton were pushing outwards so I could get closer to him. My breasts ached for the stroke of his hands, for the rasp of his tongue, for the suck and pull of his mouth. I looked at his mouth and felt another wave of need ricochet through me.

'Here's the thing,' I said, forcing my gaze back to his. 'I don't hand out second chances. It's another rule I like to adhere to.'

His eyes stayed locked on mine. 'I'm not offering you the same relationship as before, so strictly speaking your rule doesn't apply.'

He was good at the countermoves, I had to admit. But what exactly *was* he offering? And why was I even considering it? Although, come to think of it, maybe that wasn't so hard to answer.

'How would it be different from what we had before?' I asked.

'It would be temporary.'

I'm not sure why those four words should have hurt but they did. *Wham*. It was like a knockout punch to the solar plexus. Not that I showed it on my face or anything. I was Too Cool For School. No pun intended.

'A fling, then.' I stated it without emotion. Like a robot processing data.

He shifted his gaze and stared out at the rain-lashed street with a frown pulling at his brow. 'It's all I can offer now.'

I wiped my hand across my brow. 'Phew! That's a relief. So I won't have to worry about you suddenly springing a romantic proposal on me that I'll have to refuse on principle.'

His gaze cut back to mine. 'Marriage is out of the question.'

I lifted one of my eyebrows. 'That's quite some turn-around from the guy who once couldn't wait to get hitched and make babies.'

His jaw worked for a moment and his gaze swung back to the road. His hands gripped the steering wheel for a beat or two before he leaned forward to restart the engine.

'We'd better get a move on,' he said. 'If we don't show up on time we might lose our booking at the restaurant.'

I sat back in my seat—actually I was thrown back by the g-force of his car—and remained silent for the rest of the journey.

The restaurant was not far from the Roman Baths, and it had more stars than the Milky Way—or so it appeared to me. Even after all this time I still get a little starstruck when I go to posh restaurants. It's because Bertie and I didn't eat out when we were kids. Our parents wouldn't allow it. We weren't taken to fast-food restaurants, let alone fine dining ones.

I was seventeen and Bertie sixteen when we went to our first proper restaurant. Our parents were away on a rebirthing retreat, and thankfully we were left at home. Personally, I could think of nothing worse than returning to my mother's birth canal, as apparently I'd come out upside down and back to front and caused quite a bit of damage on the way through. A fact she likes to remind me of from time to time.

Anyway, Bertie and I rocked up to a mid-priced restaurant—we didn't want to look foolish using the wrong cutlery or something—and we both ordered big juicy steaks. It's kind of a sisterly tradition between us now. Of course we don't tell our parents what we get up to…although if my mother opens my fridge at home I guess the game will be well and truly up.

The *maître d'* showed Alessandro and me to our table as if we were the guests of honour. I suddenly felt self-conscious. Were all the other diners looking at me and wondering what I was doing with Alessandro? Wondering how a plain and ordinary, conservatively dressed primary schoolteacher could possibly interest a man as clever and sophisticated as him? Then I had another thought. Were there any parents from school in the restaurant? I did a quick covert sweep of the room, but thankfully didn't recognise anyone.

We sat down and the waiter took our drinks order. I'm not a big drinker. I'm too much of a control freak. I like to be fully in charge of my faculties at all times and in all places. There's nothing quite like a drink spike when you're thirteen to teach you *that* lesson once and for all.

Alessandro wasn't a big drinker either. At least that hadn't changed, even if his views on marriage and kids had. He had a glass of mineral water while I had a glass of cola. I know it's bad for you. Twenty-two teaspoons of sugar and all that. But if I have the diet variety then there's all those ghastly chemicals to think about. The way I see it, I can't win.

Mind you, I'm lucky it doesn't come back to bite me on the bottom. I'm happy to say my bottom is exactly the same size it has been since I was eighteen. Bertie hates me for it. I can eat and drink pretty much what I want.

I reckon it's the nervous energy that burns all the calories off. I look like I've got it all sorted on the surface, but underneath my ice-maiden mask I'm a basket case. I ruminate. I fret. I chew my nails and pick at my cuticles when no one is looking. I would thumb-suck if I could get away with it. I've been known to roll into the foetal position and rock, but not for a while. Months, actually.

Alessandro looked up from perusing the gourmet menu. 'What do you fancy?'

You, I wanted to say.

I dipped my head and made a show of examining my menu like it was a newly discovered addition to the Dead Sea Scrolls. 'Hmm, let me see.' I even tapped my fingertip against my lips. 'Aha! Beef Wellington with scalloped potatoes and green beans.' I closed my menu and sent him a 'that's settled' smile. 'You?'

He was looking at me as if I were the most fascinating thing on the menu. But then I realised I *was* on the menu. We hadn't said it in so many words, but we'd more or less agreed on a fling. *Hadn't we?* Would we race through dinner and go back to his place? We certainly couldn't go back to mine. Not with my parents there. My mother would have her ear to the wall, listening to make sure I was having tantric sex or counting my orgasms or something.

Alessandro reached for my hand across the table, his long tanned fingers closing gently around mine, his eyes holding my gaze in a sensual tether I could feel tugging on me all the way to my core.

'I've thought about you a lot, *ma petite*,' he said.

'Why do you speak French so much?' I said. 'Why not Italian, given your Sicilian heritage?'

I thought I saw something brittle come and go in his gaze before it shifted to watch his thumb stroking the back of my hand in slow rhythmic strokes.

'I haven't been back to Sicily since I left when I was eighteen.'

'Because of your father?'

His gaze met mine once more. 'My life is in England now. This is home.'

I searched his coal-black gaze for a beat or two. Was he distancing himself from his father by becoming more English than Italian? Had his year in Paris been another part of that distancing plan?

'What sort of work does your father do? Or is he retired?' I asked into the brooding silence.

His hand released mine and he picked up his glass and drank a draught of his water before answering. 'He's a property developer.'

'Successful?'

'Very.'

'Was he disappointed you didn't follow him into the business?' I asked.

That hard look came back into his eyes. 'I didn't ask you out to dinner to talk about my father. Let's talk about something else.'

'I'd like to know more about you,' I said. 'I feel like I'm only now starting to get to know you. You kept so much hidden from me in the past.'

His hand reached for mine again and gave it a tiny squeeze. 'Some things are best not talked about.'

Who was I to argue about that? I had my own dirty little secret.

I must have shown something of my conflicted feelings on my face, for Alessandro picked up my hand from where it was resting on the table and brought it to his mouth. He pressed a soft kiss to my bent knuckles, his eyes still holding mine.

'Tell me about you.'

I could feel every muscle in my body shrinking back from the table, like a snail retreating into its shell, but there was only so far I could go with Alessandro's hand anchoring me to him. 'What about me?'

'Tell me why you chose to teach in Bath.'

I flicked the tip of my tongue over my lips. 'I've always liked the area. I love the Regency period and Georgian architecture. I guess this sounds a bit weird, but I felt kind of drawn to the place. I had other options, but I felt compelled to take the job at Emily Sudgrove. Of course my mother would say it was cosmic intervention, or some such nonsense.'

His smile was crooked and heart-stoppingly gorgeous. 'Maybe it was destined that we would meet again, if only for me to apologise for how I handled things.' He stroked the back of my hand again. 'I've missed you, Jem. Really missed you. I've never met anyone else quite like you.'

I felt a sudden contraction in my chest. Had he loved me? Truly loved me? Or was it his pride that had taken the biggest hit? He had lost his ex just weeks before he met me. Would I be fooling myself to think I was somehow special? Had I been The One? He hadn't actually formally asked me to marry him. But he'd hinted he was going to. The talk of making babies and so on had made me believe I was in with a chance.

'I think you're mistaking a holiday fling for something else,' I said.

His eyes meshed with mine. 'Was that what it was for you?'

I carefully screened my features. 'In hindsight, yes, I think it was.' I gave a not very convincing little laugh. 'It was Paris, don't forget. That city's bound to make anyone think they're head over heels in love.'

His gaze was unnervingly steady on mine. 'So you're not interested in marriage and having a family now?'

'God, no.'

I probably shouldn't have answered so quickly and emphatically. Or given a theatrical shudder. I kept my expression composed, but inside I was thinking of babies. Tiny little squirmy pink bodies with ten little fingers and ten little toes. Soft downy heads and fat little bellies and dimples on elbows and knees. Cute button noses and cupid's bow mouths. Little starfish hands reaching out for mine. Little gummy smiles and happy, contented chortles. The sweet, innocent smell of their milky breath.

I'd always wanted at least three or four kids when I was growing up. I liked the idea of being a family. Of having my own tribe. I wanted the security of marriage because my parents' open relationship had always deeply troubled me as a child. I was worried one or both of them would take off with someone else, and Bertie and I would be left. Or, worse, one parent would take Bertie and leave me with the other.

Even though our parents assured us we would always come first, children don't always believe what they're told. They believe what they feel. What they sense. What they fear. What they dread.

Alessandro's thumb moved over the back of my hand again. 'I always thought you'd make a beautiful bride.'

I could feel a prickly heat coming into my cheeks. 'Weddings are such a ridiculous waste of money,' I said. 'It's just a piece of paper. Look at my parents. They've been together for thirty-one years. They're no less married than any other couple who walks down the aisle of a church.'

'True, but don't most girls dream of being a princess for the day?'

I had been one of those girls. I'd planned my wedding day since I was seven years old. I didn't tell Bertie. I didn't tell anyone, in case they thought I was a soppy fool. It was my private fantasy. A flower-filled cathedral. A beautiful gown with an elegant train and a long flowing veil. A bouquet of orange blossom and white peonies and gypsophila. Rose petals being thrown as I came out of the church with my smiling and adoring husband by my side.

I was jolted back to the moment when I realised Alessandro was still waiting for my response to his question. The heat was lingering in my cheeks.

I fanned my face with my hand. 'Is it just me or is it ridiculously hot in here?' I said. 'They should turn the heating down. It's not good for business. That's why fast-food chains have the air-con on cool. It makes people eat more.'

A half smile kicked up one corner of his mouth. 'Let's order, shall we?'

CHAPTER SEVEN

I BLAME IT on the wine. I only had one glass after I gave up on the cola. I suddenly found the cola too sweet—or maybe it was because I wanted to sit opposite Alessandro and appear sophisticated and cool instead of nervous and on edge. He had unsettled me by asking me such probing questions.

So I sipped the wine and because I hadn't had alcohol in ages it went straight to my head... Or should I say straight to my tongue.

Alessandro took one of my hands—the one that wasn't holding my glass to my lips and all but draining it—and asked, 'Why were you so uneasy about sex when we first met?'

I gulped the last mouthful of wine down in an audible swallow—which is really saying something, as there was background music playing: romantic and emotionally stirring ballads that were just as powerful as the wine.

'P-pardon?'

His hand was so gentle against my fingers it was like he was cradling a rare and precious butterfly. As if it was the very last one on earth. His gaze was soft. Supportive. Understanding.

'I know you told me your first time wasn't great, but it

was more than that, wasn't it?' he said, and when I didn't say anything he went on, 'I've thought about it a lot over the years. It's haunted me, actually.'

I swallowed again and wished I could have another glass of wine. Brandy, even. A whole bottle. No, make that a whole distillery.

'Don't use that sort of language around my mother,' I said, in an attempt to lighten the atmosphere between us. I didn't want to do deep and serious with him. I had to keep things light and casual. Under my control.

He gave me one of those lopsided smiles that tugged so painfully on my heartstrings. 'You do that a lot,' he said.

'I do what a lot?'

'Use wisecracks and humour to escape intimacy.'

I laughed—which kind of proved his point. But then I blushed, and felt stupid and exposed and more than a little tipsy. I put my wine glass down but misjudged the edge of the table, and it would have fallen to the floor if he hadn't reached out and steadied it with his free hand.

'Jem.'

Maybe it wasn't the wine's fault. It was the way he said my name…the velvet quality to his voice that was like a warm, protective cloak over my scraped raw nerves. I looked at his hand sheltering mine, the long tanned fingers capable of such strength and yet such gentleness. Or maybe it was his melted chocolate gaze…holding mine in that tender way that made me wonder all over again if he had a remnant or two of feeling for me even after all this time.

I felt like I had a wishbone stuck in my throat. I had to swallow a couple more times to clear it. And then it all came tumbling out. Once I started I couldn't stop. It was like I had been waiting years—sixteen years, to be exact—to tell someone what had happened.

'I was living in a commune with my parents when I was thirteen,' I said. 'I hated it. I didn't belong there and neither did my sister.' I took a breath that scored my already tight throat. 'I was worried about Bertie because she always got teased. She didn't know how to stand up for herself. The other kids were feral, but there was this one boy…a bit older than me…who seemed really nice. I felt like I could talk to him, you know? I felt like he understood because his parents were like mine… Although looking back I think they were much worse. They were stoned out of their minds most of the time. They didn't have a clue what their precious son was up to when their backs were turned.'

I looked up at Alessandro's expression and it gave me the courage to continue. I got the feeling if *he* had been at that commune no one would have laid a finger on me.

Not on his watch.

'I was too naive to know I was being manipulated,' I said in a hollow-sounding voice. 'He made me feel safe and comfortable so he could… Well, you can probably guess the rest. He must have slipped something into my glass of orange juice because I woke up to find him…' I blinked a couple of times and swallowed again before I could continue. 'It was over in seconds. Thank God for trigger-happy teenage boys, huh?'

Alessandro's hand gripped mine, as if he was pulling me back from a thousand-metre drop. His expression was full of anger and disgust at what had happened to me, and yet there was compassion for me all at the same time. The muscles on his face twitched. Tensed. Pulsed.

His jaw locked. His mouth flattened. His eyes flashed and then flickered with pain. Flashed again.

'If I knew who he was I would tear him apart with my bare hands,' he said.

I'm not one for violence or revenge or anything, but his words gave me a sense of closure I had never felt before. Or maybe it was because I felt safe. Finally.

'Karma's probably got him by now,' I said. 'He's probably died of a drug overdose or is languishing in prison over some heinous crime.'

'Did you tell anyone?'

I bit my lip until I felt pain. 'I considered it…but who was going to listen? My parents weren't the over-protective sort. They were—still are—into free love. I was terrified they might think I was making too big a deal out of it. That I was too uptight and probably gave out the wrong signals and should get over myself…blah-blah-blah. The usual victim blaming that goes on. I didn't tell Bertie because… Well, she's my little sister and I didn't want her worrying about me.'

His fingers gently stroked my hand. 'So you bottled it all up and put on your tough face?'

I wasn't anywhere near locating my tough face right then. It was like suddenly finding myself naked at a black-tie function. I don't think I've ever felt quite so exposed. And yet oddly enough I didn't feel shame. Not in Alessandro's presence. Not while he was wearing that protective and compassionate expression.

I glanced at my empty wine glass with a rueful look. 'I should never drink alcohol. Or orange juice.'

He brought my hand up to his mouth and ever so gently placed his lips against my bent knuckles, all the while holding my gaze.

'Thank you.'

'For what?'

'For trusting me enough to tell me.'

I screwed up my mouth but for some reason I couldn't find anything funny and diverting to say. I had to swallow again and blink. Rapidly.

'I wish they wouldn't play such soppy music in restaurants.' I gave my eyes a quick swipe with the back of my free hand. 'I bet they do it so the patrons comfort eat.'

He blotted one of the tears I couldn't quite control with the blunt tip of his thumb. 'Do you want to get out of here?'

'Where would we go?' I said. 'My parents are probably working their way through the *Kama Sutra* by now.'

He looked into my eyes. I got the feeling he was seeing behind the humour. Behind the smart-ass wisecracks. It was a strange but pleasant feeling, having someone come that close and not be fooled by the facade.

'How about my place?' he said.

I gave him a speaking look. 'Do you even have electricity at your place?'

He smiled one of his heart-stopping smiles. 'We can make our own.'

It was as we were on the way to his place that the enormity of what I'd done hit me. *I Had Told Someone*. I had told Alessandro—the man I had hated for the last five years. I had unzipped my chest and retracted my ribs and laid my bleeding heart bare.

I had never done that before. Not with anyone. I am not a confidence sharer. I don't even do it with Bertie. Sure, I tell her stuff. We chat like sisters do. But I have never told her of the doubts and fears and anxieties that have plagued me since…that night. Or even before that night.

I'm the strong one in our family. I've had to be. I took on that role at a young age and no one was going to wrench it off me.

Not even some lousy scumbag of a teenage boy who didn't know the meaning of the word *consent*.

But now I had allowed Alessandro to see behind the mask of ice that had served me so well. Global warming had nothing on me. The big melt had set in. I could feel it. I had a warm, mushy feeling right in the centre of my chest. Had I made a mistake in telling him? Would it make him feel sorry for me? Pity me?

I looked down at my hands. One of my cuticles was bleeding and I hadn't even realised I'd been picking at it.

But then Alessandro's left hand reached for my right one and brought it up to his chest, laying it right over the steady beat of his heart. His eyes were still on the road but the deep burr of his voice reverberated through my palm and somehow soothed the pitching-paper-boat-in-a-whirlpool panic in my stomach.

'You're safe with me, *ma petite*.'

I didn't answer. I would have if I'd been able to locate my voice. Instead I sat there wondering how on earth I could have thought I'd hated him for the last five years.

We were almost at his house when my phone rang. I didn't hear it at all, because I'd had it on vibrate for while we were in the restaurant, but Alessandro glanced at my bag and said, 'Aren't you going to answer that?'

'Answer what?'

'Your phone.'

'Gosh, you must have excellent hearing,' I said as I fished it out.

I grimaced as I saw it was my mother. I considered not answering it, but then I thought I might as well tell her I wouldn't be home for another hour or so.

'Hi, Mum. Listen. I've had a change of plan—'

'You have to come home,' my mother said in a strained and panicky voice. 'Your father's not well and I don't know what to do.'

Alessandro must have heard my mother's voice for he asked, 'What are his symptoms?'

'Mum, what are his symptoms?' I relayed his question.

'He's got chest pain and he's sweating and pale.'

'Call an ambulance,' Alessandro said to me. 'Tell her we'll be there in five minutes.'

And then, giving me a reassuring look, he swiftly pulled in and did a U-turn to take us back to my house, not quite speeding but with measured urgency.

The ambulance hadn't yet arrived when we got there. Alessandro took charge in a manner that was both calm and professional, which went a long way to allay my panic—not to mention my mother's. But even so my inner hysteria ran on wildly for a bit.

My father sick? He was *never* sick. I can't remember the last time he was ill, apart from a brief back-pain episode when he picked up Bertie and pulled a muscle or two, which he always reminds her of when he sees her. A bit like my mother and her birth canal. My father was usually robustly, disgustingly healthy. Now he was going to hospital in an ambulance.

My stomach clenched. What if he didn't come out?

My father was in the spare bedroom, lying on the bed. He was dressed as Superman. My mother had put on my bathrobe but I had a feeling that was all she had on. I know. Dead embarrassing. But it could have been much worse. I once came home to find my dad dressed in a dungeon master's costume and my mum in a skimpy leather bikini with a whip in her hand.

To his credit, Alessandro didn't mention what either of them was wearing. He went straight into highly trained specialist mode. He took a history while at the same time measuring my father's pulse and taking his blood pressure, and listening to his heart with the stethoscope he'd produced from the doctor's bag he'd sourced from the boot of his car.

Within a few minutes the ambulance arrived and Alessandro filled in the paramedics with my father's details and directions on what should happen by way of tests when they got to hospital.

'I'll call the hospital to let them know he's coming in under me,' he added.

My mother looked at Alessandro as if *he* were Superman. 'You're going to take care of him?'

'If that's what you'd both like,' Alessandro said. 'Of course I can always refer Mr Clark to someone else if you'd prefer?'

'No!' My mother was emphatic. 'You're the best. Everyone says you are. That's what you want, isn't it, Charlie?'

My father gave a thumbs-up sign, because he was wearing an oxygen mask, and the paramedics wheeled him out to the ambulance.

'Do you want to go with him in the ambulance?' Alessandro asked my mother.

My mother clutched the edges of the bathrobe together. 'I don't want to get in the way.'

'Mum,' I said, taking her arm, 'why don't you get dressed and we'll follow in my car?'

'I'll drive you,' Alessandro said.

My practical nature had thankfully overridden my panic by now. 'But you'll need to stay in London, and I'll have to get back to school in the morning.'

He gave a brisk nod, but then reached for my hand and gave it a gentle squeeze. 'Try not to worry,' he said. 'He'll be leaping from tall buildings in a single bound in no time at all.'

The door was barely closed on his exit when I turned to my mother and hugged her. Yes, I actually hugged her. It's not something I feel comfortable doing, as my mother has a tendency to lean right in and smother me.

'He'll be fine,' I said, hoping it was true. I couldn't imagine my parents without the other. Mum and Dad. They were a team—a weird and wacky team at times, but still a team.

Mum's arms all but cut off my circulation as she wrapped them around me. 'I was so scared,' she said. 'I didn't know what to do. It was so terrifying to see him like that. I thought he was going to die while we were having—'

'Yes, well, that would certainly have been incredibly embarrassing,' I said, somehow managing to extricate myself from my mother's octopus-like hold. 'What were you *thinking*? Dressing up is for kids, not adults.'

'Don't go all preachy on me,' my mother shot back with uncharacteristic heat. 'We weren't doing anything wrong. We often dress up for sex. It makes it more exciting. I didn't even realise he was ill. He never said. He could have died.'

'And how mortifying would *that* have been, with him dressed as bloody Superman?' I said.

My mother pouted. Yes. And a woman of fifty-five pouting is even worse than one wearing a skimpy leather bikini, in my opinion.

'You're just jealous because you're not having sex,' she said. 'You're too uptight to let anyone close enough to touch you. You stand like a shop mannequin when someone hugs you. What's *wrong* with you? Loosen up, for God's sake.'

I clenched my fists. I knew it was unfair of me to rise to her bait. We were both upset by the evening's events and in no frame of mind to talk sensibly and reasonably.

'Yes, well, thanks to you almost giving Dad a heart attack, no one will be touching me tonight,' I said. 'I was going to go back to Alessandro's place and…and… hang out.'

'See?' My mother stabbed her finger at me. 'You can't even say the word "sex". You're so prudish! I sometimes wonder how you can possibly be my daughter.'

My temper was well and truly ignited. I could not pull back from the tirade now the fuse had been lit.

'Yeah, well? Guess what?' I said. 'Sometimes I wish I *wasn't* your daughter. I wish I'd been born into a *normal* family. One where people look out for each other instead of spending their time gazing into their navels or wandering around the country chanting bloody mindless mumbo jumbo while their daughters got bullied or…or…worse.'

I couldn't say the word. The ugly word that described an ugly act. My experience was mild compared to others. I knew that, and yet it didn't give me the comfort it should.

My mother's face went from attacker mode to bewildered. 'What are you talking about? You had a *lovely* childhood. You were free to explore without the suffo-cating social structure that shuts down creativity. Look at how well you and Bertie have done. Doesn't that prove our relaxed approach worked?'

'What sort of ridiculous logic is *that*?' I threw back. 'You weren't *there* for us, Mum. Nor was Dad. Not when it counted. Most of the time you let other people do what you should've been doing. Like me, for instance. I was always watching out for Bertie. But no one was watch-ing out for me.'

My mother was still shaking her head in denial. 'No. No. *No*. You sound just like your grandmother when you carry on like that. We wanted you to be independent. To be able to enjoy the magic of childhood without restric-tion.'

I drew in a breath that felt like it was full of chopped up razor blades. Bitter, angry tears prickled at the backs of my eyes. 'I was raped when I was thirteen years old. Did you hear me, Mum? *Raped*.'

My mother blinked at me as if the lights in the room were suddenly too bright. 'Are you sure?'

Typical, I thought, with a rush of bitterness so power-ful I wanted to scream the scream I hadn't been able to scream sixteen years ago out of fear and shame and shock.

'No,' I said with heavy sarcasm. 'I thought I'd just throw that in there. Of *course* I'm freaking sure. Not that you would've noticed. You and Dad were probably too busy swinging with that other couple at that stupid commune.'

There was a cavernous silence.

Then, right in front of me, my mother's face looked like a paper bag that had been crumpled. It completely folded in on itself. She pressed her lips together, but even so, I could see the bottom one had a distinct quiver.

It was a moment or two before she spoke. 'I need to get to the hospital to see your father. I have to get dressed. I have to stop by the ATM and get some money to buy him some pyjamas. He doesn't have any. He always sleeps naked. I have to get his toiletries bag. I have to—'

'I'll do it,' I said, taking her by the arm and leading her to the spare room. It was as if I was now the parent and she was the child. *So what else is new?* I thought. 'You get dressed while I pack his things.'

As I packed my father's belongings I watched my mother out of the corner of my eye. She was like a woman of ninety. She was dithery and her movements as she pulled on her clothes were shaky, as if she couldn't get her fingers to work.

I wished I hadn't told her about the… Well, you know. Maybe that's why I'd never told her. I knew this would happen. She wouldn't be able to cope with it.

As usual, I would have to cope alone.

I left her for a moment while I called Bertie. 'Don't panic, but Dad's just been taken to hospital with some chest pain.'

'Oh, no!' Bertie said. 'Is he all right? Which hospital? Who's he coming in under? Do you want me or Matt to refer him to—?'

'It's all under control,' I said. 'Alessandro is dealing with everything.'

Suddenly I realised how comforting it was to know that. I wouldn't have to be the grown-up with him. I could collapse in a heap and sob like a little kid if I needed to. Not that I would ever do that, but still…

I could practically hear the light bulb going on in my

sister's head. 'Alessandro Lucioni is taking care of Dad?' she said. '*The* Dr Lucioni? Cardiac surgeon to the stars?'

'He's just another heart surgeon, Bertie,' I said, in my sensible big-sister voice. 'I bet you have five or six at St Iggy's.'

'None quite of his calibre,' Bertie said. 'How come you got him so quickly? He has a waiting time of months. A year, even.'

Here comes the tricky bit, I thought. 'Yes, well…he happened to be in the area and I was able to call in a favour.'

'I *knew* it!' Bertie said. 'I didn't recognise him at first. I was too busy paying the bill after you shot out of that restaurant the other week. You and Alessandro Lucioni. *Wow*. Double wow. Wait till I tell Matt.'

'Don't get ahead of yourself,' I said. 'We're not seeing each other or anything. His niece is in my class, that's all.'

'That's *all*?'

There used to be a time when I could fob Bertie off with a look or a clipped word or two. But since she's fallen in love and gotten engaged to Matt she's grown some serious backbone. It's kind of scary.

'We'll talk about Alessandro and you some other time,' Bertie said. 'I'll meet you at the hospital. Mum will need some support. So will you. What a horrible fright you must've had, you poor darling. Is that where you both are now?'

'Not quite,' I said. 'Mum couldn't go with Dad in the ambulance. She had to get dressed first.'

I could almost see Bertie rolling her eyes. 'Right. Well, drive safely. And don't worry. Dad is in fabulous hands.'

I for one could more than vouch for that.

CHAPTER EIGHT

My MOTHER AND I drove to Alessandro's hospital in London in a bruised silence. I opened my mouth a couple of times to apologise for upsetting her but then I stopped. Why should *I* apologise? My timing might be a little off but I'd said what needed to be said. Not that it made me feel any better or anything.

I felt miserable.

Bertie and Matt were there when we arrived, which made it easier for me to blend into the background. They gave my mother a hot drink—not coffee or tea, because my parents were currently off caffeine—and sat with her and explained everything that was going on. Matt and Bertie were both doctors, so this was their territory, and although it wasn't their hospital at least they knew the language.

Bertie is good at the emotional support stuff. She's also an excellent hugger. She gave our mother the sort of hug I wish I knew how to give. And kisses. Lots of them. She even did some hair stroking. Mum soaked it up and gave Bertie a grateful, wobbly little smile that made me feel even more of a cow.

Alessandro came out to the relatives' room where we had gathered. Introductions were made and I watched as

Bertie eyed him as if assessing his suitability as brother-in-law material. I kid you not. My sister is totally obsessed about weddings. She surreptitiously gave Matt a nudge before glancing at me.

I was poker-faced.

'Your dad has a badly leaking mitral valve,' Alessandro was saying. 'Probably as a result of a childhood respiratory infection. He badly needs mitral valve replacement, so we've scheduled surgery for the morning. A valve replacement is normally straightforward these days…'

He stated the risks and benefits but I was barely listening. All I could hear was his doctor-in-control voice. The competent-man-in-charge voice. The knight who had come to the rescue. My very own Superman…

Erm…come to think of it, maybe not Superman.

I looked at Alessandro's hands and imagined where they might be right now on my body if it hadn't been for my father being taken ill.

So much for my poker face. Bertie winked at me and I felt a blush crawl like fire all over my cheeks.

Alessandro spoke to Matt while Bertie leaned in closer to me. 'That's *all*?' she said, in a you-can't-fool-me voice.

I tried my prim and proper look, because it suddenly occurred to me that I needed to talk to her before my mother got there first. 'Look, there's something I need to tell you.'

Bertie led me to another room, further down the hall. 'What?' she said, once we were out of earshot.

Telling Bertie was like telling Alessandro. Once I'd finished I wished I'd done it years ago. Why hadn't I realised before now that she would be strong enough to cope with it? She might be a little scatty at times, and get herself into crazy farcical situations now and again, but she was a warm-hearted, compassionate person who loved me unreservedly.

She hugged me, and for once I didn't stand stiffly like a cardboard cut-out version of myself. I relaxed into the flower-scented warmth of her and might even have let a tear or two escape, but I had it under control once she pulled back to look at me.

'Does Alessandro know?' she said.

'I told him earlier this evening.'

'Wow.'

I frowned. 'What's with all the wows? I told you, there's nothing—'

'Not yet,' she said, brown eyes twinkling.

I hiked a shoulder up and down. 'I might consider a fling with him, just to get him out of my system.'

This time Bertie frowned. 'A fling? Don't you think you're worth more than that?'

'It's all he's offering,' I said. 'And I'm fine with it. I don't want what you want. You know that.'

Bertie put her hands on her hips like she was suddenly the older sister. 'You *do* want it. You just don't want to risk losing your heart a second time.'

I gave her a hardened look. 'I wasn't in love with him then and I'm certainly not now.'

'You are *so* in love with him—otherwise why would you have avoided him all this time?' Bertie said.

I shouldered open the door. I didn't want to discuss the feelings I could feel tiptoeing around the edges of my heart as if they were looking for some sort of entry point. Where was my cynical carapace when I needed it? The crust of my heart had softened like hospital toast. *Urgh.*

'We'd better see what Mum's up to,' I said.

Bertie gave a light, affectionate laugh that twisted my guilt screw another notch. 'God, yes,' she said, and followed me out. 'She's probably rearranging all the bedpans for better feng shui or something.'

'Someone should tell her it's a load of crap,' I quipped.

Alessandro waited until everyone else had left before he spoke to me. He took me to his office on another floor of the hospital. It was a neat and ordered room, with loads of surgical textbooks and his degree certificates set in simple but elegant frames on the walls. If he didn't stop it with the studying he was going to run out of wall space, I thought. How many qualifications did one man need? His desk was made of polished timber, and a computer and a stack of paperwork took up two thirds of it.

'Sorry about the mess,' he said.

'If this is a mess, I'd hate to see you on a tidy day.'

He studied me for a quiet moment. 'You okay?'

I stopped picking at that same hangnail I hadn't even been aware I was torturing and faced him squarely.

'Sure. Fine. Just brilliant. My dad almost had a heart attack having sex while dressed as Superman—which every doctor, intern, resident, registrar, orderly, nurse and cleaner in this hospital now knows—but, hey, all in a day's work, right?'

His expression had that soft and compassionate look about it. 'They're quite a pair, aren't they?'

I rolled my eyes and huddled into myself by wrapping my arms around my body. 'That's not all...' I took a breath and let it out in a whoosh. 'I kind of attacked my mum after you left.'

His brows drew together. 'Attacked in what way?'

'Verbally.'

He gave an understanding nod. 'It happens. Emotions often run high in a crisis.'

I chewed at my lip for a beat or two. 'I told her what happened when I was thirteen. I kind of blamed her and my father for it.'

His frown deepened. 'How did she take it?'

'The way I expected she would—which is why I didn't tell her before.' I started to pace the floor like a parrot on a perch. In a finch's cage. 'Why can't she be like other mothers? Why can't she be normal, for God's sake? Why can't *both* my parents be normal?'

He came over and put his hands on my shoulders from behind me and held me close. The shelter of his tall frame standing at my back was comforting and yet headily arousing. I wanted to turn around and slam myself into him—slake the need that was clamouring inside me. I don't know how I refrained from doing it. Maybe it was the way he was holding me just slightly apart from his body, as if he knew this was not the time and place.

'You're tired and overwrought, *ma chérie*,' he said. 'Come back to my place with me and get some rest.'

I turned to face him. 'But I have school tomorrow.'

He brushed a corkscrew of hair off my face and anchored it behind my ear. 'You could take the day off—or drive down in the morning.'

I bit my lip again. I was sorely tempted, but I kept thinking about little Claudia. She was still so new to the school. I wanted her to be able to rely on me. I was her teacher. I took that responsibility seriously.

'I can't,' I said. 'I might get held up in traffic and then Claudia will panic at having to deal with a fill-in teacher.'

He slid his hand to the nape of my neck and tilted my face up. His eyes had that tender, lustrous quality to them. 'Will you be able to drive home now? It's a two-hour journey at least. Aren't you exhausted?'

'I'm fine,' I said. 'I had three coffees in the waiting room. I'll be awake for the next week. Anyway, it'll be quicker driving at this time of night.'

He slowly brought his head down until his mouth was just above mine. 'Until tomorrow night, then.'

'What are we doing tomorrow night?' I asked.

He smiled against my lips. 'Guess.'

And without waiting for me to answer he kissed me.

I was right about those coffees. I barely closed my eyes all night, even though I had a good run back to Bath in record time. I tossed and turned and fidgeted. I relived that kiss a thousand times. The way his mouth had moved against mine—tenderly, in an exploratory way, as if re-discovering a taste for something he had long given up and now craved.

It had been a kiss of promised passion, an anticipatory kiss that had made every cell in my body quake with need. His tongue was gentle with mine. Not pushy or too overpowering. I got the feeling he was kissing me as if it were my first kiss. The kiss I should have had as a teenager.

I was drifting into dangerous territory with him. I knew it and yet I couldn't stop myself from dreaming about him... Well, I would have dreamed about him if I'd been able to get to sleep.

I gave up in the end, and got showered and ready for school by six a.m.

Bertie sent me a text, bless her, asking if I was okay. I sent her one assuring her that I was fine. We often communicate using emoticons. But this time I couldn't find one to adequately describe how I was feeling. I felt worried about my father, guilty about my mother, and full of excitement about seeing Alessandro tonight.

There was one other thing I was feeling, but I wasn't going to acknowledge it in case it took a foothold.

There was no way I was going to fall in love with Alessandro.

I wasn't *that* stupid.

After lunch I did a drama lesson with my class. The other children were excited but Claudia hung back, obviously intimidated by the thought of having to act in front of the class. I had it all planned, though. The exercises would be whole-class exercises at first. There would be non-speaking roles to begin with, and then I would up the ante.

It worked like a charm. She was a brilliant little pot plant for the first scene—in fact much better than some of the other more outgoing pupils. She stood with her little thin arms stuck out like branches. And when I said someone had forgotten to water the pot plant she visibly wilted.

I was thrilled.

Then I asked the class to pretend to be puppies that wanted someone standing outside the pet shop to come in and buy them. Claudia was amazing at it. She put on this little take-me-home-with-you face that made me feel like taking her home right then and there.

Then I asked individual pupils to act out certain emotions. I told them to use words or gestures or expressions—whatever they wanted. We did sadness, anger, excitement and happiness. The only one Claudia had trouble with was happiness. Her smile looked a little forced.

I knew the feeling.

Then I moved on to speaking parts. I told the children to work in pairs and I asked Claudia to pretend to be someone who was unhappy with a gift she'd bought from a store. Her partner was to be the unhelpful assistant. What a little champion Claudia was. She morphed into the role as if she had been born for the stage. There was no stuttering. No hesitancy. She put her hands on her hips and stared down the other pupil, insisting on getting a refund. The whole class clapped when she was done.

I can't remember a time when I felt more satisfied as a teacher.

'You're looking pretty pleased with yourself,' Lucy Gatton said when I went into the staffroom at the end of the day.

I told her about Claudia and how well she had performed. 'It was fantastic. I think we should put her in the end-of-term play. We should give her the leading role. It will be brilliant for her. She's a born actor. It's like she totally morphs into the role.'

Lucy cocked her head at me. 'This isn't a case of nepotism, is it?'

I immediately bristled. 'What do you mean?'

She gave me a knowing look. 'You and her uncle?'

I tried to look nonchalant, but right then and there I thought my six and seven-year-olds would have done a much better job. 'There's nothing going on between her uncle and me.'

'Then why were you seen having dinner with him last night?'

I wondered who had seen us. I hadn't noticed anyone— although that didn't mean no one had been there. I'd been more than a little distracted by Alessandro's company. Not to mention having that tongue-loosening glass of wine. Anyone could have seen us and reported it back to the school gossip network.

'We met to discuss Claudia's specific educational issues,' I said, with just the slightest elevation of my chin.

Lucy snorted. 'And what did you do *after* that?'

I pressed my lips together and then blew out a breath. 'Actually, he came back to my place and sorted out a health issue of my father's. He transferred him to London and operated on him this morning.'

Lucy looked a little taken aback. 'Is your father all right?'

'He's fine,' I said. 'Al—Dr Lucioni texted me during break.'

In fact, Alessandro had called me and left a very reassuring voicemail, telling me how much he was looking forward to seeing me tonight, but I didn't want her to know that.

'Everything went well. My father will be out of hospital in a couple of days.'

Lucy was still looking at me as if she wasn't sure whether to believe me or not. 'You're a seriously dark horse, Jem Clark. You could be sleeping with the guy and your own mother wouldn't know.'

You can bet on that, I thought as I collected my things before I left.

CHAPTER NINE

I WAS STILL running on caffeine when the doorbell rang to announce Alessandro's arrival. I opened the door to see him standing there with a bunch of creamy tea-roses. How on earth had he remembered I wasn't a red roses girl?

The delicacy, the subtle fragrance and the old-fashioned quality of those blooms took my breath away. I buried my head in the bouquet to disguise my reaction. Not that it worked. If I'd wanted to disguise how much his gesture meant to me I probably should have tossed them aside as if they were a bunch of cheap supermarket fragrance-free blooms. But it was too late now. I breathed in the gorgeous scent while the velvet-soft petals tickled my face.

'Your father is making an amazing recovery,' he said.

'Which he and my mother no doubt put down to the fact that they haven't eaten meat or been anywhere near a processed item of food in the last thirty-odd years,' I said.

He smiled. 'Your mother has been down to the kitchen and revamped the hospital menu—or at least tried to.'

I rolled my eyes and carried the roses to the sink, so I could put them in water before they could wilt.

'I had a breakthrough with Claudia today.'

'So she said.'

I swung around to face him. 'You've seen her?'

'I called in to the boarding house on my way past,' he said. 'She was just getting ready for bed. She told me about the drama lesson. She loved it, by the way.'

I turned on the tap to fill the vase I'd selected. *Selected?* Snort. I only had one. Just shows how often anyone brings me flowers. I made a little fuss over the way the blooms were positioned rather than look at him. I had a feeling he was getting far too good at reading me.

'She was a natural,' I said. 'She didn't stutter at all. I want her to take the lead role in the end-of-term play. It'll be great for her confidence. I just know she'll be brilliant.'

He came up behind me, put his hands on my shoulders and turned me. His eyes held mine with such warmth I felt something slip inside my stomach.

'I don't know how to thank you for what you're doing.'

'Yes, well—when it comes to thanks, what about what you did today?' I countered. 'You saved my father's life.'

He shrugged one of his shoulders. 'Any decent cardiac surgeon could've done that.'

I reached up with my hand and stroked his stubble-covered jaw. 'Yes, but *you* did it—and then drove all the way back down here to call in on Claudia and catch up with me.'

'Ah, yes, but I have an ulterior motive when it comes to you.'

'Let me guess. You want to get laid?'

He cupped my face in both his hands, his expression so darkly serious and intent it made something inside my chest quiver like a moth was trapped between my ribs.

'I don't want to pressure you into something you're not ready for,' he said, in that gravel-and-honey tone.

I'm ready! I wanted to shout. But the thirteen-year-old girl inside me appreciated his sensitivity. Oh, how she appreciated it! Adored it. Clung to it. Was healed by it.

'I want you,' I said, shocked at how much truth there was in that bald statement. I had never wanted anyone before him or since. I had no sex drive. Zero. Zilch. *Nada.* But when it came to him it was like a switch had been turned to 'on'. And not just on but flashing with neon lights.

I put my hands on the top of his shoulders, drawing him closer, feeling the heat of his aroused body next to my starving, aching one. 'Make love to me,' I said, in a whisper-soft voice.

His mouth came down and covered mine, fusing it with heat, with passion, and yet with such excruciating tenderness I felt tears gather at the back of my eyes. I kissed him back, with all the passion I had suppressed for so long. It came bursting out of me like a centuries-old fountain that had been blocked.

I heard him groan as our tongues met and tangled. I felt his erection surge against me as he gathered me closer. The heat that flared between us was like a wild-fire. And yet he kept control of it. He held me as if I was a delicate bloom that would be bruised and crushed by rough handling.

I could feel my frozen heart melting, as if someone had aimed a laser-hot beam at it. I desperately tried to keep the crusty old armour that had guarded my heart for so long in place, but it was like trying to defend an ice cream cone from a naked flame. I was oozing with feeling. With feelings I'd locked away for years.

He kissed my mouth with aching tenderness. Then he trailed his mouth down my neck, lingering over my collarbone, moving to the valley of my cleavage. His tongue lit a fire beneath my flesh, making every nerve go off like a firecracker. I could feel that racing river of fire running along my nerve-endings. It was running out of control—along with my pulse.

His hands moved down my body, skating over my breasts without lingering. I wanted more. I wanted him to possess them, to palpate them as he had done in the past. I whimpered and pressed closer, urging him to take things to the next level.

He put his hands on my hips, holding me to his arousal. Letting me know how much he wanted me and yet letting me set the pace. There was no pressure. Not like I'd felt in the past. Wasn't that why I had struggled with anyone else as a sexual partner? I had never trusted them. I had never trusted them to gauge when I was out of my comfort zone.

Only Alessandro had done that. Had intuited that even without knowing what had happened to me.

I moaned with approval against his mouth as it covered mine again. I opened it to welcome his tongue back in, stroked mine along it and around it, sucking on it to make him aware of how much I wanted him.

He made a similar sound of approval as he released my hair from its tie. It cascaded around my shoulders and he took a handful of it as he angled my head for a deeper kiss.

I got to work on his clothes, but my fingers were in too much of a hurry. His hands came to the rescue, releasing buttons so I could slide my hands over the sexy planes and contours of his chest. He had just the right amount of chest hair. Call me old-fashioned, but I love a man who isn't 'manscaped'. My fingers spread through those tight whorls and then I pressed my mouth to his sternum, running my tongue down and then over and around each of his flat nipples.

He tipped my head back up and slowly slid my shirt off my shoulders, revealing just enough skin for his mouth to tease and tempt. I shivered as his lips moved over my bare flesh. My nipples tightened in anticipation inside the lacy cups of my bra. He slid the strap of my bra over my shoulder and trailed his hot mouth over the upper curve of my breast.

He didn't go anywhere near my nipple. He explored every other slope, leaving me in a state of frenzied sexual excitement. I pushed myself towards him. Wanton, I know, but I was going to die if he didn't take my breast—or what he could get of it—in his mouth.

And then he did it.

It was just as breathtaking as I remembered. Maybe even more so. His lips closed around my nipple, softly at first—a teasing little touch that made my sensitive nerves go haywire. Then he used his teeth in a light graze that made the hairs on the back of my neck dance at their roots. He did the same thing to my other breast, his touch so mind-blowing, I whimpered in delight.

He kissed his way back to my mouth, subjecting it to another passionate exchange that made my inner core coil with want. I put my arms around his neck, linking them behind his head, kissing him with such vigour I could feel the rasp of his stubble on my chin.

He eased back and lifted me in his arms, then carried me to the bedroom. You might wonder how he knew which one was mine, but the detritus of my parents' aborted stay was still evident in the spare room. I hadn't had the time or the inclination to clean it up.

Alessandro laid me down on the bed, but he didn't come down on top of me as he might have done in the past. He sat to one side of me, stroked my face as if I were young child.

'Are you sure you want to do this?' he said.

'What part of *I want you* are you not getting?' I said, tugging at the collar of his shirt so his head came down.

He kissed me softly as he joined me on the bed.

We were still wearing way too many clothes. I started on his trousers and he got working on mine. It was a mutual journey of discovery. I loved finding him again— the heat and strength and potent power of him springing out from the confines of his underwear made something deep in my core shudder in rapture.

He slowly peeled away my clothes until I was just in my knickers. Thankfully they were my best ones. Bertie bought them for me a couple of birthdays ago, but I'd pushed them to the back of the drawer as I thought they were too girly and feminine for me. They were black lace, with little pink bows on the hips.

Alessandro obviously liked them. I saw his eyes darken as he stroked his finger down the seam of my body. The sensation of his touch through the almost sheer lace made my back arch off the bed. I could feel my dampness. I was sure he could too as he gently peeled the lace away from my body and brought his mouth down.

I shivered all over as his lips touched me. I wished I'd had time to wax, but he didn't seem to mind. He separated me so tenderly; worshipping me with such achingly poignant reverence I had to blink back tears.

I realised then that he was my first lover in all the ways that counted. He had shown me how to experience pleasure. He had shown me what my body was capable of, how it responded to touch and carefully timed caresses. He had never touched me in a way I wasn't comfortable with. He had always treated me with the utmost respect and consideration. He had not selfishly satisfied his needs with no thought to mine.

He must have sensed my emotional response, for he stopped his gentle ministrations and came back up to look deeply into my eyes.

'Too much?'

I bit my lip and shook my head, suddenly incapable of speech.

He stroked the underside of my chin. 'I've given you beard rash.'

I could feel my chin wobbling, so I bit down even harder on my lip. His hand cradled my cheek, his eyes so dark and meltingly soft I knew I was a goner.

'You have the most beautiful mouth,' he said, stroking my bottom lip so I could no longer savage it. 'So soft…so sweet.'

'I like yours too.' My voice was so husky it didn't sound like me at all.

He kissed me again, softly and leisurely, until he sensed I was ready to continue. I let my body do the talking because it was easier that way. I didn't want to suddenly blurt out how much I'd missed him or how great he made me feel—how I wished we could rewind the past and do things differently. I just wanted to be as close to him as physically possible. I wanted to lose myself in his body, to feel the magnificence of sexual pleasure with him—only with him. I wanted to break free, to escape from everything that had been so tightly bound up inside me like a giant, prickly ball of bitterness.

Alessandro moved down my body again, taking me

on a sensual quest that unmoored me from my foundations. I could feel myself being shaken loose with each stroke and flutter of his tongue against my hungry, aching, greedy flesh. The tremors of feeling moved through me until I was rolling, crashing like a wave against a shore. I was washed over with the sensations. Flooded with them. Drowned in delight. And then floating like a bit of flotsam in that blessed afterglow of release.

But I didn't want to be the only one to experience such amazing sensations. I wanted to give pleasure to him. It was my gift—the only thing I had to give him. I could no longer—*would* no longer—give him my heart, but my body was his for the asking.

I moved my hand down his shaft, rediscovering the shape and heft of him. Delighting in the way he sucked in a sharp-sounding breath, as if my touch ignited him like no other. His skin was silky and smooth, and yet the weight and thickness of him was as strong as steel. My body quivered with the memory of how it had felt to have him thrust inside me, losing himself in me.

He was fighting to control himself. I could feel the tension building in him. I could hear the hectic pace of his breathing as his need for release increased.

'Wait.'

He suddenly pulled back and reached over the side of the bed for his discarded trousers. I was glad one of us was being responsible about safe sex, because I can tell you right then it was the furthest thing from my mind. But I appreciated his concern—particularly as I wasn't currently taking the pill. I hadn't seen the need to pump myself full of hormones when I was basically celibate.

Alessandro came back safely sheathed and poised himself at my entrance. But still he didn't rush for completion. He caressed my breasts, using his hands, his lips and his tongue. He moved down my body, leaving a trail of blistering heat in his wake. I felt the pressure building inside me again as he came to my pubic bone. My nerve-endings began to twitch as his mouth came inexorably closer. I felt the warm gust of his breath against my labia, then the gentle glide of one of his fingers as he tested my moisture to see if I was ready for him.

I guided him with my hand, lifting my pelvis, making a pleading noise that was unintelligible but crossed all language barriers. He knew what I wanted and he gave it.

I gasped as he took that first slow but sure thrust. He could have gone much deeper and much harder, but he didn't. The measured pace was just right for me to find my own rhythm before I tried to keep up with his.

And then it all fell magically into place.

Somehow it was like beautiful choreography—a ballet of limbs and lips and lust and longing that built to a stunning, heart-stopping climax.

I closed my eyes to give myself up fully to the storm of passion that ricocheted through me. Tiny bright lights like a fistful of carelessly flung diamonds sparkled behind my eyelids. My flesh tingled from head to foot and my heart raced in time with Alessandro's. I could feel it pumping against my crushed breasts, where his body was pressed as the final waves of release washed over him.

I could have used one or two of Bertie's 'wows' just then, but I decided to stay silent. Talking would break the spell that had fallen around and over us like a velvet blanket.

My fingers started moving up and down the length of his strong spine like a lapsed pianist working on her scales.

'"Twinkle, Twinkle, Little Star"?' Alessandro said after a moment, his voice a deep rumble against my neck, where his face was pressed.

I couldn't stop a laugh escaping. 'Good guess. How about this one?' I tapped out the rhythm to 'Three Blind Mice'.

I felt his lips move against my neck as he spoke. 'Play it again.'

I played it again, slower this time. 'Come on,' I said, laughing again. 'It's an easy one.'

His lips started to nibble on my earlobe. 'Give me a clue.'

I shivered all over as his tongue traced the cartilage of ear. My fingers stopped playing their tune and started weaving their way through the thickness of his hair. 'I'm tired of that game,' I said in a breathy whisper. 'Let's play something else.'

He propped himself up on his elbows, his eyes glinting at me smoulderingly. 'Any suggestions?'

I circled his mouth with one of my fingertips, the sound of his skin rasping against mine making something topple inside my belly. 'Three Questions?'

He lifted one dark eyebrow. 'I haven't heard of that game. How does it go?'

I traced the right angle of his jaw with my finger. 'I get to ask you three questions. Anything I want. And you have to answer.'

A flicker of tension passed across his cheek before he got it under control. 'And do I get to ask *you* three questions of my choice too?'

'Of course.'

Now, you might ask why I was playing such a potentially dangerous game, but I had already told him my worst secret. What did I have to lose? Besides, I had a feeling there was something he wasn't telling me about his sister Bianca. Don't ask me how I knew. I'm not psychic…or at least I hope not.

'O-kay,' he said, but his tone was unmistakably cautious.

'What's the most difficult operation you've ever done?' No point in starting with the big one, I thought. I'd work up to it.

He didn't hesitate in answering. 'It was a heart transplant on a seventeen-year-old when I was a registrar. Things didn't go according to plan. To be fair, it was a risky case. But the consultant was one of those instrument-throwing ones. He was out of his depth but refused to admit it. He sent me out to tell the relatives their son hadn't made it. I'll never forget their faces. They leapt to their feet, eager for good news, and I had to tell them the opposite.'

I looked at his face, saw the anguish of that remembered tragic encounter playing out over his features— the shadows in his eyes, the ghosts of lost patients who lingered to haunt him. 'That must have been awful for them—and for you,' I said. 'And cowardly of the consultant to leave it up to you.'

He brushed a stray strand of hair away from my face. 'It was a good lesson to learn. I make a point of dealing directly with relatives. Not to mention keeping a cool head under pressure. Things *can* go wrong. No one—no matter how skilled or how much experience they have— is exempt from that. But staying calm in the middle of a crisis can be the difference between life and death.'

Somehow we had shifted our bodies so we were lying

side by side, one of his legs draped over one of mine, our hands loosely entwined.

'Next question?'

I had to remind myself of the game. I was so taken aback by the quality of him, the strength and courage he exhibited under pressure. Was that why he hadn't acted the way I'd expected when I'd accused him of using me five years ago? He had faced down my spitting tirade with what I'd thought was cool indifference. But what if that had been his way of keeping calm when the unexpected was thrown at him?

It was a sobering thought.

'Did you have a pet as a child?' I said.

A shadow passed over his features like a cloud crossing the path of the moon. 'Yes. His name was Cico.'

'What happened to him?'

'He died.'

'When?'

'That's question number four,' he said. 'Now it's my turn.'

'Hang on a minute.' I gave his chest a playful shove. 'I want to know what happened to him.'

Alessandro captured my hand and came back over me, all but pinning me to the bed. 'You're the one who made the rules, *ma petite*. You can't go changing them now.'

I gave up with good grace…well, good for me—if you overlook the quick tongue poke and the childish pout. 'Okay, fire away,' I said.

'Do you want to have dinner or make love again?'

'Make love.'

He smiled and brought his head down. I grabbed a fistful of his hair and pulled him away from his mission.

'Hang on. Don't you want to ask another two questions?' I said.

'I'm getting to that.' He sent his mouth on a hot trail down to my breasts. 'Does that feel good?'

'Yes…' It was part gasp, part groan.

He moved down my body and kissed the sensitive skin of my inner thigh. 'How about that?'

Somehow I lost count of the questions, and suddenly I was incapable of answering. Anything.

CHAPTER TEN

My FATHER MADE a spectacular recovery—which, as I'd predicted, my mother and to some degree my father took all the credit for. However, they *did* think to organise a thank-you card for Alessandro and a bottle of wine. It wasn't a top-shelf one, but it was organic.

They came back to my place to collect their things, but they didn't hang around.

I was awkward with my mother. Nothing new there, but now there was another layer of awkwardness. She obviously hadn't said anything to my father about our discussion/argument, which showed at least she had *some* sensitivity, given he was still getting over heart surgery. But I had a feeling she might never tell him. She would do what she had always done when things got too confrontational or threatening for her. She would bury her head in the sand, or in her navel, or take up with yet another guru to distract herself from facing reality.

I stood on my front step and waved my parents off, feeling that mixture of guilt and relief that so perplexed and frustrated me.

They had not long gone when I heard the unmistakable roar of Alessandro's car turning the corner.

I couldn't wait to tell him how well Claudia was

doing. The drama therapy was going gangbusters. Even the speech therapist was stunned by Claudia's progress in such a short space of time. Although Claudia's stutter was still present, the boost in her confidence from doing those drama exercises had helped her to be not so distressed about the words and sounds she couldn't say, but to concentrate on what she could.

The only thing that still troubled me now was how she never mentioned her mother. It was unusual in a child so young. She didn't show any signs of homesickness either. She had settled into the boarding house routine as if she'd been boarding for years. That sort of quiet self-reliance in an older child would have been laudable. However, in a child of Claudia's age it was faintly disturbing.

But then I thought of my tricky relationship with *my* mother. Kids soon learn who they can rely on and make the necessary adjustments. I for one knew all about making adjustments. I swear I could moonlight as a spanner.

I watched as Alessandro's powerful car growled into one of the few parking spaces at the front of my flat. He had spent the last few days working in London. I knew he was finding it tough, balancing his supervision of the renovations on his house here in Bath and his commitment to his niece, not to mention our 'relationship'— which I automatically put in quotation marks because I didn't know what else to call it.

It didn't feel like a fling, but neither did it feel like a proper commitment. He had made it clear he wasn't able to offer anything permanent, and I had made it equally clear I didn't want to settle down. The trouble was I was having wayward thoughts that would catch me totally off guard.

Like when I went to my wardrobe to get dressed for

school and my wedding dress, hidden in its silk bag, kind of stared at me. For all that it was covered in a sack—hidden, stashed away—it had an annoying habit of reminding me of the hopes and dreams I had once clung to. It was like I had shoved a part of myself into the dark recesses of my wardrobe but now that part was getting restless…agitated.

I decided I would give the damn dress away or stuff it in a charity bin the first chance I got.

As Alessandro walked towards me from his car, I could see he wasn't having the best of days. His eyes had dark circles beneath them and his skin looked too tightly drawn over his face. And there I was thinking teaching was stressful. At least I had never had to tell a parent their kid had died under my care.

'Tough day slaving over a hot pericardium?' I said.

The corners of his mouth lifted in a half smile. 'No surgery today—just a clinic that went on for ages.'

He bent down and pressed a kiss to my lips. I breathed in the tangy citrus scent of him and my senses spun as his mouth increased its pressure. He made a low, deep sound and put his arms around me, drawing me to him until our bodies were flush against each other. Somehow him hugging me or me hugging him wasn't a problem for me. We fitted together like two pieces of one of those complicated Mensa puzzles.

I wondered what my neighbours would make of it. I normally lived such a boring, uneventful life that for them to see a handsome man drive up in a top-model Maserati and take me in his arms and kiss me soundly was probably much better viewing than what was currently on the television. Out of the corner of my eye I saw a couple of curtains twitch, which more or less confirmed my suspicions. Honestly. Some people need to get a life.

Alessandro raised his mouth just high enough to speak. 'It is just me, or do you get the feeling we're being watched?'

'Maybe we should go inside and let their imaginations take over?' I said.

He brushed his lips across mine again. 'Good plan.'

I must have fallen asleep after we made love, because I woke to find Alessandro sitting on the edge of my bed watching me. He was fully dressed, which wasn't how I'd left him. He had even put some order to his hair—presumably with his fingers, for I could see the track marks in between those jet-black strands.

I pushed myself up on my elbows and shook my head so my hair went back behind my shoulders. 'You're leaving?' I tried to strip my voice of any trace of disappointment, but I'm not sure I managed it.

He trailed an idle finger down the slope of my cheek. 'What are you doing next weekend?'

A big fat nothing—just like I did every weekend. But I didn't want to admit that. I didn't want to sound too eager. I didn't want to appear too available. A girl had her pride, after all.

'I have a couple of things on,' I said. 'Why?'

A frown had formed a crease on his forehead. 'The school is shut next weekend, and I still haven't found a suitable nanny for Claudia.'

I could see where this was going and stayed silent. My sister is the opposite with silences. She hates them. She babbles whatever comes into her head if there's one to fill. I am more for waiting to see how long it takes for the other person to get to the point.

Alessandro got to the point a whole lot faster than most.

'Would you be able to do it? Look after her for the weekend? I should be back late on Saturday night. I have a commitment in London. I have to be there. It's a research meeting I've had booked for months. If I pull out, the project could fall over.'

I looked at where his hand was resting on the bed, within touching distance of mine. I could feel the magnetic force of it. It was all I could do not to reach out and touch him.

I brought my gaze up to his. 'Will she want to come and stay with me?'

His tense features visibly relaxed. 'She'll love it. She talks about you all the time.'

I lifted my eyebrows. 'Talks?'

He smiled. 'Yes. Talks. With the occasional stutter, but at least she's talking.'

I dragged at my lower lip with my teeth and glanced at our hands, so close but still not touching. Was he feeling the same gravitational pull as I was?

'Yes, she's come ahead in leaps and bounds, but there's one thing that troubles me…' I looked into his eyes again. 'She never mentions her mother. *Never*. It's as if she's forgotten she *has* a mother or is deliberately *not* thinking about her. Why is that?'

He let out a long sigh as he sent one of his hands through his hair. 'I suspect Claudia has learnt from an early age that she can't always rely on her mother,' he said. 'It's as if she knows Bianca is incapable of being present emotionally, even if she's able to be there physically—although of course just now that's impossible.'

I slipped my hand over his and gave it a gentle squeeze. 'What's wrong with Bianca? I mean apart from the drug problem?'

He looked at me—such a bleak look that I felt my chest tighten as if it was caught in a vice.

'She's had a mental breakdown,' he said. 'I think it's been coming on for months—years, more like. I had to have her sectioned. In layman's terms that means admitted to a mental health facility for her own safety.'

I swallowed and gripped his hand a little tighter. 'I know what it means… I'm so sorry…'

His fingers somehow turned, so that it was his hand holding mine. 'My priority is to keep Claudia safe, no matter what.'

'Hence my school?'

His eyes met mine. 'I knew you would be the one person I could rely on to make sure my niece got the care and attention she needed,' he said. 'I'm not an expert on small children. I've got my sister's situation to prove that.'

I frowned at him. 'Why are you blaming yourself? Your sister's problems have nothing to do with you. Mental illness can be due to so many factors. Genetics or—'

He got up so abruptly from the bed that I stopped speaking. It was like a guillotine had come down on my sentence.

'They have *everything* to do with me,' he said as he paced the small area of floor available. 'I blame myself. I should've seen the signs.'

I rolled my lips together, shocked at how dry they had suddenly become. I didn't fill the silence. I have a feeling even Bertie the obsessive silence filler would have left this one open, for Alessandro to continue when he was good and ready.

He turned and looked at me with a harrowed look. 'My father is responsible for Bianca's problems. All of them. Every single one.'

I felt my throat move over another tight swallow. 'Was he…violent towards her too?'

'It depends what you mean by violence.'

He turned away from me, to inspect something on my dressing table. I knew it wasn't that he was interested in my hairbrush or the perfume atomiser. He was gathering himself. Drawing on his inner reserve to contain the anger he felt against his father.

And then suddenly I got it.

The ugliness of it crept into the silence like a loathsome creature, reaching out with long, slithering tentacles to strangle every atom of oxygen out of the room.

'He sexually abused her.'

I didn't say it as a question. I didn't need to. The ghastly truth was written on Alessandro's face when I met his eyes in my dressing table mirror.

He turned and faced me. 'I only found out a month ago. It explained everything. Her rebellion during her childhood and teens, the drugs, the drink, the promiscuous behaviour.' He dragged a hand down his face, momentarily distorting his features. 'I could have stopped it if I'd known earlier. I *would* have stopped it. I would've made sure he was sent to rot in prison. But she didn't tell me.'

'When did the abuse start?'

'It started when we were sent to live with him, after our mother died. He groomed her for years. I can never forgive myself for not protecting her. Now he's denying everything and he's got himself a hot-shot defence lawyer who'll pull apart my sister's life until they take everything away from her—including Claudia.'

My heart ached for Alessandro's sister. I was all too well aware of the silence of shame that could go on for decades. I thought of her as a motherless little girl, unable to protect herself. Alessandro was blaming himself, but he'd been a kid too. How could he have possibly known what was going on? Perpetrators made sure such dirty secrets remained secret. It was part of the power they had over their victims.

'A lot of victims find it very difficult to speak of what's happened to them—even to those closest to them,' I said. 'And when the abuse has been happening for a long time, and from a young age…well, there are other factors. Fear of not being believed. Fear of reprisal from the perpetrator. It's terribly complex. The fact is you know now. So you can keep her and Claudia safe—which you're doing to the best of your ability.'

One of his hands pushed through his hair. 'I couldn't even keep a *dog* safe from him. What hope did I have to keep my sister safe?'

My stomach clenched. Cico. The dog Alessandro had mentioned when we played Three Questions. *Oh, dear God.* What a ghastly childhood he'd had. I felt a sudden rush of shame for all the times I'd criticised my parents. There were far worse things than having hippie parents. Far, *far* worse.

Alessandro came over and sat beside me on the bed again. He put his hand over mine. 'I want to help my sister move beyond this,' he said. 'I want her to be a proper mother to Claudia. I want justice for her. But she's not strong enough to cope with the judicial system. I'm worried if I push too hard she'll do something even more drastic than she's already done.'

I turned my hand over and curled my fingers around his. 'You're doing all you can. If and when she feels ready to press charges then you'll be by her side to help her through it. If she can't face it then you have to accept that. It's her choice. It *has* to be her choice.'

His thumb moved back and forth across my index finger tendon. 'Did *you* ever consider pressing charges?'

I dropped my gaze to where our hands were joined.

'For a long while I pretended it hadn't happened. I blocked it out. I refused to think about it. I didn't want it to define me. It's too late now anyway. It would be his word against mine. We were both kids without the proper guidance of responsible parents. Why would I put myself through it? I have better things to do.'

He eased up my chin so our eyes could meet. 'You must never blame yourself.'

'I don't,' I said. 'Men like that boy and your father are pond scum. They'll get what's coming to them eventually—at least that's what I hope.'

He let out another long breath and laid my hand back down on the bedcovers. 'I have to get going. I have a couple of things to check at my house.'

Take me with you.

The words were on the tip of my tongue but I closed my lips over them. No point in imagining a romantic candlelit picnic in his gorgeous old house. No point in imagining he might want to spend the whole night with me instead of a couple of hours. No point imagining anything other than what we had here and now. Sex without strings. Without commitment. A day-by-day affair.

I waited a beat before saying, 'I'll bring Claudia home

with me on Friday after school. There'll be paperwork for you to sign, to give me authority. Can you drop by the school office in the next day or so?'

'Sure.'

He leaned closer to press a soft kiss to my lips. I was so tempted to lengthen the contact with him but I needed to keep perspective. We had already crossed a few boundaries I had never crossed with anyone before. The deep and meaningful—and painful—conversations were a totally new thing for me.

I suspected they were a new thing for him too.

Claudia was clearly excited about coming home with me the following Friday, but was trying her best not to show it. Her big brown eyes followed me all day during class time with a distinctive gleam. Every time I caught her looking at me her little cheeks would blush as red as an apple. She would bury her chin into her neck, or hunch over her desk and pretend to be busy with whatever task I had set.

The thought of her being pleased about spending the weekend with me thrilled me in a way I had not expected to feel. Don't get me wrong. I have the occasional child I warm to, in spite of all of my efforts to avoid playing favourites. But there was something about Claudia that awoke a dormant mothering instinct in me.

Ever since I had broken up with Alessandro I had put all thoughts of motherhood aside. I had drawn a line through it with a thick red pen like someone does on a mistake in a document. I had erased it. Deleted it. But like indelible ink it was seeping back into my focus.

I was nearly thirty years old. I didn't even have a cat to go home to. I used to have a rat once, but Bertie hates them and they're not exactly the easiest pet to farm out when you want to go on holiday. No amount of telling people how intelligent rats are has ever overcome their image problem. Sad, but true.

Claudia's lack of mothering reminded me of my issues with *my* mother. I know mothers take the rap for a lot of the world's problems—which is grossly unfair because it takes two to make a child—but kids need someone watching out for them. They need to feel secure in the knowledge that someone is there for them, no matter what.

Claudia had gravitated towards me even though she had an uncle who clearly adored her. But Alessandro had work pressures and concerns about his sister—Claudia's mother. I wondered if Claudia had turned to me because I was someone she saw each day…someone who was reliable and consistent and there for her no matter what.

I hadn't seen Alessandro since he'd organised the paperwork to allow me to take Claudia home with me. He had been called away to London over a patient who had developed a complication after a stent insertion. I was becoming more and more aware of the stresses he was under. It's not that I hadn't thought about it before—over the years I'd seen the sort of pressures Bertie had been under in her work as an anaesthetist. When she puts people to sleep she wants them to wake up. When Alessandro operates on someone he wants them to get better.

The tragic reality is not everyone does.

Finally it was time to leave school. I went over to the boarding house to find Claudia with a little overnight case packed and sitting on her bed, swinging her legs as if she couldn't keep still.

'Ready?' I said.

She nodded and jumped off the bed, and went to pick up her bag from where it was on the floor.

'Here,' I said, and reached for it. 'Let me take it for you. It looks heavy.'

It wasn't—but I wondered wryly if I would turn out to be one of those musical-instrument-and-sports-equipment-carrying parents I had so roundly criticised.

You're not going to be a parent.

The internal voice was a jarring reminder of the obdurate stance I had taken as a result of my heartbreak. Five years on and I was still punishing myself for being naive. I was denying myself a lifetime of joy and fulfilment because I had been let down by a man who hadn't loved me the way I thought he should have.

But the more I knew of Alessandro the more I worried that I might have got it wrong about him. He was not a man to turn his back on responsibility or a commitment he had made to someone.

Yes, we'd had a whirlwind affair, but people *did* fall in love quickly. It wasn't unusual. Sometimes the most passionate and enduring relationships were the result of instant attraction.

And it didn't come much more instant that ours.

I had allowed bitterness to cloud my judgement. Not only bitterness—insecurity. Loads and loads of insecurity. I swear if anyone knew how much baggage I was carrying around I'd be charged extra on flights. I had always thought of myself as damaged goods. It was what I'd believed since I was thirteen years old. I wasn't worthy. I didn't deserve to have it all because I felt it had all been taken away from me.

But what if I could get myself to the stage of wanting it all again? Believing I was not only worthy of it but actively *seeking* it? Expressing my needs without fear of rejection or ridicule?

Scary thought.

Claudia was silent for most of the journey to my flat. But then, just as I pulled into the one available space on my street, she turned to me and asked, 'Are you going to marry Un-c-c-c-le Alessandro?'

My chest gave a tight squeeze as she struggled over the word 'uncle'. The hard consonants were still a problem for her, but at least she wasn't avoiding saying them. 'What makes you ask that?' I said, in the most casual tone I could muster.

She gave a little shrug that would have looked out of place on a sixteen-year-old, let alone a six-year-old. 'Just wondering.'

'We're…friends.'

Her big brown eyes were trained on me. '*Best* friends?'

I opened my mouth and then closed it. I had told Alessandro more than I had told anyone. *Ever.* Not even my sister, Bertie, had been privy to my darkest secrets. Did that make him and me best friends?

'Why don't you ask him?' I said.

'I will.'

Another scary thought.

CHAPTER ELEVEN

I CLOSED THE BOOK I had been reading to Claudia as a bedtime story and set it on the bedside table in my spare room. I'd read the same story to her four times because she'd said it was her favourite.

The Three Billy Goats Gruff was a favourite of mine when I was a kid too. To tell you the truth it's still a favourite. Particularly since the advent of social media, where there are more trolls around than ever.

But don't get me started.

I watched Claudia's dark spider-leg-like lashes resting on her cheeks. Her soft little rosebud mouth was parted slightly as she drifted into deep sleep. I had the most compelling urge to press a kiss to her little forehead.

Teachers these days aren't supposed to have unnecessary physical contact with their pupils.

But right then I didn't feel like her teacher.

We'd decided she was to call me Jem while she was with me. She would have to go back to addressing me as Miss Clark when she was at school. But I didn't want her to be worried the whole weekend about her lisp and her stutter.

I tiptoed out of the spare room and gently closed the door. I had a sudden flashback to when my mother would sometimes tell Bertie and me a story when she put us to bed…or whatever it was we were sleeping on during that phase of our lives. I seem to remember a hammock at one point, and a yoga mat on the floor of a circus-sized tent.

My mother didn't read the standard children's books of the day. No way. She made stuff up. Fantastical stuff—whimsical tales that went on and on until Bertie and I were roaring with laughter at the absurdity of the characters and their adventures and mishaps. She even let us offer alternative endings. That had been so much fun.

How could I have forgotten those times? It was so easy to concentrate on the bad things, the times when things hadn't felt right for me, but there were many times when things had been good.

I had never felt unloved. I had never been abused in any way. I had never been smacked. I had never been spoken to with harsh or punitive or shaming words. I had long lamented and criticised the lack of structure in our lives, but I had overlooked the benefits of being allowed to find my own personal boundaries. I hadn't had control and discipline enforced upon me externally. I had been allowed to develop it internally, which surely was far more powerful and lasting.

I looked at my phone, lying on the kitchen bench. Actually, it sort of looked at me—a bit like my wedding dress. Should I call my mother and apologise? I chewed at my lip. I hate apologising. I hate being wrong. Call it pride. Call it stubbornness. Call it avoidance. I had climbed so far up on my high horse I had vertigo.

But before I could call my mother, my phone started to ring. It was Bertie, who'd called to tell me about a bridesmaid dress fitting.

'I hope you're not going to make me wear some frothy, frilly thing I'll never be able to wear again?' I said.

'I've got a lovely design picked out,' Bertie said. 'How do you feel about pink?'

'What shade of pink?'

'Hot pink. Fluorescent hot.'

I smothered a groan. 'You're going to make me wear fluorescent hot pink and stand in front of how many people, for how many hours, with a rictus smile on my face for all the photographs? That's taking sisterly love *way* too far.'

Bertie giggled. 'Just wait till Alessandro sees you in it. He'll be knocked sideways.'

'What makes you think *he's* going to see me in it?' I said.

'You'll bring him to the wedding, won't you?'

'Why would I do that?'

'Because you're seeing him.'

'Your wedding is four months away,' I said. 'He hasn't had a relationship last longer than a month since we broke up five years ago.'

'Isn't that telling you something?'

'Yes—he's a playboy who doesn't want to settle down,' I said. 'He's told me he's not in it for the long haul. But then neither am I.'

Bertie made a tut-tutting noise.

'What?' I said.

'You're going to end up one of those crazy old ladies with a hundred cats for company in her dotage.'

'Maybe I'll have rats.'

'Euueew!' Bertie said, and then quickly changed the subject. 'So, what are you doing this weekend? Are you seeing Alessandro?'

'I'm minding his niece.'

'Wow!'

'There's nothing "wow" about it,' I said. 'He's got a research meeting in London and the school is closed. Claudia has nowhere else to go. It's the least I could do. She's a great little kid. No trouble at all.'

'Wow.'

'Will you stop it with the "wows", already?' I said.

'So when will you see him again?'

'Late tomorrow night, if he gets back in time, or maybe Sunday.'

'Are you in love with him?'

'Why are you asking me such a ridiculous question?' I said.

Bertie gave a dreamy-sounding sigh. 'I thought so.'

'You *thought* so?' I said. 'What's that supposed to mean?'

'I have to go,' Bertie said. 'Matt's just got back from the hospital. We're heading out for dinner. 'Bye-ee!'

I stared at my phone's blank screen for a moment before putting it on the coffee table. I had barely sat back against the sofa cushions when it rang again and the screen indicated it was Alessandro.

I put on my cool and businesslike voice as I answered it. 'Jem Clark speaking.'

'Hi.'

I wasn't sure how he could make one syllable of greeting sound so sexy, but he did. I felt a shivery frisson go right through my body. 'Hello,' I said. 'Did you want to talk to Claudia? I'm sorry—she's fast asleep. She stayed up later than normal, because it's not a school night, but—'

'I should've called earlier but I was held up in Theatre.'

'It's fine—she understands,' I said. 'We've talked about your job. She likes the fact you save lives. It gives her street cred with the other girls. Not every girl has a famous uncle.'

'Has she talked about her mother?'

'A little.'

'What did she say?'

'It was when we were choosing a book to read before bed,' I said. 'She told me her mother used to read to her at night. I got the feeling it was quite a while ago. I didn't press her on it. I figure she'll talk when she's ready to talk.'

'Thanks again for minding her. I'm not sure how to make it up to you.'

'It's not a problem—really. She's an angel.'

There was a little silence. But then I heard a phone or a pager ringing in the background.

'Sorry, Jem,' he said. 'I have to go. I'll call you tomorrow if I get held up. *Ciao*.'

I looked at my blank screen for the second time that evening. ''Bye,' I said, and sat back against the sofa cushions with a sigh.

I spent a fun day on Saturday with Claudia. I had some grocery shopping to do in the morning, and Claudia seemed to enjoy helping me with it. I planned to do some baking with her during the afternoon, as it was something I'd missed out on as a child. My mother would have freaked out at the sight of white sugar, white flour and butter. I never got to lick the beaters or scrape out the bowl after making cupcakes or brownies.

Not that I'm bitter about it. *Much*. I really had to stop harping on about my mother. Anyone would think I

needed a therapist. I still hadn't called her. My mother—
not my therapist. I don't have one. But I was starting to
think maybe I should.

After we dropped the shopping at home Claudia and
I went for a walk to my favourite park, where we fed
the ducks and ate a picnic lunch. Then we spent a lovely
afternoon baking. The smells coming from my kitchen
were amazing.

I had never really thought of my flat as a home before. It was just my accommodation. My place of resi-
dence. But filled with the smell of cupcakes and chocolate
crunch slices and lemon meringue pies—I'd gone a little
overboard on the sweet stuff, but Claudia didn't seem to
mind—my flat began to feel like home. Especially with a
little girl propped at my kitchen bench, with sticky hands
and cake batter around her smiling mouth and a swipe of
flour across her cheek.

I had another flashback. Mum and me at a campsite,
with the warm glow of the fire and the smell of a delicious beany sort of curry that she was showing me how to
cook. It was a Mum-and-me moment. We didn't have too
many of them, as there were always a lot of other people
around. It's like that in communes. No privacy. But that
time we had the campfire to ourselves.

I can't remember how old I was…maybe seven or
eight. But I do remember the way she made sure I wasn't
too close to the hot coals—made sure I kept my sleeve
away from the heat as I stirred the pot that was propped
on the stones that surrounded the fire. I remember thinking at the time how many generations of people must
have done that, from way back in primitive times to the
present day. Cooked around a campfire. Swapped stories.
Shared wisdom. Shared recipes for food, for life, for love.

I looked at my phone but didn't pick it up. The excuses were there, like scouts turning up for a parade. The kitchen was a mess. My arms were up to the elbows in flour. I had Claudia to mind. I had a cake just about ready to come out of the oven.

Truth was—I was a coward.

I think it was all the sugar that made Claudia resist going to bed that night. Or maybe it was because she was hoping her uncle would make it back in time to say goodnight before she went to bed.

I'd read several stories, and even made up one or two of my own, thinking of my mother with a sharp little pang. But after a while I realised it was pointless unless Claudia was tired.

I left her playing with some of the toys I'd managed to salvage from my childhood. There wasn't much. My parents hadn't believed in giving Bertie and I gender-specific toys. We'd made our own out of sticks and twigs and bits of fabric—which, now that I thought about it, was pretty cool. Kids today get given so much they don't have to use their imaginations. Bertie and I had played shops with shells and stones and sea glass behind a sandcastle counter. It had been brilliant fun.

'Do you have a dress-up box?' Claudia asked when I went in to check on her after I'd done the dishes from supper.

'Give me a second,' I said, and went to my bedroom.

I heard the soft pad of her little feet following me. She was like a loyal little puppy, following its new owner. I couldn't help feeling chuffed that she'd bonded so well to me.

I slid the wardrobe door back just far enough to get out

a pair of heels and a hippie kaftan my mother had given me for my birthday. Needless to say I had never worn it. It was a bright vomit-coloured swirl, but I thought Claudia wouldn't mind so long as it was long and floaty and grown-up. There was also a hat I'd worn to a friend's wedding, a couple of handbags and scarves, and a long string of fake pearls.

The satin bag with my wedding dress inside was still safely at the back of the wardrobe, still behind my hiking jacket. Even though I knew it would be the ultimate in dress-up for a six-year-old girl, I left it where it was.

The doorbell sounded, but Claudia was too engrossed in putting her tiny feet into a pair of my heels so I left her there while I answered it.

Alessandro was standing there, with a box of handmade chocolates and another bunch of flowers. Lovely old-fashioned cottage flowers—white lilacs and blush-pink peonies that would have filled my flat with their gorgeous fragrance if it wasn't for the lingering smell of home baking.

I saw his nostrils dilate. 'You've been baking?'

'Guilty as charged.' I took the flowers from him with a smile. 'Claudia loved it. She was a great little assistant. I hardly needed to wash the beaters or the bowls after she'd been to work on them.'

His smile was warm, his dark brown eyes soft. 'Is she asleep now?'

I gave him a rolled-eye look. 'Yeah, well… Here's the thing about baking with six-year-olds. She's in sugar overload. I couldn't get her to go to bed. She's still up playing.' I nodded my head in the direction of my room. 'Go in and say hello to her. I'll just find a jar or something to put these in.'

I sorted out the flowers and stepped back to inspect my handiwork. Yep. I was definitely improving in my flower-arranging skills.

I heard a sound behind me and turned from the flowers to see Claudia swishing into the room. I say 'swishing' because the voluminous folds of my wedding dress were swamping her tiny frame in spite of the pair of heels she'd put on.

She shuffled towards me with a big smile on her face. 'Look what I found in your wardrobe!' she crowed with excitement.

I didn't have the heart to burst her bubble by giving her a stern lecture about rummaging in other people's wardrobes without permission. Besides, her uncle was standing there with an unreadable expression on his face.

'Well, look at you,' I said. 'Don't you look gorgeous in my sister's wedding dress?'

I know. Lying to a little kid. How low could I go?

'Do you have a veil?' Claudia asked.

'No, I didn't buy—'

I realised my mistake halfway through the sentence. Alessandro was now looking at me with a frown, but I soldiered on regardless.

'I didn't buy one for her. *For my sister.* Yet. But I intend to. It's next on my list of things to do. We'll do it when we sort out my bridesmaid dress. Did I tell you I'm going to be her bridesmaid? My dress is pink. Hot pink. Not a colour I would have chosen for myself, but it's my sister's special day and I wouldn't want anything to spoil it.'

I was done.

I was out of breath, for one thing. My heart was hammering like a demented timepiece in my chest. I was sweating as if the temperature had risen forty degrees. I glanced again at Alessandro, but his expression was back to being indecipherable.

I gave Claudia a bright smile. 'Well, young lady, I think it might be time to make your uncle a nice cup of tea and see if he'd like to sample some of our baking. What do you think?'

It was a strange little tea party. I was on tenterhooks and overcompensating by talking too much. Bertie would have rolled about the floor laughing. Claudia had helped Alessandro to some lemon meringue pie and was chatting about how she had been allowed to whip up the egg whites for the meringue all by herself.

'It's delicious,' he said, smiling at her.

After a while Claudia tried to disguise a huge yawn. I was all for ignoring it, as I dreaded being alone with Alessandro once she was safely tucked in bed. But he was clearly of the opinion that adults needed time alone without the presence of young children. *Oh, joy.*

I was still in clean-up mode in the kitchen when he came back. My kitchen was spotless, but that didn't stop me. I was polishing every surface with an antibacterial spray like someone with severe OCD.

'We need to talk.'

'We do?' I took one look at him and put my spray bottle down. 'So, how was your research meeting? Did it all go to plan? Is your project secure? Do you have to ask for funding or is that already—?'

'Jem.'

I pressed my lips together and gripped the kitchen bench rather than face him. 'It's not what you think.'

'I've given you no promises,' he said. 'No guarantees.

I've spelled it out for you in the bluntest terms possible. I'm not offering marriage.'

I let go of the bench to look at him. 'You think I bought that dress *recently*?'

His frown made his eyebrows meet over his eyes. 'Didn't you?'

I laughed.

I know. I sound like a complete nutcase. But I couldn't help it. The irony of it was amusing even though it was also tragic.

I finally got control of myself enough to speak. 'I bought it five years ago. Three days before we broke up, to be precise. I thought you were going to ask me to marry you. I was ridiculously naive, and I completely misread the signs because there was no way you were going—'

'I was.'

I blinked. I swallowed what felt like a fishhook stuck in my throat. 'You were?'

He scraped his hand through his hair. 'I was going to ask you to marry me because back then I could think of no one I would rather spend my life with than you…'

I could sense a big *but* coming.

He drew in a breath and let it out in a rush. 'But I realise I wasn't ready for that level of commitment. I was too career-focused. I didn't have the right priorities. Which was why all my other relationships had failed.'

'So what about now?'

I shouldn't have asked. I shouldn't have revealed any sign of my yearnings. The yearnings I hadn't even been able to admit to myself. Until now.

'Marriage is out of the question now.'

'Why?'

I couldn't believe I was flogging such a lame horse. It was nothing short of cruel.

A flicker of pain passed over his features. 'Don't you see?'

All I was seeing was a life devoid of happiness, with no intimacy, spending my end days with a house full of cats or rats or…budgerigars. I figured at least they could talk.

'What am I supposed to be seeing?' I said.

He closed his eyes for a moment. Shook his head. Opened his eyes again and gave me a grimace of a smile.

'You act so tough and street-wise and smart, but inside you're still that sweet, innocent girl outside that Paris café.'

Was I?

No-freaking-José-way!

'I'm not after marriage,' I said. 'I'm happy with a fling. We can fling all we like. No one is going to stop us.'

He came over and took me by the shoulders. 'You deserve more than a fling, *ma petite*. You deserve your day as a princess. You deserve to wear your pretty dress and dream of happy-ever-after. I can't give you that.'

I frowned. 'But you do care for me…don't you?'

He gave me such a wistful look, my chest seized.

'I have too many people in my life who need me right now. My sister. Claudia. My patients. I'm not capable of giving you what you need. I can't juggle all of that *and* you.'

'I don't need to be juggled,' I said. 'I need to be loved. That's all I'm asking for.'

I couldn't believe I was asking. Make that *begging*.

His hands fell from my shoulders. His expression was painful to witness. He wore his determination, his sense of responsibility and his inner loneliness like scars carved deeply into his features.

'Sometimes love isn't enough.'

'Is this about your father?' I asked. 'Are you worried about turning out like—?'

'No.'

'You're nothing like him,' I said. 'You could *never* be like him.'

'It's not about my father. It's about me. I can't do it and fail. It would hurt too many people. I don't want that on my conscience as well as everything else.'

'Why do you think you'll fail?'

I was all fired up. I had put my heart on the line. I had nothing to lose. Well, I had *everything* to lose—but I wasn't able to stop myself from being honest and up-front.

'You and I belong together. We're a great team. Look at how well we handle little Claudia. Your sister would always have us at her back, to step in if she couldn't cope. We could have our *own* children. We could build a life together. Can't you see that?'

His face had that boxed-up look I dreaded. The drawbridge was up. The subject was closed. He had made up his mind.

'I can't marry you, Jem,' he said. 'I'm sorry. Any relationship between us has to be informal. Casual. That's all I can offer.'

'I want more.'

I was shocked at the way I was drawing a line in the sand. Not just a line, but a big deep trench. Seeing Claudia in my wedding dress had made me realise how much I wanted to be a bride. Not just any bride, but Alessandro's bride. How could I settle for anyone else? How could I want anyone else when he was the only one who had ever made me feel alive?

'Then maybe it's best if we don't see each other again,' he said, with a note of finality that slammed into my heart like a wrecking ball.

'How am I going to explain that to Claudia?' I asked. 'How are *you* going to explain it? She thinks we're best friends.'

He let out a long, uneven breath. 'I'll enrol her in a different school.'

'But she's doing so *well*!' I said. 'She's made friends. She's secure—probably for the first time in her little life. How can you uproot her just because you can't face a bit of commitment?'

His jaw locked and he snatched up his keys from where he'd left them on the kitchen bench. 'I have to go. I'll be back in the morning to pick up Claudia. It wouldn't be fair to wake her up now.'

I folded my arms across my chest and jerked my chin towards the door. 'That's right. You go. Walk away when it all gets too difficult. That's what I did. I didn't stay around long enough to hear your explanation of why you hadn't told me about your ex. It takes guts to stick around and hear the truth. It takes guts to step out of your comfort zone. To admit you need and love someone.'

Our gazes collided. Then meshed. My heart contracted. I could already read his mind. Apparently my mother isn't the only one in our family with psychic abilities.

'I wish I could give you what you want but I can't,' he said. 'There's too much at stake. I think it's best if we end our…fling. It will be fairer on you. On me and on Claudia.'

'Fine.'

I said it so matter-of-factly I almost believed it. Almost.

I was even brave enough to follow him to the door and wave him off, as if he was just another tea-party guest who had enjoyed the result of my labours in the kitchen.

It was only when the door had closed that I allowed myself to let a couple of tears squeeze past my eyelids. I blinked to stem the flow, took a deep breath, and brushed my hand across my face.

It was only then that I saw Claudia standing in the doorway, with the bundle of her bedding and a woebegone look on her face.

'I'm sorry,' she said in a whisper-soft voice. 'I had a bad d-d-dream and I wet the bed.'

CHAPTER TWELVE

IT TOOK A WHILE to sort out the bed, Claudia's shower, and an explanation of why her uncle and I were apparently not best friends any more. I sat beside her as I tucked her in and tried my best to explain.

'It's not that we don't love each other. It's…complicated.'

'Is it because you're my teacher?'

'No, nothing like that,' I said, wishing it was that simple.

'Then why c-c-can't you be together?'

Good question.

'Because there are other issues,' I said.

'Is it because of my mummy?'

I looked down at her earnest little face. How much did she know? How much had she guessed?

'Your uncle is doing everything he can to help your mummy get better,' I said.

Claudia's little fingers plucked at the hem of the sheet. 'My mummy might never get better.'

My chest tightened at the worldly pragmatism in her statement. She was six years old. *Six!* How had she become so jaded?

'We should never give up hope,' I said, hugging her close and resting my chin on her little head. 'On anybody.'

Good advice, I thought.

If only I had the courage to believe it.

Once Claudia was asleep I went back to the sitting room. I glanced at my phone. Suddenly I could think of no viable excuse not to call my mother.

I reached for it just as it began to ring.

'Mum?' I said. 'I was just about to call you. I'm sorry for what I said. It was so insensitive of me, given the circumstances, and I—'

'Poppet, I'm the one who's supposed to be apologising,' my mother said. 'I had no idea that horrible thing had happened to you.'

She began to cry, and the rest became a bit garbled as we swapped apologies and sorted out some stuff.

I hadn't realised how terribly controlling my grandparents had been towards my mother. They dictated everything to her. She'd felt like an item on an assembly line. By the age of five her whole life had been mapped out for her. What friends she would play with. What subjects she would study at school and at university. What career she would have. What man she would marry. Where she would live.

She wasn't just a square peg in a round hole. She was a feather that needed to float free. My father had much the same kind of upbringing, which was why he had bonded with my mother. They weren't perfect. But they were my parents and it was about time I accepted them for all their foibles.

We ended the call with a lot of 'I love you's and kissy smoochy noises.

Yes. Even some from me.

* * *

Alessandro arrived the next morning to pick up Claudia. We were so polite to each other it was nauseating. It was back to Dr Lucioni and Miss Clark.

I stood back as he led Claudia to his car, but just before he closed the car door she jumped back out and ran towards me. Her little body cannoned into mine and hugged me so tightly I couldn't breathe. Or maybe that was because my emotions had taken up all the space inside my chest.

'I love you, Jem,' she said.

I bent and hugged her back, and kissed the top of her head. 'I love you too, sweetie. But you have to call me Miss Clark tomorrow, remember?'

She looked up at me with those big brown eyes that so reminded me of her uncle's.

'I want to live with you for ever and ever. I want to be with you instead of at the boarding house. C-c-c-can't I stay with you?'

I glanced at Alessandro's face. His jaw was tight, but I noticed his throat was moving up and down over a swallow. His eyes looked red and pained, as if the sunlight was too bright—even though there wasn't any sunlight. Well, not much to speak of. It was a grey morning, with clouds that hung oppressively overhead in clotted knots of gloom.

I bent down so I was face to face with Claudia. 'Sweetie, I'll see you every day at school. I'm not going anywhere.'

Claudia's bottom lip wobbled. 'But I heard Uncle Alessandro say last night I'm going to a new school.

I don't want to go to another school. I want to stay at *your* school.'

Alessandro bent down and put his arm around Claudia's thin little shoulders. His knees were almost touching mine. This close, I could smell the clean sharp citrus of his aftershave. I could also see a tiny nick on his jaw where he'd cut himself shaving.

A top-notch surgeon who's cut himself shaving? I thought. He was definitely having a bad day.

'If you want to stay at Miss Clark's school that's fine, *mio piccolo*,' he said.

I pushed in Claudia's pouting bottom lip with my fingertip. 'No more tears, okay? Everything's going to work out just fine.'

Alessandro met my gaze. 'Jem… Can I see you tonight?'

I was conscious of little ears listening eagerly. 'I think we've said all that needs to be said. No point dragging things on unnecessarily.'

His eyes refused to let mine go. The intensity of his gaze made something in my heart give a little jerk.

'All right,' he said. 'I'll say it now. I love you. I fell in love with you that day in Paris, when you spilled the contents of your handbag at my feet.'

Claudia's little face started to beam and she clasped her hands together like she was mentally saying a prayer.

I moistened my lips and tried to look casually indifferent. *So what?* I wanted to say. *You obviously don't love me enough to marry me.* But instead I retreated into one of my stubborn silences.

'I couldn't believe I'd found someone so funny, so intelligent, so witty—so perfect for me,' he went on. 'I should never have let you go. I'm still not sure why I did.

But one thing I do know. I'm not going to do it again. I don't want to lose you a second time. It would be like losing my future, losing any chance of happiness. I can't bear to face the rest of my life without you in it. I want to see you every day. I want you to make me laugh every day, with your twisted sense of humour. I want to make *you* laugh. I want to take away the hurts you've hidden away for all this time. Will you marry me, my darling?'

I was having trouble seeing past the blurry tears in my eyes. Claudia was looking up at me expectantly. Alessandro was looking at me like a man who was wearing his heart on his sleeve. A tricky manoeuvre even for a top-notch heart surgeon, I thought.

'What changed your mind?' I asked.

I'm all for a bit of grovelling. I figured he owed me that much after the hellish nights without sleep I'd been through. Make that five years of hellish nights.

'I went back to my house last night,' he said. 'That great old empty shell of a house I'm spending so much money and time and effort on—but for what? What's the point of me making it into something special when I have no one special to share it with? My *life's* like an empty shell without you in it. I don't want to spend the rest of my life without you. The last five years have been bad enough. I know it's hard to juggle stuff, but other people seem to manage. We'll find a way to manage. *I'll* find a way. Please say yes. Please say you'll marry me.'

My heart was so full of love and joy it was leaving me little room to breathe. I'm pretty sure my face was radiant with happiness. I figured it wouldn't matter if the sun never came out again. I was doing its job for it. Everyone would be blaming *me* for global warming before too long.

'I've always wanted a man to get down on bended knee

to propose to me,' I said. 'I didn't realise I'd be on bended knee as well, with half the street watching.'

Alessandro grinned. 'Are the curtains twitching?'

'Numbers four to ten,' I said. 'Number three and seven are out on their front steps.'

His brow suddenly wrinkled in puzzlement. 'How do you know when you've got your back to them?'

Actually, I had no idea how I knew. Freaky!

'A wild guess,' I said.

'Then we'd better not disappoint them,' he said. 'Will you do me the honour of being my wife and the mother of my children?'

'*And* being my aunty!' Claudia piped up.

I laughed and cuddled her close—which brought me even closer to Alessandro, so our mouths were just about touching. 'Yes,' I said. 'Yes, to both of you.'

Alessandro's mouth sealed mine. Claudia's little rose-bud lips kissed my cheek and then his. Moistly. Noisily. My mother was going to *love* this little kid, I thought.

My neighbours clapped and cheered.

Our kiss went on for such a long time even Claudia got fed up.

She tapped each of us on the shoulder. 'Aren't you finished *yet*?' she said, eyes rolling.

Alessandro cupped my face in his hands, his dark brown gaze glinting. 'I'm just getting started,' he said.

My phone rang before he could kiss me again. I know. Crap timing. I *knew* it was my mother. Don't ask me how. Maybe I *am* a little psychic.

'Mum,' I said. 'I have something to tell you—'

'I know, poppet,' my mother said. 'You're getting married.'

'How on earth do you know *that*?' I asked, glancing

at Alessandro again to see if he was responsible. But he gave a 'beats me' gesture with his upturned hands.

It kind of showed how much he 'got' my parents. They would have been appalled if he'd gone to ask my father for my hand in marriage. How I would get my father to give me away was going to be an exercise in diplomacy or bribery…or something. Then there was the issue of getting my parents inside a church…

Yikes. Fun times ahead.

'I had a vision last night,' my mother said. 'You were wearing this gorgeous white taffeta and tulle dress and you had a little girl with dark hair and big brown eyes as your flower girl.'

I smiled at Claudia and whispered, 'Will you be my flower girl?'

Her little face lit up like a beacon. *'Yes!'*

But there was one person my mother left out of her vision.

Five months later I had *two* bridesmaids, as well as a flower girl—my sister, Bertie, and Alessandro's sister Bianca.

I couldn't have asked for more.

* * * * *

HER GREEK
DOCTOR'S PROPOSAL

BY

ROBIN GIANNA

MILLS & BOON

Published in Great Britain 2015
by Mills & Boon, an imprint of Harlequin (UK) Limited,
Eton House, 18-24 Paradise Road, Richmond, Surrey, TW9 1SR

© 2015 Robin Gianakopoulos

ISBN: 978-0-263-24712-1

Harlequin (UK) Limited's policy is to use papers that are natural, renewable and recyclable products and made from wood grown in sustainable forests. The logging and manufacturing processes conform to the legal environmental regulations of the country of origin.

Printed and bound in Spain
by CPI, Barcelona

Dear Reader,

My family and I were lucky enough to spend two weeks in Greece this summer, and we had an amazing time—along with a few challenges that made the trip even more memorable! Like when our rental car broke down (twice) and the mechanic spent hours chatting to my husband and then sent a soda pop bottle filled with surprisingly good homemade wine back with him. :)

The people are charming and interesting—and of course the history is amazing and the entire country incredibly beautiful. I knew I wanted to set a book or two there, and since one of the many places I'd loved was Delphi I decided this one would take place there.

Andros, my hero, is a sexy Greek doctor who was training in the US until the shock of learning he had a small daughter sent him back to his hometown to raise her there. And, of course, archaeology had to be part of the story—so that's my heroine Laurel's passion! But she has a tragic reason for wanting to find the treasure her parents believed would be found there, and with only weeks left to make that happen she shouldn't let herself be distracted by a certain hunky doctor.

Except she *is* distracted! And avoiding spending time with him is impossible when several members of the archaeological team become seriously ill and Andros tries to figure out why.

This story is about both characters learning who they truly are and finally putting their pasts behind them so they can start a new beginning together. And there's an archaeological secret and a medical mystery thrown in for good measure!

I hope you enjoy Andros and Laurel's story. I'd love to hear any feedback you'd like to offer—you can write to me at Robin@RobinGianna.com or find me on my website or Facebook.

Thanks for reading!

Robin

Praise for
Robin Gianna

'If you're looking for a story sweet but exciting, characters loving but cautious, if you're a fan of Mills & Boon® Medical Romances™ or looking for a story to try and see if you like the medical genre, *Changed by His Son's Smile* is the story for you! I would never have guessed Robin is a debut author: the story flowed brilliantly, the dialogue was believable and I was thoroughly engaged in the medical dramas.'
—*Contemporary Romance Reviews*

A huge thank-you to my SWs:
Sheri, Susan, Natalie, Margaret and Mel. You helped me through some tough times with steadfast support and love. I appreciate it, and all of you, so, so much!

A thank-you, as always, to Dr Meta Carroll, for helping me with medical scenes and always being there for me!

Thanks to my husband, George, for his infectious disease expertise and endless patience and support. Love you!

CHAPTER ONE

LAUREL EVANS GASPED as the pinhead-sized gleam of gold revealed itself, winking at her through the layers of dirt she'd painstakingly removed. Even mostly still buried in this pit they'd dug on Mount Parnassus, the glow was unmistakable.

Laurel's heart danced wildly in her chest as she grabbed her pick and brush, forcing herself to go slow as she gently worked to free the treasure. It took only a moment to realize it was something small, not the item she'd hoped to find, and she shoved down her brief disappointment. Oh so carefully, she used the delicate tools until the ancient find was finally loosened completely from the earth it had been long buried in.

A ring. Likely worn and possibly loved by someone thousands of years earlier. Even the smallest pieces of pottery, tools and partial bits of art they'd unearthed, reassembled and cataloged in the past weeks stepped up her pulse, but this? Nothing beat the thrill of finding a treasure like this one.

No, scratch that. There was one thing she could think of that would be way beyond thrilling, and the weeks were ticking away on her hopes of finding it. Of getting it on the cover of archaeological magazines all over

the world, along with her parents' faces, crowning the
pages of her PhD dissertation, and ensuring funding for
the next project that would get her own belated career
launched at last.

She closed her fingers around the ring in her palm
and breathed in the dusty, sweltering air. Too soon to
panic. There were still a few weeks left before the end
of this dig, and she, the rest of the crew and volunteers
just needed to work harder and smarter. She looked up
the mountain where the ruins of Delphi lay hidden from
her view. Why couldn't the oracle still be there to advise
her where the heck the mythical treasure might be deeply
hidden on this mountain?

Laurel wanted to show Melanie what she'd found, but
as she looked around at the crew working the numerous rectangular pits dug into the mountainside she didn't
see her anywhere. Where could the woman be? Usually
she was up early and on the mountain to enthusiastically
guide her and the volunteers. Could she have gone to the
caves with Tom? Seemed unlikely she wouldn't tell Laurel
she'd be working with her husband instead of leading the
mountain portion of the dig. Maybe the cold she'd been
fighting had gotten worse, and she'd decided to sleep in.

Laurel swiped a trickle of sweat that persisted in rolling down her temple, despite the wide-brimmed canvas
hat shielding her from the insistent sun. She tucked her
exciting find into a sample bag, but before she could start
to label it, her palm began to bleed again from under the
bandage she'd put on it.

"Damn it," she muttered, trying to reposition the pad
to cover it better, then ripped off a piece of duct tape to
slap over the whole thing. So annoying that she'd stupidly
jabbed herself while unearthing a sharp piece of what was

likely part of a cup. She was just glad she hadn't further broken the artifact in the process. She started to label the ring bag again only to stop midword as her peripheral vision caught a movement nearby.

She glanced over to see a man walking up the steep, rocky mountain path that wound between dried brown scrub scattered with tufts of thriving green plants, as steady and sure-footed as the goats that sometimes trotted by with their neck bells ringing. As he grew closer, she blinked, then stared. The brilliant sunshine gleamed on his short black hair and sent shadows and light across his chiseled cheekbones and jaw, his straight nose and sculptured lips. His face was so startlingly beautiful, so classically Greek, she thought he might be a mirage. That it was the god Apollo himself walking up Mount Parnassus to visit the temple built to honor him.

She gave her head a little shake, wondering if the blistering heat was getting to her. She narrowed her eyes against the sunlight and looked again.

Not her imagination. And not Apollo, but most definitely a real man. Greek gods didn't normally wear khaki-colored dress pants and a short-sleeved, blue, button-down shirt that was open at the collar. A shirt that emphasized the obvious fitness of his torso and the deep tan of his skin. A steel wristwatch caught and reflected the sun in little white diamonds that danced on the craggy ground with each measured step he took.

The one word that came to mind was *wowza*. Who in the world was he? And why was he wearing such a surprising choice of clothing for hiking the mountain in ninety-five degrees Fahrenheit? Must be a local businessman, or possibly a reporter come to check out the dig. Or, with his knockout looks, a movie star planning his next film. She didn't normally watch many movies, but if that was the case she'd definitely find time to fit in a viewing or ten of him on the big screen.

Laurel snapped out of her fixation on the man and finished her notation on the ring bag. She stood and quickly tucked the bag inside her canvas apron, next to her trowel. Tom and Melanie wouldn't be happy if she yakked to a reporter or anyone else before they even knew about her find.

He stopped to speak to one of the volunteers on the dig, who pointed at Laurel. The man's gaze turned to her, and even with twenty feet between them she could see his eyes were so dark they were nearly black, with a surprising intensity that seemed to stare right into her.

He resumed his trek toward her. He wasn't a tall man—probably an inch or two shy of six feet. But the broad muscularity of his physique, which she'd noticed wasn't unusual among Greek men, made him seem larger. Or was it the sheer power of his good looks and intelligent gaze that made him seem that way?

"Are you Laurel Evans?" he asked with only a slight accent to his otherwise American-sounding words.

"Yes. Can I help you?"

"I'm Dr. Andros Drakoulias." He reached out to grasp her hand in a firm handshake. His palm felt wide and warm, slightly rough and not at all sweaty as she knew hers was. She pulled her hand loose and swiped it down the side of her shorts, hoping he hadn't noticed the sweat or that just the simple touch made her feel a little breathless. "Your colleagues, the two Drs. Wagner, asked me to let you know what was going on."

"Going on?" She realized it was a rather stupid echo of his words, but there was something about the serious expression she now saw in his eyes that sent her pulse into an alarmed acceleration. "Why? Is something wrong?"

"They came to the clinic early this morning feeling feverish and ill. I've done some tests, and both have pneumonia."

"Pneumonia?" Laurel stared at him in shock. *Pneumonia?* How was that possible? "Melanie and Tom both had colds the past couple of days, but that seemed to be all it was."

"Unfortunately not. I have them on IV fluids and antibiotics, and I plan to keep them today and overnight at the clinic to see how they do."

Did this guy really know what he was talking about? Handsome didn't necessarily translate to smart. She studied him. Maybe it was wrong of her, but she couldn't help but wonder if the local town doctor had the knowledge and equipment to properly diagnose the problem. Should she take them to the closest large town instead, to be sure? "What makes you think it's pneumonia?"

A small smile touched his beautifully shaped lips. "Hippocrates could diagnose pneumonia by listening to a patient's chest, Ms. Evans. Ancient Greeks were at the forefront of medicine, after all. But believe it or not, even in our small-town clinic we have X-ray equipment and pulse oximetry to measure a patient's oxygen saturation."

Somehow, her face flushed hotter than it already was beneath the scorching noon sun. "I'm sorry. I didn't mean to be insulting." Maybe inserting a little light humor into the awkward moment she'd created was in order. "But I must say, despite the Greeks putting the Omphalos stone at Delphi to show it was the center of the world, many believe Egyptian physicians adopted an ethical code of medical care centuries before Hippocrates."

His smile broadened; he was seemingly amused instead of offended, thank heavens. "Don't say that out loud, Ms. Evans, or you may find yourself in a no-win argument with angry locals."

"Is there any other kind of argument with Greeks?"

"Probably not." The amusement in his eyes became a dangerously appealing twinkle. "I lived in the United States for fifteen years. I know Americans think everyone outside the US and Western Europe are somewhat backward and simple. If you like, I could go up to the temple and consult Apollo. Or perhaps pray to Asclepios for guidance?"

"Not necessary. I'm sure you're very experienced, Dr. Drakoulias. I just…" Her voice trailed off, because she didn't know what else to say and had a feeling she might stick her foot in her mouth all over again. She sent him a grateful smile, hoping that would make him look past her blunder. "Thank you for walking all the way up here to let me know. Right now, I need to stay at the site to supervise since Mel's not going to be here. But I'd like to come down this evening to see them. Where's your clinic?"

"In Kastorini, which is at the base of the mountain above the gulf waters. Just follow the old bell tower to the center of town—you can't miss us."

"What's the address?"

His straight teeth showed in a smile that gleamed white against his brown skin. An unexpected dimple appeared in one cheek, which added another attractive layer to the man who sure didn't need it. "There are no addresses in Kastorini, Ms. Evans. We're small enough that everyone finds their way around without."

No addresses? How did people get their mail and things? She wasn't about to ask, though, and make even more of a fool of herself. "Well, I'm sure I can then, too. Thanks."

"I do have a question for you." All the teasing humor left his face. "Were both of the Drs. Wagner working in one spot? Somewhere they might have been exposed to a fungus of some kind?"

"Not really. Melanie is in charge of this part of the dig, and Tom leads the dig in the adjacent cave discovered a few years after the initial excavation. Why?"

"Just that it's unusual for two healthy people to come down with pneumonia at nearly the same time. Which makes looking for an external cause something we need to think about. Has Melanie been in the caves recently?"

Laurel thought hard about what they'd excavated and where they'd dug, but couldn't come up with anything that might have made them sick. "I'm almost certain she hasn't been in the caves at all. At least, not since the first days of the dig two months ago. At team meetings, Tom shares the cave dig results weekly, and Melanie shares our results. It's more efficient that way."

"All right. We'll see how they're both doing tomorrow and decide then if it makes sense to look harder for some connection." He looked around at the extensive excavation. "I wasn't living here when Peter Manago tried building a house in this spot and they found the ruins. When was that—five or six years ago?"

Had it been that long? Five years since her family's shocking loss that had turned her world upside down? A loss that seemed like yesterday, and yet, in other ways, felt like forever ago.

"I think that's about right." She swallowed hard at the intense ache that stung her throat. "Have you been up here to check it out?"

"No, but I've been wanting to. Is it filled with treasures offered to Apollo and the oracle?" His eyes crinkled at the corners. "Everyone who grew up around here used to dig giant holes—or at least giant to us—that we were sure would expose a sphinx, or the Charioteer's horses, or something else that would make us rich."

"And were you one of them?"

"Oh, yes. Born and raised in Kastorini. Many a goat has likely fallen into one of my 'digs.' But after finding only rocks and more rocks and the occasional very exciting animal bone, I decided becoming a doctor might be a better way to make money."

She had to laugh. Money was definitely not the reason anyone dug in the dirt for a living. "No doubt about that."

"You must be finding something, though, or they wouldn't have been working at it for so long. What's here?" He looked around at the carefully plotted-out sections of earth. "Tell me about these squares you have marked off."

"Much of the time when you unearth a site that's several thousand years old, it's a bit like a layer cake. The oldest part of a settlement is at the bottom, with artifacts that reflect how the people lived then. Vessels used for cooking, style of art that's found, even the way a wall might be built, all can change a lot from the bottom of the cake to the top. But this site?" She loved sharing the excitement of this place with people who were interested. "The layers aren't there. There's no cemetery. No human remains, despite the number of buildings that housed probably a hundred people at a time. Which convinces us that it was temporary housing for pilgrims visiting Delphi."

"Interesting. How long, do you think?"

He stopped scanning the site to look at her with rapt attention in his beautiful eyes, and a dazzling smile that momentarily short-circuited her brain. What had she been talking about, exactly? "How long what?"

"How many centuries did the pilgrims come to stay here?"

"Oh." The man probably thought she was dense. "About five hundred years, we think. Amazing that people came here to consult the oracle and worship Apollo all that time."

"Did the small earthquake we had a couple weeks ago damage anything?"

That earthquake had scared everyone, but especially Laurel. When the earth had rumbled around them, her heart had about stopped as the vision of how she'd been told her parents had died had surged to the forefront of her mind. The quake had lasted only a few minutes, but her insides had shaken for hours.

"Some rocks and earth loosened and fell into the pits, but it wasn't too bad, thankfully."

"That's good." He seemed to be studying her and she wondered what her expression was, quickly giving him a smile to banish whatever might be there. "Do you have any photos of the things you've found?"

"We do. A number of tools and potsherds have been re-assembled and I have pictures in a binder in that box. This section here," she said, showing him a large, cordoned-off rectangle, "is where several inscribed stones were found that are similar to the ones at the Temple of Apollo." And one of those stones was etched with the cryptic words that had convinced her mom and dad they'd find the price-less artifact Laurel was still looking for. That part had to be kept secret from most people, but she could show him the rest.

She pulled the reference binder from the supply box and flipped through it to show him a few of the best photos. They stood close together, the hair on his muscular forearm tickling her skin, his thick shoulder nudging hers, his head angled close enough to nearly skim his cheek against her temple. He smelled so wonderful, like aftershave and hunky man, that she found herself breathing him in. So enjoying his interested attention, she suddenly realized she'd gone on way too long.

"Sorry." She closed the book, feeling her face flush yet again, and not just from the blasting heat on the mountain. "I get a little overexcited sometimes."

"No. I'm fascinated." There was something about his low tone and the way he was looking at her with a kind of glint in the dark depths of his eyes that had her wondering if he meant something other than the dig. That thought, along with how close he still stood to her, kicked her heart into a faster rhythm and made her short of breath, which she knew was absurd. But surely there wasn't a woman alive who wouldn't swoon at least a little over Andros Drakoulias.

"My sisters tell me that when I talk about my work, I need to remember to look for eyes glazing over when I go on and on. Sorry."

"Had you been looking, you'd have seen my eyes were most attentive. And you should never apologize for talking about something you love."

The deep rumble of his voice, the warmth in it, seemed to slip inside her, and for a long moment they just looked at one another, standing only inches apart, before Laurel managed to snap out of whatever trance he'd sent her into. She sucked in a mind-clearing breath and turned to shove the binder back into its box.

"You've hurt yourself." His strong arm came around her side, brushing against her as he reached for her hand. His head dipped close to hers again as he turned her palm upward, his fingers gently tugging loose the tape and bandage to expose the darn gash that had started bleeding again.

"It's nothing." She swiped at the trickle of blood, trying to tug her hand from his, but he held it tight. "I cut it on a potsherd. I'll bandage it up better when I'm done for the day."

"When was your last tetanus shot?"

"Just before I came here, Dr. Drakoulias. Cuts and scrapes are one of the hazards of this job."

"I know. Last summer, I had to treat one of the workers on this dig for sepsis." His gaze pinned hers, his former warmth replaced by a stern, no-nonsense look. "When you come to see the Wagners, I'll clean and bandage it for you."

She opened her mouth to assure him she could take care of it just fine, but the words died on her tongue. The wide palm that held hers was firm yet gentle, and something about his authoritative expression told her any protest would fall on deaf ears. Part of her didn't want to protest, anyway. She realized, ridiculously, that it felt… nice to have someone want to take care of it for her. Probably because, for a long time, she'd been the nurse, cook, decision maker and overall helper for her sisters, without a soul to assist with all their challenges. Or, except for Tom and Mel, her own.

She reminded herself it wasn't as if there were anything personal about it, the man was just doing his job.

"Not necessary. I have everything I need to clean and bandage it at my hotel."

"Necessary." His eyes still on hers, he slowly released her hand. "I'll see you at the clinic at, say, six o'clock?"

It was loud and clear she'd be in for an argument if she refused, and what sane woman would anyway? "Thank you. I'll be there."

The warmth of his palm lingered along with a little flutter of her heart as she watched him steadily stride back down the path, and she shook her head at herself. Mooning after the man was ridiculous, supersexy or not, since the dig was over in a matter of weeks and every second of her focus had to be on what she'd come here to accomplish.

She was already so late getting her career started. By the time her parents were her age, their accomplishments had been featured in numerous archaeological magazines. She could still hear them pointing out how they'd finished their PhDs in just four years, chiding their oldest about her schoolwork and GPA, about how important it was to be a role model to her sisters. Doubtless they would be disappointed in her if they were still alive. She dropped to her knees to get digging again.

The best way, the only way, she could begin to catch up, keep their memory alive, and make them proud, was by doing whatever she could to finish their work then finally get going on her own.

CHAPTER TWO

HOURS LATER LAUREL was finally able to shower off the film of dirt that clung to every bit of exposed skin, before studying the cut on her hand. It was less than an inch long, but deeper than she'd realized, which was probably why it kept opening up and bleeding. She washed it out with peroxide and knew that it wouldn't be a bad idea to have Andros Drakoulias make sure it was clean. Which of course had nothing to do with liking the feel of her hand in his.

The feeble hair dryer in the old, rambling Delphi hotel that the excavation team had rented rooms in for the summer blew about as much air as she would trying to cool a bowl of soup. The impact on the dampness of her long blond hair was practically nil, and she had to wonder why she'd decided to dry it anyway, when she usually just pulled it back.

She shook her head as she wrapped an elastic around her ponytail. Who was she kidding? She knew the reason, which was a certain megahunky Greek doctor her vain side wanted to look good for.

She threw on a sundress, swiped on a gloss of lipstick, and headed out of the door. Already perspiring again from the shimmering heat, she slipped inside the group's equally hot rented sedan. She nosed the car down the winding road out of Delphi, and, before she turned onto the highway, paused for a moment to take in the incredible view.

On every horizon, partly sheer cliffs scattered with pines met tumbles of boulders that looked as though they'd been broken apart then glued back together by some giant hand, or perhaps the gods and goddesses of Greek lore. The mountains cradled the valley below, filled with the distinctive silvery-gray leaves of an endless, undulating sea of olive trees that went on as far as she could see. Where the valley ended, the trees seemed to flow right into the Gulf of Corinth, the water such an incredible azure blue that, every time she saw it, she felt amazed all over again. And beyond that azure sea, another range of mountains met the sky that today was equally blue, but at times reflected an ethereal beauty when mistiness embraced the entire scene.

Just looking at it filled her with a reassuring sense of tranquility, the same way walking the ancient Delphi ruins did, hearing the voices of the past. Before she left, she'd take her camera on one last hike of this historic place that still felt so untamed. To remember it by.

With a last, lingering look, she turned onto the highway, her thoughts turning to Tom and Melanie. A bead of sweat slid down her spine as she wondered how they would be feeling when she saw them. Surely they'd have improved by now, since they'd been on antibiotics for hours.

For the first time all day, she let the niggle of worry she'd pushed aside grab hold and squeeze. After her parents had died, Mel and Tom had wrapped their arms around her as if she'd become their surrogate daughter.

Advised her on grad school and now her PhD program. Helped set her up at digs close to home so she could still care for her sisters. Got her here as a paid assistant to work on her parents' project and her dissertation.

They were such special people. What if they were seriously ill?

No. Borrowing trouble was a sure way to have trouble take over, as her dad used to say. She'd had to be in charge at home whenever her parents were gone on digs, and full-time after they died. That had taught her a lot about leadership, and it was time to lead, not fret.

She had to get up to speed on what Tom's crew was supposed to be doing in the caves to make sure it happened. With so little time left on the dig schedule, not a single hour could be wasted by worrying. She knew Tom and Mel would agree, and that her parents would have too.

The sign for Kastorini was in both Greek and English, thank goodness. Laurel turned off the highway, concentrating on driving the steeply curving road that sported the occasional rock that had rolled down from the mountainside. And the term "hairpin curve"? Now she knew exactly what that meant.

If she hadn't already been sweating from the heat, this crazy trek would have done it. The road finally flattened and swooped toward a thick stone archway flanked by high, obviously ancient walls, and passing through it was like entering a different world. One minute she was driving with the mountain soaring on one side and dropping off on the other, the next she was surrounded by stone and stucco buildings sporting terracotta rooftops and draped with vines and magenta bougainvillea. Cheerful pots of flowers lined balconies and sat by inviting front doors. Farther down the narrow, cobbled street, men with small cups of coffee relaxed on patios in front of several tavernas, engaged in lively conversation as they watched her drive by.

The utter charm of the place made Laurel smile. And as Andros had promised, she easily spotted the ancient-looking clock tower and found the medical clinic with a few bona fide parking spaces right in front of it.

The building looked as old as the rest of Kastorini, and she wasn't sure what to expect when she went inside. A small, fairly modern-looking waiting room was currently empty, but within moments a young woman appeared.

"May I help you?" she asked.

The fact that, right away, the woman spoke English instead of Greek, proved Laurel's foreignness was more than obvious, though she'd accepted months ago that she didn't exactly blend in as a local.

"Hello. I'm Laurel Evans, working with the Wagners. I believe they're patients here? Dr. Drakoulias told me I could come see them."

"Ah, yes." Her pleasant smile faded to seriousness. "He is with a patient right now and wanted to talk to you before you see them. I am Christina, one of the nurses here. I will take you to Dr. Drakoulias's office."

Laurel followed the woman down the hallway. A side door opened, and she immediately recognized the deep rumble of Dr. Drakoulias's voice.

She couldn't follow many of his quickly spoken Greek words, but saw his hand was cupped beneath the elbow of a stooped-over elderly woman as they stepped from what looked like an examination room, obviously helping her stay steady as she walked. A small frown creased his brow just as it had when he'd been looking at Laurel's gash.

Whatever the woman said in return made him laugh, banishing the frown and making him look younger. His eyes twinkled as he shook his head, saying something else in a teasing tone, making her laugh in return. She lifted a gnarled hand to his cheek and gave it a pat, then a pinch that looked as if it had to hurt, but he didn't seem fazed.

Christina was chuckling too, as she took hold of the woman's other arm to walk with her back down the hall.

Laurel wanted to ask what the woman had said that was so amusing, and if she always pinched people like that, but didn't want to sound nosy. Dr. Drakoulias turned his attention to Laurel, and she felt the power of those eyes and that magnetic smile clear down to her toes. "Very punctual, I see. In my experience, the workers on the dig usually show up late. Or not at all."

"I admit it's easy to get distracted up there. But I had to learn fast how to keep track of time." Her own and everyone else's.

"So apparently you didn't find a gold statue today."

Her heart lurched hard in her chest and she stared at him, relaxing when she realized he was just kidding. "Not today, I'm afraid."

"Just so you know, I'd consider that a good reason to miss an appointment." He gave her a teasing smile that sent her attention to his beautiful mouth, which was not a good place for it to be. Thankfully, he reached for her hand and she followed his gaze to the new bandage. "Let's get this cleaned up."

"It's all right, really. I put peroxide on it and a clean bandage."

He grasped her elbow and walked to the sink, her injured hand still in his. "That's good, but I'd like to clean it again, nonetheless. Better to prevent an infection than have to treat one."

She couldn't argue with that, and again watched his fingers gently and carefully remove the bandage. He looked closely at her palm for a long moment before he spoke. "It's going to hurt a little, I'm sorry to say, but thoroughly washing this out is important. Are you ready?"

She nodded and braced herself as he turned on the faucet, holding the open cut directly underneath the cool stream. He was right, it definitely hurt, but no way was she going to be a baby about it. Biting her lip, she'd have sworn he about drained the town's entire water supply and was just about to yell, *Enough already!* when he finally turned it off.

He wrapped her hand with a towel and gently dried it. "You were very brave. I appreciate that you didn't scream in my ear like the last patient I did that to."

The eyes that met hers held a pleasing mix of humor, warmth and admiration in their dark depths. "I reserve screaming for activities that truly warrant it," she said. Then wanted to sink into the floor when his eyebrows lifted and something else mingled with the humor in his eyes. "Things like bungee-jumping, for example," she added hastily.

"I see. So you're a daredevil."

"Um, not really." Not about to admit she wouldn't bungee-jump unless her life depended on it, and definitely wouldn't admit the direction her thoughts had suddenly gone, she quickly changed the subject. "What is that stuff you're putting on there?"

"Just a topical antibiotic." With nowhere else to look, her gaze again got stuck on his face instead of his work on her hand. On his dark lashes, lowered over his eyes;

his ridiculously sculpted cheekbones; his lips twisting a little as he wrapped white gauze over the cut. "This gauze bandage will keep it clean and dry, but I'd like to check it in a couple days."

"It'll be fine. Thank you." It suddenly struck her that she probably needed to pay him. "What do I owe you, Dr. Drakoulias?"

"First, I'd like you to call me Andros, since Dr. Drakoulias reminds me of my father and I don't want to feel old around a beautiful woman. Second, I'm the one who insisted on treating you, so it's on the house. I might get a bad reputation if I chase ambulances, then hand unsuspecting patients a bill."

She had to grin at the picture that conjured, and the smile in his eyes and on his lips grew in response. "So if anybody on the dig team gets hurt, I need to find a way to lure you to the site, then when your Hippocratic Oath kicks in, we'll get free medical care? Good to know."

"I'm pretty sure you'd have no trouble at all luring me there."

Did he mean, because he was interested in archaeology? Or something else altogether? After all, he'd called her "beautiful." She shoved aside the intriguing question, reminding herself she had work to focus on, and luring dreamy Dr. Drakoulias couldn't be on the agenda, even if he was willing to be lured.

Though the thought alone put a hitch in her breath and sent a little electric zing from the top of her head to her toes.

"Are we going to see Mel and Tom now? Where are they?"

His expression instantly became neutral and professional. "They're in the clinic hospital, which is attached to this building. But before you see them, I'd like to talk to you in my office."

"Why?"

"Because," he said, his lips tightening into a grim line, "they are both seriously ill."

CHAPTER THREE

ANDROS WAS ALL too aware of the woman following close behind him down the clinic corridor. She smelled good. Like sweet lemons or grapefruit strewn with flowers, and he had an urge to bury his nose in the softness of her neck and breathe her in.

Something about her had stopped him in his tracks the first second he'd seen her on the mountain. Her blonde hair was the color of sunshine, pulled back into a thick, untidy ponytail that had flowed from beneath a creased canvas hat that was definitely for function, not style. The blue eyes that had met his were sharp and intelligent, and there was an exotic look to her features that made him want to keep looking. Maybe not a classic kind of beauty, but there was something intangible and appealing about her. Her skin was practically luminous without any makeup at all. He hadn't thought much about it until this moment, but, compared to the carefully put-together women he used to date, he liked her natural look a lot.

Down, boy, he reminded himself. Now wasn't the time to forget he was trying to reform the man who'd liked women far too much in the past, made-up, natural or anywhere in between.

Andros opened the door to his office and gestured

for Laurel to go inside, wishing there were a little more room to move around. Usually he didn't notice how his father's old wooden desk that Christina joked was the size of an aircraft carrier practically filled the small space. At that moment, however, he was intensely aware of the close quarters.

Standing or sitting within inches of Laurel wasn't the best idea, since he kept finding himself distracted by her scent and her smooth skin and soft-looking hair. There wasn't much he could do about any of those problems, though, and he wanted privacy for this conversation. The last thing he needed was for a local to come into the clinic and overhear that there might be a contagion nearby.

"Have a seat."

She sat and turned to him as he lowered himself into the chair next to her, trying not to bump his knees into hers. He pondered for a moment, wondering how much detail he should give her about the Wagners' condition. She had to be worried, but instead of bombarding him with questions like a lot of people would, she waited patiently. He looked into her serious blue eyes and decided she could handle the truth, and deserved to know.

"Unfortunately, the Wagners are no better. I'm frankly surprised and concerned about that, after having them on IV fluids and antibiotics all day. As I mentioned before, I'm keeping them here overnight for observation. With any luck, they'll improve, but we should have seen some improvement already."

"Doesn't pneumonia usually respond to antibiotics pretty fast?"

"Often, yes, especially in younger people and those with no underlying physical problems, like the Wagners. That's the good news. But sometimes it doesn't. The truth about this situation, though? The presentation of their pneumonia is unusual."

"How so?"

"According to what they told me, Tom got what he thought was a cold a couple days before Melanie did. This morning Tom's respiratory rate was about thirty breaths per minute, Mel's twenty. Which indicates to me that she may have gotten it from him, which generally doesn't happen with pneumonia. Both are showing symptoms of the pneumonia worsening." He paused, hoping she wouldn't get upset at what he had to warn her about next. "If that continues into the morning, I will recommend they be transported to a fully equipped hospital in a bigger city about an hour away. It has twenty-four-hour skilled care and equipment we don't have."

Her lush lips parted in surprise. "You really think that might be necessary? Can't you just give them a different kind of antibiotic or something?"

"It's not that simple. I'm hopeful they'll improve and we can manage it here. I'm just making you aware that's a possibility. I'd prefer you didn't mention it to them, though. No need to worry them unnecessarily."

"All right." She nodded. "Are they…are they well enough for me to talk to them? If I have to take over leadership of the dig, I need to ask some questions. Find out more about the cave dig, since we were supposed to have our team meeting for the week tomorrow."

The eyes that met his were full of worry and alarm, and he wanted to reassure her but couldn't. He hadn't seen pneumonia with quite this presentation before and figured she might as well talk to the Wagners now in case the situation slid south—which he feared very well might happen.

He stood, and she did too, biting her full lower lip as she looked up at him. Standing so close he could have tipped his head down to kiss her. The instant that thought came to mind, he looked into her eyes, the idea now so appealing, so damned near irresistible, he had to inhale a deep breath and quickly step back. "I'll take you to see them now. They're on oxygen but will be able to talk to you. I want you to wear a surgical mask."

"You think I could make them sicker?"

"No. I think they might make you sick."

"Make *me* sick?"

Her eyes widened, and he wanted to make sure she understood the possible risk, because he damned well didn't want her to end up in the hospital too. "I told you before that it's unusual they've both developed this. We just can't know if it's possibly contagious or not."

He turned and led the way down the hall, again very aware of her walking closely behind as her sweet, citrusy scent wafted around him. He grabbed surgical masks from the supply cupboard outside the hospital wing and handed her one before putting on his own.

The Wagners were the only patients in the six-bed wing, and he was thankful for that. Tom Wagner lay motionless, his eyes still closed as they came to stand between the two beds, but Melanie Wagner opened her eyes and reached out to Laurel. She held Melanie's hand between both of hers, and Andros realized too late he should have had her put gloves on. Or at least one on her good hand, and warned her not to touch the Wagners otherwise.

He mentally thrashed himself. Until they knew what they were dealing with here, every precaution had to be taken anytime someone came in contact with them.

"I'm so sorry to have to dump all the work on you, Laurel," Melanie said in a whisper. "Isn't this crazy?"

"Don't worry about a thing, Mel," Laurel said, her voice slightly muffled through the mask. "I'll handle everything until you're feeling better. Dr. Drakoulias says he hopes the antibiotics will kick in soon."

"You won't have any problems leading the team until we're better. You've impressed me since day one on this dig." Melanie gave Laurel a glimmer of a smile. "Find anything good today?"

"Mostly more potsherds. But the most exciting thing was a gold ring. I'm pretty sure it's seventh century BC, but you'll know that better than I. Can't wait for you to look at it."

"Me either. I—"

A coughing fit interrupted her speech, and when she finally stopped, her breathing was obviously more labored. Laurel turned to Andros, her eyes wide.

He glanced at the quietly beeping screen next to the bed and saw that Melanie's respiratory rate had increased a little more from the last time he'd checked, which was not a good sign.

"Let's keep this visit brief, Laurel," he said, leaning close to speak in her ear. "The more they talk, the harder they have to breathe. Did you say you need to speak to Tom? I'll wake him and you can ask him a couple quick questions before you go."

He didn't want her to feel as if he was rushing her out, but didn't like the look of either of his patients. He adjusted the oxygen flow to both of them before rousing Tom with enough difficulty that it added another layer of worry.

"How are you feeling, Tom?"

The man opened his eyes and stared up at him, his mouth open, obviously having trouble breathing. "Hard to get air."

"I know. I just gave you a little more oxygen, which will help." Damn. Might not be waiting until tomorrow to send them to the Elias Sophia hospital, if they both continued to struggle like this. Andros turned to Laurel, but, before he had to say another word, she obviously got his unspoken message, since she quickly turned to Tom.

"I'm going now, so you two can rest and get better. Real quick, though, is there anything important I need to know about the cave dig that the volunteer crew can't tell me?"

"Just that we found some human bones. Exciting. Planned…" His chest heaved a few times before he continued. "Planned to share at the next meeting. I think they're older than the artifacts at the mountain site. Probably…Minoan, but…don't know…for sure yet."

"Okay. I'll talk to the crew and have them bring me up to speed. Don't worry about a thing." She patted his shoulder, and Andros stepped behind her to wrap his hands around her lower arms. She looked over her shoulder in surprise, but he couldn't risk her touching her eyes or pulling down her mask before she'd thoroughly washed her hands.

Her soft hair and enticing scent tickled his nose as he leaned forward to whisper in her ear. "I want you to wash your hands before you touch anything, especially any part of your body. Okay?"

She stared at him, then nodded slowly, saying a quick goodbye to both patients. Still holding on to the delicate wrist of her unbandaged hand, he led her across the room to the sink, squirted soap and stuck her hand under the faucet to wash it.

"I know how to wash my hands, you know."

"Except you're a bit handicapped right now. Can't wash the way you normally would, with one hand bandaged." As his fingers moved around and between hers, it struck him what an interesting contrast her hand was, like the woman herself. Slender, delicate, feminine fingers that were also hardworking and strong. "I want to make sure it's clean. The skin exposed on your other hand too, before I change the bandage."

"Change it? You just put it on."

"'Know Thyself' is one of the famous inscriptions at the temple." He kept washing, slowly now, enjoying too much the sensual feel of their hands soapily sliding together as he looked up at her, noticing the interesting flecks of green and gold in her questioning blue eyes. "My *yiayia* used to call me Kyrie Prosektikos, which means Mr. Careful. I believe in thinking things through and being appropriately cautious." Which had been true except for one notable aspect of his life he was determined to change. "So, yeah, I'm going to put on a new bandage."

"I'd say three bandages in an hour is careful, all right. If that doesn't sterilize it, nothing will."

He liked her smile. That she didn't roll her eyes or argue with him told him she trusted him, at least a little, to know what he was doing. "Glad to see you aren't doubting my doctoring skills anymore. Some of the tourists who come to this clinic never are convinced I know what I'm doing."

"What makes you think I'm convinced? Maybe I can

just see you're hard-headed and bossy, and I don't have time to argue with you."

"Smart woman. You're right that I'd damned well get tough with you if I had to."

"Just remember I can get tough too. If I have to."

"Somehow, I don't doubt that for a second."

They stood there looking at one another, small smiles on their faces, before Andros realized he was just holding her hand in his, now, fingers entwined. He managed to refocus his attention on the job at hand instead of her captivating face and eyes, and very kissable lips.

Dried off and newly bandaged, Laurel paused as she was about to head out of the clinic door. "I'm worried, Andros."

He realized he liked the sound of his name on her tongue a lot better than the formal Dr. Drakoulias. When she looked up at him, her face filled with concern, he wished he could tell her she didn't need to be. But he was worried as well. "I know. I'm doing everything I can and will let you know how they are tomorrow. I'm planning to spend the night here to keep an eye on them. You have a cell-phone number I can call?"

"Reception is sketchy at the dig, but if you leave a message, I'll be able to get it when I'm back at the hotel." She scribbled her number on a piece of paper and pressed it into his palm, lingering there. "Promise to call me?"

"I promise." He folded his fingers over hers, squeezing gently to reassure her. It took effort to release her soft hand, to let her go. He stood there, motionless, to watch her walk to her car. Watch the gentle sway of her hips, the way her dress swung sensuously with each step of her drop-dead gorgeous legs. Watch the way her long silky ponytail caressed her back, until she'd gotten in her car and driven away.

He tucked the paper into his pocket and had a feeling he'd be tempted to call just to talk to her more about the dig. Just to hear her voice.

Which was foolish. The Wagners had told him the dig would be permanently over in just a few weeks and they'd be gone. She'd be gone.

Why did it have to be Laurel who was the first woman he'd felt this kind of interest in since he'd come home? The kind of interest that had his mind and body all stirred up. The kind of interest that made him want to take her to dinner, to wrap his arms around her, to touch her and kiss her and see where it led.

He squeezed the back of his suddenly tight neck and sighed. He had every intention of living the life of a model citizen—and a good father—putting behind him the wild reputation of his youth. Last thing he needed was attraction to a woman who would be leaving soon, tempting him to enjoy a quickie affair that would grease the town gossip machine all over again. Gossip he didn't want his daughter to have to hear about her dad.

He'd keep his distance. But he couldn't deny that the thought of spending even a short time with interesting and beautiful Laurel Evans sounded pretty irresistible.

"I know it's early, Dimitri." Andros paced up and down the hall of the clinic as he spoke to the infection specialist, barely noticing the dawn that rose over the mountain, filling the sky with pink and gold. "I wish I'd sent them last night. I wanted to give them time to possibly stabilize, but their respiratory rate's gone to thirty and forty breaths per minute. New chest films show dramatic worsening to progressive multilobar pneumonia."

"What's their oxygen saturation?" Dimitri asked.

"Both were hypoxic when they arrived. Now pulse ox says their sats have gone from ninety to eighty, even after giving them four liters of oxygen. This is acute respiratory failure, Di, and they may need intubation."

"Nikolaos will be here in an hour, and I'll send him right out."

Andros nearly slammed his hand to the wall. "We can't wait until the hospital's driver feels like rolling out of bed. Get him out here with portable oxygen now, or I'll bring them there. If they code on me, it'll be on your shoulders, since I don't have damned IV hookups in my car."

"All right, all right. He'll gripe like hell, but I'll have him there in an hour and fifteen."

"Good." He stopped his pacing to stare out of the window. "Get a blood test for fungal infection when they get there. I'm going to talk to the hotel management, and the archaeological crew they've worked with. See if I can figure out if there's some environmental cause."

"You think there might be?"

"Maybe. It's strange that they both fell ill days apart with the same symptoms. So make sure Nikolaos and the EMTs use infection control precautions, just in case."

"Will do. Talk to you after they get here."

Andros shoved his phone into his pocket, called Christina to come in early and keep a close eye on the Wagners, then caught up on paperwork in his office. He tried not to constantly check his watch. After forty-five minutes that felt like hours, he decided to make sure the Wagners were ready to go the second Nikolaos got there. He took a quick right out of his office, practically knocking down Laurel Evans, who was standing just outside his door. How had he missed her presence, when he'd been so acutely aware of it yesterday?

"Whoa, sorry!" he said, grabbing her arms to steady her. "Didn't see you there. Hope I didn't bruise you."

"No bruises. Though I did wonder for a second if I was on a football field instead of in a medical clinic." Her hands rested on his biceps as though they belonged there, and he had to stop himself from tugging her closer. "Now I see your real MO. Forget chasing ambulances. You injure people, fix them up, then bill them."

He smiled. "Not my MO. But I did play football in college in the US. Glad to know I still have the moves." Though knocking her down wasn't the move he'd like to make on her. "What are you doing here?"

"I couldn't sleep. So I came to see how they're doing."

The pale smudges beneath her eyes didn't detract one bit from her pretty face, and he again nearly pulled her against him instead of letting her go. To comfort and reassure her, of course.

"Not good." He gave her arms a gentle, bolstering squeeze before dropping his hands. "I've called the Elias Sophia hospital, which is about an hour away. The ambulance is coming to get them now."

"Oh, no!" Her hands flew to cover her heart. "They're worse?"

"I'm afraid so." He didn't feel it was necessary to tell her exactly how much worse they were. With any luck, they'd soon be fine and she'd never have to know the seriousness of the situation. "Sometime today, I'd like to talk to some of your people who've worked in the caves."

"To see if there's something there that made them sick." It was a statement, not a question.

"Yes."

"I'll be heading up when I leave here. The crew should be there soon, and I need to talk to them anyway. If you have time, you can come with me."

"Once the Wagners leave for the hospital, I can go. Even though Melanie hasn't been up there recently, it's worth asking a few questions."

"If it's contagious, just being in the same hotel room might have exposed her to it, right?"

"Right." He'd considered the same thing. The woman was smart, no doubt about that. "I'm also going to check with the hotel management, see if any tourists were ill, or if any staff that live elsewhere have been out sick."

"Can I see Mel and Tom now?"

"I'd prefer you didn't." Andros managed to temper the vehement *hell, no* he'd nearly responded with. But her being exposed to them again wouldn't accomplish anything. "Talking is difficult for them right now. After they're settled in at the hospital, we can go see them there together."

She tipped her head sideways and seemed to study him. Was she wondering if he had some ulterior motive in wanting them to go together? Again, smart woman. He hadn't said it for that reason, but as soon as the words were out of his mouth, the small rush of anticipation he felt spelled out loud and clear that, even if they were just driving to see his patients, and despite his concern for them, he'd more than enjoy the time with her.

"All right. But—"

"Dr. Drakoulias!" Christina came hurrying out of

the doors of the hospital wing. "The hospital transport is here."

"Finally." He turned to Laurel. "Stay here. I'll be back shortly."

With Christina's help, he, the EMT and Nikolaos got both patients loaded in a matter of minutes. About to shut the ambulance doors, the scent of sweet citrus reached his nose. He looked over his shoulder, and saw Laurel standing right behind him, waving to the Wagners as they lay inside on their gurneys.

"Don't worry about a thing," she said, the smile on her face obviously strained. "I'll come see you with updates."

He shut the ambulance doors, yanked down his mask, and barely stopped himself from raising his voice at the woman next to him. "What part of 'stay here' and 'possibly contagious' are you not understanding?"

"I was a good six feet from them. It seems to me you're overreacting a little, since you don't know if they're contagious or not."

"There's a difference between overreaction and caution."

"Maybe that's just something you tell yourself." She folded her arms and stared him down. "Are you going to be bossy like this when we go up to the caves?"

"I'm only bossy when I have good reason to be." In spite of his frustration with her, he nearly smiled at the mulish expression on her face. She was toughness all wrapped up in softness. "So the answer is yes. I'm staying outside the caves and you are too."

"I'm an archaeologist, Dr. Drakoulias. Detective work is part of what we do. The Wagners are my bosses and my friends, and I'm going to do whatever I can to help. The caves are part of the excavation I'm doing my dissertation on, and, with Mel and Tom sick, I'm in charge now. I have to learn exactly what they're doing there and maybe in the process spot something that could have made them ill. Since I'm pretty sure you don't own Mount Parnassus, I'm going into the caves."

"You say I'm bossy? How about I say you're stubborn?" He let out an exasperated breath. "If there's a fungal contagion, possibly connected to the caves, no one should go in who hasn't been there already. Hell, no one should go in there, period, until we have some answers. But if they have to, they need to wear masks. Which I'll provide. You, though, have to stay out for now."

"Are you afraid Apollo's python may be lurking in there too, ready to strangle me?" Her voice was silky sweet, at odds with the sparking blue flash in her eyes. "Don't worry, I'll bring my bow and arrows just in case."

Clearly, the woman had serious issues with being told what to do. "Listen, Laurel, you—"

"Daddy!"

He swung around in horror when he heard his daughter's little voice, and the sight of her standing just inside the door of the hospital wing with his sister and nephew, smiling her big bright smile, sent his heart pounding and adrenaline surging. His baby could not be in there when God knew what contagion might be in the very air. "Cassie. You can't be here right now."

"Why, Daddy?" Her eyes shone with excitement. "Is there really a python? I want to see!"

CHAPTER FOUR

LAUREL HAD BARELY blinked in shock at the little girl calling Andros "Daddy" when he'd strode to the child, snatched her up in his arms, hustled out the woman and little boy, too, and shoved the hospital doors closed behind them.

Heat surged into Laurel's face when she realized the man she'd been thinking of as dreamy Dr. Drakoulias, the man she'd been having some pretty exciting fantasies about all last night when she couldn't sleep, was apparently a married family man.

Why in the world had she just assumed he was single? Clearly, her instant attraction to him, along with wishful thinking, had blotted any other possibility from her mind.

Disgusted with herself, and, okay, disappointed too, she watched Andros crouch down next to the little girl. Surprisingly, he spoke to her in English. Why wouldn't the child speak Greek, instead?

"Cassie. There's no python. The pretty lady was just talking about the old story of god Apollo slaying the python dragon with arrows. Remember it?" The little girl nodded and Andros flicked her nose. "Know what, though? Remember when you didn't feel good with your tummy bug? There might be some germs in the clinic I don't want you to be around. I want you to go back with Petros and Thea Taryn, and I'll be home later."

Thea Taryn? Laurel didn't know a lot of Greek words, but she did know *thea* meant *aunt*. Which presumably meant the attractive, dark-haired woman was either Andros's sister or sister-in-law. Not that Laurel cared one way or the other, she thought with a twist of her lips. Married was married, and the thought of tromping over Mount Parnassus with him to talk to the crew together didn't seem nearly as appealing now.

Despite what she'd boldly stated, the truth was she didn't have a clue how to look for a fungus or whatever else could cause the kind of illness Mel and Tom had. She hadn't been in a lot of caves, but weren't most filled with all kinds of biological life she didn't know much about? Probably, she should simply focus on getting the excavation finished and hope no one else got sick. Getting it done was critical for a number of reasons, and Mel and Tom would doubtless want her to concentrate on that as well.

The cute little girl wrapped her arms around Andros's neck as he folded her close. Laurel's throat tightened as she watched the sweet moment, thinking of her own dad and all the times he'd held her exactly the same way. Thinking of how much he'd loved his four daughters, and how much they'd loved and admired him. Thinking how lucky the child was that Andros seemed to be a supportive and involved dad. One whose work enabled him to be with her all the time, and not away for months as her own parents had been.

She began to turn away at the same time Andros's head came up, and his eyes—dark and alive—met hers. He gestured to her to come over. She hesitated, then realized it was silly to feel embarrassed at her former hot fantasies. After all, he didn't know about them, thank heavens, and she was already over it. It wasn't as if she had time for any kind of relationship anyway, hot doc or not.

He stood. "Laurel Evans, this is my sister, Taryn Drakoulias, and her son, Petros."

That answered that question, she thought as they shook hands, though she should have seen the resemblance. Same dark hair, nearly black eyes and a slightly amused smile that implied maybe they both were privy to secrets no one else was privy to. His daughter had the same dark eyes, but her hair was a much lighter brown.

Laurel wondered if Taryn was divorced or had been a single mom, since she still used her maiden name. Or if she'd simply kept her name, but that seemed less likely, since Greece was still a very traditional country.

"This is my daughter, Cassandra." Andros smiled down at the girl, his eyes and face softened from the intense concern that had been on it just a moment ago. "Cassie, I'd like you to meet Laurel. She's an archaeologist, working on the dig up the mountain. You've learned a little about that, haven't you?"

"Yes! I have!" The child's eyes, so like her dad's, stared up at her. "Have you found lots of statues and gold treasures?"

If only. "Many things that are treasures to archaeologists, but not much gold, I'm afraid. Like father, like daughter, I see." Laurel smiled up at Andros then turned back to Cassie. "Do you dig holes trying to find ancient treasure, Cassie, like your dad said he used to do?"

"Oh, no." She shook her head, her chin-length hair sliding across her cheeks as she did. "Fairies are scared of big holes. I don't want to scare them. I want them to sleep under our plants so they're in the shade and live in the little houses they build in the ground under special rocks. They stay cool that way."

"I see." Laurel's smile grew, remembering how much she'd loved pretend things as a little girl. Probably part of the reason she still loved classical myths today. "Have you seen the fairies?"

"Oh, yes." She nodded, very serious. "Sometimes they dance at night when there's a moon, and you can see them better. Sometimes they dance on my bed too, when they think I'm asleep."

Laurel looked at Andros again to see what he thought of his daughter's imagination. The lips she'd fantasized about were curved, and his eyes had attractively crinkled at the corners again.

No. Not attractively. Married, remember? Then again, he wasn't wearing a ring, so maybe he wasn't. That thought perked her up so much she nearly chuckled at how ridiculous she was being.

"We've made a fairy house out of stones, haven't we, Cassie? Have you seen any go in yet?" Taryn asked.

"No." Her little voice was filled with regret. "I think maybe I need to move the furniture around. Or put in something else. I don't think they like it the way it is."

Petros, who looked to be about five, chimed in, speaking Greek, but his mother stopped him with a hand on his shoulder. "English, please. It's good practice for you, and I don't think Ms. Evans speaks Greek." She turned to Laurel. "Do you?"

"Not much, I'm afraid. Trying, since I expect to spend a lot of time in various parts of the country on future digs, but it's not as easy as I'd hoped. I plan to study it more when the dig is over and I'm back at the university."

"Your work must be very interesting."

"It is. It also can be hot and dirty and takes a lot of patience, but the reward is worth it."

"Hot and dirty sounds like fun!" Petros exclaimed.

The adults' eyes all met, with Taryn looking slightly embarrassed and Andros quite amused at the sexual connotation of what were, really, innocent words. Laurel should have felt a little embarrassed too, since she was the first to use the unfortunate phrase, but instead found the fantasies she'd enjoyed last night popped front and center into her mind. *Dang it.*

"What were you going to say about the fairy house?" Taryn hastily asked her son.

"I told Cassie we should make toad or snake houses instead. There's no fairies around here."

"Oh, there definitely are, Petros," Laurel said. "I'm sure there are plenty nearby." As soon as the words were out of her mouth, she regretted them. How ridiculous to defend Cassie's belief in fairies, when the child had her aunt and parents to pretend with her, and it was just cousin dynamics anyway, which made it none of her business. Must be habit from the fun she'd had making up stories for her little sisters. From defending them, too, she supposed.

"You know about fairies?" Cassie stared at her, wide-eyed.

"Ancient stories of fairies and nymphs and all kinds of things are part of what I do." The child was adorable, and she found herself wishing she could play fairies with her right then. But it was high time to change the subject and get back to work. "Speaking of which, I've got to get going. The students and volunteers are probably already at the sites by now."

"I'll go with you." Andros turned to his sister and spoke in a low tone. "The dig leaders are pretty sick, and I'm going to ask the workers some questions about where they've all been. For now, don't go into the hospital wing until it's been sterilized. I'll let you know when I'm done seeing patients this afternoon. I'll pick Cassie up then."

Taryn looked surprised, but nodded without comment before turning to Laurel. "Nice to meet you. Perhaps before the dig is over, you can come for dinner and tell us about all you've found in our backyard."

"Thank you, I appreciate the invitation." Having dinner with the happy Drakoulias family would be interesting, and she had to admit she was curious to meet Andros's wife. If he had one. So long as she could keep from drooling when she stared at the man the lucky woman was married to. "Nice for you to have all of Mount Parnassus as your backyard."

"Yes, Miss Laurel! And you can see our fairy house," Cassie said. "And help me get the fairies to come."

"I'd like that, Cassie." The child's bright eyes and smile would melt anyone's heart. It made her think of her sisters with a sudden longing to hug them. She was surprised at how much she missed them, considering she'd practically danced with joy when the youngest had started college this year and Laurel could finally get to this dig.

The dig. She glanced at her watch, dismayed to realize how much time she'd lost this morning. Time she couldn't afford to lose.

She turned to Andros. "Are you able to leave right now?"

He nodded. "Let me grab—"

"Dr. Drakoulias." Christina stuck her head out of the door. "We have a patient with a possible broken arm."

His lips twisted as his eyes met Laurel's. "Guess I'm not. How about I find you at the other site when I can, then we'll head over to the caves?"

"Okay." A mix of both relief and disappointment battled inside her as she said her goodbyes and headed to her car. She didn't particularly want him looking over her shoulder as she took over what would hopefully be temporary leadership and talked to all the dig workers. But she'd like to have him with her to ask the cave-dig volunteers questions she wouldn't know to ask.

And of course it had nothing to do with wishing she could just look at him and talk to him all day long...

The temperature thankfully dropped a few degrees when the sun sank behind the mountain. Laurel kept carefully digging and cataloging, ignoring the stinging ache in her palm, even though she'd let most of the crew leave long ago. Shoveling dirt and rocks and working in this kind of heat wore everyone down by the end of the day, and she couldn't expect them to be as intensely committed as she was. This dig hadn't been their parents' baby, and they didn't know about what Laurel still hoped was here somewhere, just waiting to be found.

Between her time at the clinic and meeting with different crew members, she'd lost more than half the day, and if she had to work until nearly dark to make it up, she would. So disappointing that Andros apparently hadn't been able to get away. She'd asked the volunteers at the cave dig to stick around later than usual, but, as far as she knew, he hadn't shown. Every time she'd seen someone move into her vision, her silly heart had kicked a little, until she'd realized it wasn't him after all.

Time to go to the cave site to tell everyone they were

through for the day. Hopefully it didn't matter that Andros hadn't been able to talk with any of them. Maybe Mel and Tom would be better after their hospital stay, and they could all quit worrying about why they'd gotten sick in the first place.

She stood and stretched her tired back, shoved her things into her backpack, and turned to walk the half mile to the cave site, realizing too late how dusk was closing in fast. With her head down, she concentrated on staying on the goat path, well-worn through the scrub, her mind moving from Mel and Tom, to how she could possibly pick up the pace of the excavation without them, then to Andros and how unfair it was that a man she was attracted to more than any she could think of in recent memory was likely a married man.

"You make a habit of working until it's so dark you can barely see?"

Startled, Laurel nearly tripped over her feet, heart pounding as she looked up to see Andros's unmistakable broad form moving toward her on the goat path.

She pressed her sore hand to her chest, huffing out a breath of relief and annoyance. "You make a habit of sneaking up on people to give them a heart attack?"

"Well, we did talk about my MO being injuring people, fixing them up, then billing them."

"Uh-huh. Too bad for you my heart is still in one piece."

"Good to hear. And I wasn't sneaking." He stopped in front of her. "Just hoping to find you on the way to the caves, since you've kept your poor workers imprisoned there, saying they couldn't leave until you said so."

"I didn't keep them imprisoned," she said indignantly.

"I was hoping you'd show up to talk to them, since you thought it was important."

"I'm sorry. We ended up having one injury or illness after another, and I couldn't get away. Since they're still there, I'll go tell them they can leave now. I already spoke with two of them but wanted to find you before it got dark."

"I'll come with you." Being the team leader now meant she couldn't pass off her responsibilities to anyone else. Something she'd had to learn all over again every time she'd been frustrated, even a little resentful, at having to stay home to take care of her sisters. Her parents had made it clear that, as the oldest, that was her job, when all she'd wanted was to go along on their summer digs instead.

Finally, those responsibilities were behind her, and she was here on this amazing mountain. Except her parents would never be with her too. Her new responsibility was to their memory and what they'd always expected her to achieve with her life.

"I was going to insist you do, so I'm glad I don't have to." He smiled, his teeth shining white through the dusk. "Don't want you breaking an ankle walking down this mountain to your car in the dark. I parked not too far from the caves, so I'll drive you and the crew back to it."

"Are you saying I'm clumsy? Or do you always worry like this about everyone?" She smiled back at him, feeling the same silly little glow she'd felt when they'd been together here before and he'd wanted to take care of her hand.

"Clumsy? You're as graceful as a dancer, Laurel Evans. Kyrie Prosektikos is just being cautious."

The little glow grew warmer at the sincerity in his

voice. "Because you don't want to fix another broken bone today."

"That too." He reached for her bandaged hand, rubbed his thumb across her knuckles. "How's it feeling?"

A little shiver snaked up her arm at his touch, and she nearly closed her fingers around his until she remembered she shouldn't. "Fine, thanks." She tried to tug away from his grasp, but he didn't let go. If she confessed that her cut actually hurt like blazes, he'd probably march her back to the clinic and torture her again.

"Good. Watch your step, and hang on to me." He tucked her hand into the crook of his elbow and, resting his wide palm gently on top of it, turned to head toward the caves.

They walked in an oddly companionable silence. As she held his strong arm, the way he'd tugged her close to his body as they picked their way over the uneven ground felt oddly right. The intimacy of it, the evening sky beautiful with pinkly puffy clouds, filled her chest with a sense of calm pleasure, until she suddenly wondered if he knew she'd feel that way. If he was the kind of man who used his amazing good looks and charm to solicit affairs with women from the archaeological site, knowing they'd only be around for a while.

That unpleasant thought obliterated her sense of comfortable calm. "Tell me about your wife," she said.

It seemed there was a momentary hitch in his step, probably from guilt, and the chill that had filled her chest grew downright icy. "My wife?"

"Yes. Cassie's mother. Is she from Kastorini, too?"

"Cassie's mother was American. And we were never married."

This time, the hitch was in her own step. "Was?"

"Yes."

"I'm so sorry."

"Thank you, but she and I weren't…close. It's for Cassie you should feel sorry, since she barely remembers her. She passed away when Cassie was only two, and I got custody of her then."

He didn't offer more, and Laurel knew it would be rude to ask for details. The cold tightness in her chest turned to an ache for the little girl who would never know her mother. At the same time, it absurdly lightened a little at the thought that Andros Drakoulias was single and available. All the feelings of intimacy she'd felt just moments ago came surging back, making her hyperaware of how good it felt to be tucked against his warm, masculine body.

She mentally smacked herself. Maybe she couldn't shake this powerful attraction to him, but she wouldn't act on it. There was so much work to finish in so little time, and they were down two people to boot. Hadn't her mother always admonished her about never letting a boyfriend or crush get in the way of her focus on school or work? One hundred percent of her attention had to be on this dig and the important goal she still hoped to make happen.

Dusk had nearly given way to full darkness as they arrived at the entrance to the caves, and she released Andros's arm so no one would start any gossip, which at a dig could spread like poison ivy. Becka and Jason, two of the three volunteers, were packing up by the light of electric lanterns. "Where's John?" she asked.

"He's coming. Said he was working on unearthing another human bone and wanted to finish," Becka said.

"There's something I didn't ask before," Andros said.

"Do each of you have your own section of the cave you work, or do you move around a lot?"

Becka swiped her hair from her eyes. "We keep to our own sections, mostly, unless Tom needs us to work somewhere else."

"Have you—?" Andros was interrupted by a violent coughing sound, echoing from inside the cave.

Oh, Lord, no. Laurel looked at Andros and saw his expression turn grim.

"Put these on. Now." He dug surgical masks from his pocket and quickly handed them out before putting one on himself. Another racking cough came from the cave just before John stumbled out, bending over and holding his chest for what seemed like minutes until it finally subsided, leaving him gasping.

Andros wrapped his arm around John's back, helping him stand upright. "You're burning up," Andros said, his voice slightly muffled through the mask. "How long have you been like this?"

"Had a cold the last couple days, like Tom. Got lots worse the past hour or so."

"Let's get you down to the clinic hospital and do some tests. My car's close by."

With John leaning heavily against him, Andros helped him down the path. Laurel's throat tightened when she saw Andros had taken a second to put on surgical gloves as well.

She hoped and prayed this was something completely different than what Mel and Tom were experiencing. That it was just a cold, and he'd be feeling better in the morning. Not horribly sick and hooked up to oxygen the way Mel and Tom had been. That Becka and Jason would stay healthy. That they'd all be fine.

But what if John got worse? What if his symptoms were exactly the same? And if they were, where would that leave the dig?

CHAPTER FIVE

"So what do you think?" Andros asked Dimitri in a low voice as they stood in the doorway of John Jackson's hospital room at the Elias Sophia Hospital. "Same thing as the Wagners?"

"Presents the same, but that doesn't necessarily mean it is. We'll have to wait for the blood tests to come back, and we won't have Mr. Jackson's until a few days after the Wagners'."

Andros looked at the woman standing next to the patient's bed and couldn't help but be impressed at how calm she seemed through all the activity around them. How steady, despite the incessant beep of monitors, nurses slipping in and out of the room, and techs checking the patient's vitals. Far calmer and steadier than he might have expected her to be, considering the heightened intensity in the air.

Though lines creased her brow and the blue eyes visible over the surgical mask she wore held a deep concern, her composure didn't waver. She stood straight, talking to John about the dig.

Andros had already transferred the patient here this morning, just before Laurel had shown up at the clinic. When she'd asked for directions to drive here after the day's work at the dig, he'd instantly offered to bring her instead, wanting to see the Wagners and John, too. And if an hour's car ride enjoying her scent in his nose and conversation from her lush lips was part of his motivation, what was the harm in that?

When he'd first introduced her to Dimitri, she'd asked good questions, her responses intelligent and thoughtful. She hadn't overreacted or panicked, simply displaying clear leadership in taking over for the Wagners.

Andros's heart knocked in his chest when he saw her reach out to touch John's arm, relieved when he saw her hesitate and withdraw it. John said something Andros couldn't catch, and a smile touched her eyes as she answered him back then said goodbye. She turned toward the door, and her eyes met his, held.

"You have something going with the pretty lady?" Dimitri asked.

The surprising question had him breaking eye contact with Laurel to stare at his friend. "I just met her two days ago."

"Sometimes only takes two minutes."

And damned if that wasn't the truth. Or even two seconds, which was about how long it had taken for his interest to go from zero to sixty the first moment he'd laid eyes on her.

"And if you don't, you should," Di said in a lower voice, grinning and waggling his thick eyebrows like Groucho Marx. "I'll keep you posted on our patients." He headed down the hall as Laurel joined Andros at the doorway.

"John seems to be holding his own. Doesn't he?" Her questioning eyes seemed to be willing him to reassure her. "He doesn't seem to have as much trouble breathing as Mel and Tom did when I first saw them in your clinic hospital."

"Not at the moment. Hopefully he'll stay that way." He wrapped his fingers around her arm and drew her farther into the hall. "Di told you we just don't know if this is the same thing the Wagners have or not. An influenza or some other virus. Bacterial infection or fungal infection."

"When will you know?"

"Di asked to have John's test results expedited, but that will still take a couple days."

She nodded, that pucker of worry still on her face. "I'm so relieved, though, that Mel and Tom aren't any worse. Do you think they'll be released soon?"

"Hard to say. They're getting good care, so we'll keep our fingers crossed." He wanted to banish, for at least a little while, that deep concern clouding her eyes. There was nothing more to do here, and a glance at his watch showed it was already well past 7:00 p.m. "How about we have dinner here before we head back?" He'd thought of that, wanted that, from the moment they'd left Delphi to drive here. Time spent with her away from her work and his, away from Kastorini, away from the serious problems on both their minds.

"I probably should get back. Update the team and make sure they're okay."

"Why wouldn't they be okay?"

"Well, they..." Her voice trailed off and she gave a little rueful smile. "You're right, they're adults. I forget sometimes I don't have to play mom anymore."

"When did you have to?" Surely she didn't have children. Leaving them for the entire summer for the dig.

"Oh, for my sisters. It's a wonder my hair's not prematurely gray." The tone of her voice had lightened and she smiled. "The dig team has explored a few towns outside of Delphi on weekends, but not here. So dinner sounds lovely."

"Good." He let go of her arm, resisting the urge to hold her hand instead, and they headed to his car. "You in the mood for seafood, or Greek food, or both?"

"Anything. Everything. I didn't have much lunch, and I have to admit that, next to digging, eating's one of my favorite things to do."

"Yeah?" She'd obviously decided to let herself relax with him, to let go of her worries for a time, and he grinned at the sudden enthusiasm in her voice. "Something we have in common. I know just the place you'll like."

It was only about a ten-minute drive from the hospital to the waterfront, and, since it was early yet for locals to be eating dinner, he had no trouble finding a parking spot. "Sit tight," he said to Laurel as he got out of the car, going around to her side of the car to open her door.

"More of your worrying I'm clumsy?" she asked as he held out his hand to her. "Getting out of a car isn't quite as dangerous as walking down a rocky mountain in the dark."

"Being a gentleman pleases me. And because I can see you're a woman who cares about others, you won't mind indulging me, will you?"

"Ah, the charm of Greek men." She shook her head, but a smile tugged at the corners of her lips.

She placed her soft hand in his and stepped from the car. It felt so nice to hold it, just as it had when he'd washed her palm at the clinic, and he couldn't seem to make himself let go. A little surprised that she didn't release his either, he gave in to enjoying the simple connection. Stars began to wink in the darkening sky as they strolled down the brick promenade that went for a good quarter mile along the lapping gulf waters.

"I've been in Greece two months, and I'm still amazed at all the little restaurants that line the water in every town," she said, gazing at the lanterns and lights beneath huge umbrellas connected together, one after another. "So pretty. With comfy seats too, if you want, instead of a table. I wish there were more places like this in the States."

"I went to med school in New Jersey," he said. "I admit I never got used to the beach restaurants there. Always wanting you to move on your way right after you're done. In Greece, you're expected to eat and relax for the night."

"Somehow when you said you lived in the US, I was picturing LA or Montana."

Her eyes were filled with a teasing look, and he found himself drifting closer until his shoulder brushed hers. "LA or Montana? First, I'd say those two places don't have much in common, and second, I'd ask why."

"I'm not sure." She tilted her head at him, seeming to size him up, and he grew even more curious about what she was thinking. "Maybe because you seem sophisticated and at the same time rugged. Like a Greek cowboy."

Sophisticated but rugged sounded pretty good. As if she might find him attractive, and he certainly found her very attractive. "I'm more of a Greek goat boy than a cowboy, since it was my job to look after ours when I was a kid."

"Goat boy?" She laughed. "Sorry. Doesn't work at all for you."

"You might change your mind if I show up smelling like one of Cassie's goats sometime. She and Petros like to pretend they're horses and bring them into the 'stable.' Which is her name for our living room."

"Oh, my gosh, that's adorable."

"Not when your house smells like a barn."

Her laugh, the sparkle in her eyes, were sheer temptation. The kind of temptation that left Andros wondering if he could possibly resist. If he could keep his hands and lips to himself when all he wanted at that moment was to pull her close and kiss that smiling mouth.

He drew in a deep breath, glad they'd arrived at one of his favorite restaurants, interrupting his dangerous thoughts. "Would you like to sit at a table, or have *mezedes* on these seats looking out over the water?"

"Mezedes?"

"You've been in Greece two months and don't know what *mezedes* are?" He teased her with mock astonishment. "Appetizer-sized plates for dinner, instead of one entrée. Eating various *meze* over a whole evening, preferably with ouzo to drink, is a Greek tradition."

"Ouzo? You're kidding. That stuff is awful!" He had to grin at the cute way she scrunched up her face. "Mel and Tom had us all try it at dinner in Delphi one night and I could barely swallow it."

"Don't worry. Ouzo's optional."

"Good, because the *meze* sounds wonderful. I like trying different things. And I want to enjoy seeing the water while I still can."

A reminder that she wouldn't be here for long. But when it came right down to it, what did it matter? He wasn't capable of futures or happy-ever-afters with a woman anyway. And they were far enough away that he didn't have to worry about the gossip Kastorini townsfolk used to love to share about him, back in the careless days of his youth. Which had extended into too many careless days with women in his adulthood, too.

They sat side by side in the cushioned wicker seat, and it took effort to concentrate on the menu instead of how close she was, how good she smelled, how pretty she looked. "So, no ouzo," he said. "What do you like to drink?"

"White wine, but don't let me stop you from drinking ouzo."

No way he'd be drinking ouzo. If he kissed her, he wasn't about to taste like the licorice liquor she hated. Then reminded himself that kissing wouldn't be a good idea. "Have you ever tried retsina?"

"No. That's a Greek wine, isn't it?"

"Another thing that can be an acquired taste. Some people think it tastes like turpentine, or pinesap, but by the third glass, you'd like it."

"Third glass? Are you trying to get me drunk to take advantage of me?" He hadn't seen this mischievousness in her eyes before, and his heart beat a little faster as he thought of ways they could take advantage of one another and how much fun that would be. "How about I stick with sauvignon blanc?"

"I'm a gentleman, remember?" A gentleman who wanted to kiss her, wanted to know whether this attraction, this awareness, went both ways. Except he shouldn't want to know, because if she felt any of what he was feeling he'd find it even harder to keep their relationship strictly friendly and uncomplicated. "We'll get both, since you like to try new things."

"Far be it from me to not try a drink that tastes like pinesap."

Even as he grinned he wondered how her mouth would

taste no matter what she'd been drinking, and yanked his gaze from her lips, handing her the menu. "What sounds good?"

She handed it back. "You've heard the phrase, 'it's all Greek to me'? Unfortunately, studying ancient languages doesn't help me read one word of that."

"Sorry. How about I order a few of my favorites, then we'll go from there? Grilled octopus, *keftedes*, which are fried meatballs I personally could eat a dozen of, peppers stuffed with feta, and olives from the valleys by Kastorini to start."

"Sounds wonderful, except maybe the octopus. Can't wrap my brain around eating those little suction cups."

She gave an exaggerated shudder that was almost as cute as her ouzo expression. "Maybe you haven't had them cooked properly. And I'm beginning to learn you're a little overdramatic at times, perhaps."

"Perhaps." Her lips curved. "I love that the olives are from that sea of trees. It's incredible how many there are."

"Over a million. And many are over a hundred years old."

"A hundred? That's a nanosecond in Greece."

"Says the archaeologist, not arborist."

They smiled at one another until the waiter showed up to take their order, then brought the wine. Andros let himself enjoy looking at her over his glass. Wished he could see her with that long, thick, silky hair of hers out of its restraint and spilling down her back. He nearly reached to grasp the ponytail in his palm, wanting to stroke the length of its softness with his hand, but stopped himself.

"Tell me about being mom to your sisters. How many do you have?" he asked, as much to keep from thinking about touching her as genuinely wanting to know more about her. Then instantly regretted the question, surprised to see the beautiful eyes that had been relaxed and smiling become instantly shadowed.

"Three younger. One just graduated college, one's a sophomore, and the youngest, Helen, is on a summer internship in Peru before she starts as a freshman in a few more weeks." She stayed quiet for a moment, and Andros was trying to figure out if he should start a different subject when she finally spoke. "My parents were the archaeologists who started this dig and were killed that first summer. That's how I came to take over the mom role. Did a pretty bad job of it half the time, but I tried."

"I'm so sorry. What happened?" His heart kicked at what a shocking loss that had to be. He put down his glass and rested his hand between her shoulder blades. "You must have barely been, what, twenty-two?"

She nodded. "I'd graduated college that May, and just a couple weeks later they came here to start working the dig. I was home watching my sisters. My parents were excavating a new pit and were inside it deciding how much deeper they could use machinery, when an earthquake hit. The rock walls collapsed on them."

"Dear God. I remember that earthquake's epicenter was right here on Mount Parnassus, and that some of the buildings in Delphi and Kastorini were pretty badly damaged. I can't believe your parents…" He trailed off, unable to imagine it. The shock of such a freak thing taking both of her parents at once.

"I know. It was…unbelievable. Devastating for us girls."

"That small earthquake a couple weeks ago must have scared the hell out of you. Brought it all back." She nodded, and Andros's chest squeezed at the pain on her face. "So you took over for your parents, taking care of your sisters."

"The court allowed me to become guardian. I'd watched them every summer anyway, when our parents were gone on digs. We managed. Survived. I'd planned to start grad school, but had to put it off for a few years. I hate that I'm so behind what my parents groomed me to accomplish by now. Far behind all that they'd accomplished by my age, but there wasn't another good option. It's...I knew it was what they would have expected, even though they would've been disappointed that school had to come second." The tears came then, squeezing his chest even tighter, and she quickly dabbed them before they could fall. "Sorry. Stupid to cry after all this time."

He couldn't figure out how much of her tears were from grief over her parents, or the pain of believing, somehow, that they would be disappointed with her. Surely she didn't really feel that way, considering how she'd stepped up and put her sisters first. At twenty-two, he'd been damned self-absorbed, for sure.

He took her chin in his fingers, turned her face so she was looking at him. "Never be sorry for being human and feeling pain, Laurel. Grief stays with us, sometimes for a long time. Until we learn what we have to from it to move on."

The way she forced a smile through her tears gripped his heart, and without thinking he lowered his head an inch and touched his lips to hers. Softly, gently, meaning to soothe. They were soft and pliant beneath his, and for a long moment the kiss was painfully, wonderfully, deliciously sweet.

They slowly pulled apart, separating just a few inches, staring at one another. Heat and desire rushed through his veins like a freight train just from his lips on hers. A heat and desire that had him wanting to go back for more, deeper and hotter. He fiercely reminded himself she was hurting, that he was supposed to be offering comfort. Not consumed with the need to lay her down on the cushioned seat and kiss her breathless.

Her eyes were wide, and inside that deep blue he thought he saw a flicker of what might be the same awareness, the same desire. Just as he began to ease away from her, she surprised the hell out of him, wrapping her palm behind his head, closing the gap between them and kissing him back. He found himself grasping her ponytail as he'd wanted to earlier, gently tugging her hair to tip her face to the perfect angle, letting him delve deeper. Her lips parted, drew him in as he learned the dizzying taste of Laurel Evans.

"Ahem. Your peppers and *keftedes*."

They both slowly broke apart, and Andros struggled to remember they were in a public restaurant before he turned to the waiter. "Thanks."

The waiter responded with a grin and a little wink at Andros before he moved on to another seat farther down the promenade. He looked at Laurel, not surprised to see her cheeks were a deep pink. Hell, he had a feeling his might be too, and didn't know what to say. Maybe something along the lines of, *Sorry, I didn't mean to try to suck your tongue like you were the first* meze, *but you taste so good I couldn't help myself.*

He cleared his throat. "I—"

"You were wrong, you know," she interrupted in a soft voice.

"Wrong?"

"That I'd need three glasses of retsina before I'd think

it tasted good. Just one taste from your mouth, and I know it's very, very delicious."

That surprised a short laugh out of him. "And I've come to have a new appreciation for the very appetizing flavor of sauvignon blanc." Her words, her smile, the heat in her eyes that reflected his own, nearly sent him back for another taste of her, but he somehow managed to keep his mouth to himself. He slid the plates of food closer to her. "Try the *keftedes* alone, and then with the *tziaziki*. Which, by the way, we either both have to eat, or neither of us."

"Why?"

"Because I don't want to smell like garlic if you don't. But if we both do? Nothing like a garlicky *tziaziki* kiss, I promise." And why had he brought up the subject of kissing when he was trying to behave?

He was glad to see every trace of sadness was gone, replaced by a slightly wicked smile that sent his blood pumping all over again. "Don't think it could beat the last one, but I'm more than willing to give it a try."

"I doubt it could beat the last one either. Guess we'll have to find out."

The memory of that kiss had the air practically humming as they looked at one another, and Andros knew he had to bring the conversation back to something less exciting to ratchet down his libido. Either that, or leave and steam up the windows of his car.

And that idea was so appealing, he nearly threw money on the table and grabbed her hand to get going on it.

"So," he said, stuffing half a meatball into his mouth to drown out the flavor of Laurel, "I assume you're going to shut down the cave dig for the moment."

"Shut it down?"

"Yes. With John sick now too, it's logical until we get some test results back."

"We only have a few weeks left of the dig as it is. And no one has any idea if they're sick because of something in the caves or not. For all we know it could be something a tourist brought to the hotel. Or even coincidence and not the same illness."

He was surprised as hell at her attitude and the suddenly mulish expression on her face, especially considering she'd seen how sick the three were and had seemed as worried as he was. "True. But it makes sense to wait until we get the test results. How could a few days matter?"

"Every hour matters. There'll be no more funding for this project. Which means whatever we have left to unearth has to be discovered soon, or it'll stay buried."

"Things will stay buried anyway. Unless a dig lasts indefinitely, I'd think you could never be sure what might still be there."

"True. And we have used satellite imaging and ground-penetrating radar and magnetometry to help us find what's still there. But those things are less reliable when it comes to the caves."

"So you're willing to risk someone else getting sick to give yourself a few extra days' digging." He couldn't help but feel frustrated, even angry about that, especially when an image of Laurel lying in a hospital bed, sick and nearly unable to breathe, disturbingly injected itself into his mind.

"I need to finish this dig for my parents." She frowned at him for a long moment before she finally spoke again. "But I'll compromise. I'll offer the team a choice about working on the mountain, and we'll stay out of the caves until the test results are back. Unless you can prove to me the pneumonia is definitely related to the dig, though, I'm not shutting it down."

CHAPTER SIX

"I CAN'T BELIEVE Kristin stayed at the hotel when we're already down three people." Becka sat back on her haunches and pushed her hair under her hat as she looked over at Laurel.

"It's fine, Becka." Laurel pulled a bag and pen from her apron to label the potsherd she'd dug up. "The reason I shared Dr. Drakoulias's concerns with the team was to give everyone the option to sit it out until the test results are back, if that's what they're most comfortable doing."

"But how could it have anything to do with the dig? We've been here two months with nobody getting sick."

"I agree. But until we have confirmation that it's not a fungal infection, I think everybody has the right to be extra cautious if they want, and we'll stay out of the caves for now."

"I don't get why he thinks there might be something in the caves. Mel hasn't been in there since June."

"It's possible she got something from Tom. But I figure it's more likely they got some random virus from some long-gone tourist while we had dinner in Delphi, or someone who stayed at the hotel. Though Dr. Drakoulias and I have both talked to management there, and as far as they know, nobody's been sick."

"So we should just keep at it, don't you think?"

"I'm planning to, but, again, I understand people being concerned. We all want this dig to end on a high note. Hopefully the three of them will be fine soon, and we'll find there's nothing to worry about." She prayed that was true, and that the high note was a certain big, knockout find she hadn't given up on.

"Well, I'm not worried about it. And I've gotta say, I'd rather be in the nice, cool cave than out here all day. I'd forgotten how beastly hot it is."

"Working in heat, cold and rain is part of the gig sometimes. And don't forget about the snakes up here. Gotta be tough to be a digger." Laurel smiled and tossed a water bottle to Becka. "We'll quit for the day in about an hour. Hydrate and take a little break."

Becka stood and swigged down some water. Laurel's smile grew at how much the girl reminded her of her sister Ariadne, and as she was wondering what her siblings were doing, Becka interrupted her thoughts with a chilling scream. Her heart knocked against her chest when Becka dropped the bottle and fell, writhing, onto the ground.

"What's wrong?" Laurel leaped to her feet and ran the few feet between them.

"Oh, God, my leg! What…?"

Laurel followed the girl's wide-eyed gaze, horrified to see that beneath the hand clutching at her calf, blood gushed down her leg, a shocking amount pooling around the dirt and stones she lay sprawled on.

"Becka. Let me see." Laurel's heart pounding now, she dropped to her knees and instantly saw what had happened. "I think your trowel cut you."

"I'm so stupid," the girl moaned. "You always said

never to stick our trowel in our back pocket, but I did, didn't I? Did it cut through my shorts and fall out? Is it bad?"

"It's a pretty good gash." That was an understatement, but the last thing Laurel needed was for the girl to faint or go into shock. "Let me get it wrapped up, then we'll have to get you down the mountain somehow."

Her mind frantically spun to first-aid classes she'd learned, and she prayed she remembered right. The injuries her sisters occasionally came home with had been pretty minor. Definitely nothing like this. Laurel had seen a few injuries on the digs she'd been able to go on close to home but hadn't been in charge. Why hadn't she paid more attention to how they'd stopped the bleeding?

Okay, she reminded herself grimly, freaking out and staring at it wasn't going to fix it. She ran to the supply box and dug through until she found gauze wraps on the bottom and the duct tape she'd used over her bandage. But when she kneeled next to Becka, the amount of blood pouring through the girl's fingers sent fear surging down her spine, and she knew she had to do something more than just wrap it.

"I'm going to try to hold it together and put pressure on it for a few minutes to slow the bleeding before I wrap it. Okay?"

Becka nodded. Just as Laurel began to lay a piece of gauze lengthwise on the cut, the girl let out a little moan, and Laurel looked up at her. Lord, she was staring at the blood, her face turning the ghastliest white. "Don't faint on me now." That was the last thing either of them needed, and Laurel quickly tried to move her into a sitting position.

"Sit up and put your head between your knees." It

wasn't easy to press on the wound at the same time she pushed the girl's head down with the other. "Deep breaths. I'm going to press hard on your leg to stop the bleeding, so be prepared."

Becka thankfully followed directions. Every muscle tense, Laurel tried to gently bring the edges of the wound together, then pressed hard again. Becka cried out, biting her lip until Laurel was afraid it might start bleeding too. "I'm sorry. Hang in there. Once I get it wrapped up, I'll take you to Dr. Drakoulias."

As soon as the words were out of her mouth, her heart knocked again. What if the man wasn't in Kastorini, but back at the Sophia Elias hospital or somewhere else? Then she remembered she had his phone number. She'd call him as soon as she could get a cell signal.

The fear filling her chest eased a bit, and she took a deep breath. It would be okay. No matter where he was, she'd be able to ask for his help. How much that thought calmed her was a little shocking, considering she hadn't relied on anyone else for much help in a long time.

She just hoped he wasn't still annoyed with her the way he'd been last night. Then wondered why she'd let it bother her. Her job, her responsibility to her parents and the future they'd wanted for her were all wrapped up in this dig, and she couldn't care if anyone approved of how they finished things up or not.

"Can you press down on it the way I was while I wrap it? Try not to move the gauze I already have on there."

"Okay," Becka said in a strained voice, reaching down to do as Laurel asked. Finally she had it tightly wrapped, hoping to heck it wasn't so tight that it cut off the poor girl's circulation. She sat back on her heels and stared at the gauze, relieved that it wasn't turning red with more blood.

"Okay, let's go. I'll help you stand, then we'll grab Jason so he can help us."

With Becka's arm across Laurel's shoulders, they awkwardly moved down the path toward grid eight. She couldn't see Jason, and prayed he was down in the pit where he should be. By the time they got to it, Laurel already felt nerves and muscles pinching from trying to hold Becka's weight as she limped. "Jason! Are you here?"

"I'm here," a voice said.

Laurel nearly sagged in relief. "Becka's hurt. I need your help."

In an instant, Jason came running up the makeshift stone steps from the pit, a worried frown on his face. "What happened?"

"I stupidly put my trowel in my shorts pocket, and it cut through and dove into my leg," Becka said through clenched teeth.

"Rookie mistake." Jason gave Becka a little smile as he lifted his hand and stroked her cheek, the gesture tugging at Laurel's heart. She'd thought maybe the two college kids were becoming sweet on one another, but hadn't paid that much attention. "You okay?"

"I think so. Hurts like crazy, though, and I'll probably have some ugly scar."

"Scars from a dig are a badge of honor. Makes you all the more interesting."

"You think?" The girl rolled her eyes at him, finally looking less freaked out.

"Oh, yeah. Not that you needed to be more interesting."

"Okay, enough of the mushy stuff, you two," Laurel joked, glad to be feeling less freaked out too, after the first shock of it all. "Let's get her down the mountain to my car so I can take her to the clinic. It's pretty deep, and I'm sure she'll need stitches."

It was easier with Jason's help, or, really, with Laurel helping Jason, who took on most of Becka's weight. Laurel called Andros a few times, relieved when she finally got a signal and he answered.

"Is something wrong, Laurel?"

How had he known it was her? The man must have put her contact information in his phone. That thought shouldn't have affected her, since he probably did it for professional reasons, but she couldn't help feeling absurdly pleased about it. "Becka has a serious gash in her leg from a trowel. Are you at the clinic?"

"I'm here. Bring her right in."

Jason got Becka tucked into the car and hovered there as he fastened her seat belt. "I'd like to come with you, but I better get back to work. At this rate, we're not going to finish what we've started if I don't."

"I'll be coming back to the dig after we get her fixed up and settled in at the hotel. I'll let you know how she is," Laurel promised, partly to relieve his mind and partly to get going before there was some long, drawn-out goodbye. Becka's leg needed prompt attention. And he was right—they'd never get finished at this rate unless everyone who could still work did overtime.

Andros must have been watching for them, because as soon as she pulled up in front of the clinic, he strode out of the door and helped Becka inside, Laurel following.

"You can come along if you want, or you can stay in

the waiting room," he said, speaking to Laurel over his shoulder.

"I'll come." If Becka was anything like Laurel's sisters, she'd want someone by her side. They might believe they were all grown-up, but inside they still needed someone to turn to for comfort.

Laurel's chest felt heavy when the memories unexpectedly bombarded her. She'd been Becka's age exactly when she'd fallen into the dark hole of grief her parents' deaths had left her and her sisters with. All those summers she'd been stuck home watching her sisters while her parents were working had seemed hard. Then she'd learned that had been nothing compared to what it felt like for that comforting support to be forever gone.

"After I take a look, I'll have to thoroughly wash it out, okay?" Andros settled Becka by a low sink that was really more like an open shower, before his eyes met Laurel's. "Christina's not here right now. Want to help me get some supplies?"

"Of course."

She followed him into an exam room, and he pulled gauze, pads and a bottle of some liquid from a closet, handing them to her. "Were you with her when it happened?" he asked as he grabbed some sealed bags of what looked like syringes and suture kits and who knew what.

"Yes. It's a long, pretty deep gash. Not sure exactly how deep, but it bled a lot."

"What did you do for it?"

"Tried to bring the edges of the wound together, then pressed on it a while to stop the bleeding. Seemed to work well enough, then I bandaged it and brought her here."

"Sounds like maybe you should have forgotten about digging for a living and become a doctor."

Fascinated by that unexpected dimple that poked into one cheek as he paused to look at her, she nearly dropped the gauze and bottle and fumbled to hang on to them. "Since I feared I might pass out when I first saw all that blood, I think I chose the right career path."

"Think you'll faint if you watch me stitch it up?" he asked, a mischievous twinkle in his eyes. "If so, please stay in the waiting room. Last thing either of us needs is for you to keel over and crack open your beautiful head."

"I want to be there for Becka." She was aware of a deep feeling of relief that he obviously wasn't still irritated with her. Deeper than it should have been. And how ridiculous was it that him calling her head "beautiful" gave her a little glow inside as well? "Since I'm not responsible anymore for whether she lives or dies, I think I'll be okay."

He chuckled then instantly became all business when they walked into Becka's room and Andros pulled a rolling stool up next to her. "Let's take a look."

Laurel watched him carefully peel off the layers of gauze and wouldn't admit for the world that she had to look away a couple times when she saw the long, raw slice in Becka's calf that again oozed a trickle of blood.

"Nice first-aid job, Ms. Evans," he said, glancing up at her with a smile in his dark eyes. "I'm impressed."

"Thanks. Hope I don't have to do it again."

His eyes crinkled at the corners as he held her gaze for a moment, and darned if her heart didn't skip a beat before he turned to Becka. "I'm going to put a lidocaine-epinephrine mix all around the skin, then inject it with some painkillers before I wash it out. This part's going to hurt, I'm sorry to say."

Laurel and Becka both watched him gently but efficiently smooth on a liquid with a cotton pad, all around the edges of the torn skin. When he was done, he looked up at Becka, his dark eyes sympathetic. "Going to inject the painkiller into the wound now, which isn't going to feel good either. But then it'll be nice and numb when I stitch it up. Okay?"

Becka nodded, then gave a little crying gasp before she bit her lip hard as she had on the mountain. Laurel reached for the girl's hand, not sure if she was comforting Becka or both of them, again thinking of her own sisters and how upset she'd be if they were in pain like this. She remembered many small boo-boos when they'd smothered her with grateful hugs and kisses after she'd patched them up, managing to smile at the sweet memories.

She had to turn away a couple times as he repeatedly stuck the needle down into the open wound. "Will you think less of me if I say I'm glad my parents were archaeologists and didn't groom me to be a doctor instead?"

Andros glanced up at her with a smile. "Nothing would make me think less of you. And I have a feeling you'd be great at anything you put your mind to. Even medicine." He set aside the needle and vial, and attached a hose to the faucet.

"Thank God," Becka said fervently. "That was awful."

"I know. That's no fun, but you're doing great." He patted her knee. "Washing it out isn't a picnic either, so hang in there for me."

He hosed down the angry wound, washing it thoroughly as he'd done with Laurel's hand. She started to worry that poor Becka would bite right through her lip if she chomped on it any harder.

"When Dr. Drakoulias had to wash out the cut on my hand, I thought he might drain the entire Gulf of Corinth before he was done," she said, trying to distract the girl with a joke.

Becka managed a little laugh, thankfully. "Maybe then they wouldn't be able to catch any octopus to serve up at dinner, which Jason hounds me to eat every time. I can't get why he loves them. Doesn't he understand that those little suction cups weird me out?"

"Laurel thinks octopus suckers are a delicacy, don't you? Preferably washed down with ouzo." Andros's gaze lifted to hers for a brief moment, his dark eyes filled with that mischievous twinkle again as he winked.

"A delicacy if you're a whale or a Greek."

Andros grinned, and Becka laughed before the sound morphed into a pained yelp. "Sorry. Not much longer."

Laurel sent up a prayer of thanks that the washing out was finally over, except the stitching would probably be an ordeal for the poor girl, too. Andros leaned back to pat Becka's shoulder this time. "The worst is over. Thankfully, right? The stitching is going to take a while because I need to do it in several layers. But believe it or not, it won't hurt at all."

"Find that hard to believe," Becka grumbled.

"Can't blame you. And I find it hard to believe you cut yourself this deeply with a trowel—that takes a special talent." He smiled, and that adorable dimple poked into his cheek as he began to stitch.

"Yeah, I have special talents all right. Clumsy ones."

His amused eyes met Laurel's and she found her heart beating a little harder for no reason at all. "I need to repair this cut in the muscle first, to stop it from bleeding, with stitches that will dissolve. Then the subcutaneous layer of flesh, which will reduce tension on the wound and help keep it closed and healing. Then, lastly, smaller nylon stitches that will help it look better when it heals."

"Jason said having a dig scar is a badge of honor," Becka said. "But if you can keep it from looking Frankenstein-ish, that would be great."

"Even though Laurel has no faith in the local, backwater Greek doctor, I promise no Frankenstein."

"I didn't say...oh, never mind." The amused teasing in the dark depths of his eyes told her an embarrassed protest was exactly what he'd been hoping for, and she wasn't going to go there again.

Laurel tried to keep up a bit of light conversation with Becka to take the girl's mind off her leg. Even while she was talking about the dig and asking things like what all the team had done in Delphi last night while she was out with Andros, she found her mind mostly on him.

Watching how smoothly, efficiently and impressively he stitched Becka's wound, obviously having done it hundreds of times. Noticing, as she had when he'd worked on her own hand, how dark his lashes were, how his features really were reminiscent of a classical Greek statue, how beautifully shaped his lips were as he slightly pursed them in concentration. Remembering how they'd felt against hers, which made her feel tingly and breathless and...and...

Stupid. Above and beyond any attraction she felt for the man, and there was no point in denying she had plenty, this dig came first. And with three team members in the hospital and Becka now likely out of commission for who knew how long, it was getting scarily harder to imagine she could make happen what she wanted to accomplish before they ran out of time.

She inhaled, willing her heart rate to pretend it wasn't

thrown all out of whack just from his nearness. Time to bring business back to the forefront, get Becka to the hotel and herself back on the mountain.

"Since I forgot I was supposed to lure you to the mountain so you'd feel obligated to give us free medical care, I'll need a bill from you," she said.

"I'll have the office manager get it to you. I know US universities have insurance for teams like yours. And my yacht payment is due."

She tried hard to be immune to the power of his smile, but failed miserably. "Then why...?" Her voice trailed off. She'd been about to ask why he hadn't given her a bill for her hand, then wasn't sure she wanted to hear the answer. If it was because of this attraction that simmered between them despite her wishing it didn't, she didn't want to know. Having it verbalized instead of just zinging in the air around them might make it even harder to resist.

"You have a yacht?" Becka looked wide-eyed at him as he finished slathering on the same antibiotic he'd put on Laurel's hand.

"Well, a yacht by my standards, but probably not by Aristotle Onassis's." His eyes were focused on wrapping Becka's leg with layers of gauze, a different gauze wrap and elastic bandage on top of it all. "It's a twenty-five-foot boat with a two-fifty-horsepower motor. Perfect to take you both octopus fishing on your day off."

Becka laughed, and Laurel wondered how in the world she was supposed to resist lusting after a Greek god who cared for his patients, seemed to be a good dad, had a delicious sense of humor and even more delicious mouth?

"Ready, Becka? Your leg feel okay?"

"I'm sure it'll hurt like crazy later, but right now it's

nicely numb." She turned to Andros, who was scribbling on a pad. "Thanks a lot, Dr. Drakoulias."

"You're welcome. You'll need to get crutches to keep weight off it for a few days, and I have a couple prescriptions for you that you can fill either at the pharmacy next door, or in Delphi. Just—" The sound of his phone ringing interrupted him. He fished it from his pocket, and, glancing at it, frowned. "Excuse me a minute."

His serious expression sent a little jab of concern poking at Laurel's chest. She prayed it wasn't some bad news about the Wagners or John. That kick of concern heightened her awareness of him as she watched him stride from the room, his butt perfectly encased in his dress pants, his broad shoulders tugging the fabric of his shirt, his black hair catching the bright overhead light, making it gleam.

"Wow, Laurel," Becka said, turning to her with awe in her voice. "I didn't really see him very well at the caves when John was sick. He's, like, wow."

"Yeah. He is." Hadn't that pretty much been her first thought too? Even more so now that she knew how it felt to kiss him. Though she was going to stop thinking about that if it killed her.

"Anybody could tell he's attracted to you. If you don't go for that, you're crazy."

Oh, yeah, she wanted to go for "that." It might be crazy not to, but it would be just as crazy to get into a quickie relationship right now. Except every time she was around the man, her resolve to keep her distance seemed to disintegrate, and kissing him became the forefront thought in her head. Maybe Ate, the spirit of mischief, was lurking on this mountain, luring her into infatuation and recklessness.

The thought made her smile, thinking of how her sisters always rolled their eyes when she said things like that, as though mythical beings just might be real after all. "This dig is important to me, Becka." No one but the Wagners knew exactly how important. "I admit I'm tempted. Really tempted. But I just don't have time, and we'll be out of here in a few weeks."

"Yeah, I know. But still, you could—"

They both turned to the door as Andros walked back in, his expression seeming lighter, yet at the same time hard to read.

"That was Dr. Dimitri Galanos. He has interesting news."

Laurel stood and moved next to him, practically holding her breath. "What news?"

"First, John is unfortunately still on the ventilator, though they're taking good care of him. But the Wagners continue to improve, and their test results are back."

"And?"

"It's apparently some type of virus, though they're still not sure what." His eyes met Laurel's. "However, it's definitely not a fungal infection. So it appears they didn't get it from the caves."

CHAPTER SEVEN

"So IF IT's not a fungal infection, why do you still have that look on your face? I thought—" Taryn interrupted herself to tug her son's shirt as he stood on his chair. "Petros, sit down, please, and play your game. Lunch will be here soon."

"What look?" Andros rebooted the tablet his wriggling daughter held, pulled up a new game to occupy Petros, then gave his attention back to Taryn. "This is why we should've just cleaned your fridge out and eaten leftovers. Our children are monsters when we go out."

"Not monsters, Daddy! Fairies!"

"Uh-uh! I'm a monster, Uncle Andros!"

Both their protests and dark frowns were so indignant, he had to laugh. "Okay, an impatient ants-in-her-pants fairy, and a messy monster. Have another olive."

He handed both the kids olives. He watched his daughter pop it into her mouth, then fish the pit out with her small fingers, filled all over again with amazement that she belonged to him. His own flesh and blood in the adorable little package that was Cassandra Anne Drakoulias.

It hadn't been the way he'd expected to start a family someday. Making a baby with a woman he hardly remembered, and who hadn't felt a need to tell him about his own daughter. If Alison hadn't died, he might *never* have known. That tore at his heart and sent the guilt of how carelessly he'd lived his life even deeper into his bones.

But from the very first instant he'd met his child, he'd realized what an incredible blessing she was. God's way of helping him rethink how he lived his life when he hadn't even realized he needed to.

"Mom would be horrified if we ate leftovers after church. She'd hop the next plane from Scotland and be fixing her usual massive feast for us like she does every Sunday. And scold me for not spending the day cooking."

He chuckled, because it was true. "She'd be almost as horrified to see us in a restaurant. Good news is she will never know, and she'll be back to cook and fuss over us in no time. In fact, I'm dying for her *avgolemono* soup, which you refuse to fix for me."

"Fix it for yourself." His sister smirked, because she knew his cooking skills were practically nil. Something he should probably work on. "Anyway, tell me why you're still frowning and deep in thought about the pneumonia," she said, bringing back the original subject, as usual. Once his sister had something she wanted to talk about, she was going to finish no matter what. "It's not a fungal infection, so it's not from the archaeological dig, and not something the workers are going to spread around town. Right?"

"We may know what it isn't, but we don't know what it is. Maybe they were just in the wrong place at the wrong time and sat next to somebody who passed it on. But maybe it's something else."

"Like what?"

Exactly what was bothering him. "I don't know. Di

doesn't know. But I have a strange gut feeling that this isn't over."

"I remember a lot of your gut feelings just being hunger pangs," his sister said.

"Which is why you should have let me eat your *pastitsio* instead of coming all the way to Delphi for lunch." He grinned, willing his brain to stop thinking about the mystery. Time would tell whether he was right or wrong, and he hoped like hell he was wrong.

"Daddy, it's your pretty friend who knows lots about fairies!" Cassie said excitedly, pointing to the doorway.

He looked up and his heart gave a kick when he saw Laurel standing there with a few others from the dig, startlingly elegant in a long blue dress that skimmed her ankles and loosely hugged her curves. Elegant, and at the same time natural, with her beautiful hair in that thick ponytail she always wore it in, and little makeup on her exotic features.

Almost as though she felt his eyes on her, her gaze lifted to his and held, her lush lips parted in surprise until someone jabbed her arm and she turned to follow the host to their table. He had the urge to catch up with her, talk her into having lunch with them, but stopped himself. He knew a number of people in this place, and it wouldn't take much for elbows to nudge and knowing smiles and winks to be sent his way, starting gossip that no longer applied now that he had Cassie to think about.

"Can we ask her to eat with us, Daddy?"

Was his daughter a mind reader now? "Looks like she's eating with the dig crew, so let's not bother her."

"I won't bother her. I just want to ask a couple things."

Before he even realized what she was doing, Cassie slid from the chair and ran across the room to Laurel's table, with Petros following on her heels. "Cassie, you—ah, hell."

"Why 'ah, hell'?" His sister tipped her head at him with a quizzical look. "Seemed like she likes kids when I met her. She have the hots for you? Or is it mutual?"

"Why either one of those? Maybe we dislike each other."

"Yeah, right." His sister gave an indelicate snort. "I've never known a single girl to meet you and not be interested. And for the record, I've seen the way you look at her."

"I'm looking at her as someone connected to my patients. I'm building my reputation as an upstanding doctor and all-around good dad. Not looking for a woman."

"Uh-huh. Tell that to someone who doesn't know you that well. I'm well aware you have the occasional fling when you go out of town."

"I'm not a monk, but I only see a woman when I'm sure she just wants a fling too." He'd obviously have to try harder to keep his attraction to Laurel hidden. At least his sister couldn't see inside his brain as well, because she'd also learn that Laurel featured front and center in any number of fantasies at the moment. Then Taryn would laugh and shake her head and point out that there'd always been someone featured in his fantasies, and he'd have to point out—again—that was the old Andros, not the new, improved one.

"And of course I like to look at her," he continued. "She's a beautiful woman. But she's only here for a few weeks, and having some short thing with her wouldn't be worth the whole town gossiping about me and Cassie hearing it."

"So when are you going to give a relationship a chance to grow into something bigger than a fling?"

"You know as well as I do that I'm not capable of that kind of relationship."

"I don't believe that. Just because you used to go through women like Thea Stella goes through tissues, doesn't mean you can't have a long-term relationship. The lines to become Mrs. Andros Drakoulias started forming when you were about fifteen."

"I think you have to want one to have one."

"Maybe you just never met the right woman."

"Glad you have faith in me, but everyone in this town thinks different."

"People will always talk. I know I'm still on the subject list, having Petros without a wedding ring or a man who wanted to be involved in his life." His sister sighed. "So what if you were a bit of a playboy back in the day and gave the town some entertainment? That was a long time ago."

"Showing up in town with a two-year-old, shocking the hell out of everyone, wasn't all that long ago." After the phone call from Alison's brother, telling him about Cassie, the direction of his life had changed. Thankfully no one in Alison's family could take his little girl, or he might still not have her in his life. That second, he'd known becoming a more responsible man and moving to Kastorini with his daughter was his destiny, despite having to deal with the perennial tongue waggers. "One of these days, though, the past will be forgotten, if I behave myself."

"You never cared about the gossip before and you shouldn't now."

He glanced over at his daughter, talking animatedly to everyone at Laurel's table. "I have Cassie to think about."

"And I have Petros. We can flaunt our heathen ways together."

"We've always been experts at that." He had to grin. "How about we flaunt our newfound upstanding citizenship equally well?" The waiter brought their food, and Andros stood. "I'll get the kids."

He took one step and saw that Laurel was already headed their way, Cassie and Petros on either side of her, holding her hands.

"Lose something?" She smiled at Taryn before her eyes met his. Until he realized the moment went on a little too long and he quickly shifted his attention to Cassie.

"I did. My little fairy flitted away as soon as she saw you come in."

"And my monster followed," Taryn said.

"I asked Laurel if she'd come see our fairy house and tell us how we can get the fairies to move in."

A flood of instant pleasure filled Andros at the thought of her coming to Kastorini, spending time with him that afternoon at his home, while at the same time knowing it wasn't the best idea. "Miss Laurel probably has things she needs to do, Cassie."

"It's Sunday. Sunday is for playing," Cassie said, that cute frown on her face again. He had to smile, reaching out to smooth her brow with his fingers.

"True. But Miss Laurel may already have plans for how she wants to play today."

The second the words were out of his mouth, he knew exactly how he'd like to play with Laurel. His eyes met hers, and damned if his thoughts weren't reflected right back at him.

"At the risk of Cassie scolding me, I do have work to do today, since we're behind schedule," Laurel said, breaking the heated eye contact that somehow happened between them again. She looked down at his daughter. "But I'd enjoy stopping by for a short time to see your house and give a fairy-attracting consultation. It's the least I can do since your dad fixed up my hand for me."

"Speaking of which, I want to look at it again," Andros said.

"Thanks, but it's healing nicely."

"How did you get your boo-boo?" Cassie lifted up the hand she was holding, still wrapped in a bandage, and examined it with an interest that made Andros smile again. Who knew? Maybe his girl would become a doctor one day, carrying on the family tradition.

"I stabbed it with a potsherd. That's a piece of pottery that's broken, and we try to find all the pieces so we can put it back together again."

"I'm glad my daddy fixed it for you. He's a good fixer."

"Yes, I've seen that he is." She looked at him again, and the warm admiration in her eyes had him wondering what she saw in his own. "Your food's going to get cold. You go ahead and eat and I'll come down at, what, two o'clock?"

"Park at the clinic, and I'll meet you there. We'll walk around town some and I'll fill you in on a little of its history on the way to our house."

"I'll be there." She patted both children on their heads and walked back to her table, her rear end gorgeously round and sexy in that clingy skirt of hers as she moved across the room.

Pretty oblivious to his lunch as he chewed, he became

aware of Cassie jabbing her knife into the meat on her plate, and he quickly cut it for her as his sister softly laughed.

"What?" Though he damned well knew what. That it had been written all over his face, which he'd have to better control when Laurel came to town.

"Looking at her as someone connected to your patients?" Taryn's eyes gleamed with amusement. "Right. More like dessert."

"I want dessert, Mommy. Something really sweet," Petros said.

"Like uncle, like nephew." She chuckled, still looking at Andros with that sisterly smirk firmly in place. "Which means Kastorini's female population has much to fear in another ten years, Petros. Or much to look forward to, depending on your point of view."

Glad that Christina was on call for the clinic, Andros caught up on paperwork in his office. Not very efficiently, though, since he kept seeing Laurel's beautiful face and shapely body in that dress of hers that made him want to skim his hands along its fluid lines. Feel her curves beneath it. Kept interrupting his work and thoughts to walk to the clinic's big front window to see if she had arrived.

Since when did he act like a smitten schoolboy in the throes of his first crush? That first crush was so long ago he could barely recall it, probably because it had been followed by plenty of others before he'd left for school in the US. Even more after he'd arrived there, where the world, and the number of women in it, got a whole lot bigger than his hometown of seven thousand people.

So why had Laurel gotten so thoroughly under his

skin, making him feel so oddly restless and itchy? Could it be because he'd spent the past two years showing he was a reformed man? Somehow, he didn't think so. There was some intangible thing about her that, for whatever reason, just called to him like some irresistible siren.

About to go back to his desk, or, more accurately, the desk he shared with his father, he spotted her dusty sedan on the road that rounded the steep curve beyond the bell tower.

And just like that, his chest felt light, his work and the mysterious virus forgotten, his restlessness replaced by focus. On her.

With a sudden pep in his step, he went outside, locking the clinic door behind him. The car nosed into one of the empty parking spaces, and the smile on Laurel's face seemed as carefree as he knew his own was.

He leaned in through the car's open window. "Are you Laurel Evans, fairy consultant?"

"I am." Her beautiful smile made his own widen. "And my fee for attracting fairies is very reasonable."

"What is your fee?"

"I'm still deciding."

The way she looked at him, her eyes a brilliant, sweet, hot blue, practically melted him where he stood, and he struggled against the urge to grab her up, sit in the driver's seat and pull her onto his lap to help her decide real quickly about that fee. Show he was ready and willing to pay up however she wanted him to.

Attracting fairies? Hell, if she attracted them as easily as she attracted him, his house would be overrun with the little things. He leaned closer to her in the hot car, a breath's distance away, her sweet, citrusy scent intensified by the heat of her body. "How long will it take to decide?"

"Hard to say, but I've learned to go with a gut feeling when I get one."

The breath rushed from his lungs and his heart bumped around in some off-kilter rhythm at her words. He knew exactly what he wanted, and from the way she was looking at him, she just might want the same thing. And how was he supposed to resist kissing her to find out? The question flitted into his mind, then promptly right out as, unable to think anymore, he closed the gap between them and kissed her.

Her mouth opened to his, moving, tasting, exploring in an excruciatingly slow dance that weakened his knees. Her kiss was sweet and hot and beyond irresistible. He cupped her cheek in his hand, stroking the fine bones there, the softness of her skin and wisps of hair adding another layer to the overwhelming sensual pleasure. He could feel her response, taste the small breathy gasps that touched his moist lips and sent him deepening the kiss until the loud, grumbling chug of a truck engine cut through his foggy brain.

He pulled his mouth from hers, barely aware of the truck disappearing with a cloud of black smoke puffing behind. Laurel's eyes were half-closed, her lips parted, their panting breaths sounding nearly as loud in the car as the truck had.

A jabbing against his ribs made him realize his torso was just about completely inside her car. He inhaled to catch his breath and clear his mind, thunking his head on the door frame as he extricated himself. A brain shake was probably something he badly needed.

"Ooh." She winced, scrunching up her face in that cute way she had. "That hurt?"

"No." Not nearly as much as stopping kissing her had.

Which proved again that the woman was a siren, attracting him with her song and smile until he quit looking where he was headed, crashing on the rocks for all the world to see.

Hadn't he promised himself not to give the town any new gossip material? While getting it on with Laurel was about all he could think of at that moment, in a few weeks she'd be gone. If Cassie had to hear yakking about what a playboy her father still was, asking questions he didn't want to answer to a four-year-old, he'd hate himself for his weakness.

"Just leave your car here." He turned away from the question in her eyes, opening the car door and grasping her elbow with the hope anyone watching would just see it as a cordial gesture. "I'll be your Kastorini tour guide."

"Are you as good a tour guide as you are a doctor?"

"Not sure. You'll have to let me know if I'm good."

The heat and humor that sparked in her eyes made him think of that mind-blowing kiss, shortening his breath all over again. He wondered why he'd said it that way. Must be his subconscious thinking about the crazy chemistry between them.

Strolling the streets with her next to him felt strangely natural and right. Just as he'd felt after they'd been at the hospital in Vlychosia, reaching to hold her hand seemed a lot more normal than resisting it, which he managed only with extreme effort. The air around and between them held an odd tension, an intense awareness, that crackling spark he always felt around her. But at the same time he felt relaxed and comfortable as he told her about the various landmarks in town.

That relaxation diminished when he realized he could feel the curious stares fixed on them from houses they passed and from second-story windows of homes above the various shops. From the grinning men sitting at tables outside tavernas, drinking coffee or something stronger as they heatedly discussed whatever was the subject of the day, and enjoyed watching and talking about anyone who walked by while they were doing it.

He glanced at Laurel and could see she was aware of it too. "Living in a small town is a bit different from living in a big city. Didn't think I'd come back here because of it."

"But here you are." She looked up at him, one blond eyebrow quirked. "So why did you? Aside from the obvious charm of the place?"

She thought it was charming to be stared at? Or was she able to look beyond that to see the generations of history and how it connected all of them in a strong bond of community you couldn't find in a big city?

"Just decided it was time to come back. Take my place as town doctor beside my father." No need to tell her the whole story. How he'd never been sure he wanted that for a lot of reasons, including the embarrassment his parents felt from his actions, and his sister's too. But the sudden situation with Cassie had shown him he needed it.

"Your father is a doctor too? Why haven't I met him?"

"He and my mother have taken advantage of me being back. They're traveling around Great Britain at the moment. Were supposed to come back this week, but decided Ireland had to be added on to the itinerary."

"How long have you been back?"

"Two years. They've been to the States and Canada, on various European tours, and to Iceland since then, believe it or not."

"My parents also loved traveling," she said softly, her

eyes instantly wistful and sad, as they had been last time she'd spoken of them. "Most of it for digs without us, but we did have a few great trips to national parks and Washington, DC, and other places they deemed too important for their girls to miss."

"Glad you have those memories with them." Now that he had Cassie, he couldn't imagine leaving her all summer every year, and wondered why Laurel's parents hadn't found a way to take their daughters with them. He let his arm slide around her shoulders to give her a brief, gentle hug. If he couldn't comfort someone in need, then to hell with those watching who might want to make something of it.

"I can see you give Cassie a lot of your time," she said, looking up at him with eyes that weren't quite so sad now. "That you're a good dad."

"I try to be." Wanted to be. And her words were a reminder, again, of why he shouldn't pursue the short but doubtless incredibly sweet time he knew he and Laurel could spend together before she left. "Thanks. Not sure that's always true, but I'm working on it." Working on it damned hard, if resisting the urge to touch her and kiss her counted. He shoved his hands in his pockets. "So here's the edge of town. The stone walls were built all the way down to the beach, complete with small angled cannon openings in the walls to defend against whoever wasn't in possession of the town and fortress at that moment."

"Is that a mosque? It doesn't look like a Greek church."

"It was. Built during Turkish rule. Later used as a schoolhouse, then a taverna, and now it's owned by someone who lives in Athens and comes to stay here occasionally."

He drew her to the outer wall to look down, where its

smooth stones ended at the beach far below and swimmers lounged on large, flat rocks tossed among the boulders and slapped by gentle waves. Farther down, colorful fishing boats bobbed at the long wooden dock. "Kastorini never had the same height advantage a lot of walled cities had during the Ottoman Empire, built way up at the top of a mountain, but we had other things going for us. Back in the day, citizens could see any approaching ships from far away on the gulf, and the mountain behind is so steep and prone to rock falls that it was pretty hard for invaders to sneak up on us."

"So your ancestors were likely a mix of Ottomans and Venetians, with a little Byzantine and Turkish spice thrown in with salt and pepper. You're like a finely flavored Greek stew."

"That's very poetic. Greek mutt's probably more accurate."

Her soft laughter, the sparkle in her eyes, filled him with pleasure, and, while he didn't wrap his arm around her again as he wanted to, he moved closer until their shoulders touched.

"This place is just beautiful," she said, gazing around at the curving, narrow streets, the old homes, the arches covered with masses of vivid flowers, her expression warm and admiring. She shifted her attention to the gulf waters and the misty mountains beyond. "It's no wonder you wanted to come back."

"There was a time when I didn't want to. Now that's hard for me to imagine."

"I'm just starting my journey as an archaeologist, ready to travel all over. But I'd be lying if I didn't say it's awfully appealing to think of getting to live here forever.

Someday, when I'm ready, I think I'll look to settle in a place like this."

They stood there together for what felt like long, peaceful minutes, watching the brightly colored fishing boats and a large tour boat slice through the sapphire waters of the Gulf of Corinth. Her scent, sweetly mingling with the tumble of flowers nearby, wafted to his nose again. It reminded him of their kiss, how she'd smelled and tasted, and the memory of that sensory overload nearly had him turning to her to do it again.

He curled his fingers into his palms, trying to focus his attention on the boats below. Just as he was about to suggest they move on, she turned to him. "Must be incredible to have this kind of history be a part of who you are," she said. "Studying it, loving it and being drawn to it like I am isn't the same as being a part of it."

"I guess it is. Like anything, you take it for granted sometimes until you're reminded of it." He looked down at her, saw the sincerity in her eyes. Eyes a color close to the mesmerizing blue of the gulf. "You ready to go stir up some Greek fairies?"

"Ready. And I think you've already paid my fee in full, Dr. Tour Guide."

He wasn't going to ask if she meant the tour, or the kiss. And if it was the kiss, he'd be happy to go deep into debt. "Our place is down this street just a short way. Watch your step. These cobblestones will trip you up if you're not—"

"Andronikos!"

Ah, hell. He turned to see his aunt laboring up the street parallel to his. What was she doing in this part of town? "Good afternoon, Thea Stella."

"*Kalispera* to you as well." She folded her arms across

her ample bosom and stared at Laurel. "Who's the girl and what's she doing here?"

Always polite, his *thea*. Not. At least she'd spoken Greek, so Laurel wouldn't understand the words. "This is Laurel Evans, from the archaeological dig near Delphi. Laurel, this is my aunt, Stella Chronis."

"Nice to meet you." Laurel extended her hand with a smile, but his aunt just stared suspiciously.

"Hmph. A very pretty one, as usual, Andronikos." His aunt turned dismissively from Laurel, and the rudeness of it nearly had him pointing it out to the woman. Probably best to grit his teeth, though, since Laurel might not have thought much of it, and any comment would just call even more attention to her actions. At least she continued to speak in English instead of completely excluding Laurel from the conversation. "My friend Soula's nephew wants to meet you to talk about medical school."

"I'd be happy to."

"Good. And while you're at it, tell him about your foolish mistakes and how to keep his pants on, Andronikos. Like you are finally doing now." Frowning, she glanced at Laurel. "I hope."

He'd thought he was too old to feel embarrassed about much anymore, but now knew that wasn't true. If only she'd kept speaking in Greek, after all.

Any chance Laurel might be oblivious to what his aunt was referring to? He glanced at her and saw a small smile on her face. Since Stella was as subtle as a sledgehammer, he knew she'd probably figure it out. With his aunt's brows still lowered into a near scowl, she grabbed his face and gave him a kiss on each cheek before trudging up the steep road without a backward glance.

"Andronikos? Is that your full name?" Laurel tilted her head at him as they resumed walking toward his house.

"Yes, after my grandfather. Quite a mouthful. My aunts and mother are the only ones who use it."

"I like it. Andros for warrior and Nike for victory. It suits you."

"You think?"

"I do think." Her beautiful lips curved wider. "So does your aunt feel a need to protect you from women on the hunt?"

So much for hoping she wasn't listening. "Or women from me, maybe. I had a bit of a reputation as a young man. Sorry she was rude to you, but don't take it personally. Stella enjoys being rude to everyone."

"And here I was feeling special."

He had to laugh at that, enjoying the teasing smile in her eyes, glad she wasn't hypersensitive, or thinking less of him after his aunt's remarks. "You are, believe me. I knew that the first day I met you, and you were so stubborn about me treating your hand."

"Stubbornness is a special trait?"

"Never knew I found it attractive until I met you. But combined with beauty, brains and your unique brand of humor? Oh, yeah."

The eyes that met his had a twinkle in them but seemed to be searching too. She didn't have to look hard to see he had a major jones for her, and he didn't know what the hell to do about it, since it appeared to be mutual. Maybe some intimate time together far away from Kastorini or Delphi would burn it out, since that was pretty much his MO anyway. Laurel was leaving soon, so she wouldn't want more than that either, and just thinking about all that made his pulse quicken. "So there's my house, on the right with the—"

"Daddy! Laurel!"

Just as it had every day for the past two years, his heart warmed at the sight of his daughter tearing up the road to meet them, hair and arms flying, leaving the front door wide open behind her. It warmed even more when she flung herself at him, as though it had been days instead of hours since they'd been together.

"Koukla mou." He swung her into his arms, smiling at the excitement in her eyes, wondering how he'd gotten so incredibly lucky to have a daughter with such a sunny, happy nature. "What have you been up to since lunch?"

"Trouble with a capital T."

He heard Laurel laugh, and grinned. "Her usual answer. Gets it from her *papou*. I have a bad feeling that's going to be her answer for the next fifteen years, which strikes fear into her father's heart."

"Don't be scared, Daddy. I'm just kidding!" She wriggled from his arms and grabbed Laurel's hand. "Come on. I want to show you my fairy house."

"Cassie, let's be polite and offer Miss Laurel something to drink first. Didn't your Thea Taryn make lemonade this morning? Let's go inside and ask her for some."

"She's out back with Petros, kicking the football."

"I don't think I can wait that long to see the fairy house, Andros. Mind if we have some after?"

"It's here." Cassie tugged Laurel to the side of the house where a small strip of dirt contained various flowers his mother planted and tended for him.

"These flowers are so pretty!" Laurel turned to him. "Are you a gardener?"

"Can't tell a weed from a flower. When I bought the

house, my mother couldn't stand the weedy scrub and planted them."

"My *yiayia* is good with flowers," Cassie said. "She lets me help her grow them."

"I don't know much about flowers, Cassie. Maybe you could teach me some things."

His daughter beamed at the suggestion, pointing at various blooms as she said some plant names. Andros had a feeling she might just be making them up as she went along, and his chest filled with warmth all over again as he looked from her to the woman sniffing blooms and asking questions, pretending she thought Cassie really was an expert.

Laurel's face was lit with a smile as bright as Cassie's, and he could see she'd been an amazing big sister. A sister who'd had to take on becoming their mother. How hard must that have been for her?

"It's good you have your fairy house tucked in among your *yiayia*'s flowers, Cassie. You probably know fairies love flowers. You know what else? They love olive wood too. I found this piece of wood that looks just like a little bed, don't you think?" Laurel pulled it from her purse and Cassie reached for it in awe. "I bet if we find something soft for a mattress, and put a flower petal or pretty leaf on it for a blanket, a fairy will love to come snuggle on it."

"Do you think fairies probably live in the olive groves, then?"

"I bet they do. I bet they're really close by, just waiting for a nice bed inside this nice house."

Seeing the two of them standing close together in front of his home, Cassie plucking flower petals, gave him a strange feeling. Just as he was trying to figure out exactly what it was, a cacophony of voices made him turn. Then stare.

What the hell? Two men were striding fast down the street, one carrying a microphone, the other following with a big camera on his shoulder. Numerous townsfolk were gathered around them, walking, talking and gesturing. Pointing right at him.

"Dr. Drakoulias? Doctor, we've been told there's a mysterious illness in Delphi, and patients came here to your clinic before they got so sick they had to be moved to the hospital in Vlychosia. Is it contagious? Are others in Delphi and here in Kastorini at risk?"

The guy shoved the microphone in his face, and he stepped back, not about to be railroaded into saying something that might trigger public hysteria. "We don't believe anyone is at risk. If you give me your contact information, I'll keep you informed as we know more."

The guy got annoyingly close, with the cameraman right behind him. "Does it have something to do with the archaeological dig? We talked to some of the people working there, and they said it might. And that the dig leader is here with you today." He shifted his attention behind Andros, craning to see around him. Anger swelled in his chest. He'd be damned if the man was going to harass Laurel and possibly scare Cassie.

"Again, I'll keep you informed."

The rude-as-hell jerk shoved past him and stuck the microphone in Laurel's alarmed face. Andros didn't even hear the questions the guy started bombarding her with, he just reacted with instinct. Stepped between them and went nearly nose to nose with him, ready to shove him away from her if he had to.

"Ms. Evans doesn't know any more than you do. Now

get off my property." He turned to grasp Laurel's arm and Cassie's hand, hustling them both into the house and away from the media sharks he had a bad feeling had just begun their sniffing around for headline-grabbing blood in the water.

CHAPTER EIGHT

AFTER TALKING ABOUT the media mess with the dig crew for almost an hour, Laurel found herself tuning out the hubbub of conversation as they sat on the back deck of their hotel, darkness shrouding the misty mountains beyond.

How they could still be rehashing the afternoon's excitement with the media showing up to talk to each one of them, she didn't know. Lord knew she was beyond tired of talking about it. The shock of them showing up in front of Andros's house had faded, but she couldn't get out of her head the surprising expression on Andros's face when he'd stepped between her and that reporter. His hard-eyed, angry look and aggressive posture had her wondering if he might actually punch the irritating guy, and she was thankful he'd simply cleared them out of there before she'd had to say much.

Part of her had wanted to tell him she could handle it, but the truth was she'd been all too glad he'd hustled her and Cassie away into his house. It hadn't occurred to her she might be asked about the sick crew members. Thanks heavens she had some time now to think of how she should answer.

The intrusion had ruined what had been an otherwise beautiful day. Spending time with adorable little Cassie had been even more fun than she'd expected, making her feel all warm and fuzzy inside. Helen had been twelve when their parents had died—about to start her teen years. Adorable in her own way, she'd been a little trying at times too. That might be true for Cassie as well, though she couldn't imagine the child being anything but cute as a button.

It struck her with surprise that Helen had been even younger than Cassie when their parents started spending entire summers, rather than just weeks, away. How had they been able to leave her that long? Later leaving all three under Laurel's insufficient care and guidance?

She didn't think she could do that if she ever had children of her own someday, no matter how much she loved her work. Then fiercely shook her head, feeling a bit like a traitor to judge her parents that way. Reminded herself of how they'd both explained they were showing their girls that family life had to be balanced with work life.

Reminded herself how important their work had been to both them and the archaeological world. Reminded herself it was just as important to her, which she'd nearly forgotten today as she enjoyed herself in Kastorini.

Would this sudden media circus create yet another distraction from the job they had to get done with fewer hands and little time? She'd reminded the crew they had to focus, and they'd all agreed. Still, she knew it was human nature to love being on camera and part of a medical mystery, despite worrying about Mel, Tom and John in the midst of it.

Restlessness overcame her, and she stood. "I'm going to my room to plan where everyone will be working tomorrow. Let's get an early start. Be at breakfast at seven a.m., please."

The nods and quick good-nights they sent her way were perfunctory as they kept up the steady yakking, and she shook her head, hoping it didn't continue tomorrow when they had to get digging instead.

In truth, she'd already planned out tomorrow's schedule and decided she needed some fresh air instead of a stuffy room. The street outside the hotel was so dark she could hardly see, and she paused, wondering what might calm this strange unease. Maybe just a long walk around the tiny town of Delphi, even a little mindless shopping she hadn't taken time to do much of, would be enough to help her refocus.

Every store owner competed for the summer tourists, staying open until midnight or later if a single customer was around. One or two shopkeepers stood in their doorways, enthusiastically promising her good prices if she'd just come in and look. Others were busy with customers who had likely earlier toured the ancient sites and the wonderful museum that held the incredibly massive statues, friezes and sphinx. And of course, the stunning bronze Charioteer. That famous Delphi antiquity just might be eclipsed if she could only locate the treasure her parents believed in.

The one they'd died trying to find.

Laurel gave her head another forceful shake and stepped into a jewelry store, wanting to rid herself of thoughts of death and tragedy, of failure and unfinished dreams. At the back of the store, she peered into one of the many open cases of jewelry. A silver necklace reminded her of the one she wore at that moment—the necklace her sisters had given her for her birthday a few years back.

She reached up to grasp it in her hand, glad to have

something to think about that made her smile. The three of them had made a massive birthday cake for her, one that ended up flat on one side and such an ugly deep blue they'd all laughed themselves silly over it. But it had tasted good, and it had been a wonderful evening of sisterly togetherness. A lovely memory among so many special moments the four of them had had over the years. A lovely memory among some that were not quite so great. Memories of all the times she'd despaired over her lack of maturity and skill trying to raise them.

A pair of earrings caught her eye and she picked them up, wanting to look more closely at the silver swirls that curled around the stones, thinking they seemed similar to an ancient pattern on a bracelet they'd unearthed at the dig.

"Moonstones help protect you during your travels, I've heard," a deep voice said next to her ear. "Maybe you should get those earrings, since you'll be moving on soon."

She turned to see Andros behind her, but of course she'd known it was him. Even if she hadn't recognized his voice, every nerve in her body had, tingling and quivery and instantly alert to his nearness. Just as they had been earlier in Kastorini, when flirting with him had been so much fun, even as she'd told herself she shouldn't. When touching and kissing him had been at the forefront of her mind even as she'd been fascinated by the history of the place.

"What are you doing here?"

"Hoping to find you. Wondered if the media had harassed you anymore."

"Thankfully, no. And I don't need the moonstones quite yet."

"I thought maybe that had changed. That maybe you'd be closing down the dig sooner rather than later."

"Why would I?" She stared into his eyes, dark and serious, with a touch of something else. Puzzlement? Frustration? "I'm here until the funding ends and the university tells me I have to leave."

"Do you really want to have to deal with all the media questions now? They might not have followed you here tonight, but I promise they'll be up on the mountain, hounding you."

"I can handle it. I'm not afraid of them. Speaking of which, while I appreciate the gesture, I didn't need you to rescue me today." Didn't need it, maybe, but hoped he didn't know how much she'd been glad of it.

"I know you didn't. Just didn't want him scaring Cassie."

The way his lips curved showed that was a lie, and that he probably knew she'd been lying too. She found herself smiling back. "Got to admit, he was pretty scary."

"I do have one question."

"That sounds ominous."

"Why? Why don't you just be done with it, so you don't have to worry about whether the illness has to do with the dig or worry about the damned reporters swarming around?" His hands moved to cup her face, tilting it up as he moved closer, practically torso to torso. "Surely after five years of excavating here, it can't matter much one way or the other if you close it down now or two weeks from now."

"We don't know what amazing artifact we still might find, just like we don't know anything about Mel and Tom and John and why they got sick. I...okay, I can't deny it worries me. But since we don't know if it had anything to do with the dig, I can't justify completely closing it."

He just kept staring at her, and, despite the unsettling, irksome conversation, Laurel found she couldn't move away from his touch. From the heat of his chest so close to hers. Couldn't stop her gaze from slipping from his eyes to the oh-so-sensual shape of his lips and back. What was it about this man that shook up her libido so completely?

"Until I met you, I'd always figured archaeologists to be easygoing, steady academics who analyzed facts," he said.

"And the facts are…?"

"Three sick people with similar symptoms. Cause unknown."

"Those are pretty vague facts, if you could even call them that. I wouldn't have a chance at any kind of grant if I told them a dig site was kind of like another dig site, but I didn't really have any idea what might be found there or why."

His lips curved slightly again as he shook his head. "Who knew your head was as hard as the rocks you've unearthed?"

"Is that a compliment?"

The smile spread to his eyes, banishing the deep seriousness, and Laurel found herself relaxing and smiling too, in spite of everything. She didn't want to have to defend herself and her decisions and her goals to anyone, least of all this man she couldn't deny sent a zing with a capital Z through every part of her body whenever he was near.

Like now. Very, very near.

His lips touched her forehead, lingered, and, surprised at the deep pleasure she felt from just that simple touch, Laurel let her eyes drift closed until he dropped his hands and drew back. "If you won't listen to logic, at least let me buy you the earrings. Maybe they'll help you remember Delphi, and keep you safe on your travels into that damned cave."

"Not a good idea."

"Why? You afraid I'll expect a thank-you kiss?"

His expression was teasing and serious at the same time, and at his mention of a kiss Laurel's gaze dropped right to his mouth. She wasn't sure she should tell him about moonstone lore, but just as she decided that would be a bad idea the words came out in a near whisper. "Because for thousands of years, people have believed moonstones are a channel for passion and love from the giver to the receiver. A talisman for secret love. Carnal love. Can't risk igniting the power of a moonstone, can we?"

The scorching blaze that instantly filled his eyes weakened her knees, so it was a good thing his strong hands grasped the sides of her waist, pulling her flush against him. Everything about him seemed hot—that look in his eyes, the breath feathering across her lips, every inch of his body touching hers.

"I don't know. Can we? Seems like something's ignited even without the stones."

Whew, boy. Her body answered, *Oh, yes, we can, and right now, please*, while her brain tried not to short-circuit any more than it already was. She opened her mouth to say something—what, she wasn't sure—when she realized the shopkeeper had come to stand next to them.

"Welcome, welcome. May I assist you?" he said in a loud, robust voice. "Would you like a price for one or more of our fine pieces of jewelry?"

They both turned, and Andros dropped his hands from her. She should have welcomed the interruption to help her gather her wits, but really wanted to tell the guy to go away so they could get back to the steamy conversation that made her breathless. "No, thank you," she said. "I was just looking."

"Mister? Surely you wish to buy the beautiful miss something as beautiful as she is. At the best prices, you understand."

"We're still deciding if it's worth the risk. Thanks anyway," Andros said, his lips quirking as he looked at her, but that barely contained blaze that still smoldered in his eyes had her quivering all over again.

The man looked perplexed at Andros's answer, and kept peppering them with questions and various offers as they made their way out of the store, shouting after them to be sure to return for 'the better price' than the original ones he'd been offering.

Andros's arm was around her back, her waist again cupped in his hand as they walked to the darkest end of the street. It curved around in a U-turn to the adjacent street full of more tavernas and shops, but Andros stopped next to a stone retaining wall, beneath tall, arching shrubs that grew from behind it.

He pulled her into his arms, flashing a smile that practically lit up the dark corner he'd finagled them to. "It's not helping, you know."

She had a pretty good idea what he was talking about, but said instead, "What's not helping?"

She could feel his hands splay open on her back, pressing her close, as his warm mouth touched her cheek, moved over to her ear, giving it a tiny lick. "Not having the moonstone. Don't need that to feel a powerful desire for you. To want to share some passion with you. I've been fighting it since the second I met you, but it's been a losing battle."

The low rumble of his voice, along with the little kisses he kept placing against her ear, her neck, her cheek, managed to narrow her entire universe down to those singular sensations. She let her hands slip up his wide chest, outlining his hard pectorals as she went, gratified to feel his muscles twitch and bunch beneath her touch.

She turned her face to give him access to her other cheek, because she liked the breathless feeling it gave her and wanted more of it. Apparently amused at that, he chuckled as he softly kissed every inch of sensitive skin on that side as well.

"I don't have time to…to get involved with you." Proud of herself that she'd managed to remember that, she tipped her head back as his tongue explored the hollow of her throat.

"I know. And I can't risk getting involved with you."

"Risk?" Risk? What did that mean?

"Never mind." His mouth moved in a shivery path up her throat until it was soft against her lips. "This isn't involvement, right? Just friendship."

That startled a little laugh out of her, and she felt his lips smile against hers. "Yes. Friendship with benefits."

And then he kissed her for real. Softly at first, then harder and deeper. Dizzy from the pleasure, she moved her hands up from his chest to cling to his shoulders. There were some firm, taut muscles right there, perfectly placed for her to hold on to so she could stay on her feet and not melt into a small hot puddle on the still-steamy blacktop.

One wide hand slid farther up her back to gently cup her nape, his warm fingers slipping into the hair against her scalp that had loosened a bit from her ponytail. She thought her heart might pound right out of her chest at the thrilling barrage of every sensation he'd managed to make her feel in a matter of minutes—hot, weak, strong and slightly delirious.

A sound of need came from one of them, a little moan from one moist mouth to the other, with an answering gasp in return. The kiss got a little wilder as he pressed her so close, she felt her body mold completely with his. In the foggy recesses of her brain, a bizarrely wild sound filled her ears, and for a moment she feared it had come from her. Then realized with relief that it hadn't, that, somehow, they were surrounded by a cacophony of cat meows.

Andros seemed unaffected, kissing her with a single-minded focus that weakened her knees all over again, until the crescendo of sound was so distracting, she was finally able to break the kiss to look around.

"What in the world is that?"

His eyes, glittering through the darkness, met hers with heat and humor. When he answered, the sound was breathless and amused. "Feral cats. They're everywhere in Greece. Haven't you noticed?"

"They've stared at us and walked around while we ate dinner on the outdoor patios here, but I guess I didn't realize. Thought they were pets of the owners." Still caught close in his arms, she turned to the tangle of shrubs next to them, astonished to see a nearly uncountable number of eyes staring at them luminously through the darkness. Big, small, up close and hiding deeper in the greenery; she couldn't imagine how many there must be.

"Greeks have a love of animals. And also can turn a blind eye to their needs sometimes as well, unfortunately. But many do feed the strays, when they can." He loosened his hold on her to dig something from his pocket, tossing it to the cats, then tossing more of it deeper into the thicket. The mad scramble that ensued made Laurel's heart hurt for the poor hungry creatures.

"Are they never neutered?"

"Just by a few of us. Our secret, though."

She looked up at him, so impressed at his caring. At his warmth, which he'd now shown her extended to all creatures, great and small. "Our secret. Though I didn't know you had surgical skills, too."

"I have many mad skills you don't know about." Their eyes met and held, and it was all there, swirling between them. The intimate smiles, the banked-down heat, the connection that made her feel as if she knew the man so much better than she possibly could after only days.

Had she ever felt such a strange, sensual connection with any other man? As soon as the question came, she knew the answer.

Never.

"It's good that you help little creatures. Back at home, we—"

The harsh ring of his phone made them both jump. The instant he looked at its screen, a deep frown replaced every bit of the heat and humor that had been there before.

"Ah, hell." His gaze lasered in on hers for a moment before he took a few strides away to answer. "Di. What's the matter?"

The second she heard who it was, her gut clenched. The man wouldn't be calling on a Sunday night to catch up on the weather.

Her breath seemed to completely stop, and her hands went cold as she watched his expression get grimmer with each passing second. Finally he turned to her, and she found herself praying.

"Andros. Please don't tell me…Mel and Tom…" She gulped, not able to finish the sentence.

He reached for her hands and held them tight. "It's John. They're doing everything they can, but Di felt we should know. He's taken a turn for the worse."

CHAPTER NINE

"John is sicker?"

The blue eyes staring up at him were wide and worried. Her hands had tightened on his so hard, her short nails dug into his skin. "The breathing machine is having trouble compensating for the pneumonia in his lungs, getting him enough oxygen. But they're giving him the best care they can." He'd known John's condition was becoming more precarious but hadn't seen any reason to alarm her more than necessary.

"What about Mel and Tom?"

"They're getting better every day." He stroked her back, hoping to soothe. "They're going to be fine, and hopefully John will come around too."

"Thank God." Her stiff posture seemed to relax just a little and she dropped her head to his chest, wrapping her arms loosely around his back. "I have to tell everyone he's worse. I have to give them a choice about whether they want to work at the site anymore. I still can't imagine they got sick from the dig, for all the reasons we've talked about. But who knows?"

"Wouldn't it end your stress to just shut it down, like I said before? Let your people go on home? You wouldn't have to worry about someone else getting ill or the media badgering you."

"I can't this second. Have to think. I don't expect you to understand."

No, he didn't understand, but now wasn't the time to get on at her about it. Not when she was feeling so upset and anxious. "I'll come talk to your crew with you. Explain his condition and answer any more questions they might have."

"Thank you. I'd...I'd appreciate that."

She slipped from his hold in what seemed like slow motion, as though it was a supreme effort. He was glad she didn't feel she had to shoulder the entire burden of talking to everyone about John's health.

They walked back to the hotel, silent but for the sounds of their feet on the pavement, the breeze rustling leaves in the trees, the mewls from hidden cats. The hotel seemed equally silent, and Laurel led him through a few cavernous rooms toward a door that led to a deck. Through the floor-to-ceiling windows, it was obvious even in the low light that the deck was empty.

"When I left awhile ago, they were all back here." She nudged open the door, and he followed her outside. The deck spanned the distance along the entire back of the hotel, but the only visible people were a couple in an embrace at the far end.

"Maybe they went to a bar. Or to bed, since I told them we'd be getting an early start."

"You want me to come back in the morning to talk with them then?"

"That's sweet of you, but no." She shook her head. "It's part of my job, though if he's any better in the morning, I'd really appreciate it if you tell me early."

"I admire that you're serious about your job and your responsibilities. Taking care of your sisters." He reached for her, stroked his hands up and down her soft arms. Soft, yet strong, just like her. "You step up to any task forced on you, no matter how difficult."

"Doesn't everybody?"

"No." Quite a few had doubted he could step up when he'd found out about Cassie. "You have a lot to be proud of, Laurel."

The eyes that lifted to his were somber. "Not enough. Not yet."

He wondered what she meant, but when he opened his mouth to ask, got sidetracked completely when she suddenly twined her arms around his neck, pressed her soft curves against him. Pressed her sweet mouth to his.

Her lips plied his, gentle yet insistent. A controlled kiss, but with a slight desperation to it he knew came from her fears for the Wagners, the stress of the dig, the worry of John's worsening illness. Of her parents' deaths just a mile from where they stood. He could sense all of it, feel all of it, as though their hearts and minds had melded together along with their lips, and he hurt for her. Wanted to erase some of that hurt as best he could.

He let his hands roam down her back, to the curve of her waist, found them sliding farther south to grasp the round, firm globes of her rear, pressing her against his hardness. He'd wanted to touch her like this, hold her like this, every time they'd been near to one another, every time they'd kissed. The feel of her was everything he'd known it would be, and it was all he could do to not let his hands explore more of her. Tug the straps of her dress down her arms to cup the small mounds beneath, learn their sweet shape. Help her forget anything but this moment.

Her fingers slid to the sides of his neck, into his hair, making him shiver, sending his pulse ratcheting even higher. He knew he had to get control of himself before he lowered her into one of the deck chairs and made love to her right there under the stars.

It took Herculean effort to pull his mouth from hers and suck in a deep breath. "Don't think either of us wants to be caught out here by your dig crew or, God forbid, somebody working at this hotel who lives in Kastorini. Or, best of all, media types back for another interview and photo op." And wasn't that a hell of an understatement?

"Then let's go to my room."

His heart jolted hard at her words at the same time every muscle in his body tightened, ready to grab her hand and head there at a dead run. "Laurel. I want you. Which I'm sure you know. But not when you're hurting. Not when you might regret it tomorrow."

"I won't regret it. Just tonight. Just this once." She cupped his face in her hands. "I can't let myself be distracted from what has to get done at the dig. But right this minute I don't want to think, I just want to feel. Not feel alone, but feel good. With you. Which, if I'm honest, I've wanted to do since we first met."

"Laurel." His hands tightened on her behind, which pressed her pelvis tighter against him. He nearly groaned. All he wanted was to make her feel good. But would he be taking advantage of a weak moment? The same way he'd often thoughtlessly done, not all that long ago?

"Andros." There was a flicker of slightly amused impatience in her eyes when she said his name in return. Her hands slipped to his chest as she took a half step back. "I'm not a wilting violet you need to look out for or worry about, if that's the problem. I'm strong, and I've been on my own a long time now. You have about five seconds to say, 'yes, that sounds great' or 'no, thanks.' So which is it?"

A surprised chuckle escaped him. The woman standing in front of him definitely wasn't a needy, weepy, sad soul. She was fire and light, toughness and softness, and he was the luckiest man alive that she wanted to be with him tonight.

"Yes, that sounds great."

Her response was to grasp his hand and tug him along behind her through the foyer, up three flights of stairs and into a tiny room. He shut the door behind him and leaned against it, wanting to give her one more chance to change her mind. One more moment to decide if this was really what she wanted tonight.

When she turned to him, the desire that shone in her eyes reflected his own. He took a deliberate step toward her, keeping it slow and easy, giving her just a little more time. A little more space.

"Something about the way you're moving toward me reminds me of a lion on the hunt," she said, taking an equally slow step as the gap between them closed from four feet to three.

"And something about the way you're moving makes me think of a siren. Sending me out of my mind. Making me crazy. Which has occurred to me more than once, by the way."

"Has it?" Another step brought her close enough to touch. Her fingers reached for his shirt buttons, began flicking them open one by one, and his heart thudded thickly in his chest in response. "I never thought of being a siren, until I met you. What if I confessed that, the moment I saw you on the mountain, you made me think of a warrior god? Maybe even Apollo himself."

His laugh morphed into a low moan as her hands slid across his skin to spread open his shirt, her fingertips caressing his nipples. "Oh, yeah?"

"Yeah."

"I don't think I have much in common with Apollo."

"Are you sure? I can think of several things."

If his self-discipline hadn't already disintegrated, it would have at the way she was looking at him, smiling at him, touching him. "Such as? I'm not musical, never shot an arrow in my life and can't claim to be a prophet."

His stomach muscles hardened, along with notable other parts of his body, when her hands tracked down his skin to unbutton his pants. "You're a healer, right? Not to mention you seem to create heat and light whenever I'm around you. And as for physical beauty, you—"

"Okay, enough of this torture." He swept her hands aside, lifting his fingers to the thin straps of her dress. "Part of me wants to let you keep going, so I won't have to wonder if I'm taking advantage of you. But that concern is dwarfed by wanting to give you what you asked for." He slipped the straps down her arms. "Which is to just feel."

"Believe me, touching your skin is a good way for me to just feel."

"I have a better way. And can't wait another second to see *your* physical beauty, which I've fantasized about for days." He reached behind her, unzipped her dress. Slid it down the length of her body until it pooled at her feet, and he could see her luminous skin. He smiled at the paleness of her belly compared to her tanned arms and legs. Swept his fingertips across her stomach and over her white bra, lingering at her hardened nipples. "I like your archaeologist's version of a farmer's tan."

She gave a breathless laugh. "No time to sunbathe at the pool. Sorry."

"I love it. It's just like you. A woman of contrasts, all light and dark." He kissed her throat, moved his tongue down her delicate collarbone. "Soft." He slowly moved down over her bra to take that tempting nipple into his mouth through the fabric. "And hard."

Her hands grasped his head again, holding him against her. He reveled in the little gasping sounds she made as he moved from one breast to the other, dropping to his knees to softly suck on her belly. The scent of her arousal surrounded him, so delicious he groaned as he pressed his mouth over the silky fabric covering her mound, moistening it even more.

"Come back...up here." Her voice was a little hoarse as she grasped his arms, tugging.

He wanted to stay exactly where he was for a while longer, but he was here to make her feel good. Do what pleased her, what made her happy. He stood and flicked off her bra, thumbed her panties down her legs at the same time she shoved his pants to his ankles. Kicking them off along with his shoes, he took her into his arms and kissed her, backing her toward the bed.

He broke the kiss to flick back the covers. When he looked at her, standing there gloriously naked, he realized there was one more thing he needed to see. He reached around to her ponytail, gently tugging at the elastic band there. "I want to see your hair down. I want to see it spread over you, feel it touching my skin."

A sensuous smile curved her lips and she reached

behind to pull off the band, dragging her fingers through her hair as she brought it over her shoulders to cover her breasts, her pink nipples peeking out of the silken strands.

He touched its softness, stroking from her ears down over her breasts, and could barely speak at how beautiful she was. "I've wondered how you'd look. It's better than any of my fantasies. Just like etchings of beautiful sirens rendering men helpless with one glance."

"I hope you're not helpless." She reached for him, and he picked her up to lay her on the bed. Touched her and kissed her, wanting to give her the pleasure she deserved.

The little sounds she made nearly drove him wild, and he lay on top of her to feel all of her skin against all of his. Then suddenly froze in horror.

"I don't have a condom." *Damn it to hell.* "But I can still make you feel good."

"Well, I, um, I bought some recently. Just in case, you know?" She looked at him with an adorably embarrassed expression before leaning over to rummage in her purse, handing him one. A breath of relief whooshed from his lungs.

"Smart, beautiful, responsible and even resourceful. A woman a man can only dream of." He took care of the condom as fast as possible, because he couldn't wait another second to join with her, holding her close, slipping inside her moist heat with a groan.

They moved together, their eyes locked, and the universe narrowed to that one moment, skin to skin, breath to breath, soul to soul. Seeing her lying there, her beautiful hair billowing all across the pillow, his name on her lips, sent him over the edge. Watching her eyes, darkened with bliss, hearing and seeing her fall with him, was a moment he knew he wouldn't forget if he lived a thousand years.

* * *

Laurel stared at the pastel pink-and-blue sky, the morning sun still low over the mountains beyond their Delphi hotel. How was it possible to have so many different balls of emotions rolling all around in her stomach at the same time?

Last night, she and Andros had been lying bonelessly sated and content, skin to skin and heart to heart, when his phone had rung. A call that had obliterated every ounce of pleasure, delivering the shocking, unbelievable news that John had passed away.

Her throat and eyes filled with tears as that terrible tragedy, that horrible reality, took precedence over everything. When she'd called a late meeting to somehow tell everyone about his tragic death, the horror on their faces had been every bit as intense as her own.

Those other balls rolling around were from grief and fear. Worry and anxiety. John's death likely wasn't connected to the dig, but it was still a terrible, heavy loss. A loss that added to her determination to finish what she'd come here to do. Finish the work her parents had died for. And now John too.

She swallowed hard at the sickly churning in her stomach as she waited for the dig crew to show up again. She'd asked them to meet with her again after breakfast to give them options. A breakfast she hadn't joined them for, since she doubted she could get one bite of food down anyway.

John. Dead. How was it possible? She still couldn't wrap her brain around it.

And was that going to be Mel and Tom's fate as well? "No," she said out loud, fiercely. Willing it to be true.

Praying for it. Andros had promised her they would be fine.

Somehow, the thought calmed her stomach and helped her breathe slightly easier.

"Laurel. Are Mel and Tom...still okay?"

She looked up to see Becka hobble into the room on her crutches, looking pale and upset. Worried. As they all did, now filing quietly behind her to lower themselves into the mismatched crowd of overstuffed chairs and sofas, their faded fabrics showing varying degrees of wear.

"Yes, they're okay. Apparently anyway. Dr. Galanos told me they'll likely be released soon, which would be wonderful. I...I need to talk to them, find out what their plans are." Did their plans include coming back to the dig? Or going home? Certainly, after what they'd been through, no one could blame them for doing exactly that.

As she was interim team leader, the painful job of contacting John's family had fallen to Laurel. Tears welled in her throat again as she remembered their stunned silence, then bewildered and disbelieving questions. Then a near hysteria of grief and pain that had cracked her heart in two.

Did it make her weak and pitiful that she'd been beyond relieved to finally be done with her deliverance of the shocking news, passing the phone to Andros to further explain and try to comfort? Probably, yes. But with her own memories of receiving the nightmare call about her parents forever burned into her heart and mind, it was all she could do to maintain her composure. To not begin sobbing with them, which would have just made it all the worse for John's family.

Laurel drew in a deep breath, swallowed again at

the threatening tears. She looked at the dig team—her team—perched or sprawled on the chairs, and realized two were missing. "Where are Jason and Sarah?"

"Jason's coming in a minute," Becka said. "He's feeling a little sick to his stomach. Because, you know…"

Becka's voice faded away as a few team members looked down at the floor. Yes, they all knew. Jason had become good friends with John over the past months, even though the college boy had been seven years younger than John. Almost like a big brother to the young man, Laurel supposed, and her chest pressed in even tighter at the thought.

"Sarah didn't answer her phone when I called to ask if she was ready," one of the girls said. "Probably still in the shower or something. Or maybe she, you know, needed a little more time to compose herself."

Laurel understood. She wished she had more time, too.

"Well, let's go ahead and get started." Laurel braced herself to ask what she had to ask. Knew their answers might well mean working with a thin crew, and she'd simply have to put in even more hours on her own. In fact, she might prefer that. No matter how much she wanted to find the artifact, she couldn't feel good about possibly putting others at risk for it.

"This is a devastating thing for all of us," she said. "John was not only an enthusiastic, hardworking person, he knew a lot about archaeology after volunteering on so many digs the past few years. We'll miss him as a friend. And we'll miss him as a teammate."

All eyes on her, they sat silently, two of the girls sniffing back tears. Laurel dug her fingers into her palms, kept her eyes away from the anguish on the girls' faces, and forged on. "No one knows why John died. What he had, or where he got it, or even if it could possibly have been contagious. If it was the same thing as the Wagners or not. Dr. Galanos said the hospital is working to find out, but we just don't have those answers yet. So I must give you all the option of deciding whether or not you still want to be part of this dig."

"I do," Becka said instantly. "If it was contagious, we'd already have been exposed anyway, right? I feel fine, and it seems to me everyone else does too. What's the point of quitting now, when we're so close to the end? I mean, I found those cool coins just last week, and the day before Sarah found those amazing ivory feet, just like the ones in the Delphi museum! Think what else we still might find!"

Becka's impassioned plea lifted the weight in Laurel's chest ever so slightly and she managed a smile. "Thank you, Becka. Though you have to take a few more days off until your leg has had time to heal. I'm not asking you all to decide this minute. I'll be working on the mountain as soon as we're done here, and possibly in the cave as well. Those who want to join me are welcome, so long as you understand there may be a risk involved, and you're willing to take that risk. Any of you end up deciding you want to pack it in and schedule flights home, I completely understand and support your decisions."

Just by watching them, seeing who made eye contact with whom and what expressions they wore, made it fairly easy to figure out who wanted to go and who would stay. And who could blame them? No matter how few hands would be left, though, she had to keep believing there was still a chance to finish what she had come to do.

"Talk it over with one another. Feel free to take the day off, then sleep on it," she advised them. "You can let me know in the morning, and we'll go from there."

As she looked at the uncertain faces, her whole body felt a little numb, but jittery and anxious as well, and she knew the antidote was work. Give them time and space without them feeling as if she was hovering around to coerce them, or judge them. Last thing she'd want would be for someone to stay on from guilt. Shorthanded or not, everyone still working tomorrow needed to feel as passionate about the project as Becka did.

"I'm heading up, if anyone wants to go. If you decide to come later, you'll find me at the mountain excavation first."

She swung up her day pack, and Becka followed her to the stairwell. "Let me tell Jason you're ready to leave. I'll be right back."

Laurel's lips twisted a little that the only person still for sure on board was handicapped with a bandaged-up leg and couldn't work for days. She closed her eyes and lifted her face skyward. "Any way you two know where it is? Don't angels have special powers? I need your help, here."

"You talking to the ceiling, or yourself?"

She opened her eyes to see the dark chocolate gaze of the man she'd gotten to know, oh so intimately the night before. They were serious eyes, questioning. As he walked across the wide foyer, bronzed and strong and so gorgeous, the utter male beauty of him stole her breath. That jittery nervousness in her stomach faded away to a feeling of warmth.

Which was dangerous. If this attraction had been a distraction she couldn't afford before, she could afford it even less now.

"Just talking to my parents," she said, keeping her voice light so he wouldn't read too much into it. "Hoping for some divine intervention."

Sympathy joined the other emotions in his eyes as he came to stand in front of her. His hands stroked her arms, slowly, softly, soothingly as they had last night. "Find any?"

"No luck so far. Guess I'm on my own."

"No. Not on your own." He pressed his lips to her forehead, and she found herself briefly closing her eyes, finding that simple touch also seemed to leach away some of her stress. "I'm here to help. Starting with talking to your crew if they have questions."

"Thank you." Their eyes met, and the reassuring touch of his hands on her arms made her wish it were that easy. That poor John hadn't died, that she wasn't beyond short-handed, that she wouldn't likely have to spend time away from the dig getting the Wagners settled back in Delphi or heading home, whichever they wanted. That anyone deciding to stay wouldn't be risking their health. That she wasn't facing imminent failure at what she'd wanted so much to accomplish. "They didn't say much. It might be good if you talked to them now. Maybe they'd feel more free to say or ask things with me out of the room."

"All right." He gave her arms a squeeze. "I don't have clinic appointments until nine. If—"

"Laurel! Laurel!"

They both turned to see Becka limping down the stairs, grabbing the handrail as she stumbled in her hasty descent. Panic was etched on her face, and an echo of it filled Laurel too, making her stomach clench. What could possibly be wrong now?

Andros leapt up a few steps to grasp Becka's arm. "Steady now, before you fall."

"Oh, thank God you're here, Dr. Drakoulias!" The girl clutched at him. "It's Jason. He's really sick. I think—"

She gulped down a little sob. "I think he has what the Wagners have. And…and John. Oh, God, what are we going to do?"

CHAPTER TEN

LAUREL SAT IN the dirt on the side of the baking mountain, bagging and labeling potsherds, barely paying attention as she did. Wondering why she was even bothering.

It was over. Finished. She wasn't going to prove her parents' theory. She wasn't going to get their names in archaeological journals one last time, and her own too, to jump-start her belated, fledgling career. Probably wouldn't even receive the grant she'd wanted so badly, enabling her to get going on a project of her own. One that would inch her toward accomplishing at least an iota of what her parents had accomplished by her age.

How could they have died for nothing? Why couldn't their last excavation have been worth more than potsherds and jewelry and artifacts that, while interesting, were similar to all those already unearthed in Delphi?

She'd wanted that for them. For herself, and for her sisters, giving them a small feeling of peace over her parents' passing. And now? Now she had to wonder if this work, their work, had been worth the very high cost.

Worth all the summers they'd had only a long-distance relationship with their girls. All the times Laurel had tried to play parent, while they had dug for history. Worth the hole left in their family that had started to form even before they'd died.

She swiped her dusty hands across her wet cheeks. John's family would be feeling the same emptiness, wondering why and for what, and her chest felt even heavier.

So often when digging, she could feel the spirits of the ancient people who'd lived there, hear them speaking, see them cooking in a vessel they'd unearthed, or wearing the jewelry they'd found. Sometimes it even felt as though the hand of fate was guiding her, showing her exactly where an artifact might be, drawing her there. But today the mountain was silent.

She pushed to her feet and looked into one of the wide, deep pits. The one that had been painstakingly re-excavated after her parents had been crushed by its walls. Her throat got so tight she could barely squeeze out the words. "So this is it, Mom, Dad. This is the best I could do, and I know it's not nearly enough. Not what you would have expected of me. I'm sorry."

She gathered up the few bags, walked the worn goat path to her car and cleaned up before driving to the hospital in Vlychosia. Andros had arranged for Jason to be transported there, and, no matter how much it hurt, she owed the living more than she owed the dead. Starting with Jason, to see how he was and see if there was anything she could do to help. Then talking with Mel and Tom to tell them the dig was over. To ask what she could do for them as well.

She peeked into Mel and Tom's hospital room, surprised they weren't there, and a jolt of alarm went through her, sending her quickly back out of the room. Had they gotten worse? Were they back in the ICU?

Heart pounding, she practically ran down the hall, trying to find someone she could ask. She spotted two men in doctors' coats about to round a corner, one with thick dark hair, a sculpted jaw and a muscular frame, and knew without a doubt who it was. "Andros!"

He stopped and turned, spoke to the man with him, then moved in her direction. She jogged toward him, breathless. "Where are Mel and Tom? They're not worse, are they?"

"No, no. They're fine." He cupped her face in his warm palm for a moment before sliding it down to her shoulder. "In fact, they're being released. I was going to drive them back to the hotel after all the paperwork's done."

She took a deep breath of relief. "What about Jason?"

"Not sure yet, but so far not worse. He's getting good nursing care, so let's hope for the best." He looked at his watch. "How about a cup of coffee? They won't be ready to go for maybe another hour."

She didn't know if coffee would lift her spirits or jangle her nerves even more. Regardless, being with Andros would be the one thing sure to help her feel at least marginally better.

The coffee shop was surprisingly large, but the tables were tiny, their knees bumping against one another's beneath it. He reached for her hand, and his warm strength felt so comforting, she twined her fingers within his.

"You talked to the dig crew, right?" he asked.

"Yes. I told them to make their travel plans to go home."

"Good." His brows were pinched together in a small frown as his thumb absently stroked up and down hers. "We want them to wait a few days before getting on a plane. Or being close to other people. Quarantined, basically. And I also want blood tests from everyone. If no one else gets sick, you can all go."

"You did blood tests for the Wagners and John. You know it wasn't a fungal infection."

"We're looking at other possibilities. With John dead and three others sick, the national infection-control folks are involved. We'll be doing a battery of tests this time, a viral serology panel, looking for emerging infections. Something we maybe haven't seen before. Takes a long time to determine something that complicated, though, so I don't expect we'll know anything for a while yet."

His tone was as serious as his expression, and she realized it was a very good thing she'd shut down the dig. The pain she felt over not achieving her dream, her parents' dream, would be far worse if anyone else got sick. "It seems impossible that all this has something to do with the dig. But I know my parents wouldn't want anyone else to die trying to accomplish what they didn't have a chance to."

"Plenty's been achieved in the last five years of that dig, Laurel. Right? What more could there be to accomplish?"

She felt the supportive hold of his hand in hers, looked at the sincerity in his eyes, the caring, and nearly told him. But her lips closed and she shook her head. Even now, with the dig ending, she found she couldn't. Why, she wasn't sure, but it just seemed she should still keep the secret her parents had held close. "You never know. That's what makes you keep digging."

"I just realized I don't even know where you call home. I'd like to know, so when I think of you I can picture you there."

Home? Did she have such a thing anymore?

She'd been so consumed with everything that had happened, she hadn't even thought about leaving here in a few days. About not seeing him again. But the low, husky voice, the serious dark depths of his eyes, put that reality front and center. Added another layer of weight to her heart.

"Indiana. After my parents died, the only digs I worked on had to be close to where we lived, studying protohistoric Caborn-Welborn culture. But I recently sold the house, since my sisters don't need a place to roost anymore. And because I hope to head to Turkey soon, making that home for a while." If she could get the funding, which would be tough going, now. And why didn't that thought bother her as much as it had just last week? Must be the depressing reality of everything that had happened since.

"Protohistoric what?" His eyes crinkled at the corners, and just looking at his beautiful features caught her breath. "That's all Greek to me."

Trust him to somehow make her smile, and he did too, just before he leaned across the tiny table and kissed her. Long and slow and sweet, and when he pulled back, the eyes that met hers weren't smiling anymore.

"If you think this thing might be contagious and that some of us might have it, you shouldn't be kissing me, you know." She was trying to lighten the moment, but her chest felt even heavier, knowing it just might be their last kiss anyway.

"Too late. But even if it wasn't, it's worth the risk."

Worth the risk? Her heart fluttered, and she thought of the moonstones, and their teasing about them. Wished maybe she'd gotten them after all, to remember him by.

As though she needed anything to help her with that.

"Andros."

They looked up to see Dr. Galanos standing there.
"The Wagners are ready to go. I've arranged for them
and the whole crew to stay in quarantine here. Getting it
ready now, and it should be comfortable enough. Which
of you is going to get the Wagners' things from Delphi
and bring back the rest of the dig crew?"

"I am." Laurel stood and, with a tightness squeezing
her chest, braced herself for goodbye. "Thanks for all
you've done for us, Andros."

"Your car won't fit everybody. I'll help drive the crew
back here."

"Thank you." Only a couple more hours before she
didn't get to look at him anymore. Until they said goodbye one last time.

Their days in quarantine had seemed to drag on forever,
and Laurel was glad it was finally over. Relieved that
not a single team member had shown any symptoms at
all. Beyond relieved that Jason had improved so much,
they'd agreed to release him and let him go back to the
States with them.

Andros had stopped in once, apparently meeting with
Dr. Galanos. She and the Wagners had filled their time
going through all the dig notes, writing summaries and
outlines of the papers they'd publish, but it still hadn't
been enough distraction for her to not hope it was Andros
every time someone came in the room. For her to hope
he'd stop in one more time to say goodbye.

But, really, why should he? It was a long drive from
Kastorini, he'd likely been busy at the clinic, and it wasn't
as though they were anything more than passing friends.
Briefly lovers, though that fleeting moment was etched

in her mind far more clearly than any other love affair she'd experienced.

She and the Wagners walked to the car to pack it up before they left for the airport to go home. It struck her that the word *home* felt hollow, just as it had when Andros had asked where she'd lived. What was there for her, other than her short-term teaching-assistant position? Finishing up the final pieces to her PhD?

Somehow, she had to get that grant for the dig she'd been so enthusiastic about just months ago. The dig she knew her parents would have been proud she'd pursued. With any luck, she could find some success with that and push past this strangely restless emptiness in her chest.

"I feel like I've been in this hospital a month instead of nine days," Tom grumbled good-naturedly as he tossed their bags into the car.

"The best days of your life, considering we're still here on earth, thanks to the good care we got," Mel said.

"I know. And part of me feels odd, leaving. Like we should be going back to the dig to finish."

"Really?" Laurel stuffed her bag behind his and stared at him in surprise. "After the ordeal you've been through, I thought you'd run and never look back."

"They still don't know if it had any damn thing to do with the dig. If I felt strong enough, I'd go back right now, but I know I'm not up to it," Tom said, stopping in the midst of packing Mel's bag to give Laurel a long look that struck her as very odd.

"What? Why are you looking at me like that?"

"I just…I'm not sure I should tell you, but, ah, hell." He grabbed the back of his neck and sighed. "You know how sometimes we all get that feeling on a dig, like an invisible finger is pointing and you just have to follow it and look?"

Her heart sped up a little. "Yes. I know."

"I felt it in the cave. That last day. Real strong and compelling. Leading me toward the far left wall, just past a huge orange stalactite, about a hundred feet back. Farther in than we'd been excavating. I was going to dig some, but it got late and I wasn't feeling too good. I figured I'd be able to tackle it better the next morning."

"Which all could have been delirium, since that was the night you got really sick," Mel said. She wore a deep frown, shaking her head slightly at him.

"You think that's where it might be," Laurel said, barely able to breathe.

"I do. Mel doesn't want you to go in there, but honestly? I really think we were close. My gut just tells me it might be there."

She looked from Tom to Mel and back again, a surge of adrenaline roaring through her blood. Without one more second of thought, she yanked her bag back out of the car and could practically feel her parents pushing her on the way they so often had, even when she'd been frustrated by it. Wanting her to use these final two weeks to search a little longer.

She'd learned to listen to little voices in her head, whoever or whatever they might be. And these little voices? They might be the most important whispers she would ever hear.

"I'm going back." She leaned in to kiss Mel on the cheek, then Tom. "I'll keep you posted."

"Laurel." Mel reached for her. "I know your parents expected a lot from you. Were driven, and drove you too. And you always stepped up, no matter how hard it was.

But they wouldn't want you to risk getting sick. Risk your life. Let it go. You have other digs in your future."

"But not a dig like this one. And like Tom said, you getting sick might have had nothing to do with the dig anyway. But I'll be careful. I'll wear gloves and a mask. It'll be okay."

"I know there's no point in arguing with you when you've made up your mind." The woman who'd stepped in to do quite a bit of mothering after Laurel's parents were gone gave her a fierce hug. "Promise you'll be careful. Promise you'll stay safe."

"I will. I'll see you back at the university in two weeks, and with any luck there'll be a treasure in my pocket."

"A little too big for your pocket," Tom said, hugging her and grinning. "If you find it, they'll build a whole new room for it in the Delphi museum, with your parents' names on the plaque. So many visitors will flock to see it, the Charioteer will be damn jealous."

"We'll drive you back," Mel said.

"No, I'll rent another car. Don't worry about me. Adventure is what I live for, remember?"

Funny how the day seemed blindingly brighter. Her chest filled with an excitement and energy she hadn't felt since before the Wagners got sick. And that excitement and energy sent her thoughts to Andros. Bombarded with memories of how he made her feel exactly that way too.

By the time she got the car rented and arrived back in Delphi, there was too little daylight left to head up the mountain to the dig. Being back in town made her thoughts turn to Andros again. Of strolling through the streets, feeding the cats, kissing him until she was breathless. Walking into the hotel filled her with memories of kissing him again on the back deck and of making love with him in her slightly lumpy little bed.

Not that she hadn't thought of him more times than she could count the past three days and nights in Vlychosia anyway.

Maybe after she checked in, she should call him. Just to let him know she was back. Then again, she knew he'd be unhappy with her going back to the dig, and even more unhappy that her first stop would be the caves, which she hadn't been in even once. And that he still believed might be the source of the mysterious pneumonia.

She didn't need the man's approval or permission or lectures. She'd been on her own for a long time, so why did she feel this need, this longing, really, to get in touch with him?

No. She shook her head and grabbed up her duffel. She'd been given one more chance to find the treasure. Tonight she'd look at the map of the caves, carefully drawn over the past three years, read through all Tom's notes, and make a plan. A plan that didn't include making love with Andros Drakoulias again.

"Hello, Spiros," she said to the desk clerk. "I'm back. Can I have the same room, or do you need to move me?"

The young man looked over his shoulder twice, then finally focused on her. The expression on his face could only be described as alarmed, and she wondered if the media coverage and the quarantine had spooked everyone.

"I am sorry, miss, but there are no rooms left."

"I'm absolutely fine, Spiros. The hospital gave us all a clean bill of health." She fished in her purse for the papers they'd given her, holding them out. "See?"

"I am sorry," he repeated. "But we did not know you

were returning. We have rented every room for the next two weeks. I will call other hotels in Delphi for you, yes?"

"Thank you." She dropped her bag to the floor. Why hadn't she been smart enough to call as soon as she'd known she was coming back? Regardless, it didn't really matter. A place to stay was a place to stay, so long as she could easily get to the dig.

As the minutes ticked away and Spiros made one call after another, concern grew to alarm. She might not be able to understand a word he was saying, but the frown and worried look were plain. Finding a room wasn't happening.

"I am sorry, miss," he said yet again, looking remorseful. "It is high season, you understand. Every room is booked by tours and others. I am sorry."

"Thank you for trying. I appreciate it." So now what? She hauled her duffle over her shoulder again and went out the door and across the still-hot blacktop. There was only one solution she could think of. And how ridiculous that the solution sent happiness surging through her veins, sending her practically running to her car and jumping inside.

There was one person nearby who'd said he was there to help her any way he could. Was it her fault she needed a little more help from him now?

CHAPTER ELEVEN

"ONE MORE STORY, Daddy? Please?"

Andros slid the book from his daughter's hands, an easy accomplishment since her fingers had gone limp, her words slow and slurred. "Not tonight. If you sleep tight, I'm sure your little fairies will visit."

She smiled at the same time her eyes closed. He watched her roll to her side, pull her sheet up to her chest and fall straight to sleep. He tugged the sheet a little higher to tuck it beneath her little chin, wondering all over again how he could possibly be so blessed.

The stairs creaked as he made his way back to the living room, absently thinking he should see if he could find a way to quiet them. His handyman skills weren't up there with his doctoring skills, but surely he could figure something out.

Right now, though, there was something more important to figure out. He propped up his feet, put his laptop on his knees, and did another advanced internet search to look at various known pathogens, common and uncommon. Trying to read through it all, he found it hard to concentrate on the information. Damned difficult, in fact, because he just couldn't stop thinking of Laurel.

Di had told him the entire archaeological team had

been cleared to leave quarantine, including Jason, thankfully. Probably they were all at the airport by now, maybe even already on a plane bound for the States. Leaving unanswered questions behind them, but he and Di and the virologists would eventually figure it out. Had to, because even though no one in Delphi, Kastorini or any other nearby town had come down with anything similar, they all wanted it to stay that way.

He closed his eyes and pictured Laurel's face. Her amazing blue eyes and pretty lips that sometimes smiled or cutely twisted when she was thinking. Lips that had kissed him until he couldn't think straight. He pictured her slim figure and how sexy her rear looked in anything she wore, even those loose, dirty work shorts of hers with pockets everywhere. But his favorite had been that silky long dress. No, not quite. His favorite was how she'd looked when her hair had been released from its ponytail, spilling across the pillow and her soft skin, tangling in his fingers as he made love with her.

Damn. Just thinking about her, all of her, made his breath feel a little short and his heart feel a little empty. How was it possible he could miss a woman so much, when he'd barely spent more than a few days with her?

He'd itched to go to Vlychosia to see her, to say goodbye one last time. Nearly had gotten in his car more than once, but stopped himself. Last thing he'd want to do would be to hurt Laurel, which he hadn't even realized he'd done to some of the women who'd briefly been in his life. He wasn't made for a real relationship anyway, and, even if he had been, what was the point of getting too attached to a woman focused on spending her life at digs around the world? Or for Cassie to? A little girl who had lost her mother far too soon just might be unconsciously looking for someone to take her place.

No, it was good Laurel had moved on, leaving no possibility of anyone getting hurt, or the storm of gossip he wanted to avoid.

He tried to refocus on the internet journal and the various viral beta groups, and was startled when his cell phone rang. He hoped it wasn't an emergency, but if he had to bundle up Cassie and take her the few houses down to his sister's, he suspected his little girl wouldn't lift an eyelid.

He dug his phone from his pocket. His heart jerked hard and his breath caught in his chest. Laurel. What could she be calling about?

"Dr. Drakoulias." He'd answered that way to keep his voice sounding calm and professional. Unemotional, so she wouldn't know how much he'd been thinking of her. Missing her.

"Is this the Dr. Drakoulias who told me he was here to help if I needed it? Unfortunately, I have a little problem."

"That would be me." Her voice sounded normal, with even that touch of humor he liked so much, so there must not be some terrible problem. He relaxed at the same time he felt instantly wired, alert, elated too, because hearing her on the other end of the line was like being given an unexpected gift. "What is this little problem?"

"Well, believe it or not, I'm in Delphi. But the hotel gave my room away, and there's not another room to be had in the entire town."

"You're in Delphi?"

"Yep, I am."

"And you need a place to stay." He couldn't imagine why she'd come back, but the way his heart had jerked in his chest when she'd first called was nothing to the gymnastics it was doing now.

"I'm afraid I do. There are a few hotels in Kastorini, aren't there?"

"One's full up for a wedding this weekend, which I know because a patient talked to me about it for half an hour today. The other two usually take on overflow from Delphi, so I bet they're booked too."

"That's what Spiros at my hotel told me." She sighed in his ear. "Is there any way I can hole up in the clinic or something, just for one night while I check out nearby towns tomorrow? Or maybe even briefly stay with Taryn?"

"My house has three bedrooms. No reason to call Taryn tonight, you can just stay here." The instant the words were out of his mouth, he pictured her here with him, sitting in his cozy living room, fascinating him with stories about the dig and about her life. Tousled and sleepy when he fixed her coffee in the morning. He wondered what she wore to bed, and a vision of something silky and skimpy came to mind, or, even better, her completely naked, glorious body. But even if she slept in an oversized T-shirt, she'd look sexy as hell.

That vision faded when he realized if anyone found out he had a woman staying in his house, the tongues would flap like crazy. And what were the odds no one would know? Pretty much zero out of a hundred. But he couldn't worry about that when Laurel needed someplace to lay her head. "Cassie's in bed, but she sleeps like a rock. Won't even blink if I put her in the car to come get you."

"Thank you." Her voice got softer, warmer. "But I rented another car. I'll be there in about twenty minutes, if that's okay."

"I'll be waiting." And each minute of it would seem like two. At the moment, there was no way he'd get one thing out of the clinical information on his laptop, and he closed it, realizing the house could use some spiffing up. Cassie's toys lying all around didn't bother him, but probably making sure Laurel didn't turn an ankle stepping on one would be a good idea.

His arms were full of the last of it—multicolored plastic blocks he was trying to find the box to dump into—when there was a soft knock on the door. It opened a few inches, and beautiful blue eyes met his through the crack. "Hi. It's me. Didn't want to wake Cassie by ringing the doorbell."

"Nothing wakes that child up. Come on in."

The sight of all of her, not just those amazing eyes, caught his breath. She was wearing that dress he loved so much that embraced every curve, and her hair—God, her hair was down, out of her usual ponytail, falling in a shimmering golden waterfall over her shoulders. He stood there staring like a fool, an armload of plastic stuff preventing him from pulling her into his arms and kissing her until she was as breathless as he felt.

But maybe she didn't want that. Yes, they'd made love after the stress of learning about John's failing health, but that didn't mean she wanted to go there again. And he wanted her to feel comfortable in his house, not worried he might jump on her any moment like a flea on a kitten.

On the other hand, he might not be imagining the way she was looking at him. A way that said she might not mind him jumping on her at all.

Where was that damned box? "You don't happen to see a white box with pictures of blocks on it, do you?"

"Is this it?" She walked to the small door under the

stairs where they stored Cassie's stuff. He'd already stuck a few things in there, and she bent over to open the door wider. He got so fixated on her shapely rear in that dress, he hardly noticed she was pulling the elusive box out from behind a huge stuffed lion.

"How come I put things in there twice and didn't see it?"

"I'm good at excavating, remember?" She held out the box, and he dumped the blocks inside. She turned and bent over again to shove the thing back behind the lion, and Andros gave up trying to keep his distance.

"You do realize you bending over in that sexy dress of yours is testing the limits of my gentlemanliness?"

"Is it?" She turned to him and took a step toward him, the amusement in her eyes mingling with the same heat he was trying to bank down. "Funny. Just looking at you in your T-shirt and jeans with your hair a little messy makes me want to test it even further."

To his shock and delight, she closed the gap between them, tunneled her hands into his hair and kissed him.

He wrapped his arms around her, lost in the taste of her, the intoxicating flavor he'd thought he'd never get to taste again. Her silky hair slid over his hands, his forearms, as he pressed her even closer, loving the feel of her every soft curve pressed against his body.

Still clutching his head, she broke the kiss and stared into his eyes. "I kept hoping you'd come back to the hospital one more time. To say goodbye."

"So you came to say goodbye?" He'd thought she'd already gone. So why did the thought of a goodbye now feel so bad?

"Not yet. Right now I'm saying hello."

"I like hellos better than goodbyes," he murmured

against her lips before he kissed her again. The way she melted against him, gasping softly into his mouth as their tongues leisurely danced, made him think maybe she'd missed him too. That maybe she'd thought of him as much as he had her the past few days.

But she had a life in the States and a PhD to finish and papers to write. Grants to get and new digs to work on. Thinking of him or not, why had she come back?

"How long are you in town? And why?"

She drew back a few inches. "Well, I have some unfinished business. Don't know how long it might take, but—"

The shrill ring of his phone interrupted, and he nearly cursed it. He hated letting go of Laurel's warm body, but it would seem pretty odd to dance her over to the side table to answer the damn thing. "Dr. Drakoulias."

"Andros! It's Yanni. Dora's having the baby. Thinks it's coming soon."

"Do you think she's able to get to the clinic?"

"Yes. I think so."

"I'll meet you there." *Damn.* Timing being what it always was, Christina was in Athens for a few days. Not to mention that things just might have been leading somewhere very good with Laurel. "I'm sorry. Got to go deliver a baby that apparently is in a hurry to get here. Excuse me again."

He dialed the nurse midwife in Levadia who was on call for Christina. He huffed out an impatient breath when her husband said she'd gone to the grocery store. Didn't on call mean on call? "I need to hear from her as soon as possible."

"What's wrong?" Laurel asked. "You worried about the mother?"

"No. She's had a healthy pregnancy. But this is her fifth, and if she thinks it's coming soon, I believe her. Christina's not here, and the midwife on call isn't home. And it'll take her half an hour to get here anyway."

"Let me help. I mean, you just need an assistant, right? I don't need to be a nurse or anything?"

"Just need an assistant. Are you sure you're up for that?"

"Sounds like it would be an experience, and, hey, I'm always up for an adventure."

"Never thought of bringing a baby into the world as an adventure, but I guess it can be." He'd already seen the woman didn't back down from a challenge and had to smile. "It'll be faster if Taryn brings Petros here. I'll call her, then we can go."

"Looks like they're not here yet, which is good," Andros said as he pulled the car up to the clinic. "You can help me get stuff set up."

Nervous but excited too, Laurel followed Andros back to the hospital wing. She couldn't believe she was about to see a baby being born, maybe even be a part of bringing it into the world. Hadn't thought she'd ever want to, but, now that it was about to happen, she knew it would probably be an amazing experience.

Andros wheeled over a small cart from a corner with what looked like maybe a heating unit above it, and put a tiny little oxygen mask in the corner of the little crib, hooking it up to something. He pulled other strange things out from the supply cupboard, laid them on a thick metal table next to the hospital bed, then grabbed more items in his arms.

"I don't want to get in the way, but is there anything I can do?"

"I'm good right now, thanks." He tossed her a couple of plastic bags with what looked like blue paper inside. "Can you go see if Yanni and Dora are outside and bring them in here? Then put on that gown. Gloves too, after you come back, because I'll need you to handle the baby."

Handle the baby? What if she dropped it on its head or something? Nerves jabbed into her belly at the thought, though she should have realized she might have to take care of the newborn while he took care of the mother.

As soon as she got to the front door, a car zoomed up the street and swerved in front of the clinic, parking crooked. She rushed out of the door, hoping like heck the woman wasn't already spitting out the baby right there in the car, but if she had to catch the newborn, then, darn it, she would. A man leaped out and practically flew around to the passenger door, looking a little wild-eyed.

"Do you need help? Dr. Drakoulias is inside—do you want me to get him?"

"*Ochi.* I can bring her."

He swung the woman into his arms, and she wrapped her hands around his neck before burying her face in his chest. Her distressed cry was muffled, but Laurel's gut tightened, hearing her sound of pain. She ran to hold open the door and led the way to the clinic.

"Follow me."

Andros had already changed into scrubs and was busy putting towels next to the bed. He looked up and smiled. "Always in a hurry, Dora. Ever since we were in grade school."

The woman looked up and gave him a wavering smile back. She spoke in Greek so Laurel didn't know what she'd said in return, but apparently the woman still managed to have a sense of humor despite everything, as both men laughed.

Then just that fast, she apparently had another contraction, crying out as her face contorted. All humor was replaced by worry on her husband's face as he laid her on the bed, speaking to her soothingly. The sweetness and caring in his eyes tugged at Laurel's heart, and she wished she'd talked to her parents about what it had been like the times their own brood had been born. Made her wonder, for the first time, why they'd even had four children when their careers had been such a huge priority. Had their family been more important to them than she'd realized?

"I'm going to speak English, as Laurel doesn't speak Greek," Andros said, "so she understands what she needs to do to help. Okay?"

Both nodded, and he turned to Laurel. "Help me get her clothes off and a gown on her, please." Despite the strangeness of the situation, it felt oddly normal to work together with him, and they quickly had Dora ready. Laurel was surprised it didn't also seem uncomfortable for the lower half of the woman to be completely naked, but maybe since it was obviously the last thing the woman was concerned about, it seemed like no big deal.

"This is an external probe, to monitor the baby's heartbeat." Andros attached a belt to her swollen belly, with some electronic gadget attached to it. "It's not as accurate as an internal probe we sometimes attach to a baby's head, but since your little one wants to come soon, I think this is good, okay?"

Both nodded again, obviously having complete faith in Andros, and Laurel looked at his face. Calm, but completely in command, and she knew she'd have the same exact confidence in him no matter what the situation.

"Are you all right? Do you want pain relief, Dora?"

"*Ochi*. No time. The baby…is coming."

He glanced at the monitor and his expression was neutral, but it seemed to Laurel it tensed a bit. "Baby's heart rate is dropping a little, Dora. Called bradycardia. Could be just from contractions, but we need to keep an eye on it."

"What do you mean?"

"If there's sustained fetal bradycardia, we'll need to get the baby out as fast as possible. Not to worry, though. And see? It's already recovering a bit."

Dora gave a sudden, extended cry, so agonized, Laurel winced for her. Yanni gripped her hand, looking nearly as distressed as his wife did. Laurel was so focused on the poor woman's pain she didn't notice Andros was leaning over the woman.

"You weren't kidding about it coming soon, Dora! Baby's on the way. The head is crowning. Time to push."

Laurel stared in amazement when she saw the top of the baby's head begin to emerge. She'd wondered if it might be gross or icky to see, but it wasn't at all. It was awe inspiring. Incredible.

"Oh, my gosh, it's right there!" She hadn't meant to exclaim that out loud and looked guiltily at Andros. He kept his attention on the baby and mother, but that surprise dimple poked into his cheek and she knew he was smiling.

"Yes. He or she will be here soon. Push again, Dora."

The woman grunted and groaned and pushed as her husband murmured encouragingly to her, but the baby didn't seem to move.

"Baby's heart rate is dropping again, Dora. We need to get the baby out. Laurel, I need you to put fundal pressure on top of the uterus."

"Fundal pressure?" Laurel's heart beat harder. She hoped she was up to whatever task this was he needed her to do.

"Basically, I need you to put your hands on the top of her belly and push hard. Put your weight into it."

"Um, okay." She positioned herself next to the woman and spread her hands on Dora's belly, feeling a little weird and a lot nervous. She pushed down, worried she might hurt her. "Like this?"

"Harder. As hard as you can."

Holy crap. "I'm afraid I'll hurt her."

"You won't. And we need to get the baby out."

Andros's intense expression sent her heart pumping even harder, and she gritted her teeth and put everything she could into pushing on the surprisingly hard expanse of poor Dora's belly. In the midst of the woman panting and pushing, and her husband speaking tensely in words that were probably supposed to be encouraging, Andros suddenly said, sharply, "Stop, Laurel. Stop pushing, Dora."

"What? Why?" Dora gasped.

"Baby's heartbeat is dropping again because the cord is around its neck. Give me a minute."

Almost as short of breath as the laboring mother, Laurel stared down at the baby's head, now out of its mother's body and being held gently in Andros's hands. Then her breath stopped completely and she felt a little woozy when she saw the baby was beyond blue, and the umbilical cord was wrapped several times around its neck.

She sucked in quick breaths to calm herself. Big help

she'd be if she fainted in the middle of the birth. Andros slid his fingers carefully beneath the cord, gently loosening and unwrapping it, then finally slipping it completely off over the baby's head. "Okay, ready now. Let's have a last few good pushes, Dora. You're doing great. Can you help her, Laurel?"

Fear gave Laurel super energy, and she pushed hard on Dora's belly as the woman worked to deliver her child. After a few monumental pushes, the baby slipped from its mother's body into the waiting hands of Dr. Andros Drakoulias.

"Another girl!" Andros said, glancing up with a smile so big that that dimple of his showed again. "And she's as beautiful as her mother."

Dora sagged back, gasping and beaming, looking from the baby to her husband and back again. Yanni leaned forward to give her a lingering kiss, speaking soft words in her ear that Laurel couldn't understand, but at the same time she knew exactly what he must be saying.

Laurel felt about as wrung out as Dora, but wired too. She watched Andros rub the baby gently all over with a towel then put a bulb into her mouth to suction out fluids. The tiny thing seemed alarmingly blue, and the seconds seemed like minutes before the baby's head finally began to pink up, then her torso, as she cried out in lusty breaths.

The parents laughed and kissed, Andros grinned, and Laurel sagged, letting out a huge sigh of relief.

What an amazing experience. Scary and exhilarating and wonderful and unforgettable.

"You did a great job, Dora. Baby's had a bit of a rough time, so we need to get her warmed up and breathing well before I hand her over to mama." Andros's gaze met Laurel's. "Are you okay handling the baby, Laurel? She needs to be dried off with the towels to warm her up, wrapped with a dry one, then put under the heat lamp and given oxygen. I already have it turned on, so just position the mask over her mouth. I need to take care of Dora."

"Yes. Of course." She hurried over, not knowing exactly what to do, but whatever it was, she knew Andros would guide her through it if she messed up somehow.

He handed her the still slightly wet baby, and a moment of terror nearly stopped her heart. What if she dropped it?

"Don't worry. She's not glass." Andros gave her an encouraging smile. "Just dry her off like you would a little puppy after its bath, swaddle her up, then put her in the warmer." Andros grinned as though he'd read her mind, and she wondered what expression was on her face for him to see.

Heart thumping, she grabbed up a towel and carried the baby to the warmer. Softly, she began stroking the child with the towel, dumbstruck at the little brown eyes staring up at her as she did. As though the baby, just a few minutes old, was avidly studying her brand-new world.

"Dora, I'm going to give you some oxytocin to help your uterus clamp down and stop the bleeding. Okay?"

Laurel didn't look behind her, but knew the new mother wore the same expression on her face she'd had all along. Complete confidence that Andros would take care of everything.

She finished drying the baby, marveling at her mini fingers and feet, her tiny elbows and knees, then awkwardly swaddled her, sure any nurse would laugh at the pitiful job. The immeasurable good Andros accomplished every day struck her with awe. Yes, she loved her job. Following in her parents' footsteps. Uncovering history, learning from the past, was valuable to humankind's education. But this?

This put it in perspective. A dig wasn't life or death. It was about past lives and past deaths, but, when it came right down to it, helping others today and now was the most important thing anyone could do.

Helping her sisters become the people they'd become had been more important than getting her PhD done. More important than any dig, no matter how meaningful. She was glad to be free of the responsibility now, but postponing those things to raise and guide her sisters had been the biggest accomplishment of her life so far. How had she never appreciated that before?

The little baby staring at her from under the heat lamp raised her downy eyebrows, seeming to agree. Laurel smiled, stroking the infant's soft cheek, feeling a strangely serene, inner calm she couldn't remember feeling since before her parents died. For the first time, she realized that maybe having a baby of her own one day had its place on her list of life goals.

She'd head back to the mountain, into the caves, tomorrow. Hopefully she'd bring to a close her number-one goal. She'd leave no stone unturned to make it happen. But if she didn't?

She'd remember this sweet little baby's face, and be at peace with the outcome, knowing she'd given it everything she could.

CHAPTER TWELVE

"DID YOU REALLY help Daddy born a baby, Laurel?" Cassie asked as the three of them sat at the breakfast table, her usual excitement on her adorable face and sparkling in her brown eyes.

"I did. It was amazing. Your daddy's pretty amazing too." She looked at him over her coffee cup, struck all over again by his astonishing physical beauty, somehow magnified even more by the dark stubble on his chin and the faded T-shirt stretching across his thick chest and arms. And his inner beauty too, which she'd seen last night. Radiating competence and caring, reassuring the mother throughout even the scariest part of the birth.

"I know," Cassie said as she stuffed a piece of bread into her mouth. "How did I look when I was born, Daddy? Did I cry a lot?"

Andros stilled in midmotion, his gaze meeting Laurel's before he put his cup back down. "I wasn't there when you were born, remember, sweetie?"

Laurel's chest squeezed at his somber expression. Obviously, this was a painful subject for him, and she wondered when she'd finally find out about his relationship with Cassie's mother and how she'd died. A woman he'd said he wasn't close to. The knowledge that Cassie didn't have a mother made her heart ache for the child. But she was lucky to have a father who so obviously loved her, and an extended family too, in Taryn and Petros and her grandparents. Laurel knew from experience that could make even a terrible loss more bearable.

"Oh. I forgot." Cassie went back to eating, not seeming very bothered by the conversation, which eased the tightness in Laurel's chest. "When are we going fishing, Daddy?"

"As soon as you're done eating. I want to see that apricot go down the hatch." He picked it up and held it to her mouth and she lunged at it, nearly biting his fingers. "Ouch! Are you a wild dog this morning? I need all my fingers, you know."

Cassie giggled. "I'm a monster fairy. I have tiny teeth, but they're very sharp and hurty."

"Monster fairy? Sounds like a compromise with Petros."

His amused eyes met Laurel's, and they smiled together in an oddly intimate connection. How could sitting here at their breakfast table feel so normal, so right, when she didn't really know either of them all that well? How could it remind her of her own family, of breakfasts with her parents and her sisters that were the best memories of her life?

Moments she'd taken completely for granted until they were in the past. Until they could never happen again.

"You're not working today, Andros?" she asked, wondering how the only doctor in town had time to fish.

"Since Christina's gone a few days, I closed the clinic. Off work to play with Cassie, unless there's an emergency."

"Are you coming fishing with us, Laurel?"

"I can't. Unlike your dad, I don't have the day off." Filled with a sudden longing to join them, she fought it back. She hadn't been given this one last chance to find the treasure just to twiddle away the little time she had. Andros's brows quirked at her in a questioning look and she braced herself. The man would not be happy about her plans to go in the cave, but it wasn't his decision. Wasn't his parents' dream she had one more shot at realizing. Her chance to make them proud.

"With all the excitement, you never did tell me why you came back. What is it you still need to do?"

She opened her mouth to tell him then closed it again. Coward that she was, she didn't want to ruin this warm, pleasant moment they were sharing. And didn't she deserve just a few hours of relaxation and fun on the boat with them? Just for a little while before work took 100 percent of her time? The way it had for her parents?

"You know, work can wait a little while longer. Because, you might not believe this, but..." She leaned closer to Cassie. "I've never been fishing. Will you teach me how?"

"Yes! I will! Can I get my tackle box now, Daddy? Please?"

"All right. I'll pack up the last of your fruit for a snack."

Laurel smiled as the child leaped from the chair and ran off, her spindly little legs practically a blur. Maybe it made her nosy, but she couldn't help being curious about Cassie's mother and what Andros had said before. Now might be the only chance she had to ask without the little girl around.

"So. Maybe enjoying a little nakedness together doesn't give me the right to ask," she began, wondering why she felt suddenly nervous, like maybe she didn't want to know the answer after all, "but Cassie is the sweetest little thing, and I can't help but wonder about her mom. You said she passed away?"

Andros stared down into his coffee cup, not responding, exactly the way he'd acted when she'd brought the subject up on the mountain. That seemed like a long time ago now, but just as she was about to apologize for asking, for butting into something that wasn't her business, he looked up and fully met her gaze.

"Yes. As I said before, it's a sad thing for Cassie. But the rest of the story? It isn't one I'm particularly proud of."

Oh, Lord. Probably this really was something she didn't want to know and she wished she'd kept her mouth shut at the same time that she found herself desperately needing to hear it.

"I spent my youth going from one girlfriend to the next. Thought that was a good thing, what guys did, right? Now I wish my parents had yanked me aside and lectured me on respecting women, but they didn't. Don't know if they turned a blind eye or honestly weren't aware of it until after I left and they heard the gossip, but by the time I left Kastorini for school in the States, I had quite a reputation."

"You're a beautiful man, Andros, which I'm sure you know." Hadn't she about swooned the very first time she'd set eyes on him? "I bet it was a two-way street, with girls throwing themselves at you."

"Doesn't mean you have to take advantage of it. But I did. And when I saw the big, wide world of a college campus, then med school and residency? I felt like I'd moved from dinner to a full banquet."

"And you feel guilty about that." She could see it in his

eyes. Guilt. And while a part of her felt uncomfortable, maybe even a little cheap at being just another woman who'd offered herself up at that banquet, she also believed he was no longer that young, careless man.

"Yes. I do." His eyes met hers again, intense and sincere. "Even before I found out about Cassie, I'd started to grow up. To see that women weren't something to be enjoyed at random, even if that seemed to be all they wanted, too. I took a step back to think about who I was and who I wanted to be. Figured I just wasn't capable of a lasting relationship with a woman. Had never wanted one, but knew I needed to start being more careful about who I got involved with so no one got hurt. Then I got a phone call that brought that lesson home for good."

Laurel knew what that phone call must have been. Her heart twisted in a knot, and she covered his hand with hers and waited.

"Alison's brother—Alison was Cassie's mother— called me. Said she'd died in a car accident, and I was listed on Cassie's birth certificate as the father. Her parents were older and couldn't take care of a toddler, and the brother was single and traveled a lot. So they decided to contact me."

This time, his dark eyes were filled with pain. Remorse too, and her heart clutched even harder. "You didn't know."

"No. I didn't know. I wish she'd told me, though I hate to admit I barely remembered who she was. Maybe she didn't because she figured I'd be irresponsible."

"No, Andros, she had to know the caring man you are would have stepped up."

"Maybe, maybe not. When I first found out, there were plenty who knew me that doubted I would. And I wasn't sure I could blame them." He held her hand between both of his, his gaze not wavering from hers. "Maybe it happened later than it should have, but learning about Cassie brought me to that final step of realizing I was a man now, not a careless, self-absorbed boy. Which meant coming back to Kastorini to work with my father, as he'd always wanted me to. To raise Cassie here the way I'd been raised, to finally embrace the roots I'd been blessed to be given."

She tightened her hold on his hand, giving him a smile that she hoped showed she understood. That everyone had years they'd spent doing a whole lot of growing up, and it wasn't always tidy or pretty. Hadn't she struggled to guide her sisters, often failing miserably because of her own immaturity? "Gotta admit, I find it hard to believe there was a time you weren't sure you wanted to come back. I love it here. Your place—your town—is truly special." She had to bite back her next words, which had almost been *and you're every bit as special, too.*

"It is. Special, and hard for me to believe." A small smile played about his lips now, and she was glad to see it. Happy he'd felt able to share all that with her, and happy he saw she understood.

"By the way." He leaned in, a breath away. "Just so you know, you're not just another fling to me. You're damned special too."

Her heart knocked at the words she'd almost said to him. She saw his smile, slightly crooked and more than sexy, just before his mouth touched hers. Her eyes drifted closed to savor the sensation. Sweet and slow, tasting a little like coffee and a lot like warmth and pleasure and simple happiness. Just as she was sinking deep into all of it, a banged-open door, followed by a voice so loud it was hard to believe it came from a tiny little throat, interrupted.

"Got everything, Daddy and Laurel! Let's go feed the fishies!"

Laurel would never have believed that such a soft, comfy cocoon of a bed would have left her tossing around with not nearly enough hours of sleep.

She'd sunk deep into its comfort, enjoying reliving the beautiful day she'd spent on the water with Cassie and Andros. Smiling as she remembered the tangled fishing lines and the hook that had flown back to snag her hair when Cassie had yanked too hard at an invisible fish she'd been sure was on the line. Seeing Andros's immediate concern when he'd jumped up to carefully extricate it, the expanse of his wide chest in front of her face for a temptingly long time, making it nearly impossible to not breathe him in. To not wrap her arms around as much of him as she could and kiss him senseless.

Thank heavens Cassie had been chaperone, or she knew she couldn't possibly have resisted. And that realization knocked away all those pleasant feelings, leaving her frowning at the ceiling. Wondering about this deep contentment she felt here, and worried about it too. She had to be happy and content when she moved on from here, and each hour she stayed made her realize it might be a bigger adjustment than she'd expected to become a rolling stone, living in various places around the world as she built her career.

The only thing that had marred the day slightly were reporters showing up to sniff around. Apparently a few locals knew she'd returned and told them she was on Andros's boat. That situation had him looking beyond grim, which seemed a little unnecessary. Though she supposed having to answer questions and calm worried locals was a stress he didn't need.

She caught herself drifting back to the lovely memories of the day on the boat and opened her eyes again, annoyed with herself. She'd come back to Kastorini to find the statue, not play around with and lust after Andros Drakoulias. Really, she hadn't meant to come to Kastorini at all, and if she'd been able to get her room back wouldn't even have seen him again.

Except she had to face that this stern self-lecture was partly a lie. Consciously or unconsciously, she knew she'd have looked for a reason to come back here, even if that reason had been something lame and inane.

She flopped to her side, pinching her eyelids closed, willing herself to sleep. Tomorrow had to be cave day. Not an easy day, either, since she hadn't worked in there at all and had only Tom's map and his "feeling" to help her find that statue. "And finding it means everything, remember?" she whispered fiercely to herself. "Everything."

Everything. Everything her parents had expected her to work toward. What her parents had died for. What was wrong with her that it seemed harder and harder to keep that at the forefront of her mind?

Her bleariness faded at breakfast, with Cassie's steady, cute chatter and two cups of coffee managing to help her feel upbeat again.

"A little more coffee, Laurel? Or more fruit?" Andros asked, holding up the pot.

"No, thank you, but it was delicious. If you'll excuse me, I have some things I need to get done today." She shoved herself from her chair and left the kitchen, feeling Andros's gaze on her back. What were the odds he wouldn't ask her what she was going to do, when she came down with her pack?

She didn't have to wonder long, as he stood just a few feet away from the bottom of the stairs. Her trot down the steps slowed, and she braced herself.

"You can't be serious. Are you nuts?"

Andros stared at her with disbelief and anger etched all too clearly on his face. He folded his arms across his chest and took a step closer, as though his size and maleness would somehow intimidate her.

"What do you mean?"

"I'm not stupid, Laurel. You're obviously planning to go into the caves."

She took a step toward him and stared him down. Well, up, actually, since she was now only inches away from him.

"I know you don't understand. I don't expect you to. I'll wear a mask and gloves, just in case. But I need to look just a little longer."

"Look for what? More potsherds or a long-lost gold ring like countless others in Greek museums? Bones from thousands of years ago? I've talked to the Wagners about this dig, about the hundreds of items excavated. You've done plenty. Why can't you let it go? It's over."

"Not quite yet."

He turned to pace away a few steps, staring out of the window. His posture was stiff, and frustration practically radiated from him. Her throat tightened and her conscience tugged at her heart. The man wasn't worried about a contagion infecting Delphi or Kastorini or anywhere else.

He was upset because he was worried about her. She

couldn't stand to let him think she was just an idiot. A stubborn fool. She owed him the whole truth.

"Andros," she said softly, walking toward him to place her hand on his back. He didn't turn, didn't respond, and she inched closer until her body nearly touched his. "This isn't about a few more potsherds. There's something important my parents believed would be found at this site. Something that will rock the archaeological world. Something I want to find for them, and for myself."

He turned to look down at her, that deep frown still between his dark brows. The worry still there too, but not the anger. "What? What could be so important?"

"There's a lengthy poem inscribed on one of the stones excavated near Delphi. A poem that talks about the Pythian games and the Charioteer and a golden Artemis, Apollo's sister. After studying the interesting metaphors in this poem, Mom and Dad became convinced the golden Artemis really existed in the form of a statue."

"They've been excavating for five years here with no statue showing up, Laurel."

"I know. But…" She wrapped her fingers around the warm skin of his arms. "The Wagners always suspected it might have been hidden in the caves, to protect it from looters after people no longer worshipped at Delphi. Tom thinks he felt where it is. So I'm going to look there a few more times."

"Felt where it is? What the hell does that mean?"

"Sounds ridiculous, I know. But surely you've had moments where you just had a gut feeling about something? A diagnosis, maybe, that comes to mind and seems right?"

He looked at her, not answering. After a long, tense moment, he finally shook his head and sighed. "You may be crazy, but even you know you can't go into a cave solo. I'll go with you."

"Andros, you don't have to—"

"Yeah, I do." He pulled her against him, and the lips that touched her forehead were gentle, not at all angry, and she was so relieved, she found herself leaning against him. Slid her hands up to his strong shoulders as his mouth lowered to hers in a kiss filled with frustration and sweetness and a slowly building heat that curled her toes and sent her fingers tangling with his thick, silky hair.

The heavy-lidded eyes staring at her were utterly coal black as he pulled back and ran his thumb across her lower lip. The sensual touch sent her breathing even more haywire, and she nearly drew his thumb into her mouth. Until she quickly reminded herself that heading to the cave was her priority for the day, not having delicious, sweaty sex with the hunkiest doctor alive.

"I really appreciate you…coming with me. I'm ready to go when you are."

His gaze lingered on hers a moment longer before he wordlessly turned and headed upstairs.

CHAPTER THIRTEEN

"I WAS EXPECTING it to be wetter in here. But most of the moisture's on the stalactites and stalagmites, not the ground at all," Laurel said as they moved through the cave, the light from their lanterns and helmet lamps swinging in wide arcs on the low ceiling, rocky walls, and floor.

"There is ground water in some caves on the mountain. Wouldn't that destroy artifacts?"

"Depends on the artifact." She pulled out Tom's map and looked at it again, trying to orient herself. "I thought working in here would be better than the hot mountainside, but it's a little creepy, don't you think?"

"The big bad adventure woman thinks it's a little creepy?"

The amusement in his voice was loud and clear even through the mask he wore, and she gave his arm a playful swat. "You're telling me you like it in here?"

"Interesting formations around. But I frankly can't see how the hell you think you'll find anything. A statue like you're talking about couldn't be buried in solid rock. If it was here, surely it would have been found by now."

She wouldn't admit she'd been thinking exactly the same thing. But Tom knew a lot more than she did, and he thought it was still possible. Who was she to doubt, when they'd been inside for barely half an hour?

"He said he got his feeling when he was about a hundred feet in, on the left-hand side. Behind some orange stalactite." She held up her lantern, peering for something orange, so focused she stumbled over a small, mounded stalagmite and might have fallen if Andros's strong hand hadn't shot out to grab her arm.

"Steady, adventure girl. We're not in a big hurry, here."

"Easy for you to say. You're not the one who has to head back to the university before the start of the new term." The words sent an unexpected jab right into her solar plexus at the thought of never being here again. On this amazing mountain, or in beautifully charming Kastorini.

Of never seeing Andros and little Cassie again.

But that was the nature of the life she wanted, wasn't it? That she'd trained for. Spend months of the year somewhere, meet new and interesting people, then move on. Maybe get to see them again the following year if a dig continued. But getting attached to one place for too long? Not a good idea for an archaeologist.

Remembering that wasn't going to be easy.

Andros hadn't said a word in response, and she wondered if he was thinking what she was. That he'd miss her. That he wished they'd had a little more time together to light up, then burn out, this...thing that had formed between them.

Definitely hadn't had enough time for either. And of all her regrets, she knew that was the biggest.

So aware of his warm hand still holding her arm, she moved farther into the cave, then stopped dead. "Look! A huge orange stalactite, over there!" She pointed, looking up at Andros, and his eyes met hers above the mask, strangely dark and intense at the same time they were touched with the humor she loved to see there.

"If we find it, can we keep the discovery to ourselves so I can put it in my living room?"

"Wouldn't suit your homey decor too well, I don't think. Let's look."

The sound of his chuckle vibrated practically in her ear as he squeezed in next to her behind the stalactite, his chest touching her back in the narrow space. Her heart thumped as she scanned the area. At first it looked as if it was nestled in by more expanse of solid rock that ended in a triangular corner, covered by a thin, shimmering layer of crystal. The excitement that had bubbled up in her chest when she'd first spotted the orange formation deflated a little as she moved in close to what she could now see was obviously a dead end.

"Looks like it stops right here," she said. "I wonder if Tom could have meant a different stalactite?"

"Maybe. Or his psychic feelings were really just indigestion." Andros wrapped his arm around her, splaying his gloved hand across her belly in a squeeze. A shiver slipped across her neck and down her spine as his deep voice murmured in her ear, "Gotta say, though, this cave is starting to grow on me. I like being smashed into close quarters with you. Except it's hard to nuzzle your ear with this damn mask on."

"You're the one who insisted on the masks." She turned her face and their noses and mouths touched through the paper, making them both laugh a little breathlessly.

"Kissing you this way is still better than kissing anybody else's lips." The eyes that stared into hers were hot and amused and held an absurd sincerity that had her pressing her mask-covered mouth to his again.

"You're ridiculous," she said, forcing herself to turn back to the crevice and remember why the heck they were in this cave to begin with.

He held his lantern up above her head. "Or maybe it wasn't indigestion after all," he said softly.

"What?"

"Look. There's an opening up here. Kind of jagged and narrow, but maybe big enough for a smallish person if you're careful. Dry too, and looks like it might expand to a bigger space once you're through."

Her gaze followed his and she jumped up and down, trying to see inside. She knew it was probably nothing but couldn't help feeling a ping of excitement anyway.

"I'll give you a boost." He put down his lantern and threaded his fingers together, palms up. "Step in my hands."

"Let me take my boot off first. Or better yet, I'll get on your shoulders and climb in so you don't have to lift my full weight."

"What, you think I'm a wimpy weakling?" He stopped her as she reached for her boot. "I'm wearing gloves, and you might get your sock all wet."

Wimpy weakling? She shook her head and grinned at the man who was about as far from that description as a human could possibly be. "Fine. But don't complain if you throw out your back."

She stepped into his palms and he lifted her so high, she was able to grab onto the edges and peer inside, the glow of her headlamp lighting the space. "It's big inside here, but kind of strange. Different from the cave we just came through."

"How do you mean?"

"There are chunks of stone and broken stalactites everywhere. And like you said, the crevice is real jagged instead of smooth like the cave walls."

"Aeons of moisture and minerals have glazed these walls. Since this crevice isn't like that, there's a reason. Like maybe the earthquake a few weeks ago opened it when it had never been open before."

She looked down at him, his eyes vibrant and alive as they met hers. "Maybe you're right."

"Come back down. We'll grab the tools and open it up wider so we can both get inside."

Andros found a few sizable rocks to roll over beneath the crevice that they could stand on as they whacked at the edges of the opening. "Turn your head when you swing, so you don't end up with shards in your eyes. I hate removing stuff from people's corneas."

"And I'd hate it to be my cornea you had to remove stuff from." Looking at him balancing on that rock, a smile in his eyes as they stood close together in this corner working away, made her insides feel all gooey.

"Thanks for helping me. I really appreciate it."

"Like you left me a choice. I would've been a nervous wreck thinking of you getting lost in this cave. Not to mention I didn't want to have to spend my whole day off tomorrow hunting for you when you didn't show up for dinner."

"You don't fool me. I think you're enjoying this. It's an adventure, right?" She turned her head and closed her eyes as she gave another mighty swing at the crevice edge. Though mighty was probably an overstatement, since Andros had already bashed out a good six inches from top to bottom on his side.

"Okay, I admit it. It's intriguing." He leaned back and surveyed their work. "I think it's big enough. Come on, I'll help you up, then follow you in."

She stuck her foot in his hands again, and when she was halfway in he let go and cupped her derriere in his hands, shoving her far enough in that she was able to squirm the rest of the way and stand up. "Was that an excuse to fondle me?"

"Do I need an excuse?" He boosted himself in to stand in front of her, sliding his hand around her rear again and pulling her close.

She chuckled. "I guess not." She gave him another one of those paper-mask kisses, their eyes meeting over the top. "You realize I'm sorely tempted to pull down this stupid thing and kiss you for real."

"Me too. But we'll save that for a little later, hmm?" He grasped her hand as they picked their way over all the broken rock littering the ground. "This place definitely had a huge seismic shift just recently for there to be so much of this. I—holy Apollo, Laurel."

"What? What?" She looked all around, trying to aim her headlamp where he was looking.

"Something's back here, behind this tall half-broken wall. Gleaming, like metal."

Laurel didn't realize she'd stopped breathing, her heart pounding so hard it echoed in her head, until they stepped around the wall and every bit of air left her lungs in a gasp. "Oh, Andros."

Together, they stared silently at the stunning, life-sized gold statue of Artemis, gleaming as brightly as if it had just been polished by an ancient hand. She stood beautifully perfect beneath an arching ceiling, coins and jewels scattered around her feet in what had probably been homage to Apollo's sister.

Tears stung Laurel's eyes and throat, and a small sob burst from her mouth, muffled by the mask. She turned to Andros, and saw the same awe and amazement on his eyes she knew was in her own.

"You did it, Laurel. You didn't stop believing, didn't stop trying. This is…incredible."

"I'm not sure I didn't stop believing, but I wanted to believe, so much." She reached to touch it, reverently sliding her hand over the statue's intricately detailed gown, her ethereal face.

"Your parents would be so proud."

"They would. Yes, they would. Oh, my God, I can hardly soak it in."

She flung her arms around his neck and buried her face in his shoulder, letting the tears flow as his arms came around her. Tears of happiness and relief and joy, knowing her parents' work would be highlighted once more. Thinking how proud they'd be that she—with Andros's help—had actually found this spectacular treasure.

"Thank you, Andros," she whispered. "Thank you for helping me. For seeing the crevice. Hammering it open. For spotting…her. I…I don't think we'd be standing here in front of her if you hadn't."

His hands slowly stroked up and down her back. "Oh, you would have found her. That stubborn streak of yours would have kicked in, and who knows? Maybe that feeling Tom had would have come to guide you too."

She looked up, blinking at her tears. "I think maybe there's a part of you that believed in that feeling. That kind of guidance."

"Maybe." His eyes crinkled at the corners. "So now what, Ms. Evans? Who do you need to contact?"

"First, I—*Aahh!*"

They both ducked, startled by something swooping by their ears. Andros straightened and looked around, his brows lowered in a thoughtful frown. "I asked Tom if he'd seen bats in the cave, and he said no. But that was definitely a bat."

He released her and walked around, looking carefully at the various corners of the cave where he pointed his headlamp. "Bat guano. A lot of it." He looked upward, aiming the light around the ceiling that was much higher in this cave than the other one. "Bingo! Hundreds of bats curled up there sleeping. See them?"

"Okay, now I know for sure why I preferred working on the mountain instead of in here." She shuddered, creeped out by the creatures hanging shoulder to shoulder, as far along the cave ceiling as they could see. "Glad we found Artemis pretty fast."

"Bat guano, Laurel." He stared at her, a new excitement in his voice and gleaming in his eyes. "It can be a primary source of coronavirus infection if it's breathed into the lungs."

"Coronavirus? You mean like SARS and MERS?"

"Probably a mutated strain. Pneumonia is the most common clinical presentation of coronavirus, sometimes with nausea and diarrhea like Jason had. Renal failure and pericarditis. Sepsis, which we couldn't manage well for John. It all makes sense now!"

He grabbed her shoulders, practically dancing her around. "The reason no one got sick before the past couple weeks was because the bats were in this cave, not the one your crew was working in. Then the recent earthquake opened up that crevice, and the bats flew into the dig cave. Tom and Jason worked all day, breathing in the airborne dissemination of the virus."

"But what about Becka? She worked in the cave all day and didn't get sick. And Mel wasn't in here at all."

"Some people carry the virus, but never show symptoms, which could be the situation with Becka. And while coronavirus is primarily contracted through respiratory exposure to guano or animal secretions, like from camels carrying MERS, it can be contracted from very close person-to-person contact."

"So you've solved the mystery." Her excitement began to match his and she laughed as they did another little two-step around the cave. "Nobody in Kastorini or Delphi has to worry they'll get it. You're a genius!"

"We solved it together." He cupped the back of her head with his hand. "I never would have come in here if you hadn't."

"And Artemis might have stayed hidden forever." They looked at one another, and Laurel's heart swelled and squeezed at the same time. "Do you think she was hidden by the earthquake my parents died in? That maybe the only entrance got shut down to anything bigger than a bat?"

"More likely an earthquake from a thousand years ago, and if that's the case your parents would never have found it." He tipped his forehead against hers, speaking softly. "Maybe the gods felt bad about that, about the tragedy, and made another earthquake happen just for you in their memory."

"Yes. In their memory." She gave him a fierce hug, unable to identify all the powerful emotions swirling around inside her. They were grief and joy, sadness and amazement, and Andros was somehow wrapped up in every one of them.

"We have some work in front of us, Ms. Evans," he said, his voice that low rumble in her ear that always made her quiver inside. "I need to talk to Di and get the national infection control folks out here, take some samples. Have them check the blood work we have from your team to confirm it. And once it is, contact the media to calm the fears they stirred up before."

"And I have to call Tom and Mel and tell them we did it. They'll talk to the university while I contact the Greek Archaeological Society." She squeezed him tighter. "I can't wait to tell my sisters too."

"We should probably call the authorities to protect the statue. I doubt anyone would come in here, and it's hidden well, but, since it appears to be solid gold, I'm thinking there are one or two people who would like to get their hands on it."

"Except she probably weighs a zillion pounds."

"There's that." He chuckled. "I'll call Georgo, the police chief in Kastorini, and let him handle it however he thinks. He's an old friend and as honest as they come."

She slowly pulled herself from his arms. Holding his hand, she carefully stroked the statue one more time. "Thanks for showing yourself to us, beautiful. I know whoever created you as a gift to Apollo loved you, but it's time for the rest of the world to love you even more."

Andros gripped her hand and when she turned to him she was surprised to see his eyes were now deeply serious. "And I have a feeling the world will love her finder as well."

* * *

The rosy-gold sky was darkening around the mountains, the waters of the gulf a deeper blue from the low light, when Laurel and Andros finished what seemed like a never-ending number of calls and emails.

"Okay," Andros said, "I think we can finally relax and celebrate."

Laurel glanced up from her laptop, her heart skipping a beat as she looked at the man leaning against the kitchen doorjamb. He'd showered and changed, and his slightly damp black hair was curling a bit around his ears and at the nape of his neck. His snug jeans rode a little low on his hips, and a white polo shirt was startlingly bright against his bronzed skin.

She let herself soak in the sight of him, that uncomfortable swirl of emotions back in spades.

There was no denying she was crazy about this man. Smart, caring, and beyond beautiful inside and out. She adored his little girl and felt warmed and welcomed by this lovely town they lived in. Liked his sister too, and had a feeling she'd like his parents just as well.

But she would never know, because she had to leave. With Andros's help, she'd accomplished her goal, big time. Now could finish her PhD dissertation. Get the grant paperwork done and in, making sure the wheels were greased to get her dig in Turkey going when she got the grant money, which shouldn't be a question now. She'd assemble a team. Lots of qualified applicants would want to be a part of it after this monumental discovery. And there would be interviews galore—while she talked about her parents' conviction that they'd find the statue there, she'd take that opportunity to talk about her own upcoming dig, knowing her parents would feel satisfied and happy that she'd accomplished the dream they'd had for her.

All that should leave her feeling elated. But battling with that elation was the heavy reality that she'd be saying goodbye to this place. To Andros. She couldn't deny she wasn't ready to do that. Wasn't sure she'd ever be ready.

She managed a smile, determined to enjoy her last day or two with him. "We've earned a celebration for sure. What did you have in mind?"

His eyes took on a wicked glint, and his slow smile sent her heart rate zooming. How could a single look from a man make her feel like throwing him to the floor to have her way with him?

"Let's start with an aperitif. I got white wine for you, but of course I have retsina and ouzo as well."

"You know, believe it or not I do have a taste for retsina tonight. And maybe a little of that grilled octopus you say the restaurant down the street does so well."

"Yeah?" He took a few steps closer, and she set her laptop aside so she could stand and meet him halfway. "Sounds like you've become part Greek. Part of Kastorini."

"Maybe I have." Her eyes drifted closed as he pressed soft kisses on her temple, her cheek, the corner of her mouth. Her words echoed in her head, making her chest ache. *Maybe I have. Or maybe this place has become a part of me.*

"So, about you becoming part of Kastorini." The pads of his fingers slowly slipped across all the places he'd just kissed, ending up warmly cupping the side of her throat. His expression was surprisingly serious, at odds with his teasing voice. "You already know Greece is the epicenter of history just waiting for an archaeologist to find and share it?"

"Spoken like a true Greek, especially one born near the belly button of the entire earth," she said. "But a lot of other countries might argue with that perspective, Dr. Drakoulias. Not only in Europe, but China and South America and—"

He pressed his mouth to hers, effectively shutting her up. When he broke the kiss, his lips were curved, but his eyes still held that peculiar seriousness. Though she shouldn't think it was odd, since she found herself feeling very serious too.

"I know your passion is Greek archaeology," he said. She looked at him and nodded, though front and foremost in her mind at that moment was an entirely differently passion of hers. Passion for the man standing right in front of her. The man who stole her breath and had managed to steal a scarily large chunk of her heart as well. "But at the moment, there's a different subject on my mind."

"I might be able to guess what it is," she managed to say in a teasingly light voice.

"Probably not." His hands tightened on her. "I just wanted to say I wish we'd met in a different place in our lives. Before you had your exciting dig plans stretching out in front of you, and before I had Cassie to think about, raising her here in Kastorini. But we didn't."

"No," she whispered. "We didn't."

"I'd ask you to come back and visit sometime when you're in Greece again, but I know that's not the best idea. Cassie already likes you a lot, and since she lost her mother I don't want her to become attached to someone who's not going to be around long. And, I...well, you know I'm not a guy with a very good track record. But I want you to know that I'll really miss you."

"I'll miss you too." As she spoke she thought about what he'd said. And was filled with the bizarre thought that someday, when she worked in Greece again, she could visit Andros and see if, maybe, they might both be in a different place then. That Cassie might need another mother figure. And if they were, who knew? Maybe—

The door burst open, and they both swiveled toward it to see Taryn run in, frazzled and breathless. Andros let go of Laurel and strode to his sister. "What's wrong?"

"Have you seen the kids? They were playing in the backyard, but when I went to get them for dinner they were gone. I looked around but don't see them anywhere. And it's almost dark." She sucked in a breath. "They must be here, right?"

CHAPTER FOURTEEN

LAUREL FOUGHT DOWN her rising fear as the three of them searched for Cassie and Petros. It was nearly impossible for Laurel to keep up with Andros as he strode down streets and narrow alleyways, shining his flashlight into garden plots and patches of forest, calling the children's names in a voice loud enough to carry a long way through the inky night. Kastorini might be fairly small, but in the dark one house looked pretty much like another, so she tried to stick as close to him as she could. Last thing he needed was to worry about her being lost too.

"Let's check the schoolyard," Andros said in a controlled but obviously tense voice. "They both like to play there."

"But they've never tried to go alone, even during the day," Taryn said, sounding breathless and near tears. "I can't believe they'd go that far at night."

The terror in Taryn's voice clutched at Lauren's heart and brought back the frightening memory of her sister being missing, just a few months after her mom and dad had died. Helen had ridden her bike to a friend's house and hadn't come home for dinner. Laurel still remembered the icy panic she'd felt when she'd called and found Helen had left the friend's nearly an hour earlier.

She'd jumped into her car and driven up and down the streets Helen would have ridden on, but she wasn't anywhere to be seen. Her chest had filled with an unbearable fear as questions swirled in her head. Had Helen been abducted? Had she done something crazy in her grief over their parents? How could she have gotten lost? Laurel remembered nearly weeping in relief when it had turned out her sweet baby sister had just gotten a flat tire on her bike and decided to take a shortcut when she walked it home.

It had been the first moment, one of many to come, that Laurel had doubted she was capable of taking on the care and guidance of her sisters full-time.

"We've looked close to home," Andros said. "We need to think of where they like to go, what they might be thinking."

A number of neighbors had joined the hunt, spreading out through the town. "Cassie was excited telling me about fishing with you and Laurel," Taryn said. "Surely they wouldn't go to the boat."

Andros swung around to look at his sister, a low curse on his breath. "Neither of them can really swim. Come on."

They switched direction. Laurel thought they were heading to the stone steps down to the water and could hear the rising anxiety in both their voices. Could feel it in her own heart. An olive branch snagged her hair, and she had to stop to pull it loose. Then stared at the tree, an overwhelming conviction smacking straight between her eyes.

"The fairies!" she called out to Andros and Taryn as she hurried to catch up. "You know Cassie and Petros have been obsessed with fairies and monsters. Remember when I told her they liked olive wood, and she asked if I thought they lived in the olive groves? They both asked me about it again and if monsters might live there too."

Andros stopped and stared at her, his eyes glittering through the blackness of the night. He yanked out his phone and dialed. "Georgo, check to see if they might have gone to my boat on the water. We're going to the east olive groves." He hung up the call. "This way, Laurel." He grabbed her hand, and they backtracked up the steps and onto a dirt path. "You just might be right, and I hope to God you are."

After a five-minute near run to the grove, and another twenty minutes searching and calling, Laurel began to despair. She nearly blurted out the question she kept wondering, which was how long would it take to find them in the midst of thousands of trees? And how much time were they wasting if the kids weren't here?

But she managed to bite her lip, nearly drawing blood. Last thing Andros and Taryn needed was for her to pile on more doubt and fear with a stupid and obvious comment.

Andros came to such an abrupt stop, she nearly bumped into his back.

"What?" Taryn asked with wide eyes. "Do you—?"

He held up his hand. "Shh. I thought I heard them answer." He cupped his hands around his mouth, bellowing out to them, and Laurel's heart nearly stopped when she heard what might have been an answering cry.

"Petros!" Taryn nearly screamed her son's name and took off running through the trees, Andros moving in the same direction but veering more to the left. Laurel realized it made sense to spread out some and went in the other direction, trying to search for the kids with the flashlight, somehow watching where she was going at the same time.

Her entire heart felt lodged inside her throat as she called to them. Her ears strained to hear something, anything, and suddenly the small voices were in front of her. "Cassie! Petros!"

"Laurel!" The little girl sounded terrified.

"Oh, my God, Cassie, where are you?" She swung the flashlight through the trees, the light picking up eerie shadows she kept thinking were the children, and suddenly they were there. They rushed into the beam of light, both children grabbing her legs and crying.

"I thought I heard my mommy," Petros sobbed. "I thought I heard her and Uncle Andros."

"They're here. They're both here. You're fine. You're safe." She crouched down and hugged them against her, tears clogging her throat. She swallowed them down so she could let Andros and Taryn know she had them.

"Here! Over here!"

A dark shaped loomed out of the darkness. Andros. He swung both children into his arms, kissing their cheeks, then pressed his face against Cassie's hair. "You both scared us to death. Don't ever, ever leave the house without telling us. You hear me?"

Both nodded, and Cassie snaked her arms around his neck in what looked like a stranglehold. "I'm sorry, Daddy. Laurel told us there were fairies in the olive trees. But then it got dark and we didn't know how to get home."

The little sob in her voice stabbed straight into Laurel's heart and she took a step back, her hands clutching at her chest as Taryn ran up to hold Petros.

This was all her fault. Why hadn't she realized she shouldn't say something like that to a small child? She'd always known she hadn't truly been up to the task of raising her sisters. So how could she have just been thinking there might be a time she'd like to come back to Kastorini? To see if this something between her and Andros could blossom into something more? To mother this beautiful child?

"I have to leave," she said as she turned away, her heart feeling shredded from the anxiety of the past hour. From guilt and misery at her own inadequacy. She wasn't sure if she'd said it to herself or Andros or the fairies in the olive grove, but she now knew without a doubt she had to go.

Laurel rested her hand on the windowsill in Andros's living room, staring out at the night. Wishing she could see the charming homes with their terracotta roofs and tumble of vibrant flowers, the crooked little streets, the cats sitting grooming themselves by doors so colorful and intriguing they could have been from a story, making her want to walk through and read the next chapter.

But it was probably just as well the darkness shrouded it all. She'd be leaving in the morning, and the look and feel of this town was etched forever in her mind and heart anyway.

She heard the stairs creak but didn't turn. Sensed rather than heard Andros coming to stand behind her. His hands resting on her shoulders were warm and heavy. Adding to the weight she already felt there.

"She's sound asleep. I guess an adventure and scare like that takes it out of a little girl."

And big ones, too. "I'm willing to bet she and Petros stick close to home from now on." She turned, swallowing down the tears that formed in her throat again. "I'm so sorry I thoughtlessly talked about the fairies living in the olive groves. This was all my fault."

"Don't be ridiculous." His hands tightened on her shoulders. "You couldn't have known they'd get it in their heads to go there."

"I have three sisters. I watched them a lot when they were little. And after I took on their care full-time, I learned the hard way to be careful what I said. To think before I spoke when they talked about boyfriend crises and school dramas and plans to move to the Amazon jungle alone to study indigenous peoples."

"Laurel. Every parent does or says things they later wish they hadn't."

"I'm not a parent. Not anymore. And I can't be. I just finished that role, and I wasn't very good at it. I…I have a plan for my life, and I need to get started on that plan." A plan that, just hours earlier, she hadn't been 100 percent certain she wanted so very much anymore.

His gaze seemed to search her face for a long time before he finally nodded, tugging her closer to press the gentlest of kisses on each of her cheeks before fully pulling her into his arms and simply holding her. She wrapped her arms around his back and breathed him in, wanting to imprint his scent and the feel of his body on hers one last time.

She tilted her head up to look at him, touching his face, wanting to also imprint every beautiful feature of his face in her memories. Though she didn't really need to do that, as she'd committed it to memory weeks ago. It seemed perhaps he was doing the same, as he looked at her for long moments before he lowered his mouth to hers and kissed her.

Soft and sweet, the kiss was also filled with a melancholy, then with a growing heat until Andros pulled back and set her away from him. His chest lifted with a deep breath before he spoke. "You need me to do anything for you before you leave?"

There was only one thing that came to mind. "Yes." She stepped close again and wrapped her arms around his neck, but he grasped her forearms before she could kiss him.

"Laurel. We shouldn't. You mean more to me than a night of sex before you're out of my life forever. That's not who I am anymore, and it will just make saying goodbye even harder."

"Maybe it will. But you mean more to me too." She stroked his cheek, cupped it in her hand. "I don't think it would be wrong for two people who care about one another to make love before they say goodbye, do you?"

"Maybe it wouldn't." He pressed his lips to her palm, lingered there. "Maybe the truth is I'm just trying to keep my heart intact here. But one thing I do know is that being with you one more time would be worth a few more bruises tomorrow."

The small smile he gave her added to the pain and pleasure swirling around her heart. "I agree." She tugged his head down to her and kissed him. Long and slow and with a building passion that weakened her knees.

He drew back. "Cassie almost never gets out of bed, but in case she has a nightmare or something we should go to my room. Come on."

He grasped her hand and led her to his bedroom. A comfortable-looking masculine space she'd peeked into but hadn't been inside. He shut and locked the door behind them. Holding her gaze, he gently tugged her hair loose from her ponytail. His fingers slowly stroked down the length of it, then he touched her forehead, her cheek-bones, and chin with his fingertips as well. Much the same way she'd touched the Artemis statue, with a reverence on his face that made her ache. He finally reached for the buttons of her blouse, and with each one he flicked open, her breath grew shallower, her anticipation ratcheted higher.

"You are so beautiful, Laurel." He slipped the blouse from her shoulders, ran his fingertips across the lace of her bra until she shivered.

"As are you." She tunneled her hands beneath his shirt, loving the way his muscles tightened at her touch. Stroked her palms through the soft hair on his chest until impatience got the better of her and, with his help, she yanked it over his head and off. She wrapped her arms around him, pressed her lips to his warmth, and he seemed suddenly impatient as well, flicking off her bra and quickly undoing her pants, shoving them down and off, along with her panties, in one swift movement.

She wasn't sure how he managed to kiss her breathless, shuck his own pants and settle them onto the bed in a matter of moments, but it didn't matter. His lips caressed her throat, her collarbone, her breasts. His fingers moved over her skin and teased her everywhere, and she closed her eyes to soak in the delicious sensations one last time. And when the pressure built until it was nearly unbearable, he finally joined her. Twined his fingers with hers, palms pressed together, eyes meeting in a deep connection that went far beyond the physical one they were sharing.

"Laurel. Laurel." He whispered her name as he took her further, higher, and his name was on her lips when they fell.

CHAPTER FIFTEEN

LAUREL SAT IN the university's office for the archaeology school and stared at the letter in her hand, waiting to feel the jubilation that should have her jumping up and down. The letter announcing that her grant application had been approved, and the dig she'd planned in Turkey could begin as soon as she had the equipment scheduled, accommodations booked and a crew pulled together.

Her gaze slid to the sturdy cardboard envelope lying on her desk that held her doctorate diploma, and while she was proud of it, she didn't feel the elation she knew she should feel by having completed both those accomplishments in the past month.

And she knew why. Making love with Andros had felt so bittersweet, leaving her with even more memories of him that now filled her with more sadness than pleasure. He'd been right when he'd said it would just make it harder to say goodbye. *Had* made saying goodbye harder, or would have if she'd stayed long enough to say it.

Hours of tender kisses and lying quietly together, arms and legs entwined, had left her with too many emotions tangled up as well. And when she'd finally slipped away to the guest room so Cassie wouldn't wake up to them in bed together, she'd been unable to sleep. Thinking of leaving in a few hours, and saying goodbye to Kastorini. To everyone she'd become fond of. To Andros and Cassie, whom she'd become far more than fond of.

So she'd left, slipping out of the door and driving to the airport before dawn. Leaving a note had seemed like the best kind of closure, but now she realized it had been cowardly. She'd wanted to avoid the pain of those farewells, but the only thing that had accomplished was to leave her with a deep ache. Without a sense of closure after all.

She sighed and tried to pull her attention back to work. While she concentrated on making a long to-do list for the project in Turkey, Mel came into the office and leaned down to give her a hug.

"I heard about your grant, girl. Congratulations, you deserve it! Your parents would be so incredibly proud of all you've accomplished."

"I know. They would." And she was glad. Glad to know they'd be proud, in comparison to all the times they hadn't been so proud. All the times she hadn't quite lived up to the standards they'd set for her.

"And yet you don't seem very happy." Mel sat in the chair next to the desk and rested her elbow on it. "What's going on?"

"Nothing. I'm happy. Just tired, I guess. My moment of fame, being interviewed for magazines and on TV, has been pretty exhausting, I've got to say." She kept her voice light and joking, but knew Mel would probably see right through it.

"Mmm-hmm. More so than working ten solid hours digging rocks on a hot mountainside, which never seemed to exhaust you. So tell me the truth."

Laurel leaned back in the swivel chair, and just the thought of telling Mel made her feel like a traitor to her parents. To their dreams. "I achieved everything I wanted to this year. Got my doctorate, the grant money, and most incredibly, we found the statue. There's clearly something wrong with me that it doesn't feel like…enough."

"Maybe because it's not what you really wanted after all."

"Of course it is. I wanted to finish this dig for Mom and Dad, and I wanted to get going on the achievements they planned for me."

"What do you want for yourself?"

Laurel stared at her. "I already told you. Their work—"

"Exactly. *Their* work. Which doesn't have to be yours, Laurel. I know, as their oldest, they always expected—demanded—a lot of you. You took on the care of your sisters, which wasn't easy. Took on your grad studies, then took on the task of finishing the Delphi dig, with spectacular success. So why do you feel like that's not enough?"

She stared at Mel, gathering her thoughts. Asking herself that question. "Because it's not. For years, they talked about me heading up a dig as soon as I got my PhD. Planned to help make it happen so I'd get started in that role even younger than they were. I may be behind, but I still want to make it happen."

"For you, or for them, to fulfill their dream for you? Maybe it's time for you to ask yourself if what you thought you wanted is really just what *they* wanted." Mel reached to hold her hand. "Maybe focusing on all this has been your way of unconsciously dealing with the grief that's still inside you over your parents dying. A way to come to peace with that."

Stunned, Laurel met Mel's gaze. Was it possible she'd convinced herself she wanted to do the project in Turkey for that reason? Not because that was what called to her professionally?

"I...I don't know. But I do love archaeology. I love digging and finding and recording history. Really, I do."

"I know you do. Just think about the rest of it, will you?" Mel squeezed her hand. "By the way, Helen called me. Said she'd been trying to get hold of you and wanted me to tell you."

"Okay, thanks."

She stared at Mel as she left the room, still confused by their conversation, then dialed her sister. "Hey, sweetie, what's up?"

"Hi, Laurel! Guess what?"

She smiled at the enthusiasm in her bubbly little sister's voice. "What?"

"Professor Green said he wants me to come back to this dig next summer, after I'm finished with my first year of college! Do you really think it'll be a good thing to put on my grad-school applications?"

"Congrats! Yes, it definitely will. I'm proud of you for working hard and going for it." As soon as the words came out of her mouth, she wondered if she sounded exactly like her parents. Pushing instead of just encouraging. "But you may find other things you want to study after this coming year. Don't feel like you have to plan your whole future right this minute."

"Okay, I won't. Thanks for being the best big sister ever and for always giving me good advice."

Her heart squished at her sister's words. "I don't think I've always done that so well."

"Sure you have. I want to tell you how much I love you for that. How much all three of us do."

"I love you too." Laurel stared at the phone after they

said their goodbyes. Realizing that all her sisters had said sweet things like this before, but she hadn't really heard them. Had she been too worried about how she was "failing" at being a parent to notice the things she might be doing right?

Maybe she'd been mistaken about a lot of things she'd been so sure of. And if she had been, maybe it was time to get it right.

"There's another picture of Laurel, Daddy!"

Cassie's stubby finger pointed at the photo in the magazine, but she hadn't needed to. Most readers probably focused on the pictures of the spectacular golden statue he'd been blessed enough to help find, but he saw only Laurel. Her intelligent blue eyes, her sweet, smiling lips, her beautiful face. Her hair—hair that he knew all too well felt silky soft within his fingers—spilling in golden waves over her shoulders.

"Yes. There are quite a few pictures of her in these magazines, aren't there?"

"Why?"

"Because the statue was an amazing find. There's nothing like it in the whole world, and Laurel's the one who kept looking for it."

"You helped her. You found it too. Why isn't your picture in here with hers?"

He wished there were photos of the two of them together, but it wasn't meant to be. Probably his penance for the years he'd dismissed the idea of a real relationship with a woman. Known he didn't have it in him.

But the way he'd missed Laurel the past month had him wondering if maybe he was capable of it, after all. That maybe he'd just needed to meet the right woman to feel that kind of commitment. Except she was traveling the world, and he had Cassie to raise here.

"She's the archaeologist. I just got lucky to be with her that day." And a few other magical days. More than lucky.

"Thea Taryn showed me your picture in the other magazine. The one about people getting sick. Laurel helped you figure that out, didn't she?"

"Yes. We made a good team." And as he said the words, the hollowness he'd felt since the moment he'd woken up and found her gone seemed to widen a little more.

"Why aren't you still, Daddy? A team with Laurel?"

He looked down into her wide eyes and his lips twisted a little, thinking what a simple question it was. One with a simple answer. "Her work takes her on adventures all over the world, Cassie. Our home is here in Kastorini, with Yiayia and Papou and Thea Taryn and Petros and everyone else."

"I like adventures, Daddy. And doctors can help people anywhere. Why can't we go on adventures with Laurel and come home to visit everybody sometimes?"

Her words were so matter-of-fact, the expression in her eyes telling him she thought he might be a little dense. And as he stared at her he wondered the same damn thing.

He'd brought Cassie to Kastorini because he'd thought that was where the newly mature doctor with a daughter needed to be. Taken his place beside his father, even though the man had practiced medicine for years without any problems finding a temporary replacement when he'd needed to.

He'd disliked being judged by the town, worried about disappointing his parents, couldn't let Cassie be exposed to gossip or become attached to a woman he might selfishly date for just a short time. But didn't part of growing into a responsible adult bring with it a responsibility to himself too?

"You may be onto something there, *koukla mou*. Maybe an adventure with Laurel is exactly what we need."

Laurel's hands were sweating on the steering wheel of her rental car as she drove up Mount Parnassus and parked. She got out and stared at the mountain, which hadn't changed since she'd left a month ago. Hadn't changed in aeons. Then turned to look at the incredible blue waters of the gulf that stretched to mountains on the other side and to the sea of olive trees flowing down to meet it.

She'd loved this place the moment she'd arrived. Loved it even more after living in Kastorini for a few days.

Loved the man who'd been born here and was a part of this place, and she hoped and prayed he wanted her to be a part of it too.

He'd been silent for a moment when she'd called to tell him she'd come back to Delphi on business. Didn't tell him it was personal business, because it was too important to talk about on the phone. Too critical to her future happiness.

She walked up the goat path, stopping a few times to lift her face to the brilliant sun. To the intense heat she loved. When she finally got to the closed dig site, she moved slowly to the pit that had collapsed during the earthquake five years ago. The pit where her parents had died.

She knelt, picturing the horrific scene as she had so many times before. But this time felt different. Their spirits were there with her on the mountain, and they were smiling at her, holding her, encouraging her. Not judging her, not disappointed in her. The occasional strife of their relationship that had lodged itself too long in her brain faded away, leaving only the good memories of all their years together.

"I love you, Mom. Dad. Thank you for everything you gave me, including my love of archaeology. And most especially my sisters."

She kissed her fingers and pressed them to the ground for a moment. Then stood, and, when she turned, saw a beautiful Greek man walking sure-footed and steady up the goat path, looking exactly as he had the first time she'd seen him. She smiled and her heart swelled at the same time that nervous jitters quivered in her stomach.

She made her way back down the steep path to meet him. "Hi." It wasn't a very original greeting, but all her rehearsed words seemed to evaporate when she looked into the dark eyes she'd missed so much.

"Hi." His lips curved just a little and he took another step closer, until they nearly touched. "You called me to help you find another statue up here?"

"No. I...I hope you'll help me find something else."

"What's that?"

"I lost my happy after I left here. I'm hoping you can help me find it again."

His dark eyes stared into hers as his hands cupped her waist. "I'll do whatever I can to help you. But here's something funny. I need your help with the same damn thing."

In a sudden movement, he tugged her flat against him and kissed her. She clung to him, the heat of his mouth and the sun burning down on them making her dizzy.

"I almost fell over when the phone rang and it was

you," he said, "because I'd just pulled it from my pocket to call you. Must have been that sixth sense you and Tom believe in."

"Why were you going to call?"

"Because I realized I hadn't followed the wisdom of the stone at Delphi that says 'Know thyself.' That I believed I had, but was focused instead on who I thought I was, who I thought I needed to be. Not on who I could be."

"Me too," she whispered. "I—"

"I need you to know why I'd decided to call." He pressed his fingers to her lips. "I wanted to tell the incredible woman I'm crazy in love with that a four-year-old girl is smarter than I am. That we don't have to stay put in Kastorini. We can travel to be wherever you are, so you can do the work you love. I don't care where we live and neither does she. I just want to be with you, if you'll let me."

"Oh, Andros." She sniffed back stupid tears. "I came to tell you I love Kastorini. I love Cassie, and most of all I love you. So much. I realized I wanted to be in Kastorini with you and Cassie, which could work if I concentrate on digs in Greece instead of other places. And I realized that working around the world wouldn't make me happy if you weren't with me."

He lifted one hand to cup her cheek, tunneling his fingers into her hair. "Cassie told me we make a good team. Maybe that means we do both. We live in Kastorini when you don't have to be on a dig outside Greece, and we live wherever your work takes you when you do."

"That would...be good. Perfect, even." She reached up to kiss him but he pulled back.

"There's one more important thing I need to ask." He

grasped her hands, and went down on one knee in the dirt, wincing when his knee rolled onto a stone.

"Come back up." She tried to tug him, but it was like lifting the statue of Artemis. Or Apollo. "You don't need to do this."

"I want to do this." His eyes met hers. "Laurel Evans, I love you more than I knew it was possible to love a woman. Will you marry me? Be my wife? My forever teammate, wherever it takes us?"

The emotion in his voice had her choking back tears again. "Yes. I will. And, darn it, come up here so I can kiss you."

"One more minute." He reached into his pocket. "It's not a ring, yet, but maybe it will do until I can get one. Hold out your wrist."

She looked down and gasped when she saw a bracelet circled with gleaming moonstones. "How did you find time to run to the store to get this?" she asked as she held out her hand.

"I bought it after you left." His gaze was suddenly serious as he looked up from fastening it to her wrist. "I thought maybe if I held it close in my hand, it would keep you safe on your travels. Maybe even be that love talisman you talked about. Bring you back to me someday."

"Oh, Andros," she whispered, swallowing hard at another lump in her throat. "What did I say before about the charm of Greek men? How can I possibly resist the power of a moonstone? And of you."

"I hope you can't." He grinned as he rose, and that elusive dimple poked into his cheek. She laughed and sniffled and kissed it first, before she pressed her mouth to his to seal the deal. "Thank you," he whispered against her lips. "I promise to do everything I can to make you happy."

"Being a team of three will definitely make me happy. With maybe a few more recruits when we're ready."

As he kissed her again, the warmth of him wrapped her with joy, and she didn't think it was her imagination that she just might be hearing the music of god Apollo from the mountaintop, playing in celebration.

* * * * *

MILLS & BOON®

Why not subscribe?

Never miss a title and save money too!

Here's what's available to you if you join the exclusive **Mills & Boon Book Club** today:

✦ *Titles up to a month ahead of the shops*
✦ *Amazing discounts*
✦ *Free P&P*
✦ *Earn Bonus Book points that can be redeemed against other titles and gifts*
✦ *Choose from monthly or pre-paid plans*

Still want more?

Well, if you join today we'll even give you
50% OFF your first parcel!

So visit **www.millsandboon.co.uk/subs**
or call Customer Relations on 020 8288 2888
to be a part of this exclusive Book Club!